Here's what *Romantic Times* had to say about RITA® Award-winning author Ruth Wind and *The Last Chance Ranch*...

"Powerhouse writer Ruth Wind mesmerizes us with *The Last Chance Ranch*, an electrifying tale of love, passion and redemption you won't be able to put down."

"Ms. Wind moves us from tears to great joy in this tour de force love story."

...and *USA TODAY* bestselling author Pamela Toth and *Rocky Mountain Rancher*!

"...Ms. Toth treats us to a hero and a romance to savor."

"Ms. Toth gives readers a solid storyline, strong dialogue, engaging characters and heated passion."

RUTH WIND

is the award-winning author of both contemporary and historical romance novels. She lives in the mountains of the Southwest with her two growing sons and many animals in a hundred-year-old house the town blacksmith built. The only hobby she has since she started writing is tending the ancient garden of irises, lilies and lavender beyond her office window, and she says she can think of no more satisfying way to spend a life than growing children, books and flowers. Ruth Wind also writes women's fiction under the name Barbara Samuel. Visit her Web site at www.barbarasamuel.com.

PAMELA TOTH

USA TODAY bestselling author Pamela Toth lives on the Puget Sound area's east side. When she is not writing, she enjoys traveling with her husband, playing FreeCell on the computer, doing counted cross-stitch and researching new story ideas. She's been an active member of Romance Writers of America since 1982.

Her books have won several awards and they claim regular spots on the Waldenbooks bestselling romance list. She loves hearing from readers and can be reached at P.O. Box 436, Woodlinville, WA 980720. For a personal reply, a stamped, self-addressed envelope is appreciated.

RUTH PAMELA
WIND TOTH

HEART
OF THE
WEST

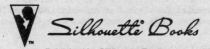
Silhouette Books

Published by Silhouette Books

America's Publisher of Contemporary Romance

SILHOUETTE BOOKS

ISBN 0-373-23018-4

by Request

HEART OF THE WEST

Copyright © 2003 by Harlequin Books S.A.

The publisher acknowledges the copyright holders of the individual works as follows:

THE LAST CHANCE RANCH
Copyright © 1995 by Barbara Samuel

ROCKY MOUNTAIN RANCHER
Copyright © 1995 by Pamela Toth

CONTENTS

Dear Reader,

The Last Chance Ranch is a very special book to me. There had been, in my town, a rash of women murdered by their estranged husbands, and I found myself more and more angry about it. I could not bring those women back, but I could create one who survived an abusive marriage and went on to find a good life.

The book has brought a huge number of letters over the years—it was also a RITA® Award finalist and the winner of a generous cash prize given to a romance dealing with a social issue.

For all of that, the book is not about an issue. It's one of my favorites because I love the tender, gentle blooming of love between Tanya and Ramon, and the rock-solid enduring love we all need to think about now and again, don't we?

Visit me on the Web at www.barbarasamuel.com. Hope to see you there!

Ruth Wind

THE LAST CHANCE RANCH
Ruth Wind

This is for the friend of my heart,
Sharon Lynn High Williams,
a tireless warrior for the lost children;
a lamp in the darkness, burning bright.
With love and admiration.

Prologue

On her twenty-second birthday, Tanya Bishop took her three-year-old son Antonio to see a Disney movie. They returned home late, and Antonio was asleep on her shoulder when she unlocked the door.

She knew Victor had found her again the minute she stepped into the house. Something just didn't feel right.

Halting on the threshold with Antonio asleep in her arms, Tanya listened to the darkness. Her instincts prickled. From the kitchen came the predictable plop of water from the leaky faucet, and the warm hum of the refrigerator. Though she waited a full minute, holding her breath, she heard nothing else.

Cautiously, she eased in far enough to flip on the lights in the living room. The lamp on the coffee table burst alive and illuminated a room that looked exactly as it had when she left. A little cluttered but basically clean.

Still she held the slack body of her son against her and waited, listening for another moment. Nothing.

Tanya walked to the kitchen, inky dark at the end of the hall. Her footsteps made the old floor creak. In her arms, Antonio stirred and lifted his head, then settled it again on her shoulder. She could feel his hot, moist breath on her neck.

In the kitchen, she lost her nerve to be still and quiet, and flipped on the light in a rush. The fluorescent tubing spluttered as it always did, the gases heating slowly, dimly, then flaring to abrupt life.

On the floor, in shattered, tiny pieces, was Tanya's china. The exquisite saucers and one-of-a-kind dinner plates that she had collected for years were shattered all over the kitchen. He'd ground some below his boots, for the china was powdered in places, and the linoleum below it gouged with the ferocity of Victor's rage.

Tanya stared at the leavings of his violence and fought back tears. She had a restraining order against him, but he ignored it. Seven times she'd called the police and signed complaints. In desperation, she had gone into hiding, moving every three months so he would never know for sure where she was. He tracked her each time, once all the way to Santa Fe.

A deep and painful ache of fear beat in her chest. This time, he would kill her. Two days ago, he'd accosted her at a supermarket, in front of witnesses, and the police had arrested him. Now he was out of jail, and he knew where to find her.

Very slowly, she backed out of the kitchen.

* * *

It all counted against her later.

Tanya settled Tonio on the couch and filled his day care bag with extra clothes, his teddy bear and the blanket he could not sleep without, plenty of underwear and his favorite toys. Then she sat down in her kitchen, brushing shards of china from the table and chair, and wrote her son a letter which she tucked in among his things.

She took him to a day care home she trusted, then drove back to her house. It was just past eleven.

In the ruins of her kitchen, she sat down to wait.

And as she waited, she remembered...Victor, winking at her across the crowded school auditorium the first time she'd seen him. The gentle trembling of his hands as he kissed her the first time. The passionate avowals of love he'd pressed upon her. The flowers he brought in apology when his temper had got the better of him. The jealous rages that had become more and more frequent....

At 2:37, she heard Victor at the back door, drunk and cursing as he jimmied the lock. She lifted the phone and dialed 911.

Victor kicked the door. "I'm gonna kill you, Annie!" He kicked it again and the windows rattled under the impact.

To the girl at the end of the emergency line, Tanya said, "I need the police at 132 Mariposa. A man is breaking into my house." She knew if she said it was her ex-husband the police wouldn't come as quickly.

Victor roared an obscenity and kicked the door.

Tanya winced. ''Please hurry,'' she begged and dropped the phone. She ran for her bedroom, hearing the threshold splinter as Victor barreled into the back room. He roared his name for her. Tanya scrambled in her drawer for the loaded revolver she'd put there, and rushed into the bathroom.

In the bathroom, she locked the door and crouched in a corner, praying in the nonsensical words of the terrified, ''Please, please, please.'' The words meant *please make him go away* and *please don't let him find me* and *please don't let him hurt me anymore.* Last time, oh, last time—

''Annie!'' In the living room, she heard things breaking, and chairs being overturned, and a low growling roar that struck a panting, mindless terror through her. He didn't even know he did it. But that animal sound meant his temper was beyond all mortal limits, that drink and rage had turned him into a beast.

A beast that had mauled her in the past.

Not again. She clasped the gun between her violently trembling, sweaty hands. In the distance, she heard sirens.

Please, please, please.

''Annie!'' Something else was turned over.

He kicked or hit the bathroom door and Tanya couldn't halt the sob of terror that escaped her lips. She closed her eyes as he began to batter the door, lifted the gun as he yelled her name again. Tears came. Tears for everything—so many good things and so many bad—ran in great washes down her cheeks. She had to use a wrist to wipe them away.

The sirens came closer. The door gave with a splintering sound. Victor, savage as a rabid bear, tumbled into the room.

Not again! her heart cried. *Not again.*

Sobbing, Tanya aimed the gun at his chest and pulled the trigger.

It was the last thing she remembered.

Chapter One

Dear Antonio,

They called him a hanging judge. Everybody says it might have gone better if I'd had the money for a real good lawyer, but I didn't, so I'm going to spend a long time behind bars.

Maybe it would be okay, if I could see you sometimes, but your dad's sisters want you protected. From me, I guess. And someone has to take care of you while I'm in here. If I do what they want, then I can pick who takes care of you. It won't be one of them.

So I signed the papers they brought to me, giving custody to your dad's cousin, Ramón Quezada. He's a fine man, and very smart. He'll take good care of you.

Be good.

Love, Mom

Eleven years later

As the bus pulled into the dun-colored adobe bus station at Manzanares, New Mexico, Tanya Bishop scanned the concrete apron for the man who was supposed to be meeting her. She remembered Ramón Quezada from a wedding reception fifteen years ago. She had danced with him. He'd been skinny then, an intense and bespectacled college student. His probing intelligence had intrigued and thrilled her even as it made her uncomfortably aware of all she wanted to understand and didn't.

Her most vivid memory of Ramón, however, was the tape that had held his glasses together after Victor hit him for dancing with her.

Peering through the bus windows, Tanya saw no one who even remotely fit her memories. She clutched her purse more tightly in her fingers, feeling the leather grow slick against her palms. What if he'd forgotten he was supposed to meet her?

No. Ridiculous. She took a steadying breath. He would not forget. Ramón was responsible, trustworthy, honest and loyal—all the things his cousin Victor had not been.

All the things Antonio needed.

As the brakes on the lumbering bus whooshed to a stop, Tanya saw a man come through the glass doors that led to the inner terminal. He was dressed all in black—black jeans, black cotton cowboy shirt with pearlescent snaps, black jean jacket lined with sheepskin. Her stomach flipped. He sort of looked like Ramón. But that couldn't be the skinny man-child she remembered.

Could it?

He was the right height—Ramón had been rather tall. He was the right age—about middle thirties now. But that lean, dangerous creature could not possibly be the same man she'd danced with so long ago. She leaned forward, frowning in disbelief.

It was him. Ramón Quezada, her late husband's cousin, the fearless leader of the Last Chance Ranch, and her son Antonio's adoptive father.

He bore the distinctive Quezada family stamp, a long-limbed grace that spoke of centuries of working with horses; hair so black it seemed to gleam with internal light; even the arrogant nose, so beautifully formed, high-bridged and straight. A conquistador's nose, Tanya thought. And the high cheekbones were Apache. A hard lot, the Quezadas. Fighting men.

Time had done good things to him. Tanya clutched her bag to the sudden ache in her chest. Ramón's long wavy hair curled in an unruly way around his neck, inviting female fingers to smooth it. He moved with the calm ease of a man at home with himself and his world. Tanya saw a woman pause at the doors and take a second look over her shoulder at him.

Passengers filed down the aisle beside her, but Tanya found herself frozen in her seat, her gaze riveted to the spot where he waited, his intense gaze fixed on the disembarking passengers. She had briefed herself on everything from the right clothes to bring to a ranch for troubled boys, to brushing up on her colloquial Spanish, to the enormous task of girding herself to see her son again after eleven years. She had even braced herself to hide her identity from that son, in order to allow a relationship to develop naturally between them.

She had not prepared herself to deal with a man who wore an aura of sex appeal like a second skin.

Had he always looked like this and she'd just been too much in love with Victor to notice? A pair of glasses might have hidden the stoked passion in his eyes, or covered the clean beauty of his bone structure, but nothing could have concealed a mouth so richly formed, so dangerously seductive.

Staring at him from the greatly mature age of thirty-three, Tanya thought—not for the first time—that she had been one of the most foolish young girls ever to inhabit the planet.

Another woman might have sighed in pleasure at the prospect of living in close quarters with such a man for the next few months. Another woman might have allowed the dark wash of desire to flow through her in anticipation of kindling the banked passion in that face. Another woman might have let her gaze wander over that lean, long-limbed body and wondered how it would feel against her own.

Tanya did not have the luxury.

For one long moment of panic, she considered just staying on the bus, letting it carry her to the next stop. From there, she'd call the ranch and tell Ramón she'd changed her mind.

On the platform, he glanced around with a frown,

and Tanya knew she couldn't walk away. He'd done a lot for her, even more for her son Antonio.

And if she didn't get off the bus now, her chances of ever seeing her son again were next to nothing.

Clutching her bag to her chest, Tanya stood up. Around her, the last passengers murmured in a musical mingling of Spanish and English. She took in a long breath and squared her shoulders, then marched down the aisle.

Outside on the platform, Tanya lost sight of Ramón. People surged around her—grandmothers gathering children, sweethearts hugging each other—and Tanya was struck unexpectedly with a sharp arrow of joy. She was free! Not as she had been at the halfway house, but truly and honestly free. Free to smell diesel fuel and hear ordinary swearing, free to touch people and be bumped. Through the garage door, she caught a glimpse of dark clouds rolling in from the west, and it occurred to her that she was free to stand in the rain if she chose. For as long as she wanted to...

A male voice sounded at her elbow, "Annie?"

The pet name was uttered in a voice almost too familiar—slightly accented and beautifully sonorous. A bolt of terror replaced her joy, and she squeezed her eyes tight. It was just a nightmare, she told herself, a nightmare like all the others she had suffered the past eleven years, dreams of Victor coming after her again. Cold sweat broke out on her body.

The man at her side touched her arm, as if to steady her, and Tanya yanked away violently, nearly stumbling in her haste to get away.

Reason belatedly waded into her terror. It wasn't

Victor, because Victor was dead. Tanya halted, then turned very slowly.

Ramón stood there, even more overwhelmingly attractive at close range. He kept his distance a little warily, his hands lifted, palms out, to show her he wouldn't hurt her. She was sure he was wondering what kind of basket case he'd saddled himself with.

"Please don't call me Annie," she said in a tone as even as she could muster. "It was Victor's name for me. No one else ever called me that."

"I'm sorry." There was genuine regret in his voice. "I didn't mean to startle you." Ramón reached for the duffel bag that contained all her earthly goods. "Let's put this in the truck, all right?"

Mutely, Tanya followed him into the dark autumn day. A sharp wind blew from the Sangre de Cristos Mountains, slicing viciously through her thin cloth coat. With a small shiver, she clutched it closer to her body, bending her head into the burst of bitter wind.

Ramón caught the movement. "Not much of a coat for this kind of weather." Reaching into the cab, he brought forth a down parka and held it out to her. "It's a nasty day, but Indian summer will be back tomorrow."

Tanya was unaccustomed to simple kindness, and for a minute, she hesitated. A gust of wind blasted them, tossing hair over Ramón's solemn face. With a dark, long-fingered hand, he brushed it away.

"Thank you," she said. Shyly, she traded coats, giving him the old one, which he tossed into the truck.

Buttoning his own jacket, he asked, "What would you like for lunch—American or Mexican? The Blue

Swan has great green chili, and Yolanda's has good fried chicken.''

Tanya shrugged. ''I don't care.''

''Me, either,'' he said. ''You choose.''

She didn't want to choose. She'd used up all her reserves of emotional energy, and there was still Antonio to think about. For herself, she'd like the green chili, but maybe Ramón would like hamburgers. She said nothing.

Nor did he. The silence between them stretched to a strained, awkward length. Tanya stuffed her hands in her pockets and waited.

At last he prodded her. ''What would you like— Tanya? Can I call you Tanya?''

''Tanya is fine.'' She took a breath and chose, watching his face carefully for subtle signs of disapproval. ''I guess green chili sounds good.''

He smiled. The expression transformed his face, giving a twinkle to the depthless eyes, adding emphasis to the high slant of cheekbones. Tanya's chest, tight with anxiety, eased with an abruptness that made her almost dizzy. She'd made the right choice.

Ramón stirred sugar into his coffee and watched Tanya carefully tear the wrapping from a straw. From the speakers in the ceiling came a soft Spanish ballad, mournful with strummed guitars and flutes. For a moment, he was transported to another day, another time, when he'd danced with this woman, when she had been a sweet, pretty young girl...and he'd fallen in love.

In those days, he'd often fallen in love. More often

than not, his passion had gone unrequited. Upon meeting Tanya for the first time, so many years ago, he'd thought his infatuation was like all the others.

But in Tanya's beautiful dark blue eyes there had been an almost painful yearning for things unnameable and unattainable. It had struck him deeply. As he'd held her loosely, her blond hair spilling over her shoulders, her youthful eighteen-year-old body swelling just slightly with the baby in her tummy, she'd told him about a book she was reading, *Tortilla Flat*. She'd said the name as if it were new, as if no one had ever discovered it before, and there had been magic and wonder in her tone, in her sweet innocence.

That she had reached the age of eighteen without knowing such a work existed, that she could find it on her own and love it with such passion, had touched Ramón in some quiet place. Until that day, he'd been too enmeshed in his anger to see what was plain if only he looked around him—a person didn't have to be brown or black or red to suffer the indignities of ignorance and poverty. The realization that social class, not race, was the great deciding factor in American society had changed his life.

They had talked all afternoon, while Victor—Tanya's husband and Ramón's cousin—drank in the bar with the wedding party. They talked about books and movies, about ideas and hopes and plans. As he listened to her sweet, soft voice, and watched her eyes shine with excitement, Ramón had fallen in love.

And when Victor, drunk and evil-tempered, broke Ramón's cheekbone, Ramón had almost felt it was deserved. Tanya was Victor's wife, after all.

Ramón had gone back to Albuquerque, to his Latin-American studies, and had tried to wipe the beautiful young girl from his mind. He hadn't known until almost a year later that Tanya, too, had paid for that golden afternoon. Victor had beaten her senseless and she'd landed in the hospital with seven broken bones, including ribs and wrist. By some miracle, the baby had survived. Tanya briefly left her husband after the hospital had released her, but Victor promised to give up drinking. Tanya had returned to him, and Victor kept his promise.

For a little while, anyway.

Looking now at the woman the girl had become, Ramón felt a little dizzy with lost chances and lost hopes and ruined dreams. She was not the softly round girl he'd been smitten with that day so long ago. Her hair was not curled and wispy, but cut straight across so it hung like a gleaming golden brown curtain at her shoulders. Her face and body were thinner and harder, lean as a coyote's. She had a long, ropy kind of muscle in her upper arms, the kind that came from sustained hard work.

Her exotically beautiful blue eyes were wary as they met his. "Do I have something on my chin?" she asked.

He shook his head, smiling. "Sorry. I was just remembering the last time I saw you."

The faintest hint of a smile curved her pretty mouth. "Boy, that was forever ago. Another lifetime."

"It was." He took a breath, trying to think of a way to pick his way through the minefield of memories.

He opted for flattery. "You were so pretty I couldn't believe you danced with me."

A small wash of rose touched her cheeks. She glanced out the window, then back to him. "What I remember is how smart you were. You talked to me like I was smart, too. It meant a lot to me."

Ramón smiled at her, feeling a warmth he'd thought far beyond his reach. "Me, too."

At that moment, the waitress brought their food. Ramón leaned back and let go of a breath as the waitress put his plate down. Things would be all right. He hadn't been sure.

Once she got some hot food inside her hollow stomach, Tanya felt stronger. The stamina and common strength she'd worked to build for eleven years seeped back, and with it, a sense of normalcy.

With a sigh, she leaned back in the turquoise vinyl booth. "Much better."

"Good."

The waitress came by with a steel coffeepot, topped their cups, and whisked away Tanya's empty bowl. "I'm sorry I seemed so strange back at the station," Tanya said. "It's just a little overwhelming."

"Don't apologize. I'm sorry I startled you." He finished the last bites of an enormous smothered burrito and pushed the plate to one side. "Let's start fresh."

"Okay." She attempted a smile, and felt the unused muscles in her face creak only a little. "Didn't you wear glasses?"

"Yeah." His grin was wry. "I'm blind as a bat, but

glasses aren't real practical on a ranch.'' He touched his lips with his napkin. ''Weren't you blonde?''

''Sort of,'' she said with a shrug. ''Victor liked my hair light, so I dyed it for him. This is the natural color.''

''I like it.'' His gaze lingered, and Tanya saw a shimmer of sexual approval in those unrelentingly black irises.

An answering spark lit somewhere deep and cold within her, and Tanya found herself noticing again his mouth—full-lipped and sensual. On another man, it would have seemed too lush, but amid the savagely beautiful planes and angles of his face, it seemed only to promise pleasure beyond all imagining.

The cinders of burned-out feelings within her flared a little brighter, stirring a soft, tiny flame of awareness she'd not known in a long, long time.

Abruptly she quenched it, stamping hard at the spark to kill it. She tore her gaze away and poked her soda with the straw. ''Why don't you tell me about my job?''

As if he understood the reason for the abrupt change of subject, Ramón replied in an impersonal tone. ''You'll be cooking. Desmary has needed someone for quite some time, but it's hard to find someone with institutional experience in such an underpopulated area.''

Tanya couldn't resist a small, wry dig at her own background. ''If it's institutional food you want, I'm a master.''

He chuckled. ''Good. Desmary, the head cook, can't move around as well as she used to, but there's no place else for her to go. You're going to be her feet and her helper.'' He paused to dip a chip in salsa. ''She's pretty independent, so if you can be discreet about helping her, I'd appreciate it.''

''No problem.''

''We've got a full house at the moment, twenty-five boys. They all have KP, so basically you're in charge of just getting them fed, and they clean up. Anybody who wants to cook can sign up to help, and you'll usually have a couple of boys every day.''

''How old are the kids?''

''The youngest right now is eight. They don't often get into serious trouble much earlier than that. The oldest is seventeen. Most of them are twelve to fifteen.''

Tanya half smiled. ''It's going to be quite a switch for me to go from an almost completely female environment to one dominated by males.''

''And teenage boys are more male than they'll ever be again.'' Ramón shook his head. ''There are few women out there. I'm trying to change that, so the boys can learn to treat women with respect.'' He lifted one shoulder. ''You may not always get it.''

''I can handle that.''

''You'll have to.''

That sounded a little intimidating. Tanya lifted her eyebrows in question.

''There are rules to create discipline and order, to teach the boys how to behave themselves. If one of them is disrespectful, you'll be expected to manage the situation.''

Tanya frowned. ''What constitutes disrespectful?''

He grinned. "If it wouldn't have gone over in 1920, it won't go over now."

"You're kidding."

"Not at all." His face was sober, but the dark eyes shone with intense passion. "Some of these boys are like animals when they come to me. They don't know how to eat at the table, or how to dress for regular society. They treat women and girls like sluts or possessions, like a pair of shoes."

Like a possession. Tanya felt the tightness in her chest again. That was the way Victor had treated her. And she'd allowed it for a long time. She looked away, to the calm scene beyond the windows.

"I'm trying to give them dignity, Tanya," he said. "I think you can help me."

Dignity. What dignity had she had, all these years? Had she ever known it? "I'll do my best."

"That's all I ask of anyone," he said, and picked up the check. "Are you ready?"

A swift wave of nerves and anticipation washed through her. "Yes."

Chapter Two

Dear Antonio,
You must be starting kindergarten this year. I wish I could see you. I'd tell you to be sure to stand up straight and make sure your hands are clean before you go. If you want people to respect you, you have to hold your head high.

I've started school, too. I'll get my GED, then take some classes from the college instructors who volunteer out here. I'm not sure what I want to study, but it helps to pass the time, and I'm good at it. It's something I can use to hold my head up high.

Love, Mom

The ranch was twelve miles from town, over rutted gravel roads. Ramón, seeming to sense Tanya's sudden nervousness, kept up a steady narration as they drove. She was grateful.

He'd started the boy ranch seven years before, he told her. Using grants from several sources, he established it as a place for troubled young boys. From the beginning, his intention had been to provide an alternative to the usual reform schools and foster homes in which such children were normally placed.

"You'll forgive me for saying so, but I don't see how it can be much different."

He smiled. "Ah, but it is different. Everything is different."

"Like what?"

"Like I'm trying to give them an old-fashioned sense of belonging, a sense of family." He gave her a quick glance. "When I was working with these kids in Albuquerque, the thing I saw over and over was that there was no one to take care of them—give them meals on time, make sure they brushed their teeth and wore appropriate clothing. Until someone gave them that much dignity, a probation officer couldn't do much."

Tanya nodded slowly. "So who gets to live at the Last Chance?" The name made her smile.

"Only the worst ones."

"Doesn't that mean you lose a lot of them?"

His answer was unflinching and unsentimental. "Yes."

Tanya frowned. "Isn't that painful?"

He looked at her. "Every time." The muscle on his

jaw drew tight and he cleared his throat. "We lost one last week when he went home on a weekend furlough. Tried to rob a convenience store and was shot while fleeing. Such a waste."

Tanya could tell by the roughness in his voice that he hadn't yet recovered from the loss. She wondered how he could stand to care so much, over and over again.

As if to gird himself, Ramón changed the subject. "They work hard, these kids. They plant and harvest our gardens, take care of the animals, clean the barns and rake the corrals. It makes them strong, gives them something to believe in."

"What kind of animals do you have?"

Ramón touched his chin, and Tanya picked up the faintest touch of embarrassment in the gesture. Puzzled, she waited for the answer.

"A lot of them," he said. "Goats, sheep, horses, cows, dogs, cats, rabbits, chickens. You name it, we've probably got it."

"Isn't it hard to feed all those animals?"

"Nah. We eventually butcher the chickens and rabbits, pigs and cows. Some of the boys don't like that duty, but most of them get around to appreciating the way food comes to the table after a while." He gave her a quick, amused glance. "Ever wrung a chicken's neck?"

Horrified, Tanya shook her head. "No!"

"Don't worry. Desmary will do it until you get used to the idea."

He said it as if she just naturally would get used to it. "All the food comes from the ranch?"

"As much as possible. It's part of teaching self-sufficiency." He turned onto a narrow dirt road and drove through a gate. "There's great dignity in providing for yourself."

"What about all the dogs and cats?"

He smiled. "Just for love. Nothing like a dog or a cat to love you when it seems like the whole world is against you."

Tanya looked at him. Against the cloudy sky, his profile was sharp, his expression certain and strong. "How did you make it happen?" she asked.

He glanced at her, then back to the road. On a rise, the buildings of the ranch appeared—a huge barn, a white farmhouse sitting in a copse of cottonwoods, three long wooden buildings with porches. "I worked with the probation system for six years, then my grandfather left me this land." He shrugged. "It seemed like it might be good for those boys to be closer to the land, so I wrote the proposals and got a bunch of grants."

He made it sound simple, but Tanya had a feeling the path had been far from easy.

They drew closer to the buildings, and anxiety sharp as talons clawed at Tanya. She could see figures moving in the corrals and around the house. Was Antonio among them? "I'm so scared," she blurted out. "Do you think he'll recognize me?"

"No," he replied quietly. "He was only three, Tanya."

"I just don't want him to feel he has to like me or forgive me. I just want to see him." She swallowed. "So much."

"I know." He slowed a little, as if to give her time to collect herself. "This is best, his not knowing who you are right away. He doesn't understand the court orders, so he thinks you didn't want him."

A bitterness twisted her lips. She had been vulnerable after the trial, too weary to fight Victor's family any longer, and desperate to see that Antonio had a good home with someone she trusted. To make sure it was Ramón and not one of Victor's sisters, who hated her, Tanya had agreed to sever contact with Antonio as long as she was in jail. With her lawyer's help, she had managed to have the restriction lifted upon her release from prison, but that didn't make up for the lost eleven years. If she were Antonio, she'd feel betrayed, too.

She lifted her chin, feeling suddenly stronger. This was what she had waited for—to see her son again. Whether he knew she was his mother or not was beside the point. Thanks to Ramón's kindness, she would have the chance to know her child.

"Thank you, Ramón," she said. "You didn't have to give me this chance, and I am very grateful."

"*De nada.*" He gave her a lazy wink. "I needed a cook."

Then they were pulling into the driveway, beneath the gold leaves on the branches of the cottonwood trees. A swarm of boys lifted their heads to watch. Tanya gathered her purse and put her hand on the door, scanning the faces eagerly. Would she even know him after so long?

Her gaze caught on a youth on the porch, eating an apple. Unlike Ramón, he wore his straight black hair short, combed back from his high forehead. The style showed off a dramatically carved and beautiful face—those heavy dark eyebrows, the distinctive and beautiful Quezada nose, his father's high cheekbones—and Tanya's blue eyes, striking in the dark face.

She had been afraid she might cry, that even all those years of training herself to hide her emotions couldn't help her at this moment. Instead, as she stared at the face of her son after more than four thousand days of waiting, she smiled.

Ramón watched Tanya step out of the truck. There was shyness in the angle of her head, a certain hesitancy as she glanced at the pack of boys who milled toward her, but she didn't cower. He pursed his lips, watching them take her measure, and was pleased when her chin lifted, when she met their eyes without flinching.

Good, he thought. After the way she had reacted to him in the bus station, he had been afraid she wouldn't be able to stand up to this inspection, that her abusive relationship had ruined her permanently.

Standing there, her expression carefully neutral, she met the gaze of these rough boys with a roughness of her own. She knew where they came from. She'd been there. They saw it, too, and their predatory instincts were appeased, at least for the moment.

Ramón smiled. "Gentlemen," he said, in spite of the covert glances some of them swept over Tanya's shapely form, "this is our new cook, Ms. Bishop."

There were murmurs and nods. The newer boys looked to the ones who'd been residents longer for clues to the right behavior. "You'll meet everyone sooner or later," Ramón said, rounding the truck to stand near her. He pointed out and named a few of the closest faces, knowing the only one she would remember was the last. "The one on the porch is Tonio Quezada, my son."

Tanya nodded at all of them, smiling at the younger ones. Ramón was impressed when she managed the same polite nod toward her son as she had toward the others.

Then she looked up at Ramón with a smile of singular sweetness. Joy spilled from the wide blue eyes, eyes that somehow still carried a touching innocence. High color lit her cheeks. Her expression was meant to convey to him what she could not say in front of all these witnesses—the most heartfelt gratitude he'd ever received. Her face made him think of the statue of the Madonna in the church where he'd grown up— sweet and purely carved.

"Let me show you your room," he said briskly. "Tonio! Grab the bag." He barked out other orders and the boys scurried to obey.

All except Zach, an eight-year-old with a bristly blond flattop and a smattering of freckles across his sullen face.

"What's up, Zach?" Ramón asked.

The boy tucked his thumbs into his jeans and stared at Tanya. "Nothin'," he said.

"Have you done your chores?" Tonio asked, coming up behind the adults.

"You're not the boss of me," Zach snarled.

Ramón frowned. The child was fairly new—he'd

only been there for a little more than two weeks—and had come to the ranch only after his sixteenth arrest, when no foster homes would take him. A hard case, but he was so young, Ramón intended to keep him awhile if he could. "Zach, is there something on your mind?"

His flat, hostile gaze flickered over Tanya, then to Tonio. "He's always telling me what to do. Damn Goody Two-shoes."

Ramón gave Tanya an apologetic lift of the brows. To Tonio, he said, "Son, show Ms. Bishop to her room, please."

"Sure." The long-legged teenager opened the door. "Right this way."

Tanya gave Ramón a single, terrified glance, then took a breath and followed her son.

Ramón waited until they had gone inside, then remained silent a moment longer, watching Zach carefully. The boy was very upset about something. He was fighting tears even as they stood there. "Are you having some problem, Zach? You want to tell me about it?"

Zach wavered a moment, then lifted his head and uttered an obscenity that more or less told Ramón to get lost.

Ramón sighed. "I hope you had a good lunch, son—"

"I'm not your son! I'm not anybody's son! Leave me alone!"

When he would have bolted from the porch, Ramón grabbed him firmly by the arm. Holding on just above the elbow, he headed for the dorms, Zach cursing and tugging all the way. "You know the rules, Zach. If you swear, you'll go to bed with no supper. I hate to do it, but you leave me no choice."

A dark, burly man met them at the door of the dorms. "Zach will not be dining with us tonight," Ramón said. "Will you see him to his room, Mr. Mahaney?"

"I'm real sorry to hear that, Zach."

The boy, out of control now, swore again. The two men exchanged grips. "Mozart tonight, I think," Ramón said, smiling.

"Good choice," David Mahaney said.

Tanya followed Tonio into the house. Her heart raced with a sick speed, making her feel almost faint. When the edges of her vision grew dark, she stopped abruptly, forcing herself to breathe in slow, steady breaths. It would not make a nice impression to hyperventilate and faint in the hall.

Tonio stopped and turned around. "You okay?"

Tanya nodded, breathing slowly, her hand on a carved wooden post. "It's just been a long day," she said.

He smiled, and it wasn't phoney or falsely patient. "I'll have Desmary bring you some coffee or something."

"No, that's all right," she said, straightening. "I'm fine."

"Sure?"

Oh, Ramón, you've done a fine, fine job! Tanya smiled. "Very."

By the time he'd led the way up a wide, sweeping

staircase to the third floor of the old farmhouse, Tanya
had calmed considerably. He showed her into a gra-
cious, turn-of-the-century room with wide windows
overlooking the semiarid land. Sea foam green wall-
paper graced the angles made by the dormers, and a
handmade quilt in green and white covered the bed.
For a single moment, Tanya could not quite believe
this would be her room.

With a surprising lack of self-consciousness, Tonio
pointed out the bathroom down the hall, the linen
closet and various other amenities. She drank in the
resonant tenor of his voice and found hints of the
three-year-old she'd left behind.

But she could not study him the way she wished to,
not now. She couldn't seem too curious or strange, so
it would have to be done in bits. His voice, his easy
movements—those were enough for now.

"Thanks," she said, finally, knowing she should let
him go. "I'll be fine."

"See you at dinner," Tonio said amiably, and left,
shutting the door behind him.

Tanya sank down on the bed, alone in the quiet for
the first time since she could remember. Even at the
halfway house, there had been constant noise—the
sound of a radio or a telephone or people talking, and
the rooms had been only one step above the cells at
the prison. Here, the quilt was soft with many wash-
ings and smelled faintly of dusting powder. With a
sense of sybaritic freedom, Tanya closed her eyes and
pulled the quilt around her, drowning in the delicious-
ness.

This was what she had missed, more than anything.

Pure solitude, and silence. For several long moments, she reveled in it, drowned in it, and then was startled by a knock at the door. "Just a minute!" she called.

It was Antonio, back again, a stack of magazines in his hands. "Don't tell my dad I forgot these," he said, sheepishly. "I was supposed to put them in here before you got here and I forgot."

Tanya smiled and accepted the stack. "The *New Yorker?*" she said in a puzzled voice. "Interesting."

Tonio inclined his head, putting his hands on his hips. "Yeah, well, Dad's got this thing about magazines. Everybody has magazines in their rooms— weird stuff, all of it, like that."

Tanya sensed he wasn't in a hurry to go, and held the magazines loosely against her chest. As if she were only lazily making conversation, she flipped the top magazine against her and asked, "Where do they come from?"

"In the mail. We get like twenty magazines and newspapers a week. The postman has to make a special trip."

Tanya lifted her head and smiled. "He has an unusual approach to things, doesn't he?"

"Yeah." He shrugged. "Yeah, he's a good guy once you get through all his weirdness."

"Weird?" Now she noticed the beautiful slant of her son's eyes, the deep clear blue framed with extraordinarily long, sooty lashes. As a baby, those lashes had swept over half his cheeks when he slept. No old lady in the world could resist him. "He doesn't seem weird to me."

Tonio gave her a tilted smile, and the expression

was rakish, even in a fourteen-year-old. "You'll see." There was fondness in his tone. "He's not like anybody else."

Tanya nodded. "Thanks. I won't tell you forgot."

"Desmary said you can come on down whenever you want."

"Thanks," she said again, and her hope that everything would be all right soared. Cheerfully, she changed her clothes and went down the stairs to the kitchen, humming softly under her breath.

For the most part, it didn't look as if much of the farmhouse had been altered. As she passed through the rooms of the ground floor—living room, library, what surely once would have been called a parlor, and dining room with a fireplace—she noticed the fine detail work that was the hallmark of turn-of-the-century craftsmen. All had been lovingly preserved.

Even in the kitchen, attempts had been made to keep the original flavor of the old house. A broad bank of windows looked toward the barns, and a big butcher-block table dominated the center of the room.

There the quaintness ended and the stainless steel began. Industrial-size refrigerators banked one wall, and below the windows were deep, functional sinks adjacent to a huge dishwasher in the corner.

Stirring the contents of a big pot was an old woman, almost whimsically misplaced in the gleaming kitchen. She turned at the sound of Tanya's feet on the linoleum floor, and Tanya was reminded of dolls made from apples. Her pale brown face was seamed deeply around snapping, alert blue eyes. A flour-dusted red apron covered a plump figure, and gray-and-white braids touched her hips. "Hi," Tanya said, a little shyly. "You must be Desmary."

"Hello, Tanya!" Her voice was both robust and kind. "I've been waiting to meet you. Come in and sit down."

"Oh, I'd rather help you get supper on the table, if I may."

"Today, you just watch how I do things." She pointed with a wooden spoon to the banks of cupboards along one wall. "Poke around and find out where things are, and you'll be more of a help than a hindrance tomorrow." She smiled over her shoulder.

Tanya chuckled. "Okay." Still a little hesitant, she rounded the room, opening doors and cupboards and drawers. "How long have you worked here?" she asked, memorizing the organization of the refrigerator and freezer.

"I've been a cook all my life," she said, and Tanya caught a hint of a lilt to her words. Irish or perhaps Scottish, but a long time in the past. "I've been cookin' for Ramón and his boys since he opened up the ranch to them."

"Do you like it?"

"Aye." She gestured toward the drawers. "Fetch me a slotted spoon from that top one, will you?"

Tanya hurried to comply. As Desmary turned to take the utensil, Tanya saw the rolling, limping gait of very bad feet, and nearly offered to fetch a stool as well, but remembered in time that Ramón had asked her to be discreet. Instead, she pointed through a set of double doors to a long, open room set with small, family-size tables. "Is that where everyone eats?"

"The boys and the counselors eat there," she said. "The rest of us use the other dining room—you'll eat with us." Lifting chicken pieces from broth, she added, "Ramón would give everything to the boys. But I told him he needs to have a time he isn't with them."

Tanya smiled. "You take care of him, then."

"Aye, since he has no wife or mother to do it." She gave Tanya a mischievous grin. "Men can't do it by themselves, as I'm sure you're aware."

The back door opened and as if their conversation had called him, Ramón strode in. Tanya noticed again the sense of energy that surrounded him, a vigor she found deeply appealing. "Ah, you've met! Good."

"Aye, we've met, no thanks to you, lad." Desmary turned, her movements as laborious as before, and Tanya caught Ramón's eye above the old woman's head. Quick knowledge passed between them—Tanya would happily share his cause to protect and make comfortable this delightful woman.

He joined them beside the stove and reached for a shred of chicken, which he popped into his mouth before Desmary could slap his hand. "Not bad," he said with a wink toward Tanya. "Needs salt."

"Leave my food alone, boy, or I'll feed you porridge for dinner."

Ramón chuckled. "No, you won't, old woman," he said, touching her shoulder fondly. "I brought you a helper today."

He touched Tanya's shoulder, too. The gesture was meant to be inclusive and comforting, and she could tell from even such short acquaintance that Ramón was the sort of man who touched people easily and often.

She told herself all those things, feeling the light, friendly grip of that beautiful, long-fingered hand against her skin. But reason warred with emotion, and even the emotions warred with each other. In eleven years, she'd not been touched in friendliness, and her first impulse was to pull away violently, as she had at the bus station. She quelled the impulse by staring at the piles of steaming chicken on a plate.

Ramón's fingers moved on her shoulder and on Desmary's. Inclusive, gentle, meant to comfort. She swallowed, hearing only the voices that flowed around her in easy camaraderie as a second emotion swelled through her: need. Not need as in desire, although his warm palm sparked the same rustling of cinders she'd experienced earlier. No, this need was more dangerous even than desire. It was the oldest and most devastating need of the human spirit, the need to be enfolded, held close to the heart and soul of another, mingling comfort and quiet and...

Pressing her lips together, she eased away from him, pretending to need to find something from a drawer. When she looked up, Ramón was gazing at her silently, a measuring expression in his dark eyes.

Hastily, she looked away, wondering how in the world she was going to gird herself to resist him.

Chapter Three

Dear Antonio,

I've taken up running. It's strange to be doing it—me, who could never play any sport, who was always the last one chosen for a game in school—but I love it. I love moving in the morning air, feeling the wind cool my hot skin. I love the taste of morning on my tongue. But mostly, I like feeling strong. I like feeling as if no one could catch me unless I wanted them to.

Maybe if I'd learned to run before this, you and I would be running somewhere together. Maybe I'd be the one taking you to first grade, instead of your uncle Ramón. Maybe—

No, thinking that way makes a person crazy. I love running. I'm glad I found it. Perhaps one

day, you and I will have a chance to run on a
track or in a park somewhere. Anywhere. Be
good, *hijo*.

Love, Mom

Dinner that first night was awkward. Tanya ate with
Ramón and Tonio and Desmary in the warm, wood-
trimmed dining room with its built-in buffet and lace
curtains hanging at the windows. She tried to appear
alert and interested in the conversation, but the truth
was, waves of exhaustion and emotion—shock, joy,
and if she allowed it, attraction—rocked her.

Putting peas on her plate, she tried to ignore that
last thought and the way it sneaked in, like a boy in
the trunk of a car at a drive-in movie. She couldn't
allow herself the luxury of even considering Ramón
Quezada attractive. She couldn't let herself be that vulnerable.

In prison, she had learned to stay alert, to live in
the moment. It had been the only way she could quell
the periodic attacks of panic she experienced there. By
focusing on the very instant in which she found herself, she could manage anything. Such an approach
helped her handle terrible things by taking them one
at a time. It also gave her an ability to treasure the
joyous moments, to really be present in them when
they happened. Taking in a calming, deep breath, she
looked around. In this moment she saw Tonio at fourteen, his hair black and gleaming, his teeth even and
big and white in his planed face. A beautiful man-child
who'd once shared her very blood. He shared this mo-

ment with her, after so many years of her wishing it could be so.

A miracle.

At the edge of her peripheral vision, Ramón laughed. She saw his long, dark throat move with his pleasure, saw his lips turn up, his teeth shine white.

Tanya willed her focus to the other side of the table, where Desmary sat, her hair gone wispy with the heat of the kitchen, her apple-doll face shadowed in the low light. Tanya knew she would like the old woman.

But women were always easier. She understood women. Men had such different signals and ways of being. Their customs and language were a thing apart.

Ramón moved. Tanya glanced over, and watched as he bent to give a tidbit of food to a cat who waited patiently at the side of his chair. The cat delicately accepted the morsel from his long fingers, and Ramón patiently waited until the cat was finished before he straightened.

He caught her gaze and gave her a sheepish grin. "Sorry about that. Do you hate to see animals fed from the table? I know a lot of people don't like it."

"I don't mind," she said. "I never had pets."

"Never?" Tonio echoed. As if stunned, he looked around the room. A border collie slept by the door, a canary sang in a corner, and the tortoiseshell cat kept vigil at Ramón's chair. "How sad."

Tanya smiled. "It was. I'm glad I can get to know so many animals here."

Ramón chuckled. "I think Merlin would be a good dog for Tanya, don't you? He likes women a lot."

"Merlin?"

"I bet we won't even have to introduce you," Ramón said. "Merlin will find you." A twinkle shone in his dark eyes. "He's a character, I warn you."

The chuckle and the twinkle and his mesmerizing voice combined to envelope Tanya in a powerful field of sexual awareness. It was bold and clear and true—and all the more overwhelming because it had been so long since she'd experienced the feeling. With effort, she looked away. "I'll look forward to it," she mumbled.

Focus, she told herself. Candles burned in old brass candlesticks on the mantel, their flames reflecting in the high mirror over the fireplace. A small table by the hearth held a very elaborate chess set, made of carved silver-and-brass figures set with faux jewels. A woman had made this room, she thought, and wondered who. Ramón's mother? Grandmother? A sister?

On the table were handmade rolls and a bowl of peas and a nice slab of roast beef, and a pot of coffee and a pitcher of water.

Tanya tried to keep her focus on those things, but every time she turned her head even a little, there he was again, filling her vision. It astonished her that he'd grown so fully into himself, so rich a feast for her senses that she could barely stand to look at him.

Focus. On Antonio. Her son. What an amazing thought that was sometimes! She liked his voice. Not too deep, not too high—a pleasant tenor faintly lilting with a southwest accent. That accent had delighted her upon her arrival in Albuquerque so many years ago, and it would have surprised her deeply if he'd escaped it. He spoke now of his girlfriend, Teresa, who was fourteen and very smart.

Tanya smiled at that. "Does she get good grades?" she asked, buttering a roll.

"No. She's not real good at school but she's smart about everything. She knows stuff." He brightened. "She likes to read."

It was impossible to avoid sharing a smile with Ramón over that. He'd been so impressed with her taste in reading—and Tanya hadn't even known enough to know she was slowly working her way through most of the classics of the English language. She just read because she liked it, because books were safe and took her away from the strains of daily life.

And not even Victor could be jealous of a book.

Ramón winked at her. His expression was gentle and kind, his fathomless eyes like the night sky, endless and vast beyond all imagining. He had a great face, Tanya thought, admiring again the cut of cheekbones, the high-bridged nose and elegantly carved nostrils. She avoided his mouth this time. It was just too—well, *sexy.*

As if he sensed her thoughts, something in his face changed. It was slight and almost indefinable, but definite. It was a penetrating expression that made her aware of her female parts. Aware of her skin, and her limbs. It made her aware, too, of *his* skin and limbs and male parts.

The thought was unexpected and oddly erotic. Trying to appear composed, she reached for the bowl of mashed potatoes. The bowl was not a problem, but she had terrible trouble grasping the spoon between her thumb and forefinger. It was only a matter of seconds, but it seemed like hours before she could hold it properly and ladle potatoes on her plate.

"This food is wonderful, Desmary," she said. Her voice croaked a little. Embarrassed, she vowed to be quiet, and keep her eyes to herself.

In a few days, she'd be used to everything, she told herself. She'd be used to the smells of the farmhouse, age and cooking and maleness. She'd be used to the sound of Ramón's voice, rich with inflections, rolling around her like a musical composition. She'd be used to catching sight of Antonio, blue-eyed and dark and so beautiful.

Feeling close to tears, she put her fork carefully beside her plate and looked at Ramón. "I think I'm very tired. I'd like to go to my room."

A flicker of concern touched his eyes. "Are you all right?"

"Yes." She stood. "It's just been a very long day."

Ramón put his napkin aside. "I'll walk up with you."

"No. Please, just enjoy your dinner."

"I'll be back in a minute, Desmary. Don't let the boys take my plate."

His solicitousness made her feel even more vulnerable, and therefore panicky. She'd spent too many long years learning how to hide her feelings, how to appear strong when she felt like a marshmallow inside.

But in all that time, she'd not had to confront her past in such concrete ways. Nor had she been attracted to anyone. In fact, she'd believed that part of her dead forever until she'd seen Ramón standing on the platform this afternoon.

Now he stood there, beautiful and kind, holding out one long-fingered brown hand toward her. "I'm okay," she said, and bolted.

She ran all the way to her room on the third floor and slammed the door closed. The soft, soft bed with its piles of pillows looked as inviting as a mother's arms. She kicked off her shoes and dived into the comforting mass, making a cocoon of pillows and coverlet, shutting out all thought with the same picture that had given her comfort so many nights in prison...a simple open meadow, surrounded with tall pines. In the middle of it was a tent. Her tent. When she went in, nothing could harm her.

Thus comforted, she fell asleep.

Ramón cursed himself as Tanya ran away from him. Once again, he'd frightened her. It was going to be a lot more difficult than he thought to learn his way around her.

She didn't reappear that evening, and just before he turned in, Ramón knocked on her door, softly. Light spilled out from below it, and he knocked again, a little louder, when she didn't answer.

Still no sound from beyond. Concerned, he pursed his lips and weighed his choices. Although she'd tried to seem calm, he'd seen her distress earlier, and he knew he wouldn't sleep until he found out she was all right. He knocked again, firmly. Again, no answer.

He could go down the stairs and get Desmary, but that would mean making the old woman walk up three flights of stairs on her bad feet. He didn't have the heart. There were no other women in the house.

But what if he opened the door and Tanya wasn't dressed?

He'd just peek in, carefully. If she was all right, he'd just close the door and go on his way. If not, he'd be glad he looked in on her.

Turning the handle very slowly, he pushed the door open a crack and peered inside. For a moment, he could see no sign of her at all. Then he spied her, on the bed and mostly dressed.

She was sound asleep. A small snore wheezed in and out of her slightly parted lips. She'd evidentially started out curled in the covers, but the house was warm, and she'd flung parts of the covers off. Her shirt was unbuttoned a little, and a swell of breast spilled from the opening, as if anxious to be freed. One arm and one bare leg were uncovered.

Ramón stood at the bedside admiring her with a feeling he couldn't quite identify. How many times had he thought of her sleeping in the cold, dead confines of a prison cot while he lay alone in a double bed, a pillow clasped to his chest? How many times had he wondered how time had changed her, molded her?

Every day. Every day he had thought of her.

As he stood there, she turned, muttering to herself, and a spill of hair fell over her face. Gently, he reached out to push it away, unwilling to leave her alone just yet. He wanted to just watch her sleep, knowing she was finally safe here.

His touch startled her. She came awake with an eerie, sharp suddenness, sitting straight up and bumping his mouth with her head. He made a noise and moved back, bringing his fingers to his lip, and tasted blood. He stumbled backward, out of her way.

She blinked, staring at him, at her room in disorientation. Slowly, she seemed to get her bearings, and Ramón felt guilty for disturbing her. "What are you doing in here?" she asked at last.

"I was worried about you."

Tanya rubbed her head, eyeing his mouth. "I'd suggest in the future that you don't touch me when you wake me up. Just say my name."

"No problem." He gave her a rueful smile. "Sorry. Soon enough you won't need a worrywart checking on you."

She rubbed her face, pulling back her hair in an unconsciously sexy gesture that put her breasts in relief against the lamplight shining through her blouse. He looked away, but his gaze snagged on her bare knees, smooth and neat-looking. He backed toward the door. "I'll leave you alone now," he said.

She looked at him soberly. "I'm sorry about the way I left the dinner table, Ramón. I just got scared all of a sudden."

"I know," he said. All at once, he was struck with her isolation here. Who did she have to lean on in this new time of her life?

Who had she ever had?

Ramón pointed to the bed, nearby her. "Do you mind if I sit down for a minute?"

The smallest hesitation marked her response. "No," she said quietly. "No, I don't mind."

He sat down next to her. Felt the warmth of her leg

against his own. "You're as jumpy as a cricket," he said, looking at her. "What scares you the most?"

She gazed up at him steadily for a minute, and in the dark blue waters of her eyes, he saw a thousand moving thoughts. "You," she said at last. "You scare me."

The answer was so unexpected, Ramón found himself speechless. Finally he asked, "Why me?"

But the first honesty had been all she could manage. With a diffident lift of her shoulder, she looked at her hands. "I don't know."

He ached to put his arm around her, as he would one of the lost boys he took in. He wanted to hold her until the cold places inside her could thaw. But he'd seen her reaction to his touch earlier and knew it would take some time before she could allow her walls to be breached.

Instead, he bent almost sideways to look into her face from an exaggeratedly silly angle. "I'm a clown, *grilla*. You don't have to be afraid of me."

"Gria?"

"Cricket," he said, smiling.

A reluctant grin touched her mouth, and he saw a flash of the impossibly young girl he'd danced with at a wedding reception so long ago. "No, I'm not afraid of you like that. I know you aren't mean," she said.

He knew what she meant, but didn't know if it should be acknowledged between them or left to lie. Acting out of pure instinct, he said, "Ah, you mean because I'm so gorgeous!"

It was the right thing to say. She laughed. "Yes. That's it."

"Well, don't worry," he said briskly, and patted her knee. Standing to take his leave, he winked. "It happens to all the girls. You'll get used to it."

The open, trusting smile on her face just then was worth anything. He wished with all of himself that he could bend and put his mouth to hers, that he could taste that sweet smile.

But he could no more do it now than he could have done it fifteen years ago. Before he could be further tempted, he bowed with a flourish. "Good night, Tanya."

"Good night, Ramón."

Ten days later, in the crisp ghostly air of early October, Tanya stepped onto the wooden porch of the farmhouse. Above the Sangre de Cristos, pale dawn had begun to bleed the night from the sky. Tanya gazed at the peaks as she methodically stretched her calves and arches and hamstrings, getting ready for her morning run.

Around the corner from the barns came a dog. It was gold and white, with patches of gray. One of the counselors said he was a blue heeler mix with more good nature than good sense. She didn't care if he wasn't smart—he'd run with her every day so far, and his companionship was one of the most pleasant things she'd ever discovered.

"Good morning, Merlin," Tanya said, moving from side to side to stretch her spine. He lifted his nose at her and sat at the bottom of the steps to wait.

Her days since her arrival had settled into a pattern. Mornings she ran her usual three miles, then got back in time to shower and help Desmary get breakfast on the table before the bus came for the boys who had clearance to go to public school. The rest went to classes held in rooms set aside for such purposes in the dorms.

The days she spent working with Desmary and whatever boys happened to be on KP that week or just drifted in to sit at the table and steal nibbles of carrot or apple or cake batter. Sometimes Tonio was one of them.

They seemed so hungry to just sit in the kitchen with the women that Tanya asked Desmary about it.

"They miss their mothers," Desmary had replied simply.

"You ready, Merlin?" Tanya skipped down the steps and paused to scratch the dog's ears. He made a soft, whining yip to signal his impatience.

"Come on, then," she said with a laugh.

Tanya began to run loosely, past the barns and the corrals, the pens with their sheep, the vast gardens with tangles of yellowing squash and melon vines, and pepper and tomato plants still heavily laden with fruit. Behind them grew stands of corn.

The air tasted like leaf smoke, and Tanya smiled, thinking it had been a long time since she'd smelled that particular aroma. Out here, some agricultural burning was allowed.

Her body fell into its natural, loping rhythm. She didn't run fast, just steadfastly. This morning, she took particular joy in the sturdy new running shoes on her feet. They had cost almost half her first paycheck, but even after one day, Tanya could feel the difference. In the prison yard, where she'd run in the grass along the perimeters of the fence, a pair of ordinary sneakers had been fine. Here there were cacti and thorny goatheads and the possibility of snakes, and she'd quickly seen the need for better shoes.

Aside from the protection they offered from pointy invasions, they made her feet feel embraced. Bouncing, she tested the sensations once again. A hug around her arch, a cushion under the balls of her feet. Quite luxurious.

She'd also purchased a pair of sweats and a sweatshirt in dark blue, and she was grateful for their warmth this chilly morning. Her cheeks tingled with a sharp breeze sweeping down from the northern mountains.

Merlin crisscrossed the path in front of her like a vigilant scout, and it made her feel safe. The fine thin mountain air tasted as cool and sweet as apples, and she breathed in with gratitude.

Glorious.

As a girl, Tanya had never been athletic. She was hopelessly incapable of doing anything with a ball, whether it be basket, bowling or tennis balls. There was just some short circuit in her brain that made it impossible for her. In school she'd suffered endless humiliations at the hands of gestapo teachers and cruel classmates. She flunked PE her junior year and vowed she'd never go back.

And she hadn't.

In prison, however, she'd discovered the deep pleasure of solitary noncompetitive exercise. At first, she'd simply walked the perimeters of the yard, over and over and over, walking away her grief and fury so she wouldn't lose her mind inside the walls of he cell. That had gone on for a long time, her restless, endless walking. One day, almost crazy with missing her son, she bent her head down and leaned into a run. When she stopped twenty minutes later, her heart pounding, her breath ragged, she had felt a strange peace.

Sometimes, she didn't feel like running, so she walked. Sometimes she didn't feel like even walking, but she did it anyway. Over a long, long time, her body had grown lean and ropy, like the body of an antelope, and she moved with a loose freedom she'd never known. Running made her strong.

She and Merlin made their circle and returned to the main buildings just as the sun came over the horizon. At the barn, she slowed to a walk to let her body cool down, feeling a pleasant tingle in her limbs, as if her blood were seltzer. Next to her, Merlin gave a little dancing leap and licked her fingers. She patted his head. "Good dog."

When she came into the yard near the house, she saw Ramón standing on the porch. He wore jeans and well-used riding boots, a black jean jacket and a flannel shirt. Ready for a day in the yard, she thought calmly. But it was only attempted calm. She couldn't catch a glimpse of him without feeling a small, electric charge at the sensual promise of that face, that mouth, those hands. To hide her discomfort, she tugged the fat band out of her hair and shook her hair loose. "Good morning," she said.

"Did you have a good run?"

"Yes." She smiled. "Always."

He didn't say anything more, but Tanya could sense there was something on his mind. At last he said, "There is going to be a harvest dance here. I wonder if you would help me plan it."

Tanya gaped. "A dance?"

"Yes. The boys can ask girls from school. We'll clear the dining room and let one of the kids play DJ. Serve food." He smiled. "You know. A dance."

For one small moment, Tanya looked at him, remembering the reception at which she had danced with him so long ago. Remembered the feeling of his strong, lean arms around her, the press of his flat stomach against her swelling one. How odd, she thought now, that the child in her at that moment had gone to him for safekeeping. "I don't know a lot about that kind of thing," she said at last. "Next to nothing. I got married pretty young."

"I know." He cocked his head in a purely Latin gesture, lifting one shoulder at the same time. "We can learn together."

It would be churlish to refuse. He'd been nothing but kind to her. "All right."

His smile—white and fast in his dark face—flashed suddenly. It struck her as forcefully as always, right in the knees. A tingling that had nothing to do with her run crept through private parts of her body. "Good." He shifted to let her pass on the steps. "Be ready about 2:00 and we can go into town for some books."

"Town?" she echoed. She'd been very, very careful to avoid his company. A cozy little ride into town didn't seem exactly the best idea. "I—"

"You haven't been to the library yet. You'll like it." His gaze was steady, fathomless. Somehow Tanya knew that he sensed all her objections and silenced them. "See you at 2:00."

There was nothing to say to that. Tanya gave him a half smile of capitulation. "Okay."

He gave her a wink and headed toward the barns. Into the quiet air rang his jaunty, tuneful whistle, and Tanya had to smile. He was the most relentlessly good-natured man she'd ever met. In ten days, she'd never heard him raise his voice or snap at a child, or get annoyed with a task. Relentlessly good-natured.

But as she watched him walk away, Tanya had to admit it was not his nature upon which she feasted her eyes. He had a rear end like a quarterback, taut and high and round.

"You gonna stand there all mornin' watching his behind," Desmary said in a droll tone from the back door, "or you gonna come help me cook sometime today?"

Tanya gave a quick laugh and turned around, aware her color was high. The old woman winked. "I'm still inclined to admire it myself." She gave a quick flick of her head toward the interior of the house. "Go get your shower. I'm all right for a little while."

"Thanks."

Chapter Four

Dear Antonio,

One of the last warm days of the year. I spent the last few days roasting and peeling chilies, and my fingers are blistered. I don't mind, though. I love the smell of them roasting.

I wonder what foods you like to eat. When you were a baby, you ate so many strawberries you got allergic to them. And you liked pork and beans and McDonald's hamburgers and candy. But you were still so little then, it isn't like big kid eating. Like having your own set of favorites and dislikes that isn't like anyone else's. I hate egg whites, you know that? And milk and okra. I love chilies and tomatoes and lots of fresh vegetables. I'm pretty good in the kitchen, too. That's where I've been working lately. It's a good place.

You be sure to eat all your vegetables. They give you clear skin and good vision and strong bones.

Love, Mom

After breakfast, Tanya chopped vegetables for the stew they would all eat for supper—fresh green peppers, some late cabbage and broccoli, and tender fresh carrots. Desmary, sitting on her high stool, gazed out the window as she kneaded bread on the counter. Tanya hummed softly a tune from childhood, about a woman who got married the day before she died.

"That's such a happy sound, that humming," Desmary said, flashing a smile over her shoulder. "Makes me think of my youth."

Tanya grinned. "Not everyone shares your enjoyment. I've been told very bluntly to shut up."

"People just get used to things being a certain way. The kids now, they don't have people sing to them. Their mothers turn on the radio when they do chores. Mine used to sing." With a deft move of her wrists, she flipped the bread dough twist and looked at Tanya. "'Amazing Grace.'"

From the short hallway that led to the communal dining room for the boys and the counselors came a child. It was the same little boy who'd been on the porch the day of Tanya's arrival. His name was Zach and he was in trouble almost all the time, and Tanya felt sorry for him. She had asked if he could be assigned to the kitchen more often, and the counselors had only been too happy to do it. For some reason, Zach calmed a little in her presence.

In his arms he carried a basket of green Anaheim peppers, long and shiny and freshly picked. Behind him came a second boy and two counselors, all bearing bushels of peppers. Desmary caught sight of them and made a noise of frustration. "I haven't seen so many peppers in one season in years!" She put her knife down and came over, her rolling gait obviously more painful than usual. With a gnarled finger, she poked the flesh of the peppers and sighed. "They have to get done right away. We'll have the apples to do this weekend."

"Apples?" Tanya echoed.

With a gloomy look, Desmary nodded. "We'll sell most of them, but some get put up in cider and butter." She snapped her fingers in annoyance. "Which reminds me—I've got to get Ramón to pick up some canning jars for me."

Tanya looked at the piles of peppers and realized she couldn't leave Desmary to fend for herself. She couldn't possibly go with Ramón to town this afternoon. She wasn't sure if she was disappointed or relieved.

To the counselors, she said, "We need a few boys to peel chilies this evening. Can you send about four or five over after supper?"

David winked. "Sure." He touched Zach's head. "Come on, kid."

Zach shot the man a glowering look and didn't move. His bristly blond flattop had been recently trimmed and stood at rigid attention over the top of his head. Freckles dotted his small nose.

"Can I keep him in here a little while?" Tanya asked. "I need some help getting these washed."

"I guess it won't hurt. Zach, you'll be in reading class in an hour—are we clear?"

"Yessir."

The counselors left. Desmary peered at the table with a look of great doom on her face. "I hate chilies," she said. "What kind of fool vegetable is that, anyway? One that burns you?"

Tanya touched her shoulder. "I'll take care of them. Why don't you take a little rest?"

"No, you need help this morning."

"No I don't." Gently, she turned Desmary around. "I'll get Ramón in here to help me with lunch. Zach is going to help me with washing the chilies, and I can get them roasted this afternoon. The boys will peel them tonight."

Desmary looked at Tanya for a long moment. "You're supposed to go to town with Ramón today."

She shrugged. "We'll go tomorrow. And I'll get you some canning jars."

Moving with deep stiffness, Desmary removed her apron and limped toward her rooms. "Call me if you need anything."

"We'll be fine," Tanya said, giving Zach a wink.

When they were alone, she lifted a bushel basket of chilies and carried them to the big stainless steel sink. "You bring them over here, Zach, and I'll wash."

"Okay."

"What are you doing home this morning?"

He carefully put the basket at her feet and straightened. "Got suspended yesterday."

"Uh-oh." Giving him an exaggerated frown over her shoulder, Tanya turned on the water in the sink and upturned a basket of chilies. "What happened?"

"That jerk Jimmy Trujillo called me names again."

"And you got suspended?"

A frown drew his sandy-colored brows into a V. "No. I hit him and broke one of his teeth."

"Didn't that hurt your hand?"

Zach leaned forward. "Look," he said, pointing to a gash on his knuckles. "That's what happened."

Very seriously, Tanya took the proffered hand and peered at the cut. It was healing nicely, but she hung on to his hand while she patted her apron pocket. "I think you need a bandage."

"Naw," Zach protested, but he didn't pull away.

Tanya located a Band-Aid—she kept them there for the small cutting knife wounds that inexperienced cooks naturally acquired—and covered the gash on Zach's knuckles. Still she didn't let go, examining his fingers and palm. "Your hands are getting chapped. You need to keep lotion on them."

"Okay." He leaned on the counter to watch her wash the chilies. "Whatcha gonna do with those?"

"Roast and peel them," she said.

"Can I help?"

"For a little while." Tanya looked at the clock. "You mustn't forget your class."

"I won't," he promised.

Tanya smiled at him, feeling a warm stir touch her heart. "I know."

Ramón found himself rushing through his chores, anxious to get everything done in time to give himself a little break this afternoon with Tanya. For several days, he'd been searching for an excuse to be with her for a few hours—just to see how she was adjusting.

Yeah, right.

He sucked in a breath. Truth was, this morning she'd been almost more gorgeous than a woman had a right to be, her hair swinging, her color high with her exercise, her legs hard beneath the sweats, her breasts moving under the—

No, he'd leave that thought alone.

Pounding a nail into the broken bit of fence he was mending, Ramón cursed. It wasn't as if he hadn't had his share of women, although he did have to be discreet. In order to provide a good example, he didn't stay out all night or bring women out here to sleep with him.

Not that a man had to stay out all night to have his needs met. But the truth was, Ramón didn't like to have sex casually. It always seemed to him sex was too intimate and revealing for anything except the deepest of relationships. Last spring, he'd broken off a long-term relationship with a teacher in Manzanares when she had finally admitted she didn't think she could stand to live at the ranch with all those boys and still pursue her own career in teaching as well as raise kids of her own. He'd understood, and had not been particularly brokenhearted. Their relationship had been close and well matched, but had there ever really been a fire?

Slam, slam, slam. He pounded nails into the fence, scaring a pair of quails from a nearby scrub oak. They flittered into the morning with noises of surprise and alarm.

Ten days Tanya had been here. Only ten days, and already Ramón had started spinning naughty fantasies about her naked body. Which would have been all right except for a couple of small details.

The most difficult aspect of the whole thing was that she was Tonio's mother—and Tonio didn't know that. When and if he found out, if they felt right about revealing that to him, things might go well or they might not. If Tonio felt betrayed—and the possibility definitely existed—then Ramón's first obligation was to Tonio. It had to be.

He took a nail from the bag around his waist and positioned it. Tonio had been told his mother's story...and professed an understanding of it, but Ramón knew the understanding was purely intellectual. Emotionally, the boy still felt his mother hadn't wanted him. Only time and maturity could change that.

The other problem was much larger and had to do with Tanya herself. When Ramón met her, she'd been eighteen and pregnant. She and Victor had been together for more than three years even then—since a fourteen-year-old Tanya had moved to Albuquerque. At nineteen, she'd divorced him. At barely twenty-two, after more than two solid years of being stalked unceasingly, Tanya had killed him.

And went to prison.

Eleven years later, the girl was a woman, but a woman who'd never had a chance to experience the full freedom of adulthood. Living on her own, making her own choices, being in charge of everything. He wanted her to have that if she wanted it. He didn't want to take advantage of her trust in him, or her gratitude to him for caring for Antonio all these years. What he wanted was impossible—an unencumbered Tanya and unfettered Ramón to meet when he was twenty-three and she was twenty. He wanted to go back in time, to rescue her from her nightmare before it ruined her life.

Impossible.

He stopped pounding and looked at the bright blue New Mexico sky above the dun and red and sage of the land. Was he chasing some dream of the past? Was he acting out of guilt? Were his feelings even genuine?

He didn't know. Until he did, he'd do his best to keep his physical attraction to himself. There was no reason in the world they couldn't just be friends for now. It was the best choice.

A boy on horseback approached. "Mr. Quezada, they need you in the kitchen."

"Did they say why?"

The boy grinned. "They've got chilies to the ceiling. Ms. Bishop says she can't go to town today, but maybe you could come help with the chilies."

Ramón was aware of a sharp, pricking sense of disappointment in his chest. But he nodded. "Thanks, Porfie."

With Ramón's help, Tanya got lunch on the table and cleaned up without incident. Afterward, they started roasting chilies.

Tanya peeked into the oven, careful to keep her face

back from the wave of heat that rolled out. The chilies swelled and made tiny noises as steam escaped from within, the green tubes rising and falling as air escaped. The skin was beginning to toast, but this batch wasn't quite done.

From behind her, almost directly at her shoulder, Ramón said, "They look like they're breathing, don't they?"

She looked at the chilies again. Rising and falling, like little green lungs. "I never noticed that before. You're right."

"They scream, too—listen."

A soft high sound of escaping air slowly filtered from the chilies. Tanya straightened with an exaggerated wince of horror. "Yuck!"

He stood rather close, close enough for her arm to brush his as she stood up, but he didn't move away. "I used to run away and hide in my room when my *abuelita* roasted chilies. I think someone should write a story about the chili monster for kids in the Southwest."

Tanya smiled up at him, drawing warm pleasure from the sense of his body so close to hers. On his chin, there was a tiny nick from his morning shave. She wanted to touch it. "Maybe you should write one," she said lightly.

A starry twinkle lit his irises. "Maybe I should." With mock seriousness, he drew his brows together. "I'll call him Diablo Chili, and give him a big shaggy mustache. He'll be one of those monsters that drag themselves up the stairs at night, panting."

"I'm never going to eat chilies again!" Tanya protested.

He laughed. "Sure you will. Smell that!"

Aware that she hadn't moved, Tanya bowed her head and shifted away, reaching automatically for the next batch of chilies and spreading them over a foil-covered cookie sheet.

"So how bad is Desmary?" Ramón asked, moving to lean one hip against the sink.

"I think she's just tired. She's resting." As if she didn't mind, as if it were nothing at all, Tanya glanced at him. "I hope you don't mind—but we have to postpone our trip to town under the circumstances."

"I understand. I'll help you finish today and we can go to town tomorrow."

Tanya couldn't help but smile at the irony. She'd seized the idea of staying here today in hopes he'd go on to town without her and she'd be spared the constant vigilance she had to maintain against his magnetic aura.

Instead, she would be trapped with him in the kitchen all day. "I can manage," she said. "Really."

"I don't mind."

"I know, but—"

His grin, white and swift, flashed on his face again. "Ah—my extreme handsomeness is making you nervous again, hmm?"

From anyone else, Tanya might have resented his pseudoarrogant teasing, but it was impossible to mind it from Ramón. For one thing, he really was devastatingly handsome. For another, she liked the idea of him defusing the tension between them like that. With a mocking smile, she said, "You've caught me again."

"I'd try to be as ugly as the chili man, but you know it's hard to hide a face like this."

Tanya laughed. "It must tough. I feel for you."

He flung up his hands in mock despair. "You have no idea!" From a basket hanging near the stove, he took four onions, two in each large hand, and put them on the counter. "I go to the store and the poor girls at the registers can't even get the numbers right. Little girls giggle behind their hands."

Following his lead, Tanya opened the freezer and took out two trays of cold, roasted chilies. She put them on the table next to a glass bowl. She flashed him a smile. "The trials and tribulations of being the most handsome man in the land."

He inclined his head and gave her a wink. Raising his chin toward the trays of chili, he asked, "What are you doing? Are you freezing them with the skins on?"

"No. If you chill them for a while, the skins come off more easily—and you don't get blisters. I had blisters so bad once that I couldn't do anything for two days."

"Me, too." He began to peel the onions deftly.

Tanya settled at the table to start skinning chilies. Under her breath, she hummed "Amazing Grace," which had been planted in her mind by Desmary's comment. Ramón didn't seem to mind it. He peeled and chopped onions, and peeked into the oven several times to shake a tray of chilies. It was very companionable.

When he finished chopping onions, he left them in

a neat pile on the counter and sat down with Tanya. "So, how is it going, anyway? Are you settling in okay?"

She smiled. "Sure. I've never had a bedroom like that in my life. It's like living in a fancy hotel."

"I always liked that room," he said. "It seemed like it would fit you. Of course, I had no idea how much you'd changed."

"It still suits me, though."

"Maybe." He lifted a shoulder. "After seeing you, I might have left it a little simpler."

"I'm glad you didn't," Tanya said. "I really missed pretty things like that."

"Yeah, you were a real girly girl back in the old days. You even had a bow in your hair."

"Not fair—I was a bridesmaid. Bridesmaids always have to wear ridiculous dresses and silly bows and dyed pink shoes." She rolled her eyes. "Ick."

Adroitly he skimmed a skin from the body of a chili and put the limp and naked flesh into the bowl with the others. One black brow lifted. "I seem to remember the dress was just fine."

"It was purple lace!" Tanya remembered her dismay over the dress, and that morning, had fretted about the fit. Her breasts and tummy had been swollen with pregnancy. They'd cut the dress a little wide to start with, knowing she was pregnant, but it was still tight when she put it on.

"All I remember is the way it fit you."

"That was all Victor saw, too. He wasn't going to let me be in the wedding at all."

"I'm sorry, Tanya, if you don't want to remember some of these things—"

"Don't apologize." To her amazement, Tanya had to physically halt herself from putting her hand on his arm. She had not voluntarily touched anyone in a long, long time. For a split second, she looked at the place where her finger had nearly lit—a smooth dark expanse of elegant skin, almost hairless and threaded with a sexy river of vein.

"I sometimes forget," he said, "that the day was so bad in the end."

Tanya nodded. "Me, too," she said, smiling. "Isn't that weird? That was probably the worst beating he ever gave me, but what I remember is talking with you for so long."

He said nothing, but his fathomless, milk-chocolate eyes were fixed on her face, waiting.

"You talked about Peru," she said, plucking another chili from the bowl.

"Did I?" he said, smiling. "I was planning my trip at that time."

Tanya felt the doors of memory creak open. Ramón then had been very thin—he'd probably not quite finished his growing, after all, and he was a lean man now. His glasses had made his eyes owlish and obscured the lines of his face that she could see now—the high cheekbones and clean jaw.

Her gaze flickered over his mouth—that impossibly sensual mouth. She still didn't quite understand how she'd missed seeing how sexy his mouth was, even at an inexperienced eighteen. A dangerous ripple of longing moved through her body.

Hastily, she jumped up to check on the chilies in the oven. "Did you ever go?"

"To Peru? Yes."

Tanya took out the cooked peppers and set them on the counter. They sighed, as if exhausted, and she glanced up to see if Ramón noticed. She found his gaze on her body, lingering with appreciation on the curves of breasts and hips. It was a delicious sensation, and with a cocky little smile, she put a hand on her hip. "I have the same trouble you do," she said, flicking an imaginary crumb from her shirt. "Everywhere I go, men fall at my feet."

He met her gaze, and now there was only the smallest hint of a smile lurking at the edges of his mouth. The dark eyes in their fringe of black starry lashes were steady and secretive and inviting. As if to drive his point home, he let his gaze drop to her lips. "I would fall at your feet," he said, "but I can think of better places to land." The smile broke free.

Tanya flicked him with a dish towel. "Behave," she said and loaded another batch of chilies into the oven.

"I'll do my best."

But as she sat back down at the table, Tanya wondered if that was the kind of best she wanted. What was his other best? How could she bear to find out? How could she bear not to?

Resolutely, she said, "Tell me about Peru."

Chapter Five

Dear Antonio,

You don't realize what you'll miss until you don't have it anymore. I miss fall evenings, when the air smells like frost, and there are the sounds of wind in the leaves. And you pull your sweater close around you deliciously, even though it isn't cold enough yet for a coat, and it's only the anticipation that makes you shiver. I miss the way the stars look on such crisp apple nights, and the way home feels so cozy when you go back inside.

I used to read to you on those crisp nights. I hope Ramón reads to you all the time. It's so important. But I think he knows that.

Be good, Antonito.

Love, Mom

They peeled and chopped chilies all afternoon, just Ramón and Tanya. As the hours passed, the day grew dark, and a storm threatened over the mountains. Lightning flashed and thunder rolled, but it was distant and untroublesome. Soon the yellow school bus would come down the road and stop at the narrow path which the boys' feet had made through the fields, and a tumble of young blue-jeaned, flannel-shirted bodies would pour out.

It made her feel very cozy to think of it.

"So," Tanya said into a lull. "We started to talk about Peru, but all you said was that you got to go. Why did you want to go there?"

"I don't know," he said slowly. "I can't really remember anymore. I think there was a film in school or something and I liked the way the mountains looked." He gave her a rueful look. "I didn't like Anglos very much and I liked the thought of going to a place where I'd be a part of the majority."

Tanya looked at him. "And was it what you thought?"

"No. It was more and it was less, but no place is ever really what you think it is."

"What was more?"

"The land. It's almost impossible to tell you how beautiful it is there. The mountains and the people and the customs—I loved it. I loved hearing Spanish being spoken all the time, too. Like a lot of children around here at that time, I spoke Spanish before I spoke English."

"And what was less?"

He smiled, and she liked the way small sun lines

crinkled around the edges of his eyes. They were living lines, evidence of his maturity and his time on the planet. "I was still an outsider."

Tanya nodded. "Odd man out. I know that feeling." She paused, then found herself saying, "One of the things I liked about Victor was the way he made me belong to him. I wasn't on the outside anymore. If he could have inhaled me, he would have. It sounds weird, in light of what happened later, but he really made me feel safe."

"It doesn't sound weird." His hand moved on the table, as if he would touch her, then stilled. "It's like me and Peru. Same thing. We just needed different kinds of safety."

She gave him a sardonic little grin. "Some safety, huh?"

He acknowledged her irony with a quick lift of his brows. Beyond the kitchen, they could hear the sound of boys coming in from school, the uncertain tenors and altos mixing with the more certain bass of the older boys. Laughter and jests punctured the air as the boys shuffled toward the dining room to read the chores list and pick up the snacks waiting on the sideboard—cinnamon rolls and raisins this afternoon.

One of the counselors stuck his head into the kitchen. "Ramón, can I see you in here?"

"Be right there." He stood up and washed his hands. "Are you all right for dinner? Shall I send some more help?"

"I'll be fine," she said. "You've been a big help already. Thanks."

He winked. "My pleasure."

At the door to the dining room, he paused. "Tomorrow, barring bad weather, we're slated to harvest apples, so what about Monday for our trip to the library?"

"Fine."

"Have you ever harvested apples?"

Tanya shook her head. "Can't say that I have."

"You might like it. Why don't you plan to come with us down to the orchards."

"Great." Several boys had filtered into the room, dropping book bags in the usual corner before putting on aprons. Tanya lifted her chin to Ramón, and he left.

The boys who had drawn KP today ranged in age from ten to sixteen. Tonio was not with them, she noted with a little sense of disappointment. Sometimes he stayed in town to visit his girlfriend or go to debate practice. A van from the ranch would pick him up just before supper, along with athletes and others who had to stay at school for one reason or another.

One boy who did show up made Tanya considerably less happy, particularly since Desmary wasn't here. At fifteen, Edwin Salazar was not the oldest boy at the ranch, but he was the biggest, both in terms of size and height. He had a brilliantly handsome face and shiny ebony hair combed straight back from his forehead. His eyes were beautiful and mean. A three-inch scar marred his cheek.

He also knew he made Tanya nervous. Coming into the kitchen today, he met her gaze with that almost invisible, insolent smirk. "Hey, teach."

"Hi, boys," she said, wiping her hands on a towel.

The timer dinged and she bent to look at the chilies in the oven. In the bald light of the oven bulb, they swelled and shivered, and she had to smile. How had she avoided noticing their breathing before this?

Behind her, the boys snickered at something Edwin said. She realized she was bent over in a rather provocative position. But just how else would she get the chilies out of the oven? A tight knot of fear tied itself in her chest. This was the kind of dilemma Victor had made impossible. He would become insanely jealous if a man looked at her—and woe be to Tanya if she had encouraged him. But bending over? In a work environment?

She breathed in the strong scent of chilies for a moment. Edwin, speaking in Spanish, made a filthy comment about her. A spark of old anger, ignited by the wind of self-respect, burst into flame. Very, very slowly, she straightened. And turned.

In prison she had learned the best way to deal with the inevitable bullies and bosses was to meet them head-on. The more you ducked, the more they singled you out. You had to stand up to bullies—and that's all Edwin was, a big bully who'd never been taught any manners.

Narrowing her eyes, she simply stared at him for a moment. His little friend, standing alongside, snickered, and Edwin lifted his chin. He didn't speak.

Tanya said, "Bad language is against the rules here. Did you think it didn't count in Spanish?"

"How was I supposed to know you understood it?"

"Maybe you should assume people can always understand you."

Again the little friend snickered. Tanya cocked her head at him. ''Disrespectfulness is also against the rules. Go. Tell the dorm master you have to have another chore today.''

The smallest flash of triumph crossed Edwin's face. He started toward the door. ''Not you, Edwin,'' she said. ''Your friend. What's your name?''

The youth lifted his chin. ''Mike.''

''Mike, you're dismissed.''

''Why? What did I—''

''Go.''

He didn't argue anymore, but she could tell he was angry. So be it.

The other boys hung back, pretending to get started on the dishes, but she could see them watching how she would handle this big, mean boy.

She didn't know. She didn't want to make a mistake, ruin whatever chance he had to make his life better here. But especially in light of the harshly sexual aspect his comments took, she couldn't let him think he was getting away with something, either.

The beautiful mean eyes glittered. Fear touched her and just the faintest wisp of memory...Victor making that panting animal sound in his throat when he was going to beat her severely.

The memory lent her insight. She reacted strongly to this boy because he reminded her in some way of Victor. Fair enough—as long as she knew it, she could make decisions with clarity.

She willed herself not to cross her arms. He stood still as a sword, returning her gaze implacably.

"C'mon, teach," he said. "What do you want me to do?"

Trust your instincts, a little voice told her. If she sent him away, he'd get what he wanted—out of KP. If she didn't, she'd have to deal with him here for more than two hours.

In a split second, she chose. "Wash your hands. You can peel chilies. Another word and you'll be in the kitchen every day for the rest of your stay here."

"You can't do that."

"Try me."

His eyes flashed, but he turned the water on in the sink, washed his hands, then flung himself down at the table. Tanya put a new bowl of roasted chilies on the table. Then she leaned close. "Let me tell you something. Where I've been, they eat babies like you for a late-night snack. Mind your manners with me. Is that clear?"

Without Edwin lifting his eyes, Tanya couldn't tell what expression they held, but he said in a voice seemly devoid of emotion, "Yes, ma'am."

The battle was over, Tanya thought, an old blues song running through her mind. The war would continue.

But today she had fought well.

Desmary was still tired at dinnertime, and took supper on a tray in her room. Tanya sat with her for a little while, listening to stories of the ranch in the old days as Desmary drank an herb tea the *curandera* in the hills above Manzanares had prepared for her.

When she was finished with the tea, she said, "Go

on, child. I'll be fine in the morning. A battery this old just needs some recharging from time to time.''

Tanya laughed. Collecting the dishes, she said, ''You'll call me if you need anything, right?''

''Sure.'' She wiggled into her pillows more fully. ''Thanks for your help with the chilies, Annie.''

Tanya froze, her hands gripped tightly on the tray. Annie. The name carried painful associations with the past. ''What did you call me?''

''You don't like it? It suits you, you know.''

''No, I don't.'' She leaned on the door. ''How does it suit me?''

''Annie is softer. Tanya just isn't the right name for you.''

She swallowed. ''I appreciate what you're saying, but please don't call me that anymore. It brings back bad memories.''

''Put those dishes down and come here.''

Tanya reluctantly did as she was told. Desmary took one smooth hand into her gnarled grip. ''Don't let the past hold you. Not even a tiny piece of it, you understand?''

''You don't understand, Desmary, that name—''

''Oh, I understand all right. I remember Annie Quezada and how they clucked their tongues over her being in the hospital.''

''How did you know?''

''I've been around forever, child. Back then, Ramón's mother lived here, taking care of her father. We gossiped like old women will about our children and nieces and nephews and dead husbands. She used to worry about you.''

"I don't really remember meeting her."

"It's hard when you don't come from such a big family, to keep everyone straight. She met you several times, though, at family things. Victor was the child she worried about even when he was little. He stayed at the ranch sometimes when they were all children. He was mean, Annie. Mean to the bone. And jealous of every scrap of attention anyone else ever got."

The soft conversation brought too many things bubbling to the top of the steaming caldron of memory. "I really don't like to think about these things any more," she breathed. She thought of Edwin in the kitchen this afternoon, his beautiful eyes hard, and knew that many adults had probably seen the same thing in Victor's eyes.

And yet—

"I really loved him, you know," she said to Desmary. "A lot of people don't understand that. But I did."

"I know you did, child."

"If there had been any other way to free Antonio and me from him, I would have taken it. I tried."

Desmary stroked her hand, slowly, and the gesture was deeply comforting. "I know."

Tanya looked down. "Every time I hear of some woman being gunned down in a parking lot, or at work, I'm so thankful that didn't happen to me."

To her amazement, Tanya felt tears streaming over her face. Tears of relief. Tears of anger—outrage for all those girls and women who still lived with that paralyzing terror. "You know what's evil? When I hear those stories, I get so angry I want to get a gun and kill all of those men who think they can love you to death.''

"That's not the way, Annie. Violence begets violence.''

"I know.'' She nodded, bowing her head against her arm, which was still stretched to meet Desmary's hand. How could it still hurt so much after so many years? How could there still be tears inside of her? "I know. I know it does.''

Slowly the papery thumb moved on Tanya's knuckles. "You need to know that when Ramón brought Tonio here, he didn't speak for almost a year. We worried for a while that he'd been beaten, too. That he would be retarded.''

Tanya frowned, sniffing. "He was talking pretty well by then.''

Desmary nodded. "It hurt him, losing you. He didn't understand. One day, I was making cookies with him, and he just looked up and said, 'Mamma's dead.'''

Tanya looked down.

"I told him you'd just gone away for a long time. He would see you again one day. 'No,' he said. 'Mamma's gone.'''

"I don't know why you're telling me this.''

"For one thing, you get as old as me, you know you could go in the blink of an eye.'' Desmary pursed her lips. "And if somebody doesn't give you some little pushes here and there, Annie, you're gonna live on the very edge of your life, scared to live, forever. That would be a shame.''

Tanya nodded. It was true. She was afraid of everything. Except survival. Surviving she knew.

"Tonio never talked about you. Ramón brought you up sometimes, just to keep you in his mind. Tonio just ignored him. He never wanted to talk about it at all. When he was ten, Ramón sat him down and made him listen to the story of what really happened to you. It didn't help. Tonio still felt unwanted."

An ache burned in Tanya's chest. "I wanted him safe."

"One day, he'll understand that." Desmary's rheumy eyes were compassionate. "First, he needs to remember his mama, the one he loved. Her name was Annie. That's what I'm going to call you."

Surprised, Tanya smiled. "All that for one declaration?"

Desmary chuckled. "I'm an old woman. I'm allowed to take my time rambling around the point of my stories."

"I guess you are." Tanya kissed her forehead. "Thank you. My own mother was always too afraid of my father to be much of a comfort to me." At the look on Desmary's face, Tanya hastened to add, "Oh, he wasn't physically abusive—he was just a jerk."

"Ah." She slapped Tanya's thigh. "Go on out there now. Grab on to your new life and start living it."

"I'll try."

Ramón was a little late coming in to dinner. He found Tonio and Tanya already seated. "Sorry. I got caught up," he said, sitting down.

Tonio shrugged. Tanya stood to ladle stew into his bowl. "No," he said, "I'll serve myself. You eat."

"I don't mind," she said simply, and filled the bowl, then gave him a napkin-lined basket of rolls. Their hands brushed on the basket. Silly as it was, Ramón thought he felt a charge of something—it startled and pleased him. He looked at Tanya. She simply smoothed her hair back from her face and sat down.

He was an idiot.

Spreading margarine on the roll, Ramón looked at his son. "How was school? Did you get that report done on time?"

Tonio scowled. "Why do we have to talk about school every time? Don't you have anything else you want to talk about?"

Ramón frowned. "Sure—after you tell me about school. Is there something wrong?"

"No." Tonio's utterly sullen teenage scowl darkened. "I just want to talk about something else. Is that a crime?"

From the corner of his eye, Ramón saw Tanya lower her head and cover her mouth. For a minute he thought she was upset, then he caught her eye and saw the dancing light in the dark blue irises. Her nostrils flared dangerously.

Ramón looked away hastily, afraid her amusement would trigger his own and they'd both laugh, making a vulnerable teenager feel even worse. "We don't have to talk about school then." He wondered if the annoyance had to do with the report he had mentioned. "How is your girlfriend—Teresa?"

"I don't have a girlfriend," he said. "She's going out with Edwin Salazar now."

Tanya's head came up. Ramón saw the wary coyote expression cross her face—alert and skittish. He frowned. Edwin was the worst case they had at the ranch, and there had been a lot of debate over whether to let him come in. In the end, Ramón had voted to allow him at the recommendation of a social worker he trusted. Edwin had been abused by not only his father, but also other relatives, and the social worker hoped that Edwin had a chance at rehabilitation if he could see a normal environment. Ramón made a mental note to ask Tanya about the boy, but in the meantime, he had a wounded child. "I'm sorry, son," he said.

Tonio shrugged, his face thunderous.

"That doesn't help much, does it?"

"No." He lifted his eyes. "I want to know how to get her back."

Ramón took a breath. "Is that what you really want? She's chosen someone else—that means her feelings aren't the same as yours, right?"

"I guess."

"So wouldn't it be more satisfying in the long run to let her go and find somebody who likes you as much as you like her?"

Tonio's lip curled. "Jeez, Dad, do you think you could be any more wise?"

Ramón glanced at Tanya. "You're a female," he said. "Tell him what you think."

The wariness had made a mask of invisibility over her features. Her mouth was without expression, her eyes opaque as if there was nothing at all behind them. A single wisp of streaked hair hung next her cheek. Her gaze slid from Ramón's to Tonio's. "I think there's nothing that will make it better except time. And nothing we say will make it hurt any less. Just let it hurt and go on."

Tonio stared at her for a long minute, then abruptly, he stood up and left the table. Ramón started to go after him for his lack of manners, but Tanya stood with him and touched his arm. She shook her head. "He doesn't want to cry in front of us."

Her nearness slammed into him. She was so much smaller than he—her head just came to his shoulder— and her body was lean on a frame of surprising strength. Her hand was on his upper arm and he could feel the press of her fingers against his muscle like four small round brands.

Slowly, he looked at her, looked down into her piquant face and thought again of the Madonna in his old parish church. As he looked into her eyes, the opaque shield fragmented, and he saw the heat below. She wanted him, too. While he was thinking of her mouth, she was thinking of his. While he imagined lifting his hand to gauge the weight of her breasts against his palm, she was thinking of his chest and what it would be like bared. He wanted to offer a trade, but she was still far too skittish.

Instead, he just looked at her, and let the heat of their close bodies mingle, let his gaze touch her mouth and her neck, let her fingers move on his arm ever so tentatively. He let his desire show. And waited for her to run away.

For a long time, she didn't. She just looked up at him with that stricken expression, her fingers lingering on his arm. He didn't move.

At last she looked at her hand on his arm and removed it. "That's twice today I've touched someone willingly," she said. "I don't do that."

He winked. "I'm irresistible."

In gratitude, she smiled. "Let's eat, O Magnificent One," she said. "My eyes are well fed, but my stomach still needs some filling."

For an instant, he wondered if he could make her forget her stomach. He wanted to try. Instead, he sat down and put his napkin in his lap.

After dinner, they played chess and told jokes. And it wasn't until he was turning out his light many hours later that he realized he'd forgotten to ask her about Edwin.

Chapter Six

Dear Antonio,

The leaves are falling again—another cycle passing. I sometimes watch the wind blow across the desert and wonder what you're doing. Third grade now. You're probably a pretty big boy. My friend Naomi's boy was in to visit her last week, and I saw him. He was up to her chin.

Sometimes, now, I get so angry. For a long time, I didn't feel anything at all. But now I get so mad at the unfairness of all of this that I can't breathe. I just want to see you. For five minutes. I wouldn't even have to talk to you. I could just see you walk by.

I get angry at Victor's sisters for pushing to keep you away from me. I'm angry with myself for agreeing to a legal adoption. I thought it was the right thing, but I don't think it is anymore. I just want to see you. It hurts like a wound.

There's nothing to be done about it now. I guess I can hope to get out of here and see you. They're moving me to medium security next week. It's a step in the right direction.

Love, Mom

The weather Saturday morning was overcast and cool, perfect for picking apples, Desmary told Tanya, who felt a little thrill of anticipation at the coming activities. She wore her new blue sweatshirt and her good running shoes and a pair of jeans, her hair pulled back in a barrette. With good cheer, she put on a pair of silver feather earrings and took pleasure in the swing of them against her neck.

Tonio came into the kitchen as Tanya was mixing a second batch of pancakes. The flesh around his eyes was a little swollen, as if he'd slept very hard. For the first time, Tanya glimpsed the little boy he'd been, and her heart pinched a little. "Hi," she said with a small smile.

"Hi." He stepped close to her. He was taller than she by three or four inches and she looked up, taking deep pleasure in the arrangement of his features, the blueness of his eyes, the blackness of his hair. Such a handsome young man.

"You mind if I give you a hug?" he asked.

Startled, she said, "No, not at all."

He bent and awkwardly put his arms around her shoulders, elbows sticking out, the rest of his body held away from her. It was clumsy and self-conscious, but for one hard, strong minute, Tanya touched the shoulder of her son and smelled the soap on his skin and the shampoo in his hair. It was so sudden and sharply pleasant she couldn't breathe.

"Thanks for what you said last night," he said, and straightened, ducking his head as if he were embarrassed. "It helped a lot."

"I'm glad."

He shoved his hands in the pockets of his baggy jeans and shuffled backward. "I just wanted to tell you."

She smiled and nodded. "I'll send out pancakes for you and your dad in a few minutes."

When he had exited, Tanya looked at Desmary, and took a huge, clearing breath.

Desmary smiled.

Tanya shook her head, and went back to ladling pancake batter onto the grill. She couldn't think about it yet, or she'd cry.

After breakfast about twenty boys, including Tonio and Edwin, who cut each other a wide berth, along with two counselors, and Ramón and Tanya gathered outside in a little square of bare earth made by the house, the barn, the corrals and the dorms. A faint misty rain fell, hardly noticeable except for the jackets they needed to keep warm. Big stacks of bushel baskets waited by the barns.

"Listen up, everybody," Ramón said. "Some of you have been here long enough that you've done this before, and I expect you to help the others who haven't."

A voice at her elbow said, "Have you done it before?"

Tanya looked down and saw Zach standing there. The sleeves of his jean jacket were too short, the cuffs frayed, and he wore only a thin T-shirt underneath. She frowned and knelt without thinking to button his jacket. "Don't you have another coat?" she whispered.

"I'm all right."

"Okay." She stood up again to listen to Ramón explain the process of harvesting the apples. Next to her, a slim cold hand slipped into her own. She curled her fingers around Zach's hand.

The counselors passed out small canvas bags that could be slung around the shoulder. Ramón illustrated how to wear them.

"Now you all get to climb trees, but do it carefully. If you break branches, we don't get fruit from that branch next year. If you don't want to eat a bunch of bruised, disgusting apples, you also have to put them carefully into your bag, and carefully into the bushel baskets. You'll be the ones to suffer, all right?" He pointed to the baskets. "Everybody grab some baskets and let's get this done."

The group headed down the dirt road toward the small orchard. About thirty trees stood in neat rows, the grass below their branches thick and green, unlike the rest of the prairie surrounding it. A narrow irrigation ditch snaked around it.

Ramón dropped back. This morning, he wore his usual jeans and jacket, with tennis shoes instead of boots. Tanya found the change oddly sexy. "Do you think you know what to do?" he asked.

"Sure. Lift, don't yank, and don't drop them, place them in the bags."

"If you don't feel like getting up on a ladder, you can be in charge of seeing that the bags get emptied properly."

"No way. I haven't been in a tree in a long time."

Ramón looked at Zach. "Will you look out for her for me?"

Solemnly, Zach nodded.

For hours they picked apples, shinnying up and down the orchard trees. Tanya, hanging on a branch below Zach, who was far too much of a daredevil for her tastes, listened to the sounds of the boys. Chatter and laughter punctuated with the peculiarly Latin-Indian "ahhh" that was like "gotcha" in English.

Toward noon, there was a stir at one end of the orchard—shouts and the dismayed cry of other boys trying to prevent a fight. A tumble of boys rushed by below her. Over her head, Zach cried out, "Look! Tonio and Edwin!" He started to scramble down.

And slipped.

Tanya saw him lose his grip. Instinctively, she reached for him, managing to catch hold of the fabric of his jean jacket. The force of his falling body yanked her loose and she tumbled off the branch behind him.

It wasn't far, but her position was awkward and she was afraid of landing on Zach and hurting him. With a twisting reach, she flung herself clear, but the heel of her right hand struck the ground first and took all of her weight. A sharp, stabbing pain sliced her arm. With a small cry, she rolled and got to her feet, clasping her arm to her chest.

"Zach! Are you all right?"

He was on his knees, coughing, and Tanya bent over him. "Are you okay? Did anything get hurt?"

"No." He put a hand to his chest. "Just got the wind knocked out of me."

She patted his back. "That was quite a fall."

"Scared me."

"Are you okay?" Her arm stung sharply and she looked down. Blood spilled from a long jagged cut in the soft flesh of her forearm.

"You're cut!" Zach cried.

Tanya shrugged out of her jacket and wrapped it tightly around her arm to stanch the blood. A fine trembling stirred in her limbs, the first signs of shock. She looked for Ramón. The cut would need stitches.

A spate of furious Spanish curse words blued the air. Tanya and Zach whirled. A burly counselor held a struggling, yelling Tonio against his chest. Blood marred the boy's lip. Edwin stood off to one side, breathing hard. The bandanna he wore to hold his hair from his face had fallen off, and thick hair washed onto his forehead. Tanya felt chilled at the expression on his face.

A second counselor picked Edwin's bandanna from the grass and gave it to him. Edwin took it without a word, his flat gaze fixed on the counselor dragging Tonio away.

Ramón materialized beside Tanya and Zach. "I saw you fall. Are you okay?"

Finally Tanya lifted her arm and peeled back the jacket. Blood soaked the fabric. "No," she said. "Sorry. I need some stitches."

Ramón winced and reached for her. "Oh, *pobrecita*." Lightly, he took her elbow in his fingers and pulled her closer. "You're right." He tugged the jacket back around her arm. "Keep it tight, and let's get you to town."

Tanya swallowed. She licked her top lip and tasted salt. "It won't hurt much till later," she said, and heard the breathy sound of it.

She felt Ramón's gaze sharpen. "Zach, run and tell Mr. Mahaney what I'm doing, okay? Tell him he's in charge until I get back. Can you do that?"

Wide-eyed, Zach nodded. "Sorry, Ms. Bishop. It's my fault."

"Oh, no, honey, not at all!" She bent and touched his head. "I wasn't paying attention and I slipped, that's all."

The boy's mouth tightened, and Tanya knew he still felt guilty. Dull pain throbbed along her arm, and she sucked in a breath. She would deal with Zach's feelings later. To Ramón, she said, "Let's stop and get some ice at the house. That will help."

"Can you make it to the house, or do you want me to go get the truck?"

"I can walk."

"Let's go."

It was not the most fun she'd ever had, Tanya had to admit. As hard as she tried to keep her arm still, there was no way to keep her movements fluid enough so that the arm wasn't jarred at all.

But it was oddly warming to have Ramón with her. At the house, he made her sit on the porch while he went inside. A few minutes later, he returned with a plastic bag of crushed ice and a towel.

Kneeling in front of her, he made a table of his knees and spread the towel over it. On the towel he put the large bag of crushed ice and smoothed it until it was a squat, wide shape. Gently, cupping her elbow and lifting the arm with one flat finger below the straight bone, he settled her arm in the cradle of ice. The first touch burned like the devil and Tanya made a noise. Tears stung her eyes.

He covered her hand with his own and looked at her. "I'm sorry. I know it hurts."

Breathlessly, she said, "Have you had stitches?"

As if he recognized her need to shift her focus, he smiled. "Not a one, actually. It's pretty amazing, considering how much time I've spent with horses." Firmly, he wrapped the towel around and around her arm to hold the ice. "Broken bones, that's what I had. Twice on each wrist, three fingers, two toes, and—" he grinned ruefully, drawing a finger over his dented cheekbone "—my cousin broke my face."

It seemed sick to laugh about it, but Tanya did, anyway. "Yeah. Mine, too."

His liquid gaze softened. "What do you know—we have something in common."

"Broken faces?"

"Laughing in spite of broken faces."

Tanya bit her lip, a thick stirring in her chest. A light wind stirred his wavy hair, and a strand touched the small indentation below his eye. In the gray day, his skin seemed incredibly perfect—supple and smooth and golden. His gaze held hers steadily, and that was where the true beauty of him was, in those fathomless, unutterably kind eyes. The expression in them shifted as she stared at him, turned molten and rich, and Tanya found her gaze slipping to his mouth, then back up. "Laughing can save your mind," she said.

"Yes." He remained kneeling for a moment, then stood and held out a hand to her.

As she stood up, David Mahaney, the counselor who'd dragged Antonio away from the fight, came striding over the open square. "You'd better wait a minute and see if Tonio is okay," she said.

"Tonio is fine. Come on."

"Ramón!" David called. "What do you want me to do with Tonio?"

"Just treat him like you'd treat one of the others."

David scowled. "That's not fair, Ramón. He's a good kid."

"Yes, he is." A hard sinew marked his lean jaw. "I want him to stay that way. He goes to his room with no supper."

"You know what a creep Edwin is," David protested. "He probably took the kid's girlfriend just because she liked Tonio. He's been on Tonio since he got here."

Tanya's arm throbbed, and her heart ached. A cool wind touched her face. She wanted to cry for all of them—Tonio and Ramón and even Edwin, who was far, far too young to be so hard.

"Violence solves nothing," Ramón said, opening

the truck door. "Tonio has to learn that like everyone else. Now, if there's nothing else, this woman is bleeding like a stuck pig and needs stitches."

"You're making a mistake, Ramón." David put his hands on his hips. "I'm speaking as your friend. He's a good kid. Don't punish him for this."

A warm color washed over Ramón's cheekbones, and Tanya could see the mark where the bone had been broken under his right eye. "Back off," he said in a dangerous voice. "Being strict doesn't hurt kids. Being permissive hurts them."

"But—"

"A week of KP duty. That's as lenient as I'm willing to be." Ramón got in the truck and slammed the door. Tanya walked around and climbed in the other side. Without a word, he drove off toward town.

At the small clinic, Ramón waited in the front while Tanya was led back into the bowels of the place. He played with some toddlers and watched a young girl, enormously pregnant, fidget restlessly, swinging her foot back and forth. She couldn't have been more than sixteen. She should have been popping bubble gum while she doodled in the margins of her history notebook, not sitting in a clinic waiting for her baby to be born.

Looking at her pretty, ever-so-young face, he was reminded of the reasons he'd started the ranch in the first place—and he wished he could open another, for the girls who were his boys' counterpoints. Truth was, though, girls weren't often violent offenders, or even particularly criminal. Girls were arrested for shoplifting, boys for burglary. Girls were arrested for forgery, boys for armed robbery. Girls were arrested for disturbing the peace, boys for assault.

Not always, of course. He'd known some mean, bad girls in his time in the probation system. Hopeless. But girls turned their brutal anger inward. Boys turned it outward—and so boys got more help. Girls got pregnant. Hooked up with a bad guy. Ended up on welfare, or maybe even in prison, but no one noticed as long as it wasn't society toward whom the anger was directed. Boys took assault rifles into the streets.

The girl noticed his stare and turned a heavy-lidded gaze toward him, as if daring him to say a word. Her eyes were lined with thick eyeliner, black, her cheeks powdered white, her lips rouged a strong red. Her hair was meticulously styled, long and curly.

He ached for her, but forced himself to look away. Maybe one day, one of his boys would find her, and the manners and respect he'd learned would make him a good man for this girl. A man who would take care of the child she carried and make sure she didn't have to stand in a welfare line, a man who would love her. It was all he could do.

A doctor in a white coat came out of the back. "Ramón?" he said. "I need to talk to you."

Ramón got to his feet. John Arranda, the doctor, had been his friend since high school. He had a kind face and a goatee neatly trimmed, and warm dark eyes. "What's up?"

John touched his nose. "You know this woman?"

He nodded.

"I just got her X rays back." They had wanted an

X ray because of the fall. "This arm has been broken in three places at different times." He held the gray-and-black negative up to the light, pointing with the eraser end of a pencil to one heavily scarred place just above the elbow. "This one didn't get much help for a while. It healed badly. It has to hurt pretty bad in the cold."

"She was abused when she was younger."

John lowered the film. "I see. Is she out of that situation now?"

"Yes." Ramón swallowed the rising anger in his throat and looked away. "Yes, she's away from it. Has been for a long time."

"Nobody breaks this part of their arm," John said quietly, touching the place above his elbow. "He probably hit her with something."

"Yes." Ramón took a long breath and blew it out.

John regarded him without speaking for another minute. "Come on in and hold her hand while I sew her up."

Ramón followed John into the examining room. Tanya lay on the table, her eyes closed. She looked pale, but otherwise okay. As John and Ramón came in, she opened her eyes. Seeing Ramón, she smiled.

Bright emotion stabbed him, and he went to stand alongside her. "Doc said I should come hold your hand. Is that okay with you?"

Wordless, she nodded. Ramón looked down at her slim small hand lying next to her thigh on the table. He picked it up and sandwiched it between both of his own. Her fingers were cold and he rubbed them between his palms, smiling. "Cold hands, warm heart."

Tanya smiled.

It aroused him. He couldn't help it. Her smile was as sweet and ripe as a chocolate-covered cherry, and he wanted to taste it. He wanted to mold his hands to her breasts, and open his palm on her belly. He wanted her.

Her fingers jumped against his palm. Ramón closed his eyes, and smoothed his palm over her fingers again, willing his desire back to wherever it lived. It didn't help a lot.

"Ready?" John asked.

Ramón looked at Tanya. She took a breath and nodded. John removed the cotton covering the wound and gave her a shot, then took out his needle. It took twelve stitches.

"Done," John said.

Tanya sighed hugely. "That wasn't so bad."

Ramón stroked her hand. "You've been so good, I'll buy you an ice cream when we're done here."

"Rocky Road?" The blue eyes glinted.

"Whatever you want, *grilla*." He restrained himself from touching her face. "Whatever you want."

"Careful, now," she said, and her grin turned impish. "You say 'whatever' and I might ask for a lot."

Ramón chuckled. "What you want, I've got."

Tanya looked at John. "He's terrible."

"Yes. Always has been." John finished cutting a tube of gauzy material and skimmed it over Tanya's arm. "You have to watch out for his type, you know."

Tanya looked at Ramón, and a curious sobriety touched the dark blue irises. "I know."

Chapter Seven

Dear Antonio,

I have met an amazing woman. Her name is Iris, and she is in prison for three life terms for crimes I'd rather not tell a boy. She's been in prison since she was nineteen, and she's quite a bit older than me—though I couldn't tell you for sure how old. Around here, you don't ask what people don't volunteer.

The thing is, she has given me keys to cope. I've been having very hard times the past six months. I've done all the educational things they have to offer, and I read all the time, but it isn't the same. You never forget you're in prison, that it isn't a normal place or way of being. You sometimes think it would be better to die and be free than stay here another day.

Iris has shown me how to live in the moment. In the very single moment there in front of me. To smell it and taste it and enjoy or endure whatever is in that moment. It sounds so simple a thing to make such a big difference, but I know it has saved my life.

Love, Mom

"So, you want Rocky Road, huh?" Ramón asked as they came out of the clinic. The earlier drizzle threatened to turn to real rain. Tanya watched Ramón turn the collar of his jacket upward.

"You don't have to buy me ice cream."

"I want to. It'll make me feel better." He reached for and clasped her free hand, then let it go, as if remembering she didn't like it.

The funny thing was, she was getting used to being touched again. Between Tonio, Zach and Ramón, there wasn't much chance someone wouldn't be touching her at one time or another.

"I'm hungrier than ice cream," he said. "Let's get a sandwich or something. If you're feeling okay."

"I'm really hungry," she said. "Any good hamburgers in town?"

He winked. "I know just the thing. C'mon." And he took her hand again. "Do you mind?" he added, lifting their joined hands to illustrate. His long brown fingers looked strong and graceful, and she liked the way his skin felt against her own. It felt like a big deal, holding hands. "I don't mind," she said quietly.

He took her to Yolanda's, a small, happy old-fashioned diner. The floors were wooden, the booths of dark red vinyl, and the tables had ranch theme table-cloths thrown over them, little Bar S and Half Moon brands on a brown plaid background.

They settled in a booth by the front window, and Tanya looked out at the gray day, feeling snug. A waitress offered coffee, and both of them accepted with enthusiasm. "And we want a couple of ham-burgers, with fries," Ramón said. "Cheese on one. Tanya?"

"Please."

"You got it," the waitress replied, scribbling their order on a small green order pad. She picked up the laminated menus they hadn't examined and hurried away.

Gingerly, Tanya put her arm on the table and touched the bandages. "It's probably going to be a few days before I can lift anything," she said ruefully. "Good thing it wasn't my left arm—I'd hate to leave Desmary with all those apples to chop."

"Are you left-handed?"

"Yes."

"So is Tonio." He smiled. "I didn't even realize it until he started school. He eats with both hands."

Tanya inclined her head. "Is he creative, then?"

"Some. His real gifts are in the analytical realm, though. He loves numbers and formulas and engine parts."

"Victor did, too."

Ramón's dark eyes went opaque. "Tonio has a pic-ture of his dad in front of that old Fury, which Victor restored. Remember the picture?"

"Yes. I took it."

The waitress brought thick ceramic mugs of coffee. Tanya stirred in sugar. "Does Tonio ever talk about Victor or me? Does he ever see the rest of family? Any of Victor's sisters?"

"No." Ramón sighed. "They used to come to visit when he was younger, but we haven't seen any of them in a long time."

A small crackle of anger rustled on her nerves. To smooth it, she breathed in slowly. "At one time, I really believed I had acted in Tonio's best interests by agreeing to the custody arrangements." She hadn't actually seen Ramón—he had conducted his business by letter. "Even then, I was wise enough to realize you had qualifications none of the rest of them did." She frowned. "What made you come forward, Ramón? I've never asked."

"No one else wanted to adopt him."

Stunned, Tanya stared at him. "What?"

"They didn't want him because he had your blood."

The anger crackling on her nerves grew more intense. "But rather than give me any joy at all, they pushed for me to give him up to you totally." As if the anger had clotted in the swollen pathways of her arm, a sudden pulse of pain struck her wrist. "Sometimes, Ramón, I look back and can't believe how foolish I was—how weak and malleable."

"No." His jaw was hard as he reached over and put a hand on hers. "You weren't weak. Not ever. You were young and without help and you did the best you could." His nostrils flared with strong emotion. "You stayed alive."

Tanya lifted her chin. "Yes, I did."

His eyes glittered with something she couldn't read but somehow it stirred her. The rustling on her nerves turned softer and warmer. Fluid awareness pooled in her breasts and washed over her thighs, and she found herself imagining how his body would feel against her own. As she stared, it seemed he knew her thoughts, for the hand that he had allowed to rest on hers shifted, and his long, graceful fingers moved in a light, erotic pattern over her inner wrist. "I'm glad," he said.

As if aware that the conversation had taken a deeply intimate turn, he leaned back suddenly and lifted his coffee cup in a toast, offering a smile in place of the heady sensuality on his face only moments before. "To life!"

Tanya lifted her cup. "To survival."

"Not survival," he said. "There's so much more to life than that, cricket."

For a moment, she only looked at him. She didn't want the rest—no passion, no wild highs and lows, no despair or great joy—just simple, calm day-to-day survival. "I didn't mean it in the grim sense."

The waitress appeared. "Here we go," she said, but hardly paused before bustling away again. She sailed by once more, dropping a bottle of ketchup and one of mustard on the table.

"Smell that," Ramón said and smiled at Tanya. "There's a lot to be said for simple pleasures."

Tanya piled everything—pickles, lettuce, tomatoes, onions, ketchup and mustard—onto the burger. Awkwardly with the bandages, she lifted it in both hands and took one second to savor the salty, rich scent before she bit into it. Juices exploded on her tongue—a perfect melding of salt and fat and crisp cold vegetables and pungent sauces. She closed her eyes, savoring the flavor.

"Little things are everything," she said when she could speak. "Everything."

Ramón only nodded, a strangely stricken expression on his face. "Eat your cheeseburger, Tanya. And then I'll show you a bookstore I think you'll like."

"Shouldn't we get back soon?"

"They'll manage without us."

She shrugged. "Okay."

By the time they emerged from the diner, the rain had stopped, but a cold wind had blown in behind it, sharp and piercing. The sky was still gray and heavy-looking. Tanya said, "It almost feels like snow."

He lifted his chin, smelling the air. "Maybe. I think it's a little ways off yet, but you never know. Last year, there was snow on the Sangre de Cristos by the end of August."

"That's early." Tanya huddled deeper into her coat. The mild tranquilizer she had finally accepted at the hospital, combined with the terrific hamburger, made her feel warm and calm.

As they walked down the largely deserted streets, Ramón told her about the owners of the bookstore. The man had fled his native Mexico as a young man. "I think," Ramón said with a smile, "that he was wanted by the law, but it has never been said in so many words."

"Ooh," Tanya said, "a desperado."

He nodded. ''Someone wanted his skin. He ran into the mountains and fell ill. A very beautiful young woman found him and took him to her grandmother, who was a famous and powerful *curandera,* one of the local healers.''

Tanya smiled. ''And he fell in love with the young girl as the grandmother healed him.''

''You've heard this story before.'' A glitter shone in his dark eyes.

''Variations, anyway.''

''Ah, well, you know then, that the girl was as gifted as her grandmother, and became a *curandera,* too. He runs the bookstore, and she dispenses herbs and potions to everyone in town.''

''Very romantic.''

''You'll love the bookstore. You still like to read, don't you?''

She chuckled. ''Trust me—prison makes readers of non-readers. The ones who were readers to begin with turn into fanatics.''

''I can imagine.''

He stopped in front of an old building. A plate glass window had been painted with the words Walking Stick Bookstore in an arch. Below it read Cesaro Valdez, Proprietor. Across the bottom of the window were more gold letters: Knowledge is power.

''Nice,'' Tanya said.

''Are you sure you're feeling all right?'' Ramón asked, pausing outside.

''I'm fine.'' She looked at him. ''Later, I will be miserable. Tomorrow, I may be grouchy. By the day after tomorrow, life will be back to normal. Right now, I feel just fine.''

He laughed. ''Okay. I'll save my worrying for to-night.''

She gestured toward the door. ''Getting some good books to keep me company later might be just right.''

As she stepped into the store, Tanya instantly fell in love. A scent of books and dust and cinnamon tea struck her nostrils, and from hidden speakers played soft Andean flute music. A rabbit warren of book-shelves, illuminated with small lamps set alongside single chairs and small tables, stretched beyond her vision. She paused. Sighed.

A woman behind the counter smiled at them. ''Ra-mónito!'' she cried. ''Where you been keeping your-self, *hijo?*'' She came around the counter, a short, round woman with ebony hair swept with wings of white. She took Ramón's hands and looked him up and down. ''You been working too hard again. I want to see some meat on those bones.''

''Rosalia, this is my friend Tanya Bishop. She's cooking at the ranch with Desmary.'' He grinned dev-ilishly. ''Blame her for my skinniness.''

Tanya grinned and rolled her eyes. Rosalia tsked. ''Like I'd ever blame a woman for anything a man did!'' A flicker moved in the almond-shaped eyes and she took her hands from Ramón and put them close to Tanya's bandaged arm. ''May I?'' she said.

Caught in the extraordinary depth of the beautiful eyes, Tanya nodded. The woman put both her palms on her arm, one just above the elbow, one just below. Tanya felt nothing, except the extraordinary warmth of Rosalia's fingers, but it was as if Rosalia were reading something, or listening. After a minute, she pursed her lips, then opened her palm and placed it, palm down against Tanya's. She looked at Ramón and jerked her head toward the books.

He made a noise of mock outrage, but smiled. "Okay?" he said to Tanya.

She nodded.

Rosalia stared into Tanya's face. "Tell me about the sorrow of this hand," she said, leading Tanya to a comfortable deep couch set behind the counter.

"I cut it on a stick. I felt out of a tree, just a little while ago."

Rosalia smiled. "No, not this new hurt, not that hand. Longer ago. Old wound." She covered Tanya's hand with her other one, making a warm sandwich, just as Ramon had done a little earlier. "There is damage here—if you don't heal it, there will be arthritis later."

Tanya tried to think of something she'd done to the hand, but could think of nothing. Perhaps she meant repetitive motion injuries, but Tanya cut with her left hand. "I don't know. Cooking?"

Slowly, the woman shook her head. Tanya became aware of the sound of pan flutes piped in quietly through speakers in the ceiling. Soothing and haunting. They increased the feeling of stepping into another time, another world. "No, cooking is a creative thing," Rosalia said. She frowned. "It's deep." She shook her head, rubbing her open palm in a circle over the bones of Tanya's hands.

Unbidden came an image of this very hand holding

a gun up before her, and she knew that was the answer Rosalia sought. "I shot a man dead with this hand. A long time ago."

"Ah." Rosalia nodded, and slowly let Tanya go. "You go look at books."

Tanya backed away, sensing the woman was not dismissing her, but giving her room to come to terms with this new piece of self-knowledge. Iris, her friend in prison, had often done the same thing.

As she headed into the rabbit warren of bookshelves, Tanya kept her hands close to her belly, feeling bemused. The strange encounter might have been right out of "Twilight Zone," except Tanya had seen such women at work in the past. It was a gift, like any other. Like all nontraditional healers, *curanderas* relied on the harmony of body and mind and spirit.

And, too, there had been an odd thing about her right hand. For months after the shooting, she'd been unable to use it at all. It gave her terrible pain to even lift a glass of water. Repeatedly, prison doctors had examined it, but could find nothing wrong. A psychologist finally told her it was akin to hysterical blindness—when a person witnessed something too terrible to contemplate, they sometimes could not see. The hand that shot Victor carried the sorrow of the act for Tanya, who couldn't.

Moving her fingers, she remembered the terrible months just after the shooting. No one had understood how conflicted she'd been. They didn't understand that she had loved him once, that he'd fathered her child, that he could be a funny, loving man. He was evil, too, and that evil had caused his death as directly as

Tanya's lifting the gun, but no evil came in the world without some hope. It was thinking about the good in him that upset her.

She twisted her mouth. Water under the bridge now, and she would not open the wounds again. Instead, she let the wonders of the bookstore seduce her, and wandered through the stacks. She saw Ramón in an aisle of music history. Tanya ambled toward the cookbooks and fell adrift in glossy pictures of French cottages, their tables overflowing with Provençal food.

She had no idea how long they were there, how long she spent drifting through one warren and into another. Outside, a second leg of the storm moved in, and mild thunder jumped in the heavens, lending the rooms an even cozier aspect. She carried two cookbooks, three paperback novels, and a Spanish-English colloquial dictionary. Although she'd spent several years reading and writing Spanish in prison—yet another of her endless self-improvement projects—she still got lost when the conversation moved very fast. It seemed everyone at the ranch could move between the two languages at will and she didn't like being at a disadvantage.

She came around a corner and found Ramón sitting on a sofa near a window. A tiny lamp burned on the antique table, and Ramón was washed gold with the incandescent bulb on the right, silver-gray from the window on his left. The fingers of light fanned over his high, clear brow, cascaded down his elegant cheekbones, danced on his generous, seductive mouth. Such a face, she thought, struck dumb once again.

He didn't seem to notice her, and Tanya clasped her books to her chest like a schoolgirl with a crush. Her lungs felt overfilled, her body too tender for the clothes she wore. Intelligence and compassion and a sense of humor—all showed in the exquisite features, along with the alluring seductiveness. How had he managed to avoid marriage all these years? How was it that some determined female had not corralled him by now?

At the diner earlier, Tanya had said she did not want life—but she did. She wanted to dance and make love, she wanted to cry out with passion and chortle with joy. She wanted to bear another child and have another husband and—

Be young and live.

She was afraid, too. Afraid of the intensity of her nature and the combustibility of Ramón's. He was genial, a generous man who would please almost any mother or matchmaker as a suitable husband candidate.

But Tanya was not the foolish sort of woman who mistook a kind man for a bland one. In his eyes was a fierce and blazing passion, carefully banked. He was a man who controlled himself rigidly and carefully, a man who kept his passions skillfully concealed, but she knew they were there. Waiting.

For her? She didn't know and didn't know if she wanted to find out.

A fleeting image of him, naked and close, gave her a momentary weak-kneed breathlessness. Embarrassed, she ducked her head and was about to turn away when he called her name in a loud whisper.

She turned.

"Come sit with me," he said quietly, gesturing. "I want to read you something."

On stiff legs, she moved toward him, creaking slowly down to perch on the very edge of the sofa next to him. "I only bite on Saturdays," he said.

Bite—oh, that brought up some images! She clasped the books closer to her chest. "It is Saturday."

"Ah, so it is." He waggled his eyebrows wickedly. "Well, I don't bite hard."

A shiver goosewalked down her spine. "Umm, what do you want to read to me?" Her voice sounded odd in her ears, all breathy and soft.

He put his book down next to him, on the cushion between them. Outside, thunder growled over the sky, and rain pattered musically at the windows. Inside, the haunting Andean flutes floated through the room. Within Tanya's chest beat a quick, fluttery pulse. It seemed impossible such tiny beats could circulate enough blood through her body, and as if to prove it, she felt a little light-headed.

Gently, he took her books from her arms and put them on top of his own, then shifted the pile to the floor at his feet. He moved closer. Tanya shrank away from him, overwhelmed with the narcotic scent of his skin, and the way the silver and gold light caught in the long strands of his dark wavy hair. Her heart beat faster, and to her dismay, she realized her hands were shaking. When he reached for her cheek with his fingers, she started violently, her gaze flying to his face.

He halted, then stretched out his hand again and lightly put his fingertips on her jaw. "I won't do anything you don't want me to do, *grillacita,* little cricket,'' he said, his fingers moving lightly. ''But I really need to kiss you.'' His gaze touched her mouth, moved back to her eyes. ''Will you let me kiss you, Tanya?''

She stared at him, wanting him and yet, so afraid. ''Yes,'' she heard her voice whisper. And again, ''Yes.''

He opened his hand on her face, his fingers spreading to clasp her ear, his lean palm cupping her cheek. The touch was unbearably gentle, wildly arousing. To be touched at all was almost more than she could bear, and when he came closer, bending over to kiss her, Tanya panicked.

She put her hand up and stopped him, ducking her head away from him. ''Ramón, no, I—it's just—this is—'' Rising terror bolted through her and she started to stand up.

Ramón let her go instantly, but caught her good hand. ''Hey. You don't have to run away.''

Tanya swallowed, feeling faintly foolish as the panic attack eased. It was Ramón here, sitting next to her, his thigh resting against her own, looking so sensually handsome. Hesitantly, she lifted her hand to touch his face. He didn't move, just waited while she touched his jaw, his cheek, his chin. Beneath her fingers, his skin was warm and male, coarse where his light beard was shaved off his chin.

She looked where she touched, the fluttering pulse strong in her throat. He didn't move, and she was glad of his patience, glad of the heat and calm in his liquid eyes. ''It scares me to want anything,'' she said.

''A kiss isn't such a big thing.''

''Maybe not to you.'' She traced the clean, straight edge of his jaw. ''It is to me.''

Gently, slowly, he lifted a hand and smoothed hair from her face. ''Not so much to win or lose, in a kiss.''

Tanya raised her eyes to his infinitely dark, infinitely patient gaze. Suddenly she remembered sitting next to him at a card table covered with layers of blue, green and white tissue paper while a Spanish band sang a sad ballad she didn't understand, and wondering what it would be like to kiss him. The memory startled her—she must have repressed it, trying to remove any feeling of guilt she felt for that day.

Now, with small movements of her fingers, she urged him closer. Very slowly, he tilted his head and bent toward her. His breath, smelling faintly of the mint he'd eaten after lunch, brushed her face, warm and moist.

Their lips touched. His were full and firm, pliant and undemanding. Gently, he kissed her. Gently he moved ever so slightly closer, putting his hand under her hair. His thumb moved against her earlobe. She opened her eyes when he pulled back, and he met her gaze soberly, dipping to kiss her again. His hair curled around her fingers. His shoulder bumped her wrist.

It was only a dance of lips, a simple, warm exploration, and Tanya felt the terrible panic and tension leave her on a sigh.

Ramón straightened, his hand smoothing over her shoulder. ''See, not so scary.''

Tanya smiled at him, warmed clear through. ''It was just your astonishing presence that scared me.''

He laughed. ''You made a joke.''

"There's hope for me yet."

"Oh, there's always been hope for you, Tanya. Always."

Tanya looked toward the window, a pungent ache in her chest. There were two sides to every coin life passed. Victor had been the dark side; Ramón was the bright. "I'm so grateful to you, Ramón. I don't know how I would have survived all this without your help."

"Was that kiss one of gratitude, then?" he asked softly.

"I don't think so," she said. "I don't know."

"I don't think so, either." He took his hands from her shoulders and leaned over to pick up their books. He gave Tanya hers to carry. "We should get back to the ranch."

Tanya had the feeling she had disappointed him in some way, but she was not sure how.

No, that was a lie. It was dangerous to start lying to herself. She didn't have to share her feelings or observations, but she had to claim them, keep herself in touch with what she really felt. It was the only way to stay healthy and strong, able to cope with the changes her life had required.

Honesty. Clasping her books to her chest, she knew she had allowed Ramón to think she was expressing mere gratitude when she kissed him. Even more than allowing him to come to his own conclusions—she'd planted the idea.

It wasn't true, of course. Her wish to kiss him had nothing at all to do with gratitude and everything to do with desire.

He undoubtedly knew that. She rubbed her forehead. Maybe that was where the disappointment lay—in her lack of honesty. A vague, formless guilt tugged her. Maybe she shouldn't have allowed him to get so close. She shouldn't have allowed her emotions to show so blatantly on her face. Maybe—

Ramón stopped dead in the middle of a dark narrow aisle and turned around. With a suddenness that surprised her, he bent and pressed another kiss to her mouth. This time, his body touched hers, chest to chest, leg to leg. The kiss carried a strong edge of hunger. The insistent thrust of his tongue sent a sharp response through her middle.

"It wasn't gratitude, Tanya. A million years ago, we were attracted to each other and we still are." He put his forehead against hers and rubbed her jaw with his thumb. "It isn't wrong, and it also doesn't have to go anywhere."

She looked at him. "I don't know how to do that," she said.

"Do what?"

"Be lighthearted about things like kisses and feeling attracted to you."

He lifted his well-shaped head, and the devilish version of his devastating smile showed off his white teeth and made his eyes crinkle at the corners. He winked. "Stick with me, kid."

Tanya only smiled. She doubted anyone could teach her to lighten up, but if anyone could, it was Ramón.

Chapter Eight

Dear Antonio,

It's the small things that make you crazy. Like never going to the grocery store. I never liked it all that much, to tell you the truth, but right now it would be such a big pleasure to push a basket through the produce section and smell the onions and potatoes, see the pale green cabbages and dark kale and mottled butter lettuce, all piled up and dotted with silver water, reflected in the mirrors. I'd love to pick out peaches and put them in a bag to make a pound.

I'd love to examine packages of stew meat and pick out the best one, the one without too much fat. And I'd love to bring the groceries in and put them away on a stormy afternoon, knowing we were safe as I made tuna fish sandwiches and tomato soup. Little things mean a lot, Antonio. If you can focus on the little things, the big ones won't hit you so hard.

                                                     Love, Mom

As they stepped out on the street, Tanya spied a Disabled American Veteran's store on the corner, and remembered Zach's ragged jacket. "Do we have time to stop in the DAV?" she asked.

"Money burning a hole in your pocket?"

Tanya realized he might not approve of her taking a personal interest in one of the boys. "I noticed this morning that Zach's jacket is too small. I'd like to see if I could find him another one. Would that be all right?"

"Yes. Very much so."

Inside, she made her way to the racks of boy's clothes and flipped through the coats. "He seems very young to be in the program," Tanya commented, tugging an army green surplus jacket off the rack. It was in good shape, but too small. She put it back.

"Zach?" Ramón took out a long black raincoat, and Tanya watched him put his hands on it, feeling it as he looked at it. "He was arrested sixteen times on petty theft and burglary. His mother kept him out of foster homes somehow or another, but she'd been doing drugs a long time, and died last spring." He put the raincoat back and pulled out a jean jacket to show Tanya, rubbing the sleeve between his fingers as if to gauge the weight. "This one?"

She examined it, found the elbows nearly bare and shook her head. "Poor Zach."

"He's pretty angry, and doesn't have a soul in the world on his side. It may be too late, but I had to try."

"And what about Edwin? What's his story."

Ramón scratched his eyebrow before he answered. "Attempted murder."

"And he's at the ranch?"

"We don't call it the Last Chance for nothing, Tanya. He's a hard case, but a lot of them are. Chris Lansky didn't attempt—he succeeded."

"He's only twelve!"

Ramón nodded. "There were extenuating circumstances, as they say, but all the same...." He shrugged.

Tanya pulled a dark blue jean jacket from the rack. It was the right size. "Edwin scares me," she said. "I try to be calm and cool, and I've handled him, but in my bones, I know he's dangerous."

"I noticed that you're uncomfortable when his name comes up." He flipped through several boy-size coats and without looking at her, pursed his lips. "Did you agree with David this morning, that I was too hard on Antonio?"

"No, not at all. You did the right thing—violence doesn't solve anything." The jean jacket was perfect. Fully lined, without tears or badly worn places and a price tag in her range. "This will be perfect."

Ramón nodded. "David is a good counselor, but he doesn't always understand how hard some of these boys are. They've been living by the laws of the streets, which are life and death laws—'one false move and you're out' kind of laws. They have to be given the same hard laws on this side."

"Tonio hasn't lived that way."

"No." Ramón looked grim. "But he's always had a tendency to try violence first. A lot of boys do, but he's got a brooding side. I want to nip it in the bud."

"And he has to live by the same rules you've set for the other boys."

"Some, but there is a difference. He isn't in trouble—he's a member of my household, and therefore has more freedom."

They walked to the end of the aisle, and on wide shelves against the wall were dishes. Tanya paused to pick up a hand-painted china saucer, the edges rimmed with gold. The price tag was ten cents. "I used to collect these."

He took the saucer from her and turned it over. "Why?"

"I don't know." She grinned. "Does anyone have a reason to collect strange things?"

"Good point."

"They're unique and beautiful—and even when I've been very poor, they were in my price range. I can have ten for a dollar, right now."

"Or—" he bent and took a dinner plate that matched the saucer from a pile in the back "—you can have a matching set."

"Perfect."

For a moment, their eyes met, and a spark arced between them, gentle and powerful.

Ramón looked at his watch. "Desmary is going to kill us both if we don't get back pretty soon. Come on."

* * *

Tanya looked for Zach when she returned. From the foyer just inside the front door, she heard him in the kitchen, and leaving her purse on the table, headed down the hall. At the door, she paused. Zach sat at the table with Desmary and Tonio. The three of them sliced apples and dropped them in cold water for the cooking tomorrow. Dinner bubbled on the stove.

Tanya didn't realize how tired she was until she stood in the doorway. There she paused, feasting her eyes privately upon her child. He had a fat lip, the only evidence of his fight with Edwin, and his mood was considerably calmer than it had been earlier. Desmary directed with gestures more often than words. Zach, almost too small for the chair, swung his feet.

"You miss her?" Tonio was saying.

Zach nodded.

"Mad at her, too, though, huh?" There was a reedy quality to Tonio's voice, the cracked hollowness of adolescence. "What I remember about my mom is being mad."

Mothers. They were talking about mothers. Tanya shrank back, listening.

"Yeah," Zach said. "She didn't have to go and die."

"You don't know. Maybe she did." Tonio dropped a handful of apple slices into a bowl of water and grabbed another whole apple. "You gotta try and keep the good stuff."

"Is that what you did?"

"Yeah. As much as I could. I don't even have a picture of my mom—only one of my dad, so I don't remember what she looked like, but I can think of other stuff—like this perfume she used to wear, and pretty hair, really long and blond.''

Tanya smiled. Her hair had never been particularly long. Children's perceptions were so different.

"But you know what I remember?" Tonio asked. "This weird song, about a lady who gets married the day before she dies."

"Eww."

"Sounds gross, but it was real pretty. She used to sing it to me before I went to sleep at night."

Raw pain sliced through Tanya's chest, and she backed out of the kitchen, unable to breathe. She ran smack into Ramón. He took one look at her face and said, "Come on, honey, let's get you to bed."

It had been too much of a day. Way too much. The fight in the orchard, her fall from the tree, the kiss from Ramón and now this. "I'm so tired."

She let him walk her to the door of her bedroom, then firmly stepped away. The bag she handed to him. "Give it to Zach, will you?"

"Why don't you just wait and give it to him tomorrow?"

Tanya nodded.

"Is there anything you need? Can I send someone up with some tea or something?"

"No," she said and looked over her shoulder. "No, I think I'm just going to go to sleep."

Ramón smiled. "Good. If you need anything, you know where to find me."

"Yes."

She bid him good-night and shut the door firmly—against him, against the painful memories the day had roused, against confronting the realities her new life offered. She kicked off her shoes, her bra and jeans, and fell into bed.

Ramón washed up and went down to dinner. Tonio, looking even more sullen than he had the night before, waited at the table with Desmary. To his surprise, Zach was there.

Ramón gave Desmary a questioning look. She lifted a comfortably padded grandmother shoulder. "He's little," she said.

For one moment, Ramón hesitated. He had to admit Zach tugged his protective instincts the same way the kid pulled on everyone else's. He was too young to have known so much trouble, and in spite of the problems he found at school and with other children, he possessed a basic sweetness of nature that made it hard to resist him. "All right," he said, and tension drained from Zach's body visibly, as if someone had pulled a plug on his big toe.

Touching his shoulder, Ramón said, "Napkin in your lap, guy. Elbows off the table.

"Do you have homework tonight?" he asked them both.

"I have math to do," Zach said. "Not much though."

"Are you good at math?"

Zach shook his head. "Not very. It's boring."

"What do you like?" Carefully, aware of the way Zach watched him, Ramón neatly cut his meat, put the knife down and shifted his fork to his right hand. "Music, maybe?"

"Music is for sissies." He cast a glance toward Tonio, who steadfastly ignored him. "I like art."

Ramón nodded. That didn't surprise him. "I bet you draw birds, don't you?"

"How'd you know that?"

"I've seen a few of them. You're quite an artist."

Zach shrugged. Ramón repeated the process of cutting his meat, then looked at Tonio. His plate of food was largely untouched. "Is your mouth bothering you?" Ramón asked.

Tonio gave him a sullen glance and shook his head.

"I couldn't quite hear you," Ramón said.

Tonio sighed gustily and said, "No."

"You need to eat something, then. Do you have homework tonight?"

"Yes."

Ramón grinned. "Shall I guess what it is? Do you have math like our little friend here?"

Not even a hint of a smile, Ramón noted with an inward chuckle. Often he could use a little teasing to bring healing to their relationship after a sharp punishment. He tried again. "English? Science?"

"Yeah and no." The faintest ease of features erased the scowl on Tonio's brow.

Ramón decided not to push it, but after supper, he called Tonio into his office. It was an old-fashioned room, with a long window facing the mountains. Shelves filled with Ramón's beloved books lined the walls—a good many of them in Spanish by the new wave of Latin novelists. It was one of the great joys of his life that he could read such beautiful novels in their original language.

Tonio draped himself over an overstuffed chair. He didn't speak, just sprawled, working a toothpick in his mouth, and waited for Ramón.

Ramón, too, took his time. He shelved several books, then sat down in the comfortable office chair he'd bought for himself two years ago. "We should talk about this, son. It isn't like you to be out of control."

"There's nothing to talk about."

"One of the things I've always liked about you, Tonio, is your strong feelings. But you can't let those feelings rule you. It's okay to be mad. Furious, even. It's okay to be frustrated and hurt and anything else." He leaned forward earnestly. "Feel anything you want to feel—it's all okay. You just can't act on those feelings inappropriately. And you have to eventually get to the moment when you ask yourself, what do I want?"

Tonio waited.

Ramón hated these scenes. Hated them and often wondered how much benefit they were. But he had them with almost all the kids, all the time. The boys were out of control, and had no disciplinary tactics to help themselves out of the sticky situations into which their mouths or hearts or screaming hormones got them.

He tried again. "What you really want doesn't have anything to do with Edwin."

"Oh, yes, it does. You know what I feel like when I see him? I want to break his face."

"Under the circumstances, that's a very normal feeling. It just isn't okay to do anything about it."

Ramón clasped his hands. "The bottom line here is the girl. Teresa, right?"

Tonio nodded.

"Edwin could give you dirty looks from morning till night if he weren't going with the girl you want."

Tonio looked stung. "I really like her," he said with lowered eyes. "And Edwin is mean to girls. He won't be nice to her for very long."

"That may be, but if you really like this girl, you have to respect her ability to make her own decisions. Even one you think is bad."

"But what if he really is mean to her?"

Ramón pursed his lips. Here was a sticky wicket. "Unless he gets verbally abusive in public or actually hurts her physically, there aren't many options."

"That su— stinks."

"I know."

"Did you ever get a broken heart?" Tonio asked quietly.

Ramón looked out the window, remembering a day long ago, when a slim, pregnant teenager had stolen his heart. "Yes," he said. "It hurts every time. But eventually, you realize it won't kill you, even if it feels like it will."

Tonio sighed. "I hope so."

"Trust me, Antonio. Like any wound, it'll get better eventually."

The boy nodded. "Thanks, Dad. Can I go now?"

"Sure." He rubbed Tonio's arm. "Hang in there, kid."

After he left, Ramón swiveled to look out the window, thinking about wounded hearts and emotions running amok. He thought about kissing Tanya this afternoon. He couldn't remember the last time anything had made him feel so much. While their lips moved together, and he felt her hair on his hands, he'd felt dizzy, adrift. Alive like he hadn't been in a long time.

If the truth were told, he'd spent most of the day in a state of semiarousal. Everything set him off—her neat little hands, the movement of her small breasts beneath her shirt, the way she turned her head to look at the spines of books. Every move she made pleased him, aroused him, made him want to make love to her. Now.

But that state of arousal had less to do with a need to see or touch or kiss any particular body part—though he'd certainly enjoy nibbling a breast—than it did with Tanya herself. The woman she was, the woman she'd fought to save. The lean and wary survivor she'd become.

He'd told himself not thirty-six hours ago that he had to leave her alone. She needed time and space to sort out her life and options before she jumped into another relationship. She needed to live on her own and experience life without a man or the state making her decisions for her.

It killed him to think of it, though—think of her leaving the ranch after he'd waited so long to have her here. He liked the way she fit here. She was a good cook and a talented baker, but he was more impressed with her ability to mother all the lost boys in his care. They gathered around her like hummingbirds around four-o'clocks, taking nourishment from her calm voice and encouraging laughter.

For the sake of those boys, for the sake of Tonio, who would eventually learn Tanya was his mother, and for Tanya's sake, Ramón had to leave her alone. No more kisses. No more sexy teasing. None of it.

But a lonely, hungry voice in his head protested, She's the one! The One.

Tanya was right about the arm. It was painful the first night but felt much better the next day. By the time a week had passed, she not only didn't hurt anymore, but had grown so used to the stitches that she did everything she'd done without them. Soon she'd have to go to town to get them removed.

It was a peculiar week in many ways. The weather was brilliant—sunny and dry and warm. Indian summer. Her morning runs were exhilarating.

Tonio spent a lot of time in the kitchen, as did Zach. They talked, both of them, about everything and anything, as they peeled potatoes, or chopped carrots and tomatoes, or plucked freshly killed chickens of their feathers—a task Tanya particularly loathed. She'd grown used to eating animals she'd formerly seen running around the chicken coop, but didn't like being able to identify which particular chickens she was chopping into pieces.

There was one bad moment on a bright sunny afternoon. Although they sometimes played the radio, Desmary had complained of a headache and turned it off that afternoon. Outside were the sounds of other boys at their chores—feeding chickens and pigs, sweeping the barn. Tanya creamed brown sugar and eggs in a huge metal bowl while Tonio cracked walnuts from a huge bag someone had given them. It was tedious work, but he picked out nutmeats happily enough as long as he could nibble on some of them. It amazed her how much these boys ate—all of them nibbled, grazed, gulped, *ate,* all the time.

Tanya paused in her stirring to reach for vanilla and a measuring spoon, humming tunelessly to herself as was her habit. It had driven Victor around the bend, that humming, and yet she couldn't seem to drop it. It was a part of her, like having blue eyes or mousy brown hair.

One and a half teaspoons per batch, which meant four and a half teaspoons for this tripled recipe. She measured two and was pouring a third when Tonio demanded in a harsh voice, "What is that song?"

Tanya had to think. Which song was she humming today? An old folk song she'd learned at her one foray into camp when she was in sixth grade. "I don't know what it's called," she said with a grin. "We always called it 'There are suitors at my door.'" She sang the first line.

And remembered.

This song, along with "The Battle Hymn of the Republic," "The Ants Come Marching Home" and "The Cruel War," was part of her humming repertoire. It was the song Tonio had said he remembered his mother singing, the one about rivers running up hill and fish flying and a woman getting married the day before she died.

Tonio stared fiercely at her, his eyes ablaze with

anger and hurt and a thousand questions. Standing there with the scent of vanilla in her nose, the notes of a song dying between them, Tanya willed him to remember, so the lie could be over. So she could stop tiptoeing around him. Softly she sang the last verse, the one he remembered.

"Stop it," he said fiercely. "Don't sing that song anymore."

"Why?" she asked quietly.

"I just hate it, that's all." He stood up violently, nearly knocking over the chair, and bolted out of the room.

With a shaky sigh, Tanya measured another teaspoon of vanilla and couldn't remember if she had added three or four. Better too little in this instance, she decided, and stirred it in.

She wondered how long it would be before he would guess. If he guessed—she supposed there was no reason for him to do so. Her hair was not long and blond anymore. Her body was lean and hard, rather than round and soft. Her name was Tanya, not the diminutive Annie he more than likely would remember.

And yet, the song was powerful. It was one she'd sung to him before bed every night. Every night. She'd even considered putting a tape of it inside the diaper bag she took to the day care woman's house that last night, but hadn't had time.

The incident disturbed her all afternoon. That evening, wearing a jacket over her sweatshirt, she sat on the back porch gutting pumpkins to be used as jack-o'-lanterns. The seeds she put in a huge bowl for roasting later.

The night was fresh and cool, smelling of distant leaf burnings and rustling grass. Indian summer in New Mexico was truly glorious. She loved being able to sit outside after dark in October.

The screen door creaked and Tanya glanced over her shoulder to see Ramón coming to join her. He carried two mugs of coffee, and put one down beside her on an overturned orange crate. "Thought you might like this," he said.

"Thanks."

He, too, had been a little odd this week. After the kisses last Saturday, she'd known a pleasurable sense of arousal and anticipation. But he steered clear of her, and at meals or other functions when he could not avoid her, he treated her like a sister, with friendly respect.

Now, dropping on to the old wooden chair near her own, he wrinkled his nose. "Aay, that stinks. I never liked the way pumpkin smelled."

"Me, either." Tanya shook her rubber-gloved fingers to loosen a long orange string. "Has to be done. Bet you like pumpkin pie."

"Not really."

"Not even with whipped cream?"

"Nope. Custard pies are disgusting. I used to have an aunt who made about thirty of them for every family gathering, and everyone else quit bringing pies because she baked so many, but they were all pumpkin or custard types."

Tanya smiled. "I don't remember anybody making

pies when I was a child. There were no family gatherings, really. We moved so often we usually didn't even have any friends to invite over on holidays.''

"Now that you say that, I realize I don't know much about your childhood. All I know about your parents is that they wouldn't help you when you...er..''

"Killed my ex-husband?'' Tanya supplied dryly.

Ruefully, Ramón laughed. "Yes.''

"They disowned me when I married him. I actually married him so early—'' she had been one day past seventeen "—because they were moving and I was tired of going all the time. I never really had another conversation with them.''

"I would say it's hard to imagine, but I've seen all kinds of parents in my line of work.''

"Mine weren't all that terrible,'' she said. She so rarely thought of her parents it was as if they'd borne her in another lifetime. "I felt like I didn't belong with them.''

"Was your father abusive?''

"No,'' Tanya said. It was not an uncommon question, coming as it did from a professional in the field. Often the children of abusive marriages grew up to repeat the pattern. "My dad was a philanderer. Slept with any woman he could get into bed. My mother responded by moving every time he formed an attachment. I went to sixteen schools by the time we made it to Albuquerque.''

"And yet, with all of that, you turned out okay.'' He grinned, nudging her foot with his toe. "More or less.''

Tanya smiled, halfheartedly, thinking of Tonio. She

told Ramón what happened, then asked him, "What do you think he remembers? I mean about the way Victor acted."

Ramón took a breath. "He remembers some of it," he said quietly. "He used to wake up from his dreams screaming."

For a moment, Tanya considered asking what Antonio said after those nightmares, but she didn't think she could bear to know just now. "My poor baby."

"He's okay. He's a good kid."

"Yes, he is." And maybe, Tanya thought, he would forgive her the small duplicity she had practiced here. "Do you think we made a mistake by not telling him the truth about me?"

He stood up suddenly. "Come on, let's take a walk."

"Why?" She held up her gloved, pumpkin-stringed hands. "In case you haven't noticed, I'm kind of in the middle of something."

"I see." He reached over, grabbed the plastic table cloth from the table, and flung it over the pumpkins. "But it's important."

For a moment, Tanya measured him. Then she stood and stripped off the gloves. "All right," she said, and followed him down the steps into the moon-swept night.

Chapter Nine

Dear Antonio,

It came to me this morning that the man I killed was your father. I wonder if you hate me for that.

I also wonder if you're like him, and how. I wonder if you're starting to look like him as you get long-legged and lose your baby fat. I wonder how I'll feel if I see you and you're his spitting image.

Sometimes I go over that last time he found us, and I wonder what I could have done differently. I go over it and over it and over it. But we moved fourteen times in twenty months. We moved out of town. We moved into a house under an assumed name. I waited tables and dyed my hair. I signed restraining orders…I did everything I could think of. And still he found us.

The time before the last one, he found us in Santa Fe, and he was furious. I hid you in our bedroom when I saw him coming up the walk, and closed the door. You screamed the whole time. I'll never forget it. After that, I kept wondering how long you would have been stuck in that room screaming if he'd actually killed me.

That's when I bought the gun. That fear made me decide it was time to take care of it myself, since no one else would. So I bought the gun and hid it and waited for him to find us again. When he did, I killed him. It wasn't the right answer, but it was the only answer I had left. I hope, if you hate me for what I've done, you'll remember that.

They tell me that if that had happened now, I wouldn't go to jail. I guess that's some comfort—that some other woman and some other boy won't have to pay the price we've paid here. I love you, son. I just want you to know that.

Love, Mom

The night was brisk, tasting of leaves and dry grass, and the peculiar notes of the desert itself, a pungent odor of juniper and sun-heated earth. Tanya tugged her jacket close around herself. "Okay, so you *do* think we made a mistake in not telling Tonio the truth?"

"No, that's just it—I know we didn't make a mistake. He might be upset when he learns the truth, but what I see is the two of you developing a real relationship, without all the entrapments of past history, at least on Tonio's part."

Tanya nodded slowly. A high moon lit the prairie with pale fingers, and lent a halo to Ramón's dark hair. His profile was hawkish against the night, that conquistadore's nose and high brow. A little shiver touched her, starting in her spine and radiating outward. She wanted him to kiss her again.

Actually, judging by her rather heated dreams, she wanted quite a bit more than kissing. They were almost embarrassing.

"I've been worried about it. About the fact that we're not telling the truth."

"Sometimes telling the whole truth only hurts people, Tanya. You know that."

She nodded.

He nudged her with his elbow. "You worry about everything. Maybe you should try to let some of it go. Those bags of guilt you're dragging behind you have to be pretty heavy some days."

Ruefully, Tanya smiled up at him, and made a motion as if she were taking a duffel bag off her shoulder to give him. "You want one?"

"No, thanks. I have plenty of my own."

"You? What do you have to be guilty and worried about?"

"Not guilty—though I do have a bag of that. Mostly I worry. About Tonio. About you." He gestured widely. "About all the boys."

Tanya pursed her lips, stepping carefully around a prickly pear spread around the foot of a yucca. Ramón made them all sound like part of some noble quest, as if he went around rescuing boys here and there, fishing them from the river of sin and sorrow. She frowned. "Am I one of your projects?" she asked. "Is Tonio?"

"No person is a project." His voice held a note of annoyance. "There are only people and I do the best I can with them. You were one of the people I wanted to see come through the system—somehow—okay. Most of these boys will die early deaths if I don't intervene, and some of them will no matter what I do." He looked at her. "But I have to try."

They stopped on a bluff overlooking the first finger of the Rio Grande—not nearly the formidable river it would become, but nonetheless a river with a certain authority. It clucked into the hollow made by a cottonwood's roots, and rushed over rocks. Tanya let go of a sigh she was unaware she was holding. "What about Tonio?" she asked, looking at the water. "Was he a project?"

He didn't answer immediately. His voice was thick when he spoke. "Tonio was born to you and Victor, but he's my son, Tanya. I've raised him for eleven years."

"I didn't mean—"

His mouth went hard. "Don't say it, Tanya. Just leave it out there. I am Tonio's father. He is my only child."

"I'm sorry. You didn't deserve that."

He looked at her but said nothing. They stood face-to-face on the open prairie, moonlight spilling down upon them like some narcotic perfume from a broken bottle. The light washed over Ramón's high cheekbones and touched his lips and the long brown strength of his throat. She ached to touch him.

He stared back at her, and Tanya felt his gaze lick her face and hair, her shoulders and breasts. Remembering his words in the bookstore, she said, "I really need to kiss you."

"We shouldn't, Tanya." But he moved a step closer, raising a hand to brush her hair off her shoulder. "I should leave you alone and let you find your own life, but I keep circling back to you, over and over again, like some lost sheep."

Tanya, made bold by his body language, if not his words, moved closer and put her hands on his waist under his coat. His sides were lean and warm below the cotton shirt, and she felt a shifting in the muscles when he took another step toward her. His arms circled her shoulders loosely and she let hers slide around to his back. Their bodies met lightly.

Their mouths joined. It was that simple and that clean. He bent and fit his mouth to hers. It wasn't so sweet this time. Tanya's body flushed as his mouth opened, as his sensual nature—so obvious in the way he touched everything and everyone, in his deep appreciation for beauty—overtook his cautious side. He made a low, warm noise and moved closer, and she felt his hard, flat belly against her own, felt his chest against her breasts. His lips moved in an expert dance of slow savoring, as if her mouth were more delicious than anything he'd ever tasted. Pleasure made her soft all over, in her knees, her hips, her hands that stretched open on his back.

His tongue ribboned the inner edges of her lips, and that part of her, too, was soft in response to him. She inclined her head slightly and let herself relax, giving him access to her mouth. A sharp bolt of almost overwhelming desire ripped through her when his tongue met hers, when they tangled so slowly, so deliciously. His hands moved on her back, and he pressed his hips to hers, and there was another jump in her nether regions.

Heaven, she thought vaguely. Heaven to kiss and kiss and kiss under a wide open sky filled with moonlight and the smell of crushed sage, and the tiny scratchings of hidden jackrabbits the only sound. Heaven to let her body mold closer and closer to his as the kiss deepened, intensified. Heaven to feel Ramón's strong hands reaching down to cup her bottom and urge her closer, to feel the ancient rocking movements between them.

She put her hands under his shirt and heard a hushed sound—delight and excitement—escape her throat. His skin was elegant satin, hot and smooth and delectably sensitive. He caught her lip and sucked on it, as if urging her to do more.

It had been such a long, long time. A powerful urgency built in Tanya's body, an ache too long left, and hunger so wild it seemed almost wanton. She moved her hands up his back, skimming his spine and the supple expanse of his muscles. Then, dangerously, she let her hands fall to the high, round rear end she had so often admired. He groaned and she pulled him closer, thinking nothing except that she would die if she had to stop.

A sudden noise in the darkness shattered the moment. An owl screeched and a small animal made a pained noise, and as if they'd been doused with water,

Ramón and Tanya startled, clutching to each other in the primal, ancient fear of humans at the mercy of nature after dark.

They looked at each other, and Ramón lifted a hand to smooth Tanya's hair from her face. "It's La Llorona, the weeping woman, come to warn you."

"Warn me against what?"

He moved his body away from hers and took her hand. They walked alongside the river. "Do you know her story?"

"No."

"La Llorona guards the rivers—she was a very beautiful peasant girl who fell under the spell of a rich man. When he went to marry another, La Llorona threw their children in the river and drowned them, so he could have nothing, as she had nothing. Now she haunts the rivers, looking for her lost children, weeping and weeping."

Tanya felt a stinging recognition in the story. "How sad."

Ramón shrugged and lifted his face to the night, as if scenting the ghost. "It's a story to keep children away from the river," he said. "It isn't true."

A shiver ran down her spine. "You're wrong," she said quietly. "It is true. It's been true through all of time, and will be true a thousand years from now, and La Llorona is crying for all those women who were betrayed." Her voice roughened. "For me."

Ramón, who had stopped to listen, bent and put his mouth on hers again. It was a sharply heated kiss, filled with tongues and teeth and urgent need. Tanya met it eagerly, taking refuge in his sensual ways, in his demanding kiss. When he lifted his head, with a trail of one, two, three little kisses, he said, "I can't stop thinking about that, about kissing you." He brushed his lips over hers once more. "You know I think about it all the time, whenever I look at you?"

Watching his lips move, Tanya nodded, and drifted forward, her body alive and thrumming. She swayed toward him. "Don't be too hard on yourself," she said in a breathy voice, "I'm irresistible." She lifted her gaze and smiled.

"Two jokes in a single week? What's the world coming to?"

"I guess you're rubbing off on me."

He pressed against her, and Tanya pressed back. "Let's rub some more then," he said. And kissed her again. When the heat began to rise once more between them, Ramón put her firmly away. "I'm not Superman, cricket. Let's go back before I rip off your clothes right here."

Tanya backed away, and wiped her palms on her jeans. She lost herself when he kissed her. She just disappeared in pleasure.

In a companionable manner, Ramón tossed an arm around her shoulder and they walked back in the direction of the farmhouse. Tanya thought she could manage his proximity fairly well until she realized how her breast brushed his side. How their thighs touched, then didn't, then did. How his hips bumped hers. Yearning pulsed in her—the yearning to give herself to this sensual, sexy, gentle man.

With a cold sense of shock, she realized she was falling in love with him. How could that have happened? How could she have allowed her guard to slip so quickly?

As they reached the barn, Merlin came padding out and licked her hand. She bent and stroked his head. Ramón paused with her. The square was quiet. In the barn a horse nickered, and from the kitchen came the light clinking of spoons and pans and glassware. From the dorms came music, unidentifiable except for the pounding beat of rap, which seemed to be the music of choice for most of these boys. "I wonder why they like rap so much," she said aloud, trying to avoid her thoughts.

"It's angry," he said. "It expresses their feelings of betrayal and fury and violence."

"How can you approve?" Tanya asked. "It's misogynistic and violent."

"Some of it is," he said, lifting a shoulder. "So is a lot of rock and roll. Rap is like any other music—it expresses something that needs expression, whether we agree with the sentiment or not. And some of it is very powerful, very touching."

"Really?"

He nodded. "Ask Tonio to play some good songs for you. Tell him you want to learn about it. He'll show you."

"I will."

A small pause fell between them, empty, waiting for the words Tanya knew she needed to say. She took a breath, steeling herself, and said, "Ramón, I think you need to know I don't think I can give myself up to whatever this is between us. It scares me."

"Don't worry so much, Tanya."

She shook her head. "It isn't worry, Ramón. It's too intense. I just spent eleven years in prison because of an intense relationship."

"Not intense, Tanya—violent. There's a difference."

"Not to me."

His face was unreadable in the dimness, but she sensed his sudden stiffness. "I'm not Victor."

"I know that." And she did know. But they were alike in ways. There were similarities in the way they looked, and talked. The timbre of their voices was nearly the same. But most of all, the passion was the same.

No, that wasn't true. She had been so young when she and Victor got together that she'd never really even enjoyed sex all that much. Some of it was nice— the kissing and touching and all of that—but she had never liked it the way Victor did. She suspected, though of course she had no one to compare him to, that he had not been the most adept lover.

But then, he'd been very young too. And what he'd lacked in skill, he'd made up for in passion. "He wanted me so much I felt whole for the first time in my life," she said quietly. "He wanted to attach me to his body so that I'd be part of him. It's impossible to tell you how that made me feel."

"That's obsessive."

"I know," she repeated, and looked steadily at him. "I've fought so hard to be whole by myself, and when you kissed me like that...back there...I felt engulfed."

"Oh!" He sounded relieved. "Is that what's bothering you?" He lifted a hand to brush away a lock of hair from her face. "Do you think I was apart and coherent? Do you think anyone is at moments like that?" He shook his head. "They aren't."

Even his hand on her cheek made that pulsing heat burst through her body again, starting that ache low in her groin. Irritated, she turned her head. "I don't want that in my life. It's too crazy."

For a moment, his hand hung in midair. Slowly, he put it down, looking at her with measuring eyes. He nodded once. "I understand," he said. "I won't bother you anymore."

"Ramón! I didn't mean it like that."

He touched her arm, let it go. "I know you didn't." A sigh left him. "We'll just be friends, as we always have been." He cleared his throat, as if to change direction. "Will you help me put the dance together? We need to get it done—it's two weeks from this Friday."

"Of course," she said.

"Good." He lifted a hand. "See you tomorrow, then."

Tanya nodded, and clasped her arms around her chest. She should have been feeling relieved. She had seen the problem, confronted it as honestly as she could, and dealt with it. Why, then, did she feel such a sense of loss?

All the way into the house Ramón cursed himself. Or rather cursed everything—Victor, fate, timing. In his study, he closed the door and leaned against it.

Damn.

He had not intended to indulge himself like that, but

out there in the moonlight, undone by the sweet yearning in her face, he had been unable to resist her. And even then, he'd only intended to play, to tease her a little and stoke the growing hunger he saw in her eyes. He'd meant to just take one more baby step forward into her skittish world. A light kiss, a few teasing words, a little light erotic play—kissing her palm, maybe, or her neck.

But the narcotic night had seduced him. Seduced Tanya. The moonlight had washed into them, and awakened their senses. Kissing her, he felt expanded— his hearing was so acute he heard the dance of field mice in their underground dens below the prickly pears, and scented the crush of juniper berries broken underfoot like spilled gin. He had closed his eyes, unwilling to add sight to the sensory overload, and concentrated on taste—her silky tongue, swirling with his, her eager lips, her faint sighs.

And feeling—her breasts bumping into his chest, immensely giving, her slim long back and round buttocks, firm with the muscles of her daily running.

He'd simply fallen over the edge at that moment, fallen adrift in the nectar of Tanya, in the pleasure of touching her, feeling her.

She was terrified, and with good reason. He had to keep himself in complete control. Not a single breach, or she'd run off like the wounded doe she was.

But he knew tonight that he could not let it lie any more. He wanted her deeply. She wanted him, too. It was right that he should be the one to teach her men were not all violent, that passion did not always wound. Perhaps he could help free her fully, to live instead of just survive. Slowly, carefully, he would show her. And if he had to let her go when she was free of the past, he would accept that, too.

The phone rang, and with a growl of frustration, he picked it up. It was the line from the dorms. "Ramón here."

"Dave here. We need you, stat." In the background were shouts and chaos. "Couple of boys are at it again."

"I'll be right there," Ramón said, and headed for the dorms, glad to have something to distract him.

Chapter Ten

Dear Antonio,

Sometimes now—from the great old age of twenty-seven—I think about how young we were, Victor and I, when we met. When we got married, when we each made decisions that would affect us forever. I was seventeen when we got married. Eighteen when you were born. At nineteen, I was already divorced. I met him when I was fourteen, and—well, never mind. No need for you to know every little detail.

Now I watch the news and see it's only getting worse. I see some of the young girls who come in here to visit their mothers or aunts or sisters—and they're so old by the time they're fourteen. Already so grown up. And so often now, the boys just kill each other. Before they're even old enough to know how long forever is.

I wish we could make it better somehow for
all of you. I hope Ramón will teach you to treasure your childhood, then your adolescence. Once
it's gone, you can't be a kid ever again. Remember that. Be a child before you become a lover.
Be a man before you take a wife.

Love, Mom

Tanya awakened from restless dreams long before the
sun rose. A cat—this one named Snoopy—slept on her
feet. It was a young orange-and-black calico, and
stretched lazily when Tanya shifted to lie on her back
while the dreams faded.

It was not uncommon for her to dream of the night
of the shooting. She never remembered the actual moments—not the shooting itself or the police arriving.
Her memory stopped with Victor at the bathroom door
and picked up again when she was locked in a holding
cell downtown with a prostitute wearing red fishnet
stockings.

It wasn't uncommon for her to have nightmares of
all kinds, actually. In her dreams, she worked out her
sorrows and angst. In daily life, she thought she was
fairly normal. It was only in her dreams that she reacted to everything that had happened.

As she lay there in the darkness, a cat purring on
her chest as she stroked its soft, pointed ears, the
dream she'd had filtered through her mind. It wasn't
the last confrontation with Victor, or one of the other

times he'd lost control or the more recent panicky dream of being back in prison.

No, this time, she'd dreamed of dancing with Ramón. He was younger, slim to the point of skinny, his glasses hiding his beautiful eyes. But his hands had been warm on her back, his laugh infectious and teasing, and his mouth—oh, she had seen his mouth that day. In her dream, she felt his arousal against her thigh, and she smiled up at him in a knowing, womanish way, to let him know she had noticed. In her dream, he had danced them toward a secluded cove and kissed her. Tanya laughed and put her arms around his neck, pulling him closer, kissing him deeply, reveling in the feeling of his hands on her breasts and smoothing over her rounded tummy.

Then she heard a shot, and Ramón slumped against her, his hot blood burning her hands that held the gun. In her dream, Tanya screamed, "No!"

And woke up to a cat on her feet in a room of Ramón's making. For the first time, she knew she'd dreamed a piece of that blacked-out day, as well as a metaphorical wish that things could have been different. If only she'd met Ramón sooner. Or been a little wiser about things. If only he had been a grown man instead of seeking boy.

If only.

With a sigh, she tossed back the covers and put on her robe. "If only" would make her crazy. No one had any clear idea of the world at seventeen. Victor had probably understood more, in his primitive way, than either Ramón or Tanya. Victor had sensed the powerful attraction between his cousin and his wife, an attraction neither Ramón nor Tanya had admitted.

She padded down the stairs in the silent house, going to the kitchen for a cup of tea. There was a light on already, and Tanya hung back, unwilling to meet Ramón in her present state. She needed to think about him and her feelings for him before the whole thing rocketed out of control. The kisses and touches between them had been, to this point, very gentle, but Tanya wasn't fooled. There was an untamed river of passion within Ramón Quezada, and it was dangerous to her carefully dammed emotions.

Silently, she peeked around the door and saw Tonio bent over a spiral notebook. A glass of juice and scattered evidence of varied snacks littered the table—popcorn, carrot sticks, an empty candy wrapper. He'd been there awhile. She wondered if she ought to leave him alone.

Pushing the door open, she said quietly, "Hi. Am I interrupting?"

Startled, he looked up at Tanya, then looked at the clock, which read 3:15. "What are you doing up?

"I could ask you the same question. Bad dreams?"

He quirked his mouth—and the gesture was utterly Victor. Somehow, it was a relief. This awkwardly teenage boy really was the Antonio she'd left behind, the one with the long eyelashes and a fondness for peanut butter crackers. "Nah," he said. "I just couldn't sleep."

Tanya took a mug from the cupboard. "I'm making some tea. Do you want some?"

"No, thanks." He pointed to his glass of juice.

"That should promote easy sleep, all right," she said, and smiled to show she wasn't criticizing. She filled her mug with water and put it in the microwave, then leaned against the counter, hands in her robe pockets. "Are you a writer?"

He shook his head, his thumb flipping the edge of his spiral notebook. The whole page was filled with his small, neat printing. "It's, like, a letter."

The microwave dinged. Tanya took out her mug and fixed the tea. "I'll leave you alone, then," she said.

"You don't have to," he said. "I mean, you don't have to stay and keep me company, either, but I don't mind if you're in here."

Tanya took the hint and sat down, trying to find someplace for her eyes besides the white, heavily filled page. His hair, freshly washed and as yet unslicked, hung black around his face—a face that was angled and brown and beautiful, all the more startling because of his blue eyes. Her eyes, she thought proudly.

Eyes presently filled with misery. "Still feeling bad over the girl—was her name Teresa?"

"Yeah." Restlessly, he flipped his pen onto the page, off the page. "I really like her. And I know Edwin's gonna hurt her—maybe not outside, but he'll hurt her. He's a jerk."

Tanya carefully schooled her mouth to keep her opinions to herself. It wouldn't do to say, "You're right—he is a jerk." Instead she lifted a shoulder. "Maybe. But maybe he really likes her, too." She held up a hand at his protest. "I know you don't want to hear that, but it just might be true."

Tonio stubbornly shook his head. "He's already

said he slept with her. I heard him saying it in the orchard that day. He's lying. She wouldn't do that.''

Again, to remain neutral, Tanya nodded, sipping her tea. ''It sounds like a tough situation.''

''You know those really jealous guys who beat up everybody when they think their girlfriend is talking to someone else or something?''

''Sure,'' Tanya said, tongue in cheek.

''He's like that. He almost killed his own brother over some girl back in Albuquerque, and I saw him hit a girl last spring for calling him a name.''

None of the anecdotes surprised her, but Tanya still didn't know what the best advice for Tonio would be. ''Have you tried to talk to her? Maybe she just doesn't realize how dangerous he might be.''

''You believe me.''

Tanya nodded.

He put his hand on his hip, pushed the notebook an inch up on the table. ''I'm writing her a letter.''

''Good.'' She bit her lip. To say any more would be foolish.

''I tried not to say anything about how I feel about her or anything. I just want her to be safe from Edwin—he only wanted her to get to me, anyway.'' Again he flipped his pen restlessly on the page. ''I'm only going to tell her one time I'm here for her if she needs me.''

''That seems a very wise choice.''

Tonio looked at her. ''Sometimes, it's so easy to talk to you, it's like I know you already. Like I knew you when you came here.''

Tanya froze. Did he guess who she was? Was she

ready for that? He didn't seem angry. "Sometimes people just mesh. I've met people I hated on sight, too."

Color moved up his cheeks and he lowered his eyes. "I think you kinda remind me of my mom. She gave me away when I was three, to Ramón."

Words burned in her throat—words she desperately wanted to say. *I am your mother and I didn't give you away, you were taken.* To hold them back, she didn't speak, only sipped some tea and swallowed the words, bitter and whole, nodding. One thing she'd learned early in life was that people only needed a little nodding to keep talking.

Tonio included. "She was real young. It was probably too much for her—though my dad, that is, Ramón, says she wanted to keep me out of all the mess." He rubbed the paper under his hand. "I have one letter she wrote to me before she had to go to prison."

In a swift bright flash, Tanya was sitting in her kitchen in the little house in Albuquerque, amid the ruins of her carefully collected, hand-painted and mismatched china, writing a letter. She could see her hand on the paper, writing "Dear Antonio..."

"That must be comforting," Tanya said over the ache in her chest. It amazed her how calm her voice sounded. "It's nice that you kept it."

"It's all I have."

She smiled, honestly this time. "It's more than Zach has, isn't it?"

Tonio's expression lightened. "Yeah," he said. "Yeah, it is."

"Well," she said, picking up her cup. "I'll leave you to your letter."

He nodded. "Thanks for listening, Ms. Bishop."

"My pleasure." Tanya walked cooly to the door, but just beyond, she bolted. No way this could go on much longer. No way. Every time he gave her a chance to confess and she didn't, the lie got bigger. Every time she pretended not to be his mother, he would remember when the truth was revealed.

With a feeling very much like panic, Tanya went to Ramón's room. She tapped at the door and waited, her arms crossed on her chest. Nothing. She tapped again, and called him softly, although he was alone on the second floor. "Ramón!"

A groggy voice answered her. "Come in."

Within, the darkness was absolute. Tanya closed the door behind her and stumbled forward, propelled by her panic. "Ramón?" she whispered, and tripped over a pair of jeans.

"Straight ahead," he mumbled, sleepily.

Tanya moved forward gingerly, hands outstretched. The room smelled of his skin, of him, rich and faintly spicy. The front of her thighs struck the bed and she bent over involuntarily, her hands going out to stop herself.

One palm landed on his stomach—bare and hot. The other landed on the pillow near his head. His thick coarse hair brushed her inner wrist. Hastily she straightened, rubbing her hand restlessly against her leg.

Now that she stood here, the intense reality of the moment came to her. She smelled his skin and heat, and the knowledge that his torso—at the very least—was bare, made her palms burn and her breasts ache. "This was a mistake," she whispered. "I'll leave you alone. I'm sorry. I don't know what—"

A big hand snagged her wrist, and Tanya tumbled forward, landing on the bed next to him. "You don't have to rush off." His voice was rough with sleep. "I've only been in bed a half hour, so another few minutes isn't going to make any difference."

"No, I—this was—I'm sorry." She tried to move away, embarrassment flooding her. What had she been thinking? She hadn't been thinking. Only feeling. "I'll leave you alone."

"Come here and tell me what's wrong."

Waves of mortification washed through her. "No, really, Ramón—"

He tugged her again. "Lie down here with me, cricket. Let me hold you." He pressed his mouth to her hand. "Just for a minute."

Tanya resisted one more moment, but his scent permeated the room, filling her with a restless sense of need. Knowing even as she relented that it was a mistake, she gingerly eased her body down beside him.

"That's it," he said roughly, and tucked an arm around her. The heat of his length along her body gave her a wild jolt. "Tell me what's bothering you, *grillacita.*"

She remembered what had driven her here. "I have to tell Tonio the truth."

"Mmm." Lazily, his hand moved on her body as he nestled closer to her, his chest against her arm, his face tucked against her neck. The broad hand made a wide circle over her stomach, up an arm, lightly clasped a breast, then moved quickly away before she could protest. Against her buttocks pressed his arousal, pointed and hot below the covers. She was almost sure he slept with no clothes—clothes would make that feel different. Her breath caught as his mouth landed against her shoulder.

"Pretty soon, we'll tell him," he said with a rasp, and his hand slipped inside her robe, over her thin nightgown, and stroked her breast again. Her nipples leapt to full attention. His skillful fingers circled back, touched the aroused points lazily, slowly. "Soon," he said into her hair. His mouth touched her neck, hot and moist. Tanya shuddered, feeling arousal rush through her.

He planted a kiss on the vulnerable flesh below her ear, and his tongue teased the edge of her ear. She made a low noise and closed her eyes, trying to be still so she wouldn't give herself away. He felt so good, he smelled so good....

The questing fingers freed two buttons on her gown and slid inside, and all at once, his naked fingers were touching her breast, skin to skin, and she gasped. He swirled and skimmed and cupped, teasing her nipple as his mouth moved on her neck, her ear, her jaw. Lower, his hips moved against her bottom, and she found herself responding with movements of her own. A warm, pleased sound came from his throat.

He spread kisses up the side of her neck. "Turn over, sweetness, let me kiss you properly."

Tanya needed no second urging. She turned in his embrace and found him propped on one elbow, ready to bend and kiss her. Lightly, so lightly. With his free hand he unbelted her robe and flipped it open. She shivered.

His big hand stroked her breasts, then opened the rest of the buttons and spread open the gown. She felt the air against her breasts an instant before he moved his hand to clasp and caress her flesh. As his tongue opened her lips and plied her mouth, he moved his deft fingers to the points of her breasts and played there, teasing and stroking. He opened his mouth and invited her in, and Tanya entered the sacred cavern, and found herself arching against his plucking fingers, his thrusting tongue.

He made a low, dark noise. "We aren't going to make love tonight," he whispered, "because I'm not prepared, and neither are you, but there's no reason we can't do some heavy petting, is there?" In illustration, he roved over her breasts deliciously, heating her flesh with his touch. "Do you know a reason?"

She put her hands on his naked back, nearly breathless with the pleasure of it. "No reason I can think of."

"Good," he breathed. With exquisite slowness, he bent his head and put his mouth on her breast. He touched the tip lightly with his tongue. She gasped. Deliciously, he tortured her with more light flutters that sent shooting arrows of sensation through her body. Urgently, she put her hands in his thick, gloriously wavy hair, and reveled in the sensation against her fingers, silky and cool and heavy all at once. And his mouth, so hot and wet, suckled her, lightly, then more fiercely, as if he were starving. His hand moved on her body, skimming her waist and thighs, and she felt the brush of hair as he tugged her gown up and skimmed her thighs with an open palm. "Tanya," he breathed, kissing her, "you're so sweet. So sweet."

And in her turn, Tanya tasted his neck, his throat, his slightly prickly chin. She slid her tongue over the long dark column of his throat into the hollow at the base, where she could feel the pulse of his life moving, beating. He was so hot—his skin was like the dark pelt of an animal who had been sleeping in the sun— and it warmed the cold, lost places inside of her.

Somehow, her robe and panties were shed, and Ramón's hands grew urgent on her body, his kiss hot and intense. She skimmed the blanket from his body and found he was indeed bare beneath it, and she put her hands on his hips, glorying in the muscled feel against her palms.

Ramón touched her, from shoulder to knee, with his hands, and his mouth, and then he covered her with his body, the lower half still draped in a sheet, and she wanted to weep with the feeling of that sleek, naked chest moving lightly over her bared breasts. He kissed her deeply, hungrily, and she thought she would die of pleasure and need.

And then, oh, then, he slipped his hand between her legs and stroked her, only a little, ever so expertly, exactly as she would have asked him to, if she had dared. The deep heat that had been growing low in her abdomen over days of kisses and dreams simply exploded.

It was not like anything else.

She had never experienced the true pinnacle of sex,

and the experience was unbelievable, inexpressible, outrageous. She heard a low, dark moan rise into the room, and realized it was coming from her own throat, as wave after wave rocked her. After long moments of blinding pleasure, the waves slowed and faded, but Ramón made a small, joyful sound and bent his head to her breast, where he teased and lapped and nibbled, and the rocketing waves returned.

Never, never, never had she understood, she thought, overcome. As the waves subsided, leaving a wide rippling heat in her body, she knew an empty aching—and that was a sensation she recognized. She needed Ramón inside of her. She urged him closer, and he kissed her, but didn't take her invitation.

"No," he whispered finally. "I'll wait my turn. I have no condoms here. I have to buy them."

Tanya, shaking, knew there were ways to give him what he'd just given her, but she was too weak, too deeply sated. He settled next to her, his hand over her breast. "Sleep, my sweet."

And Tanya, exhausted by sexual satisfaction for the first time in her life, did just that.

Ramón awakened the next morning, his body tight and aching with desire. Against him, Tanya slept, just as he'd imagined so many times. Her hair, shiny and clean-smelling, tumbled over her cheek, and her pretty, soft mouth was almost unbearably lush in sleep. One white breast, unbelievably beautiful, was exposed.

Moving cautiously, he reached for the cover to pull it up over her, to cover her nudity. But she shifted in his arms, still soundly sleeping, and the movement put one pert, rosy nipple almost next to his mouth. He groaned and closed his eyes, willing his desire to some faraway place, but her skin was soft against him, and his breath caused her nipple to pearl, and he rationalized the heavens would not so irresistibly tempt him if he wasn't meant to act.

With a sigh, he bent his head and accepted the sweet fruit into his mouth, savoring the taste for the delicacy it was. He suckled until he felt her stir, moaning softly. Her hands fell first in his hair, and her fingers roved over his scalp. She whispered his name in a voice soft with wonder and delight, and her hands moved on his body.

She touched him. Intimately, hotly, embracing his aching shaft firmly, moving in the ancient rhythm, and he forgot himself, forgot that he was a calm grown man who could hold off until there was protection, who could resist anything.

He couldn't resist Tanya. Couldn't resist this.

She coaxed him to satisfaction, and didn't flinch when he grasped her arms and kissed her deeply. And when the violent rocking had finished, he gathered her close. Touched her delicate ears, her beautiful breasts, the hungry tips, and the sleek flat of her stomach, moving lower. She stopped him, and whispered breathily, "Let's wait, until we can make love properly." She opened her eyes. "I want all of you."

Ramón kissed her. "Tanya, I missed you." A thick pulse filled his groin, making him ready again. "I'll never be able to keep my hands off you today."

She smiled. "You'd better. There are a lot of boys down there looking up to you."

"I promise I'll illustrate the right way to touch a woman for them. Will that help?"

"No." She slapped his arm. "I can't believe I never before knew what was supposed to happen."

"I don't know what you mean."

"You know." Her voice dropped and a hot pink stain touched her cheekbones. "The whole enchilada."

He thrust his hips at her playfully. "No, you haven't had the whole enchilada, baby. Not yet."

"Ramón!" She ducked her head into his shoulder and mumbled a word into his neck.

"Orgasm!" he said, pulling back to look at her face. "You've never had an orgasm before?"

She shook her head.

Ramón smiled, broadly. "Oh, cricket, are we going to have some fun." He kissed her. "Tonight."

A flush touched her face again, but it wasn't embarrassment this time. Her eyes were awash with liquid heat. "Better find a way to hide that glow, or I'll have to reassign you. Those randy boys will catch fire."

"No," she whispered, lifting her arms around his neck. "Just keep the fire low, and we'll be fine."

"My pleasure." He kissed her, wondering how he'd fallen into such good fortune, so suddenly. "My pleasure."

Tanya moved through breakfast preparations feeling as if the world were covered with a sheer coating of pearlescent light. Everything glowed. She glowed, and she knew it, and she tried to hide it.

But she was so aware of her body this morning it was nearly impossible. As she blended ingredients for bread, she felt the press of clothes against her breasts, as if the cotton were too heavy, and her arms felt tingly, as if they were waiting, and the dark pulse low in her abdomen jolted her every time she thought of the night, of Ramón touching her...kissing her...stroking her body to such heights!

She'd almost forgotten the middle of the night conversation with Tonio until he came into the kitchen after breakfast. He showed her an envelope. "I'm gonna give it to her today," he said. "If I come home with a broken face, you'll know she showed it to Edwin."

She hadn't considered that end, and some protective motherly instinct made her say, "Maybe you should reconsider. You don't want to get hurt."

A scowl crossed his face. "That's what's wrong with this world—everybody talks about making it a better place, but nobody ever wants to stick their own neck out." He put the letter into his book bag. "Well, I'm not gonna look the other way."

"You're right," Tanya said, and put her hand on Tonio's arm. "You're doing the right thing." She smiled. "But somebody has to do the worrying for the ones who do the right thing."

"I'll be okay."

"I know you will."

He stood there one more minute, looking down at her with his deep blue eyes in their frame of sooty lashes, and he was so beautiful it made her heart hurt. An odd flicker passed over the vibrant irises, and

Tanya wondered again if he guessed who she really was. "Well," he said, "see ya."

"Good luck."

Tonio nodded and left, and for the first time, Tanya saw that his walk, too, belonged to Victor—a long-legged lope.

"Why," Tanya said to Desmary, watching him walk toward the bus stop, "would any girl in her right mind choose Edwin Salazar over a boy like Tonio?"

Desmary looked past Tanya to the road. "Bad boys are more exciting."

Tanya nodded. Who had she chosen, after all? She turned to look at the old woman. "I find myself wanting to teach them, somehow, those girls. Teach them how to choose a man who is worthy of them." On a rising tide of regret and worry, she punched the dough in her bowl. "I want to wash their faces so their pretty skin shines through, and put them in clothes that don't make them look like twenty-year-olds." She paused to look at Desmary. "I want them to know they don't have to give themselves away."

"It will come, child," Desmary said. "You'll be a fine teacher for them, when it's time. Don't be in too much of a hurry. You have things of your own to work out."

"I know." Tanya smiled. "And I have you to teach me."

"Long life doesn't necessarily make a woman wise."

"That's true. But I think you were born wise."

"No, child." Desmary sighed, and her eyes wore a

faraway look. "I earned every morsel of everything I ever knew. The hard way, just like everybody else."

Tanya smiled. "The way I'm learning it."

Desmary seemed to bring herself into focus. "He knows, I think."

"Knows what? Who?"

"Tonio knows—or is beginning to guess—that you are his mother."

A cold finger stabbed her chest. "Why do you say that? Did he say something to you?"

"No. I just sense it."

With a sigh, Tanya nodded. "I think so, too."

"Are you ready for it?"

"I don't know," she replied. "I honestly don't know."

Chapter Eleven

Dear Antonio,

I'm in a work camp now. It's not nearly as restrictive as either of the other places. We work outside sometimes, and for the first time, I can see the horizon.

Every now and then lately, I realize I might really get out of here someday. I might really see you again.

I wrote to Ramón a few weeks ago. It wasn't easy to find him, actually, but one of the Sisters who come out here to teach and minister helped me track him down. I guess you're living on a ranch now. I haven't heard from him yet, but I guess he hasn't had time, either. I feel anxious, wondering if he'll help me talk to the right people to get the restriction against seeing you lifted. The lawyer I talked to here said I have a good chance of getting it overturned. The climate for women who have committed crimes like mine is very different now.

It made it real to me, writing to Ramón. Made me try to imagine how you might look now, at fourteen. I imagined you on a horse, looking like your dad when I first met him. That probably isn't too far from the truth.

    With high spirits and lots of love, Mom

About 2:00, Ramón came into the kitchen. "Desmary, can I steal your helper this afternoon? I want to get her input on some more plans for this dance."

"About time, I'd say," Desmary replied. "You only have ten days."

"There isn't that much to do! You have the food covered, right?"

"Only a little—you haven't given me any menus."

"I'll take care of the rest," Tanya said. "Make a list of what you've already planned, and I'll fancy up the rest."

"Good girl." Desmary swiveled on her stool—she had everything set up so she had to stand or walk as little as possible—and tugged out a scrap of paper and a pencil. She licked the pencil and started scribbling.

"What else needs taking care of?" Tanya asked Ramón. She met his eyes, and blushed feverishly at the look in them. Wickedly, he winked.

"The counselors have taken care of the invitations, the letters to parents, both at the school and here. Any girl who comes out here has to have parental permission.''

"Will any of them give it?" Tanya asked.

"What do you think? We have a bus going to town to pick them up and one to take them back. The parents don't have to do a thing." He watched Desmary writing. "We have to read it, *abuelita*."

"I can read it," Tanya said, as Desmary smacked his arm.

"We have to come up with decorations and music and maybe some kind of game, so we can give prizes. I've got movie passes and roller skating passes. We ought to come up with something else, too."

"Okay." Tanya inclined her head. "Why not a dance contest or something like that?"

"That might work."

Desmary handed the list of food to Tanya, who scanned the paper quickly and folded it to put in her jeans pocket. "Sure you'll be all right without me?"

A bright twinkle brightened Desmary's eyes. "I'm fine. You two go on."

"Good."

Tanya fetched her jacket and purse from her room, and met Ramón on the front steps. "Ready."

"Me, too," he said in a husky voice.

Tanya smiled.

Edwin was in the yard, raking leaves beneath the path of cottonwoods that lined the road to town. He paused to salute ironically at the pair of them. "Don't forget to bag the leaves," Ramón called.

Edwin lifted an orange trash bag, printed with a jack-o'-lantern. "Gotcha."

As they climbed into his truck, Tanya asked Ramón, "Why isn't Edwin in school?"

"He has been suspended. And last night, there was an altercation in the dorms. Guess who was at the center of it, as usual?"

"Ah."

"He's right on the edge. Won't be long now till he either hangs himself with his behavior and ends up in the state detention center, or realizes he doesn't have a prayer unless he straightens up."

"I know where I'll put my money," Tanya said darkly.

"You really don't like him, do you?"

"No, I really don't. Gut instinct."

"Well, I'm obligated to see that he gets the same chance as everyone else."

"I know. I wasn't suggesting he should have less of a chance." She pursed her lips, wondering if she ought to mention the letter Tonio had written to Teresa. She had the feeling Tonio had spilled his emotions to her because he trusted her to say nothing, and since Edwin wouldn't be in school today, perhaps there would be no trouble over the letter anyway. She chose to keep quiet.

About a mile from the ranch, Ramón pulled the truck over under a copse of lonely trees.

"What are you doing?" Tanya asked.

"This." He moved out from behind the steering wheel and slid over the bench seat until Tanya was neatly trapped between him and the door. She smiled up at him. "You're making me a sandwich?"

"Only if I can eat you," he said with a wicked lift

of one dark brow. His lips claimed hers, wet and hungry and sensual. "Mmm," he said, rubbing her arm. "I've been dying to do that all morning."

"Maybe I ought to cool you down, then," Tanya teased in return, and stuck her cold hands under his shirt.

He jumped. "I'll get you for that, woman."

"I'm real scared."

The dark eyes sobered, and he touched her face. "Never be afraid of me, cricket. Not ever."

Tanya gripped his shirt front, thinking of what she'd told Desmary this morning about young girls. This was the sort of man she wanted for all the women of the world—a kind man, a good one, who could love children and tend animals and make love like Casanova himself. What more could any woman ask than Ramón Quezada? "I'll never be afraid of you, Ramón." She kissed him, her eyes open so she didn't have to stop looking into the depths of those rich, promising eyes.

His hand, cold as her own, snaked under her sweater and bra and closed on her breast. Tanya squealed and tried to squirm away. "Paybacks," he said, and laughing, kissed her quickly, then let her go.

The afternoon was filled with the same kind of teasing, all of it edged with a giving sensuality Tanya had never experienced. With Victor, sex had been a dark and deadly serious thing.

Not so with Ramón. At the library, he stood behind her, very close, and, making sure no one could see him, bent to nibble her ear until her knees were weak. He caught her in a deserted section and pressed her back against the wall and kissed her senseless, then walked away whistling as if he'd done nothing. At the restaurant where they stopped for coffee, he leaned over and whispered naughty descriptions of what he wanted to do to her body when he got her alone again. Tanya blushed, but his words were poetically couched and never crude—the pictures they made in her mind made her hips soft.

Under the table, she teased back, letting her hand drift higher and higher on his leg as he talked. When she neared her destination—then stopped just short—his whispering ceased and Tanya looked up mischievously. "You were saying?"

He laughed.

They stopped by the clinic so Tanya could have her stitches removed, and the cut looked red and raw, but she could tell it would be fine. A thin scar might remain, but not much of one.

The last stop was the drugstore. Tanya waited in the truck while he went in. Teenagers, recently released from school, milled in the streets of the small town. Some of them hung on the corner talking, in the ancient tradition of those too young or too poor to drive. A gaggle of girls, their eyes lined with thick black liner, hair teased over their foreheads, walked together toward the drugstore. A young couple, a slim small girl and a long-limbed boy, strolled down the street, in no hurry to be anywhere. Tanya watched them, caught in their yearning discomfort. The boy leaned close, then away. The girl swayed his direction, then caught herself. From the back, it was impossible to tell how old they were. Tanya smiled when the boy managed to capture the girl's hand, and she looked up at him, and they kissed, awkwardly at first, then with more passion.

Tanya glanced away, unwilling to intrude. But a small detail of something snagged her peripheral vision and she glanced back. The backpack the boy carried had a large green political button pinned to it—and Tanya knew just what it said: Save the Rain Forest.

It was Tonio. Now she could tell, even at this distance, even though his clothes and hair were the same as a half a dozen other boys on the street. No doubt the girl was the infamous Teresa, who looked impossibly small to be the center of such a tempest.

Ramón climbed back in the truck and patted his pocket with a wicked lift of his eyebrows. When Tanya didn't respond, he said, "What is it?"

She lifted her chin and gestured in the traditional Southwestern method of avoiding the rude point of a finger. "Tonio."

Ramón caught sight of the pair and sighed. "Ah, hell." He watched them, pursed his lips, swore again. "He's supposed to be at debate club this afternoon."

"What are you going to do?"

He shook his head. "There's no law against him taking a girl to get a soda, but I hate to think he's been lying to me."

"I don't think he has. That's surely Teresa, and she's been going with Edwin."

"How do you know so much about this?"

"Tonio talked to me about it."

Ramón measured her. "And you didn't say anything?"

"Say what, Ramón? He wanted to talk to a woman about a girl, and I was handy, that's all."

With a pensive expression, Ramón watched Tonio and Teresa join hands once more and head for the ice-cream shop on the corner. They were smiling at each other as they went inside. "I don't like this situation. At all."

Tanya shook her head. "It's trouble, all right."

"Damn." Ramón started the truck and backed out.

Ramón felt choked as they drove back to the ranch. His earlier mood of sexy playfulness evaporated, killed by the specter of the possible danger Tonio had put himself in. Or maybe the danger Ramón had put him in—because if he hadn't had his heart set on running this ranch for troubled boys, Tonio wouldn't be in this position.

Not like this.

Ramón also felt guilty about the fact that he'd been buying condoms for himself when he was about to give Tonio the standard lecture about sex.

It was true he was an adult, and therefore capable of making decisions that were beyond the capacity of a fourteen-year-old. It was also true that Ramón had not given enough thought to the consequences of a sexual relationship with Tanya. It was his libido that was engaged, his libido turning him into a version of a randy teenager. He'd been completely unable to keep his hands off her today, had thought of nothing but getting her into his bed tonight and making love to her thoroughly and completely.

He'd given no thought to what would come afterward. And when he'd seen Tonio kissing his girlfriend, a vision of himself kissing Tanya in the library flashed before his eyes.

Do as I say, not as I do.

That had never been the way Ramón did things. He believed in the old-fashioned method of providing an example for boys to emulate, not setting down a list of arbitrary rules. He didn't drink, not because he had problems with it, but because so many boys did. He didn't smoke, even though he missed it, because he wanted to be a good role model. When he had carried on his affair with the teacher in town, he'd been very discreet, and careful to handle everything away from the ranch.

But with Tanya, he'd lost control. She had come to his room trustingly to tell him something, and he'd seduced her, knowing she was vulnerable, that she was ripe to be made love to, that she needed it.

Nice justification.

On the far end of the bench seat, Tanya sat with crossed arms, staring with no expression out the window. A sorrow pierced him. There was no possible way to keep such a thing secret at the ranch. The boys would start gossiping about her. They might even make remarks to her face.

And that would hurt her.

In sudden decision, he pulled over, this time on a lonely stretch of naked road. Across a vista of dry prairie grasses and swords of yucca, the mountains were a jagged blue line under a frosting of clouds. He turned off the engine and sat quietly, trying to think of the right way to word his thoughts.

"Tanya," he began.

She looked at him, her vulnerable deep blue eyes wide in her face, a face that showed the strength of her in ways he doubted she even guessed. The authority of experience lived in the cut of her mouth. The courage that had seen her survival burned in her eyes. Character had painted a face of honor and sensitivity.

He closed his eyes. Somehow these past few weeks, he had fallen in love with Tanya Bishop. Not the infatuation of a randy boy, but the sustained and powerful love of a man who had learned what was important in a mate. Tanya had everything he ever hoped to find.

And if things were different, if fate had not cheated them so cruelly, he might have been able to say to her now, "Marry me." A marriage would be a good thing for the boys at the ranch to see, an honorable, passionate union between a man and a woman. At the thought, he felt a deep and powerful yearning to make it so.

But it wasn't fair to use Tanya's long unfulfilled hunger to be complete for his own ends. He could make love to her until she was senseless—heaven knew how much he wanted that—but she wasn't the kind of woman to take sex lightly.

Nor was he that kind of man. When he'd imagined making love to her tonight, it had been with the wish that they become one, that they create a precious and mighty union of souls.

If he actually made love to her, if he allowed them to be joined, allowed the mingling of souls that would accompany such an act for them, he would never have the strength to let her go and find her own life.

"We're going to have to cancel our appointment for tonight," he said at last.

"I know." Her voice was resigned.

"It isn't for lack of—"

"Ramón, please don't go into all kinds of explanations. Let's just leave it at this. There are complicating factors we both understand."

He caught her and tugged her close to him, putting his face against her hair. She clung to him, and he felt her take a huge, shuddering breath. "I want you, Tanya," he said into her neck. "I wanted to teach you—"

Abruptly, she lifted her head and covered his mouth with her fingers. Cold fingers. "No more. I don't want to hear any more."

She extricated herself and scooted back to her place by the window.

Ramón, feeling the weight of a box of condoms in his pocket, started the truck and drove back to the ranch. It was the right decision, the moral decision, but that didn't mean he had to like it.

An almost palpable glow hung around Tonio that evening. Ramón kept his peace throughout supper, but afterward, he asked Tonio to stay when Tanya got up to help in the kitchen. In a minute, she came back with a steaming mug of coffee for him. She set it before him, and asked Tonio if he wanted anything. When he refused, she faded away.

Some women rebelled at performing such chores for men. Some women would also find Tanya's acceptance of work in the kitchen degrading. But she seemed to take joy in the small gestures that made people comfortable—she liked taking care of people, tending them, making their lives easier. A rare and precious thing.

"What's up, Dad?" Tonio asked, shaking Ramón from his reverie.

Ramón cleared his throat and hunched forward over his coffee, putting his hands around the heat of the mug. "Did you have practice this afternoon?"

Instant guilt shuttered Tonio's features. "Uh, no."

"You were pretty late home, if you didn't go to practice. What did you do?"

Tonio frowned. "Why do I get the feeling you already know?"

Ramón sipped his coffee.

"I went to Fiddler's for an ice-cream soda. That's not so bad."

"No. Except I thought you were at practice. What if something had happened, and I needed to find you right away?" He sighed and shook his head—he promised himself he'd be honest with this child whenever he could. "That's not even the real problem for me, Tonio, although I wish you'd remember to call when you change your mind about where you'll be."

"Sorry."

"I saw you in town," Ramón said. "With the girl. Is that Teresa?"

Faint color gave warmth to Tonio's dark skin. "Yeah."

"I don't want to stick my nose in where it doesn't belong, son, but—"

"Then don't."

"I have to. You're not thinking with your head, but with your emotions. Emotions can get you into trouble."

"They won't. I'm not!" He shoved back from the table in frustration and looked away. But he didn't quite dare to leave, and that was a good thing.

"How do you think Edwin is going to react when he hears about it? And why do you want to be with a girl who can't make up her mind?"

"She can make up her mind. She's coming to the dance with me."

"Yesterday, she was going to be Edwin's date."

"That was before I told her—"

"Told her what?"

"Nothing." Tonio shook his head. Arcs of light caught in the glossy blackness of his hair. "Just leave me alone, okay?" He jumped up.

"Sit down."

Tonio sat, mutinously staring at Ramón.

"It's not just the fighting I worry about," Ramón said quietly. "I worry about you getting in over your head with this girl."

"Over my head?" he sneered.

Ramón eyed him. "I'm talking about sex, Antonio. It's too important to take lightly."

Tonio bowed his head, and Ramón knew he was right to bring it up. The thought—maybe more than the thought—had crossed the boy's mind.

"I'm not naive enough to believe you'll hold out forever, but I wish you would take time to really think it through. Sex is deep, Antonio. It's supposed to bind you to another person, soul to soul, and anything else makes it cheap."

Tonio didn't speak. He kept his head bowed.

"Just promise me you'll think about it."

The boy nodded. "I will."

"I trust you to do the right thing, you know."

"Thanks." Tonio stood up. "Can I go now? I have some homework to do."

"Sure."

A sharp gust of wind struck the farmhouse as Tonio ambled out of the room. Ramón heard the windows rattle and wondered if it would snow. It would suit his mood.

Body to body. Soul to soul. Binding and deep and important. He sipped his coffee and sighed. He wished so much for that joining with Tanya that he could barely breathe. He wanted to meld with her, become one with her. He wished there was some way to do it fairly.

Damn. He didn't want Tanya to go anywhere or find any other life. He wanted her to take the place he had for her here, in his life, in his heart, next to him.

But he couldn't ask it. Not yet. Not until she'd had some time to find her own life first. It wouldn't be fair.

Fair. What a mockery life always seemed to make of that word.

Chapter Twelve

Dear Antonio,
I saw the parole board today. They are going to let me go. I can hardly believe it. And as if that weren't enough joy for one day, Ramón has written to say it was never his wish that you and I be separated. He offered me a job at the ranch, cooking, when I'm done with the program at the halfway house. It's hard to believe I will actually see you again one day soon.

Love, Mom

On the night of the dance, Tanya dressed carefully. Her thoughts were on Ramón, and his decision to not have sex with her. She pretended to accept it.

But her body had not accepted his decision. The

night they'd seen Tonio in town with his girlfriend, when Ramón had so hastily retreated, Tanya had lain awake for hours, her body on fire. She wanted to make love to him, as they'd planned. She wanted to hear his low groans, and touch his hair and feel his mouth upon her breasts. She wanted to hold him, be joined, and shatter with him.

She wanted him. It seemed almost decadent to be so clear about it, but she didn't lie to herself. She wanted him in the worst—no, make that the best—way.

And it wasn't as if he were running from the idea. He wanted to be with her just as much, but was resisting out of some sense of mistaken nobility.

As she lay there in the darkness, remembering the feel of his hands, his body, his mouth, she made up her mind. All her life, she'd been acted upon, instead of being the actor. Her daily runs were the first thing she'd ever initiated on her own, and in turn they'd given her the courage to initiate her bid to work in the prison kitchens, so she could be in a place where she could express her creativity.

That success had led to her decision to ask for visitation rights with Antonio when she was released, which led to her position here at the ranch.

Which led to Ramón.

And she wasn't going to fade passively into the background now, either. There was something deep and rich between her and Ramón, and she would always wonder what might have happened if she didn't act.

So tonight she donned a seductively elegant dress

of black velvet, cocktail length, with cap sleeves that showed her lean arms, and a square neck that bared a good deal of chest. Not cleavage, because she lacked that particular commodity, but she thought the small swell of breast over the neckline was quite nice. She'd kept the boys in mind, of course, so it was only a little low-cut, just enough.

She left her hair loose, brushing her collarbone. Her stockings were sheer black, the shoes strappy little black sandals that showed off her slim ankles.

Stepping back to admire herself in the long mirror over her dresser, Tanya smiled. The reflection showed her a woman, strong and whole and fully grown—and for one tiny moment, she felt a shift in her awareness, as if she were part of all the women who'd ever claimed this power, as if they were all with her.

And when she came down the stairs, Ramón was standing by the fireplace in the living room, adjusting his bolero in the mirror over the mantel. He caught sight of her in the reflection, and froze, hands on his collar, then turned slowly to watch her descend. His liquid dark eyes were ablaze.

Tanya felt her stomach flip. Ramón, too, had dressed up. He wore a black shirt, cowboy cut with pearlized snaps, and close-fitting black jeans, and fancy black boots that made his legs look even longer. His hair, though it could never be entirely tamed, had been brushed back from his high forehead.

A wave of heat struck her, so fierce she wanted only to rip the clothes off him and make love right there. It didn't help that the same wish was in his face as his gaze moved over her, lingeringly, taking in the cut of

the dress, the square bodice, her legs in the black
stockings. His nostrils flared, and he met her at the
foot of the stairs. He stood close, and looked at her,
touched her shoulder with one finger. "Did you do
this to torture me?"

"Yes." Up close, he smelled of after-shave and
soap. "You smell good," she said.

He didn't move, just stood there, admiring her until
Tanya felt almost uncomfortable. "Don't you think we
should go on in? It's almost time for the buses to ar-
rive."

"I can't move," he said, shaking his head. "I'm
slain where I stand."

Tanya gave him a half grin and swung around.
"Well, I can move." She headed down the hall, hearing him come behind, his boot heels sharp against the
wooden floor. As they passed through the kitchen,
Tanya gave Desmary a broad wink.

Ramón couldn't take his eyes off her all evening.
As the kids filed in, spit-shined and shaved and buttoned, and the music started to play its pounding beat,
he watched her from the corner of his eye. How could
he hope to resist her now?

The dress was a killer. And he wasn't the only male
in the room to notice. Dave was solicitous as she approached the punch table, and two of the other counselors stood alongside her as she drank it.

When had she become such a hot-looking woman?
Always before, she was sweetly attractive. Or when
she came out of prison, attractive with that hungry
coyote edge. Now she looked like a well-groomed

tigress, sleek and lean, her hair gleaming, her skin glowing. Her breasts, softly curved above the square bodice, invited the lingering eye, the caress of a tongue....

He shifted uncomfortably, wondering if every boy in the room noticed, too. Probably not, actually. To them, Tanya was older than dirt.

Behind him, a soft voice said, "Shee! Lookit Ms. Bishop."

Maybe she wasn't so old. And the truth was, her dress was elegantly cut, very simple and attractive. It didn't show off more flesh than it should. It was just the way it fit her. Or maybe the way she moved.

Or maybe he just had it bad. She turned to put her glass on the table and her hair flowed away from her skin to clasp her face, leaving behind a bare, uncovered spot on her shoulder that was unbearably tender.

"Hey, Dad," Tonio said, next to him. "I want you to meet somebody."

Relieved at the distraction, Ramón turned.

Tonio, neat in a blue sweater that showed off his eyes, and a pair of creased khakis, held hands with a girl. "This is Teresa Guerro. Teresa, this is my dad, Mr. Quezada."

Small and neat, she lifted her shy gaze to his. She wasn't particularly beautiful, but Ramón saw instantly the quality that made Edwin and Tonio fight over her. There was a luminosity in her large dark eyes, an inviting curve to her full lips. "*Hola,* Mr. Quezada." In her words he heard the accent of a native Spanish speaker.

"Hello," Ramón said. "Tonio has told me a lot about you."

"He's talked a lot about you, too," she said, and gave Tonio a bright glance.

"Do you want to stand here with my dad for a minute while I get you some punch?" Tonio asked.

Teresa nodded. "Okay."

Which left Ramón needing to make small talk with a fourteen-year-old girl he didn't necessarily think was the best person in the world for his son. Tanya's black dress caught his eye, and he gestured for her to come over.

"So, are you from Manzanares, Teresa?" he asked. "I don't think I remember any Guerros from my days there."

"Umm, no. We just came here. We've been in Texas. But my mom wants me to finish high school in an American school." She blushed bright red. "I mean a New Mexico school."

Ramón smiled to reassure her he wouldn't pick up on her gaffe, but it told him what he needed to know about her family—and made sense of the fact Tonio said she was really smart, but not too good at schoolwork. "Is your mother a farm worker?"

Teresa nodded. "My dad, too, till he had a heart attack two years ago. It's been just me and my mom since then, but she got married this year."

"That's nice."

Tanya joined them, and Ramón introduced her. "Oh, Ms. Bishop!" Teresa said. "Tonio talks about you all the time."

"He does?" Tanya beamed. "I'm glad."

Carrying two cups of punch in clear plastic glasses, Tonio returned. He whistled at Tanya, who smiled and bowed mockingly. "Thank you, thank you."

The four of them made small talk for a minute or two, and a song came on, a loud rocking rap song. "Let's dance," Tonio said, grabbing Teresa's hand and heading toward the dance floor.

Tanya turned laughing eyes toward Ramón. "Can you dance to your precious rap?"

He smiled. "Sure. A-one an-a-two." Playfully, he danced an old-fashioned two-step.

She laughed. "That's about the only dancing I can do, too. Can't even do that very well, though I certainly did my best to learn."

"It's easy, baby," he said with an exaggerated leer. "Let me show you."

"Quit," Tanya said, holding him back just as mockingly with one hand. "You have to be a good example, remember?"

He leaned close, as if he would kiss her, and took a triumphant pleasure in the heated flare in her eyes. "If I weren't such an upstanding citizen, I might say to hell with providing examples."

"But you are upstanding."

"Very." He straightened his spine to illustrate.

She sipped the punch she held. "I haven't seen Edwin tonight."

"That's because he got suspended the same day he went back to school."

"Fighting again?"

"Smoking cigarettes in the boys' room."

Tanya frowned. "I could almost feel sorry for him. How does a child get so lost?"

"I don't know." He lifted a shoulder. "And sometimes, unfortunately, the only thing to do for them is just let them hit a wall. That's the only thing that will work for Edwin."

"Maybe."

Ramón scanned the room, keeping his eye open for trouble of any kind, or potential trouble. And spied a little. In one darkened corner, under the floating pumpkins and trailers of crepe paper, a boy and a girl were making out. "Excuse me. I have to break up Romeo and Juliet over there."

Tanya chuckled.

Putting his hand on her arm, Ramón said, "Save me a slow dance, eh?"

She gave him a slow, impossibly sexy smile. "You got it."

Tanya couldn't remember the last time she'd had so much fun. She got to call the numbers for the door prize tickets for movie and skating passes, and when the dance contest started, she was a judge. Everything about the night was just plain fun.

Zach, dressed up in a plaid shirt and jeans she had pressed for him, his hair wet-combed with a neat part, was her constant companion through the evening. She put him to work behind the punch bowl, filling glasses with a big ladle, and let him help her bring out fresh crudités when the first batch ran out. She dragged him out on the dance floor at one point and teasingly taught him the box-step, and although he blushed furiously and clung to her hand so tightly she thought he'd crack her fingers, he managed to last an entire song.

After that, she found herself dancing a lot. She cheerfully declined the fast songs, but danced with counselors and some of the other boys who were too young to have asked dates.

She was gulping a drink of water when Tonio appeared at her side. The DJ had put on some Spanish songs, to the sound of groans and protests from some of the boys, and cheers from the others. Tonio grinned. "Can you dance to this music?"

She grinned. "This is how I learned to dance—at VFW dances with—" A cool wash of realization touched her. She'd almost said, "your dad," but amended it to, "my ex-husband."

Politely, he gestured toward the open floor. "Will you dance with me?"

Startled, Tanya looked toward Ramón, who stood watching from the other side of the room. He smiled at her and nodded once. Tanya put her glass on the table. "It's been a while," she said with a lift of her eyebrows, "but if you don't mind a bruised toe, sure."

They walked onto the floor. Tonio turned and held out his hands. She put her left hand on his shoulder, her right hand into his and looked up. He smiled, paused a moment to find the beat, and they started to dance.

Tanya's heart caught, hard. As the music swirled around them, she thought about all the years she'd waited to see him, trying to imagine how he looked or talked. Now she danced with him, and could smell the clean scent of his soap, could see the way his hair grew from a widow's peak on his forehead, and his strong white teeth when he grinned down at her encouragingly. "You're good at this."

"Thanks." To stem the huge well of joyful emotion rising in her throat, she forced herself to empty her mind. Some moments in life were too beautiful to hold at once. She would have to let it all flow into her and look it over again later.

The song was a familiar ballad of love lost, as so many Spanish ballads seemed to be. "Sad song."

"Can you understand it?"

She nodded.

"You used to be married?"

Tanya looked up. "Yes, a long time ago."

"To a Spanish guy?"

Dangerous territory, this. She tripped and righted herself. "Sorry," she said, looking down at her feet in the strappy sandals. "Yes."

"You don't like to talk about it, huh?"

Relieved she raised her head. "No. It was a long time ago."

"I understand."

To change the subject, she said, "Are you having a good time tonight?"

"Yeah, I am. It was the right thing to do, writing that letter."

"I guess it was. She seems very nice."

"She is." He glanced over his shoulder to where she sat by the table, rubbing one foot. "She had to borrow the shoes from her mom. Her feet hurt her when we dance."

"Poor thing."

He nodded, his face going soft. "I like her a lot."

The song ended, and Tanya let go. "You're a good dancer," she said, clasping her hands together. "Thank you."

With a small bow, he smiled. "No, thank you. All the guys will be jealous that Ms. Bishop danced with me."

She laughed.

Ramón came up beside them. "Trying to steal my girl, eh?" he said to Tonio, feinting a punch to his upper arm.

"Yeah."

"My turn," Ramón said, taking Tanya's hand. "Excuse us," he said to Tonio.

Tonio grinned and ambled off the cleared area to sit down next to Teresa. The next song started, a mournful, slow song. Only a few couples danced. The rest were milling around, picking up coats and having one last drink of punch or stack of cookies before the danced ended at eleven.

"Finally," Ramón said, taking her into his arms. His embrace was light, leaving a respectful pillow of air between them. He looked down at her, and stepped infinitesimally closer. "I've been waiting for this all evening."

"Me, too," Tanya said, huskily.

Their forearms met in a close press, and his arm around her waist drew her near. The expression in his dark eyes was thick with desire. "I've been trying so hard not to think about you as my lover," he said very quietly, expertly leading her in the familiar steps. "But I can't stop."

She looked at his mouth, so close to her own, and edged slightly closer still, until their chests met in barest contact. Somehow their legs slipped into a woven pattern, and along the inside of her knee, Tanya felt the brush of his pant leg. "Don't stop then," she said, raising her eyes to his. "I know I haven't."

He sighed and his fingers skimmed her back. "I want you," he said. "They don't have to know."

"No one needs to know."

His thumb moved on her palm in a circle. "Do you want me, Tanya?"

"Yes," she whispered, and felt her knees brush his, her thighs against his thighs, her breasts against his chest. "Yes, I do. I want to kiss you and touch you and make love with you."

His mouth lifted in a wry, half smile. "I still have a whole box of condoms."

Tanya grinned. "Good. You might need them."

"All of them?"

"You never know."

He glanced around the room, but no one was watching them. Subtly, he pressed himself against her, and Tanya pressed back, thrilling to the evidence of his desire. They swayed in the dance, hips moving back and forth, and Ramón sighed against her ear.

"I can't wait to taste you," he whispered against her ear. His tongue snaked out and touched her earlobe. Tanya shivered against him, a low throb starting to ache in her nether regions. His voice was hoarse and quiet and low-pitched. "I'm going to unzip this dress very, very slowly." His fingers moved on the zipper. "And I'm going to kiss every inch of your back, and then your arms. And then your breasts."

"Mmm." She closed her eyes, trying desperately to remain normal-looking.

"I'm going to suckle your breasts and kiss your tummy and—"

"Stop," she whispered. "I'm going to melt right here."

"Good," he replied.

She pulled back to look at him. "Not good. Behave yourself, Mr. Quezada."

He grinned, wickedly, and she felt everything in her body go soft. "Do you really want me to?"

A crash and a scream rent the air. Tanya whirled and heard Ramón cry, "No, Edwin!" He broke free, and before Tanya had completed turning around, he was halfway across the room. "Edwin!" he bellowed.

Tanya could not immediately see what happened. A knot of chaos erupted all around her. Kids scurried here and there, away from the trouble, which centered around the place Tonio and Teresa had been sitting moments before. Another scream—a yelp, really— rang out.

Then she saw Edwin, holding Teresa, dragging her toward the door. She wore only one shoe, and her limping up and down gait caused her to stumble. Edwin yanked her up and she cried out, sobbing, trying to wrench herself free. Tanya couldn't see Tonio. Where was he?

Before she knew what she was doing, Tanya had kicked off her shoes and started toward them, some primal feeling in her chest. She walked, measuring the distance between the kitchen door—his only way out—and herself and him. Counselors herded other kids toward the edges of the room, and Tanya finally spied Tonio, flat on the floor, a mark on his forehead. He looked dazed as he got to his knees.

She looked back at Edwin—and finally saw what made the others stay back. He had a knife. Not just any old knife, but a big, ultrasharp knife with a black handle they used for cutting meat with bones—like chicken.

Like flesh.

In a blaze of confusion, she wondered how he'd gotten hold of it, for all knives were carefully locked in a cabinet at night. But he'd had KP for weeks and must have secreted it away.

Teresa stumbled again, and Edwin grabbed her by the waist, holding the knife close to her face. The wild menace in his face, the animal bloodlust in his eyes sent loathing and fear through Tanya. She'd seen that look, that mindlessness. Her heart pounded. The sound was loud and fast and hard in her ears, and still she edged toward the kitchen door.

Ramón walked close to them, and Edwin made a grunting noise, warning him away. Ramón lifted his hands, palms out, in the same gesture he'd used with Tanya the first day in the bus station. "Let her go, Edwin. You won't get anywhere with her. And all you're doing is digging yourself a deeper hole."

Edwin edged along the wall, holding the girl hard next to him. She wept soundlessly, frozen, her hands on Edwin's arm, her eyes on the knife.

At the expression on her face, something in Tanya's

gut twisted. Anger, as clear and white and hot as the desert sun, filled her. Not again. Not another one.

He was only a few feet away, his eyes on Ramón, who continued to advance. Tanya lunged. Her legs were strong with her running, her arms filled with muscle from her work in the kitchen. She had surprise on her side. She seized Edwin's wrist and kicked him squarely where it would do the most damage. He grunted and doubled over, dropping the knife. Teresa sobbed and pulled free.

Ramón grabbed the knife and looked over his shoulder. Already sirens sounded in the distance, and Tanya realized vaguely that someone must have already called the police.

Her breath came fast, still riding the wild emotion pumping through her chest. She squatted in front of Edwin. ''Don't you ever hurt another woman again. Not ever.''

With a snarl, he lifted his head and glared at her. He uttered a foul epithet about the evil nature of women.

Tanya smiled tightly. ''You got it.''

Chapter Thirteen

Dear Antonio,

I'm aching for a normal life. Everyday life. People and ordinary arguments and dust on lamp shades. I'm aching to live in a place with curtains on the windows, and a place where you don't have to hide everything that crosses your mind.

I don't let myself think much beyond that, but it would be so great to have babies again one of these days. It's really the one thing I wanted, even when I was a little girl—to grow up and have babies of my own. I like children a lot, little ones and big ones both, girls and boys. I liked being pregnant and my labor was easy, and it seemed the most natural thing in the world for me. Like when I was made, the angels looked in their little bag and said, "I think we'll make this one a mother," then gave me everything I'd need for it. Like my friend Iris, who is an artist. She sees color in a different way than the rest of us—each tiny hue and variation means something to her. Speaks to her. She takes those color voices and puts them on a canvas or a piece of paper, and makes everyone else hear the voices, too.

That's how it is with me and mothering. I know, in my deepest heart, that was what I was supposed to do. And though I'm your mother, and I got to have some time with you, and there's always going to be a special link between us, I haven't really been able to be your mother all these years. I bet your voice is changing now— you'll be more than half-grown by the time they let me out.

But maybe I'll get to do a little more mothering with you, or maybe you'll have my grandchildren and I can do it that way. Somehow, I have to believe that.

Love, Mom

Reaction set in later. As the police cuffed Edwin and took him to town, Tanya felt telltale trembling fill her limbs. Nausea rose in her stomach. Dizzy and sick, she went to the kitchen and concentrated on making a cup of tea.

As she sat down to drink it, Zach appeared. His little face was pale and stark. "Hi, honey," Tanya said, extending a hand to draw him into the kitchen. "You want to come sit in my lap for a minute?"

He looked over his shoulder, as if afraid there would

be some older boy to make fun of him if he admitted to still wanting such things.

"I need a hug," Tanya said. "That kind of scared me. Did it scare you?"

His expression eased, and he nodded, moving forward. Tanya moved back from the table to make room on her lap, and Zach eased his skinny body gingerly onto her legs. She rubbed his back. "Everything is okay now."

"I'm glad they arrested him. He was mean to me."

"He was? Did you tell anybody?"

Zach sighed and shook his head. She kept rubbing his back. "I was afraid he'd be meaner if I did."

"Oh, honey." She pulled him close. He wasn't a very large child and still fit neatly in her lap.

Almost as if against his will, he put his head on her shoulder and started to cry. "I was scared for you," he said, and suddenly put his arms around her very tightly.

"Go ahead and cry it out, sweetie. Don't believe all those people who say it doesn't help anything—it helps a lot."

"What if he had hurt you bad? Or cut your throat?"

"He didn't. I'm okay. I'm sorry you were frightened, Zach, I really am. If I'd thought for a minute..." What? She wouldn't have acted? That wasn't true. "He didn't," she repeated.

He fell silent against her, his tears drying quickly. He made no immediate move to get away, however, so Tanya relaxed, her arms around his painfully thin body. "It's nice to hold a boy again," she said after a little while. "I used to have a little boy, did I tell you that?"

Zach shook his head. "Did he die, like my mom?"

"No." Tanya sighed. "No, thank goodness. I lost him, that's all. Maybe I'll tell you about it someday." She began to rock slowly, back and forth, and began to hum. "I used to hold him and sing to him. Can I sing you a song?"

"I think I'm too big for a song."

"Who's going to know?" She felt him smile against her neck, and from the weight of his body slumped against hers, he was getting sleepy. "Even grown-up boys listen to music sometimes when they've had a bad day."

He yawned. "Okay."

Tanya hummed quietly through the song to get her voice, then very quietly, she began to sing Tonio's song to him. By the time she reached the end, Zach was slumped and snoring softly. A movement at the door caught her eye, and she looked up to see Tonio standing there, a strange expression on his face. A cool sense of shock washed through her—her guard was slipping fast. To cover her feelings of guilt, she smiled. "He's out cold."

Tonio nodded and came into the room. "I'll take him and put him to bed."

"Thanks." Tanya stood and shifted the weight of Zach into Tonio's waiting arms. She smiled. "You're really a good kid, you know it?"

He smiled, but said nothing.

With a sigh, Tanya sat back down at her tea, gone lukewarm now. She covered her face with her hands, dizzy with everything that had happened—not only tonight, but since she'd been released from prison. Her life had changed so much!

That was where Ramón found her, sitting at the kitchen table, mug between her cold hands. He looked grim. The scuffle had mussed his carefully tamed hair, and it had sprung into its natural, wild waves over his head. She thought she understood why he wore it longer than normal—cut short, it would be uncontrollable. He touched the bridge of his nose. "That was crazy, Tanya."

She winced. "I know. I didn't do it with a lot of conscious thought. I just saw the chance and..." She let the words trail off and raised her hand.

With a sigh, he sank into the chair opposite. "It was brave, too."

She said nothing, only looked at her hands.

"*I* wanted to be the hero, you know." There was teasing in his voice. "That's how it's supposed to be. The guy does the heroic stuff, the girl squeals on the sidelines.

Tanya looked up and saw his wry smile. "Sorry. I'll practice my squealing for next time."

"Let's hope there is no next time."

"There will be." She sucked in a breath of air and let it go on a sigh. "There always is."

From the dining room came the sounds of cleanup. Tonio came in. A smear of dust marked his dark blue shirt, and there was a goose egg on his forehead. "Zach's safely in bed," he said.

"You okay?" Ramón asked.

"Yeah." He looked down. "But Teresa's mom is pretty upset."

"I can understand that."

"He took me by surprise." He touched the goose egg gingerly. "I don't even know what he hit me with."

"A plain old rock," Ramón said. "It's in there by the chair where you fell."

"Jeez." His head was bowed, but he lifted it now and looked at Tanya. "Where'd you learn to fight, lady?"

"Long story. I'll tell it to you someday."

He nodded slowly. "I'm going to bed. Good night, you guys." He ambled out of the kitchen, into the main part of the house, leaving a deep silence behind him.

Tanya stared at her tea, watching the lights play over the surface in rippling waves. "We have to tell him," she said.

"Yes, we do."

"How do you think he'll take it?"

Ramón sucked his teeth, shook his head. "I really don't have any idea, Tanya. You takes yer cards and plays yer hand."

She nodded. In the dining room, a pair of voices quieted with the slam of a door, and there was silence.

"At last," Ramón said, and rubbed his face. He looked at her. "Come here, will you?"

Her heart jumped, and without knowing she would, she got up and moved around the table to his side. He took her hand and tugged her into his lap. As she put her arms around his neck and rested her head on his shoulder, pounds of tension drained suddenly from her body. He, too, sighed, as if he'd needed her closeness to ease him.

He held her loosely, his cheek against her hair, his hands joined around her waist. Tanya closed her eyes at the comfort of his touch, and breathed of his scent—faint traces of after-shave and shampoo, and deeper, the notes of his very flesh, redolent of the desert and its secrets. She shifted and pressed her forehead and the bridge of her nose against his neck.

Gently he rubbed her back, smoothing his hand over her hip, back to her waist. A strange, unfamiliar feeling crept through her, calm and sweet, so comforting she didn't recognize it at first.

Trust.

It was such a strange feeling, she raised her head to look at him. He met her gaze evenly, his fathomless eyes promising honor and gentleness. She could touch him her way, explore him according to her needs—and his, too, of course—but he'd be patient while she learned him.

Earlier, she'd wanted him, with her body and a certain yearning incompleteness she didn't know how to name. Now a bone-deep need grew in her, a need to love him and let him love her in return, a need to show him she trusted him as she'd trusted no other, a need to—

He touched her face, and his long fingers spread wide to cup her jaw, her cheekbone, her temple, and his eyes were intent on her mouth. She kissed him, or he kissed her, and there was a sighing, breathy sound that came from them both. "Ah, Tanya," he said, and pulled her closer.

They kissed for a long time, and Tanya touched him, his hair and his ears and his throat where his blood ran under the skin. He stroked her back and rubbed his open palm over her thigh, and skimmed his hand under her skirt, over the slippery stockings. They parted ever so slightly, breath mingling. "I think we should go upstairs," he said.

"Yes."

And it was so easy to stand up and let him take her hand, and go through the house, turning off lights. He paused at the foot of the stairs to kiss her, as if he were nibbling something addictive. "Mmm," he said, and took her hand again, smiling.

They stopped by his room, quietly. He took the box of condoms out of a drawer and dropped them in the pocket of his robe, which he also carried with him. Tanya watched from the doorway, leaning against the doorjamb, admiring him. His movements were fluid and easy, and she liked how he handled the things he needed to bring without embarrassment. Open. He hid nothing, so he had no fear of exposure.

When he turned off the lamp by the bed, he came to her and put his hands on either side of her face, pressing his body along the length of her, and kissed her again, long and deep, as if he could never taste it enough.

Tanya smiled up at him. "You're so...wonderful," she said, and blushed because it sounded so silly.

He dipped, smiling, and touched his tongue to her lips. "Just wait."

And seized with a sudden silliness, they raced up the rest of the stairs to Tanya's room, hissing for the other to be quiet, tripping on the tie of his robe, and each other. At last they were safely inside her room, and the door was closed, and they fell on each other.

Ramón dropped his robe on the floor and reached for her at the same moment she reached for him. She tugged open the snaps on his shirt, until his brown, bare chest was exposed to her hands and her mouth. Ramón unzipped her dress, and slipped his hands underneath the fabric. She felt her bra give way, as he unfastened the hook, and she skimmed his shirt off his shoulders. He let her push it off his arms, leaving his torso bare, then took her dress and bra from her shoulders and helped them fall to the floor. He bent to gather her close, to kiss her, and Tanya gasped at the electric sensation of his naked chest against her breasts.

He breathed her name, and his kiss grew fierce. For one instant, he let her go, and knelt to take the box from his robe pocket, then walked her backward to the bed, until the back of her knees bumped the mattress. They tumbled down together, kicking off their shoes, skimming off jeans and stockings, kissing and kissing and kissing. Ramón played her body like a fiddle, setting it to a furious, building tune, using his hands, his mouth, his limbs, to tease and tantalize and arouse.

At last, gasping with need, she grabbed his shoulders. "I want you inside me, Ramón, before I die of needing you."

"Yes." He reached for the box, flipping the lid with his thumb and dumping the contents in their slippery foil packs on the bed. Tanya grabbed one and tore the foil with her teeth and took the condom out. She paused.

"I haven't made love to anyone since Victor," she said. "We don't have to do this."

"Yes, we do." He reached for it, but Tanya moved her hand away.

She smiled. "Allow me, *señor.*"

He lifted a little to give her access, and groaned as her fingers slid over the length of him. Tanya moved, and he put himself between her thighs. For a moment he paused. "I've wanted this for more years than I can count," he whispered, and kissed her breast, then her mouth. Tanya ached, feeling him at her nethermost. His hair brushed her lips as he kissed her throat, and the sensation was erotic, tantalizing.

"Ramón," she whispered. "Come *home.*"

He let go of a ragged chuckle, and she could tell by his breathing it was not so easy for him to stay so torturously poised, either. "You sure?" He kissed her gently, bracing himself on his arms. "We won't be the same after this, not you or me, or us."

"I'm sure." She put her hands on his firm buttocks and lifted her hips, and there was no more teasing from him. He made a low pleasured sound and eased into her. Tanya heard her own moan roll into the room— it was so right! She sighed his name, her hands moving on his back and hips, and the backs of his thighs. She arched. "Ramón!"

He gathered her close and drove home and there was no thought, only wide bands of feelings, only touching as they tangled hands and mouths and legs, as they rocked in ancient rhythm. Tanya felt him all through her, all around her, and he was right—it was like nothing she'd ever known. The way they melded, the way each cry, each kiss, each small movement increased the joining until there was only one being, not two. One soul, one mind, one heart, irretrievably entwined.

Ramón kissed her and Tanya tumbled, her body pulsing around his. She cried out in a sobbing voice against his lips and heard him whisper, "Sweet, sweet Tanya." He rocked her harder, closer, his lips and movements intense and wild and so vividly pleasurable Tanya thought she could happily die.

And then his mouth was all over her face and her neck and his hands held her close and she felt him come apart, throbbing within her.

He buried his face against her neck, slowly moving, letting the waves slow in him, in her. There was sweat between their chests, and their pounding, racing hearts beat only millimeters apart. Their breath tangled in the darkness. Tanya lifted her hands from his back and touched his head, putting her fingers in that silky, springy hair. She turned her head and kissed his ear, filled with emotions too broad, too intense, too new to name. Ramón planted tiny kisses on her collarbone, her throat, her chin.

They shifted to lie side by side, and tugged the covers over them. Tanya touched his face, suddenly overwhelmed with the fact that it was Ramón here in her arms. She kissed his forehead, between his eyes, and his nose. "I'm in love with you, Ramón," she whispered, touching his jaw, his mouth.

"Don't say it," he said, and kissed her, as if to blot out the words. "You owe me nothing."

Smelling the scent of their joining, together with the notes of his skin, Tanya thought: I owe you everything, but she didn't say it. She contented herself with the feel of him warm against her and the joy of being in complete union with another human for possibly the first time in her life.

They dozed and woke up starving. Ramón tiptoed downstairs and brought back a big plate of leftovers from the party, along with cans of grape soda. When he came back into her room, he stopped just inside the door, closed his eyes, and opened them again. It wasn't a dream. Tanya, sensual as a cat, waited for him in bed, naked beneath the green sheets and blankets of her bed. Her dark golden hair tumbled in disarray around her face, and one lean bare arm held the sheets to her breasts. She was beautiful, delectable, everything he'd ever wanted. Emotion slammed him, so strong and intense, he knew he was lost.

Settling the food on the lamp table beside the bed, Ramón sat down. "Hi," he said, holding out a carrot stick.

"Hi." She chomped the carrot right from his fingers and leaned back. "Come here often?"

"Not recently." He lifted a wicked brow. "Perhaps I could be persuaded with the right incentives."

"Ah, what incentives could those be?"

He grabbed the cover and tugged it down to show one round, pink-tipped breast. He closed his mouth over the nub, moving his tongue over the eager pearling, and heard her sigh. "This is pretty tasty," he said.

"All yours." She tugged him by the hair to her mouth so she could kiss him, hard.

Ramón chuckled against her lips, moving his hand against her belly. "You know how many times I hear that in a day?"

She pulled his robe open and curled her hand around him. "It's a tough life."

"Yes, it is." He kissed her and she moved her hands on him, and Ramón felt awash on her, in their passion. At one point, he took her face in his hands and just looked at her. She opened her long, exotic blue eyes and he saw the stars there, the happiness that had been so long absent, and a physical pain touched him. Slowly, deliberately, he put his lips to hers. So in love, he thought. So in love.

But he didn't say it. He only showed her again with the most ancient of movements, the most powerful of body language.

Just before dawn, her alarm went off. Tanya moved to hit the snooze button, then turned back to Ramón, who seemed not to hear it. His heat and satin and scent of desert morning struck her forcibly, and an impossible tingling roved over her nerves. In the stillness she curled up to him, nestling her head against his arm, putting her hand on his flat belly.

Her body sang. In the pale gray light, she propped her head on her arms and watched him sleep. His face was almost unbearably handsome in sleep, his mouth full and commanding, so exotically his own. And she liked his nose, that high-bridged conquistador's nose with the elegantly shaped nostrils that flared so tellingly when he was aroused or angry.

She liked the way his hair sprang back from his forehead, defiant and wild, and liked the forehead itself, for it was high and strong and very intelligent.

She liked him—the way he moved and talked. The way he could make an entire room of surly teenage boys jump to attention with a single, hawkish lift of one brow. She liked the way he made an old woman giggle, and the devotion he inspired in the animals. A good man.

He stirred. Wickedly, Tanya took the covers off him so she could admire all of him. He shifted ever so slightly, and she put her hand on his thigh, long and lean, then his knee which was not, she had to admit, the most beautiful she'd ever seen. She moved back up and touched his dark nipples with her tongue, and then leaned over him, her breasts pressing into his arm, to kiss his throat.

Below her, he stirred, but Tanya continued to tease him awake, fluttering her hands over his manhood, over the thin line of hair on his belly and around the circle of his navel. She kissed his earlobe and stayed to suckle there.

And then he was making love to her again, his body hot on hers, in hers.

Afterward, sated once more, they lay in each other's arms. "I want to tell Tonio who I am," Tanya said. "It's important."

"Give it a day or two, huh?"

"What difference will it make?"

His eyes were grim. "We don't really know how he'll react."

"It's better than keeping up this lie, Ramón. It was okay at first, but I think he's already guessed. You and I will look a lot better in his eyes if we confess before he confronts one of us."

Ramón shifted his head on the pillow and rubbed a circle around her hip. "If he doesn't react well, you'll have to leave the ranch."

Tanya nodded.

"Let's just play it by ear, okay?" Ramón said. "There's been a lot going on the past week or two. Tonio probably doesn't need any more complications."

She sighed. "I don't like the lying."

"I know." He sighed, loudly. "You know, I'm being purely selfish. I don't want to deal with it yet, and that's the real problem."

"I'll wait a day or two, then, if you want me to."

He kissed her. "I want." As if to underscore the comment, his stomach growled, loudly. They both laughed. "Time to get up, I guess."

Tanya stretched, watching him lazily as he pulled on his robe. His body was sinewy, his flesh the color of the burnt sienna crayon she'd loved as a child. He saw her watching him and winked. "I'll see you downstairs." He bent over her in the bed and kissed her mouth, then the swell of a breast. "Mmm."

She chuckled. "Okay. I have to get moving, too, but I just want one more minute."

"Better hurry—it's almost light."

"I will."

"Same time, same place tonight?" he asked wickedly.

"Yes, please."

He winked and left her. Tanya sighed happily. This morning, life was exactly what it should be all the time. Heaven. Sheer heaven. She wouldn't think of Tonio just yet. There was time. What difference could a day or two make?

At the end?

"It's what Grace does for fun." He still sounds curt.

"You know it."

He smiled. "Not an adequate description. Flip to whatever she wrote, though. a moment to decide how much to say. But this, about happy—it was different. What happened then?" he said. "Tell me more about it."

Chapter Fourteen

Dear Antonio,

This is the last letter I will have to write to you. Tomorrow, at 10:00 a.m., I will be free of the New Mexico penal system. They've even waived parole because my record is so clean, and because I've shown myself able to handle the world by living in a halfway house for the past year. It's almost normal life, the halfway house. Not quite, but enough. I know I'm ready to put this chapter behind me and go forward.

Ramón has hired me at the ranch, and we've decided it would be best for me to ease into your life. He says you feel betrayed, and though it hurts me, I guess I understand. I was so young and broken by the time Victor's family came after me that I just let you go. I meant to keep you

safe, *hijo*. That's all. I hope you'll understand that
one of these days.

In the meantime, I get to actually put my eyes
on you again, after more than four thousand days
of waiting. Such sweetness is rare.

We survived, you and I. That's a lot.

Love, Mom

When Ramón came downstairs after a shower, even
his skin tingled with afterglow. Whistling, he took the
last turn in the stairs and headed for the kitchen, wondering how in the world he'd keep a straight face when
he looked at Tanya. How could anyone look at either
one of them and not see the newly bloomed love between them?

A noise in his office halted him and he doubled back
to push open the door. Tonio sat in his office chair, a
folder open in his hand. A file drawer gaped open—
the personnel files. Ramón didn't have to guess which
folder Tonio held.

Tonio didn't even startle as Ramón came in. He
looked up miserably, tears streaming down his face.
"How could you?" he asked, and it wasn't the sulky
challenge of a selfish teenager, but the agonized whisper of betrayal.

"Damn," Ramón said, stepping into the room.
"Don't jump to conclusions here, Tonio. Give me a
chance to explain."

"Explain what? That you lied? That you brought
my mother here without telling me and pretended she
was somebody else all this time?" He threw the file

at Ramón's feet. Tears still washed over the almost manly cheeks, and his eyes held a terrible light.

Ramón didn't move for a moment. "Don't blame Tanya. She's been wanting to tell you for weeks."

"And you stopped her? Why?"

And Ramón knew, just that quickly, that he'd been wrong. "I don't know," he said. "I'm sorry."

"She killed my father! How can you forgive her for that?"

"It isn't that simple, Tonio." He reached for him— and Tonio bolted away, as if in revulsion. Ramón halted, pursed his lips for a moment, thinking, trying to remember what it was like to be fourteen and morally outraged. "Read the whole file."

"No!" His eyes slitted. "I want her to leave. I don't want to see her."

"You're making a mistake, Antonio."

The boy abruptly sat down again and put his head in his hands. A sob, all the more painful for the manly rasp it held, broke from his chest. "How could you play such an awful trick on me?"

Ramón went to him and embraced him, pulling his head into the hollow of his shoulder. "It wasn't meant to be a trick, Tonio. I swear. I wanted you to get to know her slowly, so you wouldn't feel put upon to be nice if you didn't want to. It made a lot of sense at the time. I'm sorry. I was wrong."

A sound at the door drew his attention. Father and son both raised their heads and saw Tanya standing in the doorway, a stricken expression on her face. "It was the song, wasn't it?" she said quietly. Ramón saw her knuckles were white where she clung to the door. "You heard me singing that song to Zach last night."

Tonio jumped to his feet, and Ramón grabbed him, hard. "You gave me away!" Tonio cried, jerking hard at Ramón's hold on him.

Tanya nodded. Ramón saw her dark blue eyes fill with tears. But as she stood there, it was as if a straight line pulled her upright. She lifted her chin and met Tonio's accusatory glare. "Yes," she said, simply. "I had to."

"I hate you! Both of you!" Tonio cried, and he tore free of Ramón's grip. He bolted toward the door.

Tanya stepped out of his way. "I'm sorry, Antonio," she said quietly.

With a sound of disgust, Tonio brushed by her. They heard his heavy feet on the stairs.

Tanya took a breath and looked at Ramón. "I'll pack now. You can take me to town to find a place after breakfast."

"He'll come around."

"Maybe." Her eyes were sad. "I'm not sure I would, in his shoes."

Unable to move, Ramón only nodded. Forced to choose between the two of them, he had to choose his child. "He will," Ramón repeated.

Tanya didn't reply—she just turned around and went up the stairs.

In the quiet left behind, Ramón squatted to pick up the file Tonio had flung at him. A picture of Tanya from prison was stapled to the inside. Her features looked hard, her mouth pinched, and he realized how much she'd changed since her arrival. He moved his finger over the photo. Damn.

It didn't take Tanya very long to gather her things. Even with the new things she'd purchased with her paycheck, everything she had fit into the prison-issue suitcase the state had given her. As she packed, the tortoiseshell cat played with her things, jumping into the suitcase, then out, then in. "Come on, Snoopy, get," Tanya said, finally exasperated. She picked up the cat and held him close. His fur smelled faintly of cinnamon and sunshine, and Tanya knew Desmary had been holding the cat sometime this morning, too. It gave her an unexpected burst of homesickness.

She loved the ranch! She loved working with the boys, loved cooking with Desmary, loved her room with it's high view and beautiful curtains. She loved running in the morning across the desert, and sitting at the supper table with Tonio and Ramón.

A piercing ache moved through her. Tonio. She'd been dreading this very thing, and now there was nothing to be done but clean up the pieces. She most adamantly did not want to leave the presence of her son, not after so long a time of not seeing him, but there was no choice. At least now he knew. She could live in Manzanares and work there, and be close to him, anyway.

Close to both of them.

She would miss every tiny little thing there was about this place. In a few short weeks, it had become her home more fully than any place she'd ever lived. She wished she could let her roots settle here, grow long and deep in the sandy soil. In time, she might even have learned to pluck a chicken.

Against the ache in her heart, she placed practicality. Sometimes things didn't work out the way you wanted, but you didn't stop living because of it. She had her freedom, and the dignity of knowing she had an honest trade to offer the world. Perhaps one of the cafés in town would hire her.

However all this ended, the Last Chance Ranch had truly given her a fair chance at life, renewing her resolve and determination, giving her a chance to love herself again. In doing so, she'd reclaimed the dignity that had been lost so long ago. Whatever else happened, that was worth coming here.

From the bottom drawer of the dresser, she took a stack of letters tied with string. Each was in an envelope, just as if she were going to mail it—but of course, she hadn't. She'd only written them, and put them away. And now she'd give them to the boy for whom they'd been intended. It was all she had to give him. The only way he'd understand.

Firmly, she closed the suitcase, made her bed, and then marched downstairs, her chin up. At the very least, she'd go with dignity. Ramón, looking bleak, took the letters from her as if accepting a sacred trust. "I'll see that he gets them," he said. His voice was raw.

In town, he saw her settled into the single decent hotel, over the diner, and paid her bill for a week, then walked upstairs with her. "I can manage from here," Tanya said, taking the key from him in the hall.

He watched her open the door, and set her suitcase just inside in the foyer. "I hate this," he said.

Tanya clenched her teeth, willing herself to be as calm as she could be, but waves of lonely protest washed through her as she stood there. "Me, too."

"Damn," he said, and pulled her close. "Maybe it won't be long."

She closed her eyes, smelling the tang of autumn in his jacket. His hair touched her forehead. For one long, indulgent moment, Tanya allowed herself to glory in his touch, in the wonder that was Ramón. She loved him. Deeply. And there was nothing she could do about it. She had chosen him to raise Antonio because she'd known he would put Antonio's welfare above everything else, as any good parent would do. Now she could hardly cry foul when he was doing exactly that.

"I wish things were different," she whispered. "I wish we'd told him the truth from the beginning."

Ramón pulled back and held her by her arms. "No, you don't. He would never have spoken to you, Tanya. Not one word. You have to trust me that we did the right thing."

She nodded. Plucking at his coat, she said, "You'd better get back."

"Are you sure you're all right?"

"I'm fine."

He gave her another quick hug, and pressed a kiss to her forehead. Then, as if he didn't trust himself, he hurried away. Tanya watched until the top of his head disappeared down the stairs.

After a subdued supper through which Tonio didn't speak one word unless he was spoken to first, Ramón called the boy into his office and gave him the letters.

"What is this?"

"Tanya...your mother wrote them from prison. To you."

Tonio tossed the packet back on Ramón's desk. "I don't want them."

Grimly, Ramón picked them up and lifted Tonio's hand and put the two together. "They're all you have—your only legacy."

Tonio stared at him, unmoving, and the dark blue stillness reminded Ramón deeply of Tanya. "What am I supposed to do with them?"

"How about read them?"

"No."

"Damn, Tonio, don't be so hard." He shook his head. "I've tried to never say anything too bad about Victor, your father, but it's time you really understood the truth."

"Don't bring him into it."

"I have to, Antonio." He stood up and walked to the window, where he stared at the night beyond. "He was mean, Tonio. Meaner than Edwin by a long shot. He was insanely jealous about your mother, too. She couldn't even talk to anyone else. When she finally left him because of his cruelty, he stalked her, over and over again. You know some of this, but I don't think you've given it enough thought."

There was suspicious moisture in Tonio's eyes again, and he blinked hard, finally looking down to the packet in his hands. "I don't remember either one of them," he said. "I just remember shouting. Screaming. My mother's long blond hair."

"You're old enough to know now, Antonio," Ramón said, turning to face him.

The boy's mouth was tight. "I don't want to know."

"It won't go away, son. Better to face it and get it over with now. You take those letters and read them."

"None of this little speech changes the fact that you lied to me."

"You're right." He crossed his arms. "But let's be real honest with ourselves, eh? When I got the first letter from her, asking if she could see you when she got out, you'd just spent an afternoon with your Tía Luna, and she spent the whole time poisoning your mind against your mother. Your father's family always did that. They hate your mother. If I'd brought Tanya in here and introduced her as your mother, you would have spit on her feet and refused to try to learn anything about her."

Tonio said nothing, just rubbed a thumb over the edge of the letters.

"You know I'm right, Tonio. You just don't want to admit there might be a reason to bend the rules once in a while. I practice honesty with you as much as I can, but you don't necessarily need to know everything."

Begrudgingly, Tonio nodded.

"You can go now, if you want," Ramón said. "Unless you want to play a round of chess or something."

"No, thanks." Tonio tapped the letters with his fingers, and Ramón knew he'd won. At least Tonio would read them. At least he'd know the truth. That was a lot more than most people got.

Chapter Fifteen

Dear Antonio,

It's my birthday today. I'm twenty-two. We went to McDonald's for a Happy Meal, then I took you to a movie—Bambi, out for a special showing. I hope you remember seeing it. It's a good movie. One I've always liked, even if the part about the mother is sad.

When we got home, I found all my china plates smashed to bits, and I know Victor, your father, has been here, and that he will be back. I don't know what will happen, but I want you to have this, so you know how much I love you, how special you are. Of all the things that have happened to me, you're the best.

I remember the night you were born. It was already midnight. You just barely made it on the tenth, eight minutes before the day changed. There had been so much noise and activity, but then everyone left. All the nurses and doctors and Victor and his family. And it was just you and I. They wanted to give you a bottle because you were so big they said my milk wouldn't be enough, but one kind nurse left you with me and said it wouldn't hurt anything if I nursed you, that if you were hungry later, they could always give you a bottle then.

So there we were in that quiet room that had been so loud, just you and me. You curled your fist and put it on my breast as you nursed and looked at me with those big, big eyes. Even then you had the longest eyelashes I'd ever seen, and a thick head of hair that was still wet from being inside of me. There was this big fat lump in my chest right then, like nothing could ever go wrong again, not as long as you were my child. And just as I thought that, you let go of nursing and took a great big breath and sighed, like you felt that way, too.

Tonight, you're going to go to the baby-sitter because I'm afraid of what's going to happen here. I can't stand to let you be so afraid again, like you were last time—screaming and screaming in your room. No. No, that's not going to happen anymore. And maybe I won't be there to give you hugs and kisses in person, so I'm giving them to you now. And wherever I am, I'll always be your mother. I'll always love you. More than I can ever, ever say. Be safe. Be good.

Love, Mom

Ramón was alone in his office. Outside, light snow fell, the first of the season, and it was beautiful. It made him so achingly lonely for Tanya he wanted to die. He simply sat in the chair and stared out the window and wondered how to make things right.

"Dad?" Tonio said from the doorway. In his hands were the letters from Tanya.

Ramón swiveled, surprised. "Come on in, Tonio."

Tonio had been weeping. There was dampness still in the extraordinarily long eyelashes. He came in and sat on the long couch against the wall. "You should read these."

"No. They're private, between your mom and you."

"My mom." He moved his hand on the letters. He took one of them out. "At least this one. It's the oldest, the one she wrote to me the night she…that my father came after her." His voice sounded strangled. "At least read it."

Ramón took it. In a childish handwriting, still filled with loops and softly formed consonants, was Antonio Quezada, and the date, almost eleven years before. He steeled himself, and opened it, unfolding a single sheet of notebook paper, covered in the same unformed handwriting on both sides.

Dear Antonio, he read, *It's my birthday.*

When he finished, there was an ache in his chest and he had to bend his head and pinch the bridge of his nose for a long moment before he trusted himself to speak. "You've had this one a long time. I've read it before," he said at last. Having read it before didn't make it any less searing.

"I've read it, too," Tonio said. "But I didn't understand it until now." He paused. "Until Edwin and Teresa."

Ramón swallowed. "Yes."

Tonio's tears spilled over on his cheeks. "All this time, I've been so angry with her, and she did it all to keep me safe." He closed his eyes. "It's not fair what happened to her."

"No, it isn't." Ramón crossed the room and sat down next to him, and put an arm around him. "But it isn't your fault."

"You love her, don't you?"

Ramón paused. "Yes."

"Why didn't you do something to help her? Why didn't you save her?"

"I didn't know it was so bad. I didn't even know she'd divorced Victor until after all of it happened."

Tonio touched his chest. "I hate that I have his blood in me. That I'm from him."

"No." He tapped the letter they'd both read. "Do you think she would trade one minute of her life, one minute of anything that's happened, for you?"

Tonio's lip trembled, and another spill of silver tears fell on his face. Mutely, he shook his head.

"You're loved, son. So much."

"I know."

Tonio put his head against his dad's neck and wept. And Ramón just let him cry. There would be new grief, and new wonder, and even new anger before they were through, but the process, so long denied, had begun.

When the boy had calmed, Ramón said, "I want her back here. I want to marry her, but won't even ask it if you aren't ready." He sighed. "I don't want long, but I'll wait awhile if you want a little time to get used to the whole idea."

Tonio stared at him for a long time, and it was impossible for Ramón to read the expression in his eyes. "You mean we'll be a family? Mom and dad and kid?"

"Yeah. Yeah, I guess that's exactly it. Maybe even some more kids, brothers and sisters, eh?" Ramón gave him a half smile.

"I don't know about all that," he said with a frown. "But the rest is okay." He took a breath, blew it out hard. "Can I see her alone first, before you start all that?"

"Of course."

"Can we go now? I want to stop by the drugstore."

"Now is great."

They stood up. Tonio leaned forward, almost as tall as Ramón, and hugged him awkwardly. "Thank you."

"For what?"

Tonio shook his head. "For everything, I guess. For being my dad, for taking care of me when there was no one else. For stepping in."

"Hey, how could I resist?" He smiled. "You were the cutest little boy—not like now, when you're all surly teenagerness."

Tonio grinned, and the expression showed a lot of his mother. "Gee, thanks."

Ramón winked. "No problem."

* * *

From her room on the second floor of the hotel, Tanya had a view of the Sangre de Cristos, jagged against the horizon, very blue in contrast to the snow beginning to fall in thick flakes. It was chilly. She huddled closer in her sweater and got up to find another pair of socks.

She had spoken to the owner of both cafés to see if either of them needed a cook. The owners of the Blue Swan, the Mexican food place where she and Ramón had eaten the first day she came to town, were clearly suspicious that an Anglo would presume to cook Mexican, but she managed to convince them she wasn't telling lies, and they agreed to try her on weekends for a while. In the meantime, they needed a waitress for the lunch shift, starting the end of the week, and Tanya agreed to take the job.

On the way back to the hotel, she'd stopped at the bookstore and stocked up on paperback novels. It was depressing to find herself at such loose ends after all the motion of the ranch. Too much like prison.

But she refused to dwell on it. Munching M&M's from a big bag, drinking hot tea from a thermos, she tried to read an Agatha Christie mystery.

When the knock sounded, it took Tanya a moment to realize it was at her door. The visitor knocked a second time before she jumped to her feet and ran across the room, hoping against hope that Ramón had come to visit.

It was Tonio.

Stunned, Tanya simply stared at him.

"Hi," he said quietly. "Can I come in?"

"Sure. Yes." Tanya backed up, swinging the door wide to give him entrance. "Of course."

He came in and stood in the middle of the room, looking around. Awkwardly, Tanya closed the door and folded her arms over her chest. "You can sit down if you want to." She lifted her chin toward the table by the window. "Have some M&M's."

"Umm, thanks, but I really came to talk to you." He thrust an envelope into her hands. "To give this to you."

Tanya stared at him. Bright patches of color burned in his cheeks. He touched his nose, bowed his head. "Open it."

She looked down at the envelope, then turned it over and lifted the flap. Inside was a card. She took it out.

"Oh," she said in a small voice. It was a big card, fancy, with a rose frosted with white glitter that came off on her hands. In scrolly script, it read, Happy Mother's Day.

Trembling, Tanya opened it and had to blink several times to clear her vision before she could read the poem printed inside. "Roses are Red, Violets are blue, When I think of all you've done, Mother, I love you." Below that, Tonio had written, "I'm sorry I hurt your feelings. I hope we can start over fresh. Love, Antonio.

"P.S. I'm proud to be your son."

"I had to ask the guy at the drugstore to see if he had a Mother's Day card in the back," Tonio said.

Tanya pressed her lips together, and blinked hard. She put the card down on the table blindly and put her fingers on her mouth, but the tears had been too long repressed. She looked at her son—her son—and tears ran unchecked down her face. "I didn't expect this," she whispered, fighting desperately for control.

"I read your letters," he said. "They made me cry."

Tanya shook her head. "You can't imagine…how much I missed you," she whispered. "So much. Every day. I've waited for you for so long." Her breath caught and she covered her mouth and turned away.

A little awkwardly, Tonio moved and hugged her. "I already did all my crying. Don't be embarrassed."

Silently she hugged him, letting the tears flow down her face, hot and free and fulsome. After a moment, the huge wave subsided enough that she could step back. She touched his face. "You're still you, you know. That first day, I knew you right away in all those kids."

He gave her his cockeyed grin. "That's what my dad says, too." Stepping toward the door, he said, "And speaking of him, he's here, too."

Tanya wiped her cheeks and turned around. As if that were his cue, Ramón came into the room. "My turn," he said.

Tonio smiled and gave them a salute. "I'll be downstairs."

Tanya felt dizzy as Ramón moved toward her. "I can't believe this," she whispered. "It's just…I can't believe…"

He stopped in front of her and took her hands. "May as well have lots of things not to believe in then."

"What?"

He looked at her hands in his, then lifted his gaze to her face. "I wanted to let you find your own life," he said. "I had all these noble ideas about leaving you alone to be an adult without the state or some man telling you what do." He shook his head. "But there's been enough time wasted. I fell in love with you at first sight, Tanya."

"I don't want to be alone—"

"Shh, let me finish, because I might get tongue-tied if you stop me."

Tanya made a noise of disbelief. "Tongue-tied? You?"

"It could happen."

"Maybe." She chuckled. "If you were dead."

He tsked, but she saw the twinkle light his eyes. "You'll spoil this if you don't hush."

"Sorry." She bit her lip and shifted on her feet to assume a position of intent listening. A bubble of bright, pure happiness began to grow inside her.

"Where was I? Ah." His eyes sobered. "I want to marry you, Tanya. I want you to come live at the ranch with me and Tonio and all the children. I want to grow old holding you at night."

The bubble, iridescent with the promise of all the things she'd missed and wanted so much, expanded to fill her entire being. "I am so in love with you," she said softly, "that it almost seems like a dream."

"Is that a yes?"

"I want babies, Ramón. Do you want more children?"

He laughed, triumphantly and grabbed her, kissing

her face. "Yes, yes, yes. A dozen, if you want. Babies everywhere." He kissed her again. "Oh, yes."

"Well, okay, then." She shrugged. "I guess I'll marry you then." She flashed an evil grin.

He laughed, and hugged her. Tanya, swept into the power of his embrace, overcome with joy, leapt on him and let him swing her around. "I can't believe I found you," she whispered into his neck. "I love you."

Ramón put her down and took her face in his hands in that gentle, cherishing gesture she so loved. "Say it again."

"I love you, Ramón."

He closed his eyes and opened them again. "And I," he said, bending to touch his lips to hers, "love you, Tanya."

Epilogue

They were married in the church at Manzanares, an old Spanish adobe that had stood there for more than two hundred years. Tonio was best man, Desmary matron of honor. Zach, dressed in a new suit, was ring bearer.

Tanya wore a simple lace dress, long and white. She'd protested for weeks that she could not wear white, that it was only for first-time brides and virgins, but Ramón had unrelentingly asked her every day to change her mind. Exasperated, she asked him why white was so important to him. "A fresh beginning," he said.

She capitulated, and standing in the warm room, her hand on his arm, she was glad. Ramón had broken with his usual black to don a white tuxedo that made him look almost too handsome to be real.

The old bell rang out in celebration as they emerged from the church, and as if nature, too, wanted a fresh start, thick snow had begun to fall. "Beautiful," Tanya breathed.

"Yes, you are," Ramón said. He kissed her.

The reception was held in the boys' dining room, and it was as traditional as receptions came. A Spanish band played, and all the old ladies gossiped while children ran in circles in their patent leather shoes and toasts were lifted. The only nontraditional thing was the lack of alcohol served.

Teresa came in from town with her mother, a slim woman far younger than Tanya had expected, and Tonio danced with her all afternoon. "It's love," Ramón commented. "They seem so young."

"They are," Tanya said, and raised her eyes to her husband.

"Would you like to dance?" he said.

Gathering her veil and skirt, Tanya stood up. "Yes, I would. Very much."

He waited for her, and took her lightly into his embrace, and Tanya, hearing the reception laughter and music swirl all around her was suddenly transported to another wedding a long, long time ago. Remembering the youth who had kept her company, she said quietly, "We've come many miles to this day, haven't we?"

Soberly, he nodded. "Yes."

"Thank God you were there that day, Ramón. Think how our lives would be different if you weren't."

"No," he said. "I don't want to think of life without you, Tanyacita, never again."

"Thank you, Ramón. You're my knight in shining armor, you know."

"And you're my princess." With a grin, he bent and kissed her in full view of everyone. "And I'm so glad I don't have to pretend I'm not madly lusting for you every minute."

A trio of boys sent up some catcalls. "Eeeh, Mr. Quezada!"

He grinned at them. "See what you get if you behave and mind your manners? An intelligent and beautiful wife!"

Tanya laughed, and bowed, and they clapped. And then Ramón was swirling her away again and whispering what he would do with her when they were at last alone. And Tanya snuggled close, thinking of the days ahead with Tonio and Ramón, and babies and long winter nights. She sighed against him. "I'm home, at last."

"Yes," he replied against her temple. "Home at last."

* * * * *

Dear Reader,

In real life, the man I love would make Dr. Phil grin and Oprah swoon. He's funny and open and trusting. He takes out the garbage without prompting and he'll go to the mall without sneaking looks at his watch.

In my books, I write about heroes with flaws and rough edges. It's not the handsome prince who fuels my imagination, it's the king of the jungle with a thorn in his paw, the rogue whose trust has been shattered, the bad boy with a wounded soul. He wears an air of danger like a good cologne. He's forgotten how to love and he won't commit, but beneath that forbidding exterior is a lonely man in need of a woman's healing touch.

Ex-convict Luther Ward is one of my favorite heroes. He's broken, beaten and desperate. A woman with no place to turn has no business trusting a man like him, but kindhearted Maddy does just that. I love writing about people who find the courage to take chances and what happens when they do.

Rogues and bad boys are fine for books, but I hope that every woman looking for real-life love finds a true hero like mine.

I love to hear from readers. A stamped self-addressed envelope is appreciated for a reply.

Pamela Toth

Pamela Toth
P.O. Box 436
Woodinville, WA 98072
www.specialauthors.com

ROCKY MOUNTAIN RANCHER
Pamela Toth

To Cindy, Andy and Trevor Wicken, with love.
Thanks for keeping "Aunt Pam" in your family.

Chapter One

Luther Ward lay on his back with his hands behind his head and contemplated the underside of the bunk above him. The tan paint was chipped and scratched with graffiti, revealing the bare metal underneath. The sound of snoring filled the cell like some kind of rough, primitive music.

It was visiting day, and Luther never had visitors. He had no family, no close friends. The state prison had been his home for eight years now, and sometimes it seemed as if he had been here forever.

"Hey, Eddie, shut up!" Luther kicked at the top bunk. The steady drone stopped abruptly. After three years in the same cell, Luther had gotten used to Eddie. He didn't mess with Luther's belongings, he didn't steal Luther's cigarettes and he had never tried to crawl into Luther's bunk.

Before Luther could draw two breaths, the snoring started up again. There was no more point in trying to silence Eddie than there was in whining about the fact that Luther was stuck here for another dozen years. Neither reality was about to change.

Out of long habit, he tried to brush aside the despair and defeat that threatened to surround him like demons around a deathbed, waiting for his soul. He turned onto his side and shut his eyes.

A sudden burst of raucous laughter from a nearby cell and a steadily escalating argument from farther down the tier barely penetrated his thoughts; he was used to the noise. As well as the sour smells and the boredom.

Luther, always a loner, survived the sameness of each long day and longer night by painting pictures in his mind. Pictures of his ranch. He followed the seasons and mentally went over every chore. It had been so many years since he had walked his own land that he was no longer sure where memory ran out and imagination filled in.

When he was working in the kitchen, washing the huge cooking pots in scalding water and detergent strong enough to peel a man's skin, he reconstructed the plot of every book he could remember reading; he played back each memory of his son. He tried not to think too much about women or the last time he'd had one.

Sometimes he worked out elaborate escape plans. His latest was the most clever, one that might actually work. As he lay on his bunk and listened to Eddie snore, he tried to work out a minor problem with the timing. He was concentrating so hard that he barely noticed when one of the guards stopped outside the cell.

"Ward, you'll have to come with me." Conroy, a bulky man with a shaved head, was staring through the bars. Luther bore a scar down one cheek from Conroy's snake-head ring.

"Warden wants to see ya," he added. His grin revealed an empty space where Luther had knocked out a tooth before being subdued by Conroy and two others. "You must have screwed up bad this time."

Keeping his face expressionless, Luther took his time getting to his feet. He wondered what the warden could possibly want with him. One thing for damn sure, it wasn't going to be good news.

Buffeted by the howling prairie wind, the small ranch house creaked like an old lady's knees. The view beyond the windows, framed by homemade curtains in a sunflower floral, was bright with swirling snow despite the fact that night had fallen. Every few minutes an especially strong gust shook the house, playing hell with Maddy Landers's nerves even though she knew the structure was solid and secure against the harsh Colorado winter.

Above the relentless wail of the wind, her six-year-old daughter's sobs tore at Maddy's heart.

"I want my kitty," Chelsea cried.

Maddy wrapped an arm around her in an attempt at comfort. "I know, honey. I'm sure that Tiger has found shelter somewhere. He'll stay holed up until the storm is over." Even as she said the words, Maddy prayed they might be true. The kitten had been missing since that afternoon. By the time Chelsea had realized Tiger was gone, the snowstorm had struck full force. Maddy didn't dare risk going out again. Chelsea and her half brother, David, depended on her. Maddy was all they had left.

Gator, a German shepherd mix, thrust his head into Chelsea's lap and whined. Daisy, a collie, paced the length of the room and back. Daisy hated the wind.

Maddy was about to say something more about her daughter's missing cat when she heard a thumping noise from outside. It couldn't be David; he was upstairs doing homework. Perhaps a board had come loose.

The pounding grew louder. Chelsea hopped off the couch, her serious blue eyes still wet with tears. "Someone's here," she announced. "Maybe they found Tiger."

Chelsea's words wrenched Maddy's heart as she realized their futility. Her daughter was right about someone being at the door, though. Who would be fool enough to go out on a night like this? Their house sat a mile back from the main road, a mile of ice and drifting snow.

"Wait right here," Maddy cautioned her daughter firmly. "I'll see who's at the door." Always obedient, Chelsea stood by the couch as Maddy crossed the small living room, accompanied by both dogs. "Who is it?" she called through the door as Gator growled.

There was no response. Whoever was outside probably couldn't hear her over the wind. She checked to see that the chain lock was fastened and turned the dead bolt, opening the door just a little.

Peering through the crack into the glow from the porch light, she saw the great hulking shape of a man bundled up against the weather.

"I put my truck in the ditch back on the main road," he said in a gruff voice. "I walked the rest of the way, until I saw your light."

He wore a dark knit cap over shaggy black hair. What Maddy could see of his blunt face was red and wind-chapped, his cheeks rough with stubble. His eyes were narrowed against the blowing snow and it clung to his thick brows like bits of white cotton.

For a moment, Maddy thought longingly of the unloaded pistol deep in the back of her closet. Still, a robber would have to be truly desperate to venture out on a night like this.

Gator growled again and nosed her hand.

"I'm here about the job," the stranger added when she hesitated. A body would have to be equally desperate to go looking for work in this storm.

Maddy had no choice; if she turned him away, he might well die. She spoke to the dogs, shut the door and freed the chain. When she opened it wide, she saw that he was indeed a big man, tall and broad shouldered beneath the denim jacket that was dusted with snow. Its sheepskin collar was turned up, scant protection against the wind. One of his gloved hands seemed to be holding his side. Perhaps he had been hurt when his truck went off the road.

"Are you all right?" she asked.

He glanced down, following her gaze. "Yeah. I

came about the job,'' he repeated, as if to reassure her.
''My feet and hands are so cold they're getting numb.
Guess I forgot how bad the winters around here can
be.''

Bad was putting it mildly, Maddy thought. She had
done nothing for the past two weeks except take care
of the stock and try not to freeze. She knew what that
numbness he mentioned could mean. Frostbite.

Hoping she wasn't making a bad mistake, she released her grip on the door and stepped back. He
stomped his feet on the porch to shake off the loose
snow and removed his hat.

''Come in,'' Maddy told him. ''My husband and
two ranch hands are upstairs repairing a heater.'' She
turned to Chelsea and stifled her daughter's impending
denial with a warning glance as the stranger took off
his gloves and flexed his fingers. No reason for him
to know that her husband had died the year before,
that she and the children were really alone here. Not
until she was more confident of his intentions.

Gator stayed at Maddy's side, his gaze unwavering.
Daisy had retreated to the kitchen doorway.

''I'll make a mess,'' the man said, eyeing first Gator
and then the rag rug in front of the door.

Maddy shook her head. ''Don't worry.'' She took
his hat, wet with melted snow, and set it on the fireplace hearth to dry. ''A little water won't hurt,'' she
added, looking up at him.

He was solidly built, like a log house. One of his
cheeks bore a faint scar and his nose looked as if it
had been broken at least once. His eyes, behind a
screen of thick, short lashes, were dark and wary.

It was his eyes that got to her.

"Take off your coat," she told him. "Sit down and I'll get you some coffee." She glanced at Chelsea and then muttered a low command to Gator. He wouldn't bother the visitor unless the man made an aggressive movement.

His lips twitched. "Coffee sounds good," he said politely. "But, before you go, I have something here that might be yours." As Maddy watched, braced for trouble, he unbuttoned his jacket, and she saw a flash of orange fur cradled against his side.

"Tiger!" Chelsea squealed. The half-grown cat yowled a protest and leapt out, obviously unappreciative of its rescue. Apparently none the worse for wear, it streaked past Daisy into the kitchen.

The man lowered his hand, but not before Maddy caught a glimpse of angry red scratches on his wrist below the cuff of his green flannel shirt.

"You're hurt," she exclaimed.

In a curiously childlike gesture, he put his hand behind his back. "It's nothing."

Up close, Maddy could see that his eyes were gray. Not a light, sparkling silver but darker, the color of a gathering storm, and surprisingly opaque. Thick brows that matched his black hair did little to soften his dangerous appearance.

"Oh, thank you, thank you for saving Tiger," Chelsea cried, her face bright with excitement and relief. Not waiting for a reply, she turned and ran after the cat.

"We're so grateful," Maddy said earnestly. She

would have to check the kitten over and make sure he was okay. "Where did you find him?"

The man seemed embarrassed by her thanks. "He was down the walk a ways, under a bush," he replied, glancing once again at Gator, who remained at Maddy's side. "I saw the orange color against the snow and stopped to investigate. Good thing he was too chilled to run."

"I'm glad you bothered," Maddy said, "especially when you must have been so cold yourself. Chelsea was just heartbroken that Tiger had gotten out, but I didn't dare search for him."

The man's eyes widened. "You did the right thing. It's brutal out there." If he wondered why her husband and the ranch hands supposedly repairing the heater hadn't searched, he didn't ask.

"*You* were out in it," she couldn't resist reminding him.

He frowned. "That's different."

Maddy was tempted to challenge him. Did he think a woman's body froze faster than a man's? She had read somewhere that women had an extra layer of fat to keep them warm, but it wasn't something she felt like bragging about. "Let me see those scratches," she said instead, holding out her hand expectantly.

"I'm okay," he said, and she could hear the irritation in his voice. "I'd rather have the coffee, if you don't mind."

She let her hand drop back to her side. "Of course." She would see to his wrist later, when he had warmed up. After inviting him again to sit down, she commanded Gator to stay and then followed her daughter into the kitchen.

Footsteps thudded down the stairs. No doubt David, her stepson, had heard their voices and was coming to investigate.

He burst into the kitchen right after her.

"Who's come by in this storm?" he demanded.

Maddy couldn't help but smile. At fifteen, David was a thin, leggy copy of his father, with a long face, brown hair and dark eyes. He was surprisingly strong for his size, and Maddy couldn't have run the ranch without his help.

"It's someone about the job," she replied. Her ad for a hand to do ranch chores in exchange for room and board had been posted so long without any response that she had been caught off guard. Lord knew they needed the help, though. She hoped desperately that the man would stay. He might be big and fierce-looking, but he had rescued Chelsea's kitten. Would anyone with evil intentions bother to do that?

"He came in this storm?" David's brows rose skeptically.

"I'm not kidding," Maddy told him. "And he found Tiger hiding outside, so Chelsea's thrilled."

At her words, David's expression softened. He adored his little half sister. "I'm glad. Maybe I'd better meet him."

Smothering a grin at David's protective streak, Maddy poured some coffee. "No time like the present," she said. "Come on with me."

She took the steaming mug and a plate of brownies into the living room, where the man was perched on the edge of the couch, looking uncomfortable as he and Gator eyed each other. Tension radiated from the man's rigid frame like heat from the propane stove. His attention shifted as he took the mug from Maddy's outstretched hand.

"Thank you." His deep voice was surprisingly appealing, as was the contrast between his gray eyes and that tangle of black lashes.

She set the plate of brownies down on the table and indicated that he help himself. While he did, taking two, David sat on the arm of the old recliner. Maddy chose the rocker her husband had given her the first Christmas they were here. As she picked up her own cup of lukewarm coffee, she pretended not to notice the brownie David slipped to Gator.

Hesitating as he swallowed a mouthful of coffee, the man demanded, "Has the job been filled yet?"

The urgency in his voice startled Maddy and she almost dropped her cup. "No, it hasn't," she admitted.

He sat back on the couch, his gaze without expression. Like someone who had known so many disappointments that he no longer cared, she thought distractedly as Daisy sneaked back into the room. David gave her part of his brownie.

"You mentioned two ranch hands. I thought maybe you didn't need more help," the man said in a mild voice.

Maddy stared blindly at her coffee, ignoring David's quick glance. "Well, uh…" She wasn't sure how best to clear up the misconception she had deliberately created. Or whether she should. But she had to trust him, she realized.

If she hired him, he would be sleeping in the basement of the house. A pipe had burst, flooding the bunkhouse, and there had been no money or muscle to repair it. In the harsh Colorado winter, there were too many other priorities, like getting feed to the cattle or breaking through the ice in the water tanks. So many things like these gobbled up Maddy's time and strength.

Inexplicably she remembered the weeks she had cared for her husband after he fell ill last winter. She missed him terribly, but part of her had been relieved when he finally slipped away, freed from the pain that had been his constant companion.

Guilt, oily and unpleasant, washed over Maddy at her own mixed emotions. Was she wrong to feel the way she did?

The man was still waiting for her answer. She pulled herself together. Perhaps it was time for trust, in God, if not in the stranger.

"The job hasn't been filled," she said, lifting her chin. She could feel the heat pumping color into her cheeks. Admitting a lie had always been hard for her. "Actually, there are no ranch hands upstairs." She glanced at David. "No husband anymore, either. The children and I have been running things ourselves." She hated appearing so needy, but George's long illness had drained their resources as well as her strength. "I can't pay much. Room and board—"

Slow comprehension filled the man's eyes. His mouth remained a grim line, but she thought she saw some of the tension leave his shoulders. He must want the job badly.

"That's all right," he said with a dismissive wave of his hand. "I don't need much."

She was glad he made no comment about her vanishing menfolk. "Are you from around here?" she felt compelled to ask. She had worked in a dentist's office before she met George, and he had done all the hiring since they had moved here. Now she wasn't sure what questions to ask.

"I used to live here," the man said, "but I haven't been back in almost a decade."

That explained why he didn't look familiar. She and George had bought the ranch six years ago.

"And you've done ranch work before?"

The man's lips twisted into the semblance of a smile as he sat forward and rubbed his fingers down one grizzled cheek. "I've got plenty of experience at hard work," he said. "If you'll have me, I'll take the job." There was something in his expression as he got to his feet, a mixture of desperation and pride and another element she couldn't identify. Perhaps bitterness.

She wondered about him and his reasons for taking such a job. Perhaps, in time, he would open up a little more. Perhaps not. She sensed that he was a man with little trust left in him. It made her curious. And sad.

She rose, too, and held out her hand. "We'll give it a try, then," she said.

Chelsea slipped silently back into the room, holding Tiger. The cat was limp in her arms, like a rag toy, and purring loudly.

Maddy's new employee nodded, apparently satisfied, and enfolded her hand in his large, rough one. Without taking the time to analyze the brief flare of comfort she felt at his touch, Maddy said, "I suppose we should introduce ourselves. I'm Madeline Landers. My daughter, the one whose cat you rescued, is Chelsea." She glanced at her stepson, who had already risen and come to stand beside her.

"I'm David," he said, shaking hands. "These are Gator and Daisy."

Wordlessly the man held out his hand to the German shepherd, who sniffed it warily. When he did the same to the collie, she shied away.

Maddy looked expectantly at her new employee.

His expression was closed, revealing nothing of his thoughts. He squared his shoulders. "My name is Luther Ward."

Ice slithered down Maddy's spine as she stared in shock.

"But you're supposed to be in prison," she blurted. "For murder."

Chapter Two

Warily, Luther watched the woman standing before him, her blue eyes wide with shock. Her hair, the rich golden brown of a caramel apple, tumbled in waves around her face. She was pretty, but she looked tired. Keeping the ranch going almost single-handedly would be difficult for anyone, especially during the winter.

"You're supposed to be in prison," she repeated. She held her ground, but her cheeks had gone pale and her freckles stood out. Luther suspected that, cat or no cat, she was wishing she had left him outside to freeze.

"I won't hurt you," he said quickly. "And I promise you that I didn't break out of prison." He spread his hands, palms up. "I was released a couple of weeks ago."

As she swallowed nervously, the teenager named

David crowded closer to her in a clearly protective gesture. Luther could have flung him against the wall with a backhand swipe, but he admired the boy's courage. One of the dogs stood at her other side, eyes locked on Luther.

"Are you out on parole then?" David asked, voice breaking.

"Not exactly." Luther reached slowly around to his wallet. "I've been cleared. Let me show you something." As he dug out his papers, his throat threatened to close up on the sudden burst of feelings that ripped through him. He was free, but he had already paid a hell of a price. He'd lost everything.

He unfolded the legal documents and handed them to Mrs. Landers. Knowing he was a jailbird, she would probably snap back that job offer faster than a sprung trap, but maybe she'd at least feed him and let him wait out the storm in the barn before she kicked him out for good.

Her gaze skimmed the papers, slowing when she got to the warden's signature and the official seal.

Luther glanced around the living room. It had been redecorated since he had last been here. The furniture wasn't fancy but he liked it. As she continued to study his official release, he asked curtly, "Don't you watch television? Or read the newspaper? My story must have made the local news at least." He could imagine the gossip. Had anyone felt a twinge of regret for assuming his guilt so readily? So totally? Had any of his neighbors, his friends, entertained a single doubt about Luther's apparent willingness to take someone's life? Were they glad he was free, or did they even care?

She refolded the papers and handed them back to him. "I don't take the newspaper," she said. "And there hasn't been much time for TV lately."

Luther felt a stab of remorse at his gruffness. Had he really been so naive as to think things would change just because he had been exonerated? No matter, it wasn't this woman's fault he'd been railroaded into jail.

"You recognized my name," he said. "Just what have you heard?"

Her gaze was steady, but her hands were clasped together so tightly that her knuckles were turning white. "I know you used to own this ranch." She gestured at their surroundings. "It wasn't until after we bought it that we found out what had happened."

Luther's lips twisted into a humorless grin. He could just imagine what she'd been told. That he had killed his wife's lover in cold blood and then tried to cover it up by faking a burglary.

"Why did they let you out?" she asked. "Did they find some new evidence?"

"Someone else confessed."

"How long were you in prison?" she asked.

His jaw clenched. "I served eight years." He saw the horror in her eyes and was tempted to tell her he didn't need her pity.

"Being out must be a tremendous adjustment for you," she said. "I'm sure there have been a lot of changes."

Her perception made him nervous. "I was in prison, not marooned on a desert island."

She flushed, making him feel guilty again. "I didn't

mean to imply that I could even begin to comprehend
what you've gone through.''

"That's okay.'' He had gotten out of the habit of
considering anyone's feelings but his own. ''My social
skills are a little rusty.''

Her delicate brows rose. ''I'm sure you'll adjust.''

He wondered whether she was referring to having
his freedom or learning some manners. Or getting used
to the changes—like his ranch belonging to someone
else. Like his wife and son being gone for good.

''I suppose I will,'' he said. ''I saw your ad and
came straight here. I didn't do much looking around
on the way.'' He went on to tell her the half-truth he'd
thought out when he had first seen her notice posted
at the gas station on the main highway. ''I need a job
and a place to stay, that's all.''

He didn't tell her about the feelings that twisted
together inside him like snakes as he drove here. Impatience. Bitterness. And a fulminating rage that made
him want to strike out at something.

She must be desperate for help to consider him now.

''Mrs. Landers—'' he began.

''Call me Maddy.'' He wanted to ask her to give
him a chance, but he didn't know how. He had never
liked talking about himself and he wondered if he
would ever fit in anywhere again.

''I'll work hard,'' he said finally, swallowing his
pride.

She seemed to hesitate, and he braced himself.
''Was it your idea to sell the ranch?'' she asked.

He shook his head. ''After I was convicted, my wife
divorced me and then she sold it.'' He had been pow-

erless to stop her. His lawyer had written to give him the news; Diane hadn't bothered.

Maddy pressed her lips together. "I didn't know. For your sake, I'm sorry things worked out the way they did."

But not for her sake, he thought cynically. She was glad she owned the Double C. He wondered if she would consider giving it up.

He could still remember being taken from the courtroom in restraints. A mob of reporters had pelted him with questions, but his wife had walked away without a word. Her abandonment no longer hurt, but his anger at her subsequent betrayal still ate at him like acid.

Luther didn't realize that he had curled his hands into fists until he saw Maddy staring at them. One of her dogs, the shepherd mix she called Gator, growled low in his throat. She bent to pat his head.

"It's okay," she murmured, scratching behind his ears.

Before Luther could think of anything else to say, the little girl looked up at her mother. "Why did they put him in jail if he didn't do anything bad?"

"Sometimes mistakes happen, honey."

Luther was tempted to tell them that sometimes people just wanted a scapegoat to take the blame and make them feel safe again, but he couldn't say that in front of the little girl. "That's right," he said instead. "Sometimes people make mistakes, but I promise you that I didn't do anything bad."

"I believe you." Chelsea held up the cat he had found outside. Tiger's eyes narrowed and he flicked his tail. "Would you like to hold my kitty? When I'm sad, he makes me feel better."

It had been a long time since anyone had believed in Luther. He squatted down so that he could look right into Chelsea's eyes. They were the same bright aqua as her mother's.

"I'm not sad," he said quietly, "but thanks anyway." He gave the animal a perfunctory caress. Luther had never liked cats and he didn't have much experience with little girls.

As he straightened, Maddy suggested to her daughter that she take Tiger up to her room to play.

With a wave to Luther, she complied.

"If you didn't kill that guy, how'd they convict you in the first place?" David asked.

The question reminded Luther that not everyone was going to accept his innocence as easily as Chelsea had. "I was convicted by some circumstantial evidence, an ambitious prosecutor and a jury that wanted to go home," he said bluntly. When the trial was over, one juror had admitted that some of them didn't want to be sequestered over the weekend.

Remembering, Luther once again curled his fingers into fists. He had lost everything he had ever worked for, and then the witch who had betrayed him killed his son. Now he eyed David, who was clearly startled by his bitter reply.

"Despite what I told your little sister, sometimes people just don't try very hard to get at the truth. Sometimes they don't even want to know what it is."

"Why did you come back to Caulder Springs?" Maddy asked. "Do you have family here? Friends?"

He thought of his parents and the way they had cut off all contact when he had been found guilty. He thought of his wife and his son, closing his eyes against the pain. "There's no family left," he said. "As far as friends go, I guess time will tell, won't it?"

"I guess it will." What else could she say?

"I came back because I wanted to see the ranch again and because I needed a job." His shrug was jerky. No way would she let him stay now that she knew who he was.

For the first time since he had told her his name, Maddy smiled. "I guess I can understand that," she said.

Luther braced himself. She was going to tell him she was sorry, but she just couldn't let him stay after all. He wondered if she would make up some lame excuse or just tell him straight out that she didn't want an ex-con around, even one who had been put away by mistake.

"Unfortunately the bunkhouse isn't habitable at the moment," she said. "We'll have to put you in the basement."

Distractedly he wondered what had happened to the bunkhouse. A fire? Before he could ask, she spoke again. "The room in the basement isn't fancy, but it's private. I guess I don't need to show you how to find it."

"No." He was still stunned that she hadn't thrown him out. "That will be fine." It was more than he had expected.

Her smile was slightly warmer. "Good. I'll get you

some fresh sheets and towels. You can use the bathroom on this floor. My husband put in a shower stall. He liked to clean up when he came in.''

''What happened to your husband?'' he asked abruptly. ''Are you divorced?''

''No, he died,'' Maddy replied, glancing at the boy. ''He had liver cancer.''

The anger drained from Luther as suddenly as it had come. He wasn't the only one who'd had a tough time. Oh, hell, now he was plotting against widows and orphans. ''I'm sorry to hear it,'' he muttered.

For a moment, Maddy looked sad. He wondered how long ago her husband had died. Then he ignored his sudden twinge of conscience. He couldn't afford to think about anyone else's needs. Not now. And maybe never again. His own needs were too overwhelming.

''Will it bother you to work here?'' Again she surprised him with her perception. ''I mean, you used to be the boss and now you'll be taking orders from a woman.''

He gave her the only reply he could. ''I can stand it if you can.''

She stuck out her hand and he shook it. ''Welcome to the Double C, Mr. Ward.'' She turned his hand over and looked at his wrist. ''Now how about letting me tend to those scratches Tiger gave you?''

''Do you think he'll like sleeping in the basement?'' Chelsea asked later that same evening after Maddy had finished brushing out her daughter's hair and tucked her in. After the storm had blown itself abruptly out,

David and Luther had taken the tractor down the road to see if they could pull his truck out of the ditch and to retrieve Luther's gear.

"I don't imagine he'll mind." Maddy prayed that he really was telling the truth and she wasn't putting her family in danger.

"I think it's spooky in the basement," Chelsea continued as Maddy put down the hairbrush and opened the book they had been reading each night before bed. Maddy had a love of books that she dearly wanted to pass on. Even David had become more of a reader since she had married his father seven years ago.

She stared into eyes that were the exact same shade of blue, rimmed with green, as her own. Chelsea had her coloring as well as her freckles. Pennies from heaven, Maddy's father had called them when Maddy was Chelsea's age.

"Mr. Ward doesn't look like a man who's easily frightened." Maddy wondered if he had ever been scared while he was in prison. Surely he had. She'd heard the horror stories. "Besides, it's warm in the room down there and the bed's comfortable." She imagined him trying to fit his big body into the narrow twin bed, and then, as if she were invading his privacy, she veered away from the tantalizing picture her mind conjured up.

Anything must surely be an improvement on a prison cell with its total lack of privacy. Eight years! He had been locked up since before she had even met George. How had Luther stood it?

He had saved Chelsea's kitten. Was Maddy being naive to think a man who would do that was no threat?

In case she was wrong, there was always Gator to protect them. He had gotten his name because of his sharp teeth. And she could keep the pistol under her pillow for a while, just until she got to know Luther a little better.

She needed someone to help with the ranch, that was all, and she had no ulterior motives in wanting so badly to trust him.

"Is the basement nicer than prison?" Chelsea asked as she settled herself under the quilt Maddy had made for her when she was a baby. It was covered with little girls in sunbonnets and flowered dresses.

"Yes, sweetie, the basement is much nicer than prison." Forestalling any further questions and her own morbid thoughts, Maddy opened the book and began to read.

David and Luther had winched up his battered truck and pulled it from the icy ditch.

"Can't see any real damage," Luther shouted as he slid out from underneath the pickup and stood, switching off his flashlight. Despite the sheepskin-lined jacket he had bought at a thrift store in Greeley, he had felt the cold sinking into his marrow as he lay on the ground.

"Thanks for the help," he told David. Luther's breath turned to a white cloud. He was grateful for somewhere to sleep tonight besides the cold, cramped cab.

With a wave of one gloved hand, David steered the tractor back down the road.

The pickup motor caught at the first turn of Luther's

key. Relieved, he eased the old Jimmy into gear, listening for any clue that might tell him the undercarriage had been damaged by its violent meeting with the icy ditch. The ride was no worse than usual, so he let himself relax.

His duffel bag and black Stetson were still on the bench seat where he had left them; apparently the storm had been too brutal for anyone with larceny in his heart to venture outside. He would have to amend his thinking, he realized. The crime rate in northeastern Colorado was no match for that back in the joint. There you guarded your back and your few possessions with your life.

He glanced at the battered nylon bag that held his worldly goods. All those hours in the prison kitchen had earned him enough for the pickup, with a little left over. His share from the sale of the Double C was still sitting in the bank where Diane had left it, but Luther had no intention of spending the money on anything but his ranch. Of course, he didn't have nearly enough to buy it outright. Diane had left her share to her mother, and the woman had never liked Luther. He'd have to get a loan—the minute he persuaded Maddy Landers to sell.

Driving through the gate and down the road after so many years and seeing the light from the moon glistening on the snowy fields brought back a flood of memories. When he'd walked here during the storm, he had been too busy putting one foot in front of the other to notice. Now he had to keep reminding himself that he no longer owned the place. He was just a hired hand. Still, he had never expected to set foot here again or to breathe the air that was so pure it hurt his chest. The realization turned the feelings churning inside him bittersweet.

Later, when he had wished his new boss good-night and descended the stairs to his quarters, he wondered again how he ever hoped to reclaim the land into which he had poured so much of his sweat and blood. He had to believe it would happen, though; it was all he had left. Before his thoughts could wander any further, exhaustion claimed him as sharply as a blow to the head, and he plunged headlong into a dreamless sleep.

Maddy had fed the dogs and was almost done cooking breakfast when she heard the water quit in the shower down the hall. Ignoring her flutter of apprehension, she went to the foot of the stairs.

"Chelsea! Come on, honey. Breakfast is ready." There was oatmeal with a sprinkle of brown sugar, leftover ham that she'd sliced and fried, a stack of toast, apple juice and strong, hot coffee.

As soon as Maddy realized she was examining the table with a critical eye, she made herself turn away to finish packing school lunches. He was a cowhand, not a visiting VIP. Why should she care what he thought anyway? Even though he was attractive in a rough-hewn way, he was still an unknown quantity at best. And big trouble at the very worst.

Maddy heard Chelsea's footsteps on the stairs. David was already outside, feeding the chickens.

"What's for breakfast?" Chelsea asked. Tiger, who slept on the foot of her bed, was right behind her, orange tail sticking up like a flag. Maddy gave Chelsea a quick hug and patted Tiger's head.

"We're having oatmeal. You look really pretty this morning, sweetie."

"So do you. Why are you wearing that sweater?" Chelsea asked as she got out the cat food. Tiger began to bellow as if he hadn't been fed for days.

Heat warmed Maddy's cheeks. Ordinarily she wore a sweatshirt around the house, but this morning her hand had strayed to a sweater she usually saved for trips to town.

"I felt like wearing red today."

After she fed Tiger, Chelsea looked around the kitchen, clearly disappointed. "Where's Luther?" He had asked her and David to use his first name. "He didn't leave, did he?"

Maddy wondered if Chelsea missed her father so much that she would be drawn to any man who paid her a bit of attention—even a drifter with a questionable past. The thought was a disquieting one.

"I haven't seen him yet this morning, but I heard the shower running." Before Maddy could say anything more, the subject of their conversation appeared in the doorway.

"Mornin'."

She had convinced herself that her mind must have added its own embellishments to the husky attraction of his deep voice. It was disconcerting to realize now that it hadn't. As she looked up about to return his greeting, her jaw dropped and her reply dried up in her throat. Astonishment held her fast.

Luther's smoothly shaved face went pink and she

realized she was staring rudely at his drastically altered appearance. His whiskers had blurred the strong line of his jaw and the length of the faint scar that ran down his cheek to the bottom of his ear.

"G-good morning," she managed when he hesitated. "Sit down, please."

He pulled out the chair next to Chelsea, who began to pepper him with questions about his missing whiskers. Maddy's hand shook as she reached for his coffee mug. Good heavens! Neither the scar nor the creases around his eyes could detract from his dangerous appeal. She filled his mug and set it back down beside his bowl of oatmeal not daring to look at him again. She didn't want to make him more uncomfortable than he already was.

"Chelsea, eat your breakfast, or you'll miss the bus."

Just then, David came in from outside, stomping the snow from his boots and hanging up his jacket in the mudroom.

"Wash your hands," Maddy told him when he started to pull out his chair.

As he exchanged greetings with his sister and Luther, Maddy took the opportunity to sneak another look. Luther's head was down, his damp black hair already starting to curl. As he dipped his spoon into the bowl of oatmeal, she wondered how he had gotten the scar.

"I hope oatmeal is okay." The words slipped out before she remembered that she shouldn't be trying so hard.

He glanced up, clearly startled. "It's fine, thanks."

Before Maddy could react to the force of his gaze, he had returned his attention to the food before him.

"It's not okay with me," David grumbled. "I hate oatmeal."

"Oatmeal is good for you in this cold weather," she countered automatically, unwilling to be drawn into an old argument. "Tomorrow we're having porridge and grits."

David's head shot up. "Huh?" He saw the teasing grin on her face and gave her a disgusted look in return.

"What's grits?" Chelsea asked.

"She's just kidding," David told her around a mouthful of ham.

Luther took a drink of his coffee. Maddy thought she saw a hint of amusement in his storm-colored eyes, but couldn't be sure. She refilled her own cup and sat down.

During the rest of the meal, eaten hurriedly, she managed to sneak several more glances his way. He ate methodically, without looking up again.

She would have to be very careful, she realized. She must be lonelier than she would have guessed to be drawn to such a troubled man. Funny, she hadn't felt this spark of interest toward any of the local opportunists who had come sniffing around the moment George drew his last breath.

Best she not forget that the last thing she needed was to become interested in her own hired hand. And one who had just gotten out of jail besides. She had no idea what he'd been through, but prison was bound to have changed even an innocent man, and not for the better.

Maddy looked at the yellow plastic wall clock that George had given her. "Hurry up," she told David and Chelsea, who had a tendency to dawdle. "It's almost time to go."

"Are you driving us to the bus?" David asked, rising. She usually did when the weather was bad, since it was a mile to the main road.

Before she could answer, Luther glanced up. "I could take them, if you want." As soon as the words were out, he looked as if he would have liked to call them back.

It took Maddy a moment to figure out why. "Thanks. That's a good idea," she said. Did he think she would have hired him if she wasn't willing to trust him around her children? If anything were to happen to either of them, she would make him wish he had stayed in prison. "It will give me a chance to clean up the kitchen and then we'll go feed the stock."

His gaze stayed on hers for an extra beat, as if he recognized the bit of trust she had offered. Then his shoulders relaxed and he scraped back his chair. "When does the bus come?" he asked after he had thanked her politely for breakfast.

"Seven o'clock," David replied, gulping down the last of his juice. "Come on, Chelsea. Hurry up."

As soon as they had donned coats, hats and gloves, Maddy handed them each a lunch sack and watched the three of them troop out the door.

"I'll see you in a few minutes," Luther said before he shut it behind him.

Maddy watched through the window as both dogs approached him, tails wagging. He extended his hand for them to sniff before he gave them each a rough caress. Then he followed the children around the corner of the house.

Before he got back, Maddy hastened to get the kitchen cleaned up, pack them a lunch and change out of her good red sweater.

She was tough, Luther thought, watching Maddy break the bales he tossed off the tailgate of the truck to feed the hungry cattle. She had an air of fragility about her and she reached only to his chin, but it was obvious that she was used to hard work. Still, she must be exhausted from running the ranch with only a couple of kids to help her. Luther hoped she would be ready to sell it back to him as soon as he got the money. Suing the state would take years; his best chance was a mortgage loan if he could get one.

Maddy was watching him expectantly, so he stuck the hay hook into another bale and hefted it. He couldn't figure her out. Even though he knew he made her nervous, she was willing to give him a chance. Did that make her a saint or just a fool?

All around them, the hungry heifers crowded close, bawling out their impatience. Scattering protein cakes to supplement the hay, Luther ignored the noise, just as he ignored the icy wind that came up to chill him through his heavy clothing.

"I can do that," he suggested as she wrestled with another bale. "Before one of your cows knocks you over."

Maddy shook her head stubbornly. "Thanks, but I can manage. David and I do this every morning, and the cattle have never hurt me." She squinted up at him and he could see tiny lines around her blue eyes. "I think they know I'm their meal ticket."

As he watched, she finished with the bale and started to move aside. The packed-down snow was as slippery as a skating rink and her feet flew out from under her. She let out a shriek and went down hard on one hip.

Luther swore and leapt off the tailgate, ready to help her up. She scrambled to her feet before he could reach her.

"You okay?"

Her eyes were watery and her Stetson had come off. He picked it up and held it out to her as she stood rubbing her hip.

"I'm fine." She took the hat with a muttered thanks, jammed it onto her head and bent to break another bale. Maybe she was one of those women who didn't accept a man's help easily. Or maybe she was a little scared, worried that he had been without a woman for so long that he might suddenly jump her, as mindless as one of her breeding bulls. He almost snorted with disdain until he noticed the sweetly rounded curve of her backside.

His body's immediate reaction was as mindless as any bull alive. Despite the cold, he could feel sweat breaking out and his heart began thudding against the wall of his chest.

Ruthlessly he set his jaw and got himself back under control. As he did, he realized that Maddy was alone out here with him, miles from help. Perhaps she was more trusting than he had first thought.

There was no way he could assure her that she was safe with him, but maybe he didn't have to. What he should be doing instead was remembering why he was here and figuring out how to get what he wanted—without feeling like a total heel for wanting a widow and two kids out of the only home they had. Hell, life would be a whole lot easier for her in town anyway. The thought made him feel better.

He had climbed back into the truck and was reaching for the next bale, telling himself that Maddy Landers and her brood weren't his problem, when her bare hand reached up and snagged his wrist, right where his glove didn't quite meet his shirt cuff.

Reaction to her touch shot up his arm like the jolt from an electric prod, making him straighten abruptly and pull away.

Her cheeks, already rosy from the cold, went crimson. "You're bleeding," she said quietly.

Thoroughly rattled, Luther glanced down at his wrist. Sure enough, the deepest of the scabbed-over cat scratches he had refused to let her doctor had broken open again.

"It's nothing," he said brusquely. The skin she'd touched still tingled.

"You know how easy it is for something like that to get infected," she scolded, ignoring his rudeness. "You should have let me put some antiseptic cream and a bandage on it last night."

Luther glared. She stared back, unflinching.

"When we get to the house, you can give me the

stuff and I'll treat it myself,'' he finally told her, making it clear that he didn't want her touching him.

Maddy nodded and turned away, but not before he had glimpsed the raw hurt on her face. She had only been trying to help. It wasn't her fault that any civilized qualities he might have had to start with had been long since stomped out of him.

Feeling lower than a junkyard dog, Luther once more began hooking the heavy bales and heaving them over the end of the dropped tailgate.

''Stand clear.''

His growled warning was unnecessary. Maddy had already moved away. Her back was to him and she was giving every indication of examining something on one of the cow's necks while it chewed a mouthful of hay. Swearing under his breath, Luther jumped down and started breaking bales. Even when he was done, she kept her back to him.

For a moment, chest heaving from the sudden exertion, he studied her. Noticed how small and slight she really was. Saw how the wind sifted through the ends of her hair like a curious lover, making it shimmer and writhe with a life of its own. He wondered if it was as silky soft as it looked. At that thought, he realized the dumbest thing he could do was to try to find out.

When she moved away from the cow she had been studying and began smoothing her gloved hands over another one, Luther stomped around to the cab of the truck. Getting in, he started the engine and let the warmth of the heater wash over him. She could stand out in the cold and pretend to check on her cows until she froze, he thought. It was sure as hell nothing to him.

Maddy was in the kitchen that afternoon, making a dried apple pie, when she started thinking about the papers that Luther had shown her. Watching him work all morning, realizing how powerful his big body was and seeing nothing but distance and coldness in his eyes, she had begun to worry.

What if those official-looking documents weren't authentic? How did she know whether that gold seal was the real thing, or if the warden's signature was a forgery? Luther could have signed them himself, although one would think the last place a rational fugitive would go back to was home.

What if he wasn't rational? What if his only goal was revenge and the people living in his house were the targets? The idea made her shiver.

Once she allowed the first doubt past her defenses, they came faster and faster. It wasn't just her own safety she was gambling with, but that of her daughter and her stepson, too. What if she had been wrong to trust Luther? Dead wrong? Maybe he really had escaped and planned to murder them in their beds in some horribly misguided plot to get back his ranch.

She glanced up at the wall clock. If he really was some crazed killer bent on revenge, she didn't want him to catch her checking out his story. There was time, though, to call the prison while he was at the barn with the horses.

She really had no choice, she told herself as she dialed the number she had obtained from directory assistance. She was crazy to think Luther would in some way be disappointed if he found out. She hardly knew him; she didn't owe him any trust. Even though something in his eyes had told her he needed to be trusted— that it had been a very long time since anyone had.

Well, he wouldn't have to know that she called. Let him think she believed him one hundred percent. It was a harmless deception.

The phone at the prison rang several times and she was about to give up when a male voice answered. Warden Bingham was tied up in a meeting for the rest of the day, so Maddy left a message. She would keep Luther busy outside tomorrow until she could verify that what he had told her was the truth.

She was at the sink cutting up a chicken for supper when he knocked briefly and came in the back door, almost filling the opening with his bulk. He took off his gloves and his hat, raking one bare hand through his tangle of black hair. The bandage Maddy had given him gleamed white against his injured wrist. His cheeks were red from the cold and his eyes were as shuttered as ever.

"Trouble?" Maddy asked.

He held up one glove and she could see that the side seam was split. "I caught it on a nail."

"Did you scratch your hand?" she asked, though why she should concern herself was a mystery, considering his earlier rudeness.

"No, it's okay." His expression was grim and she wondered if he was annoyed at her about something. Did he sense her reservations about him? "I just came in to get my spare gloves,'' he said as he went around her. "Then I'll be out of your way.''

Maddy didn't bother telling him that he wasn't in her way to begin with. "No problem,'' she said instead as she disjointed a chicken leg with the point of her knife. "There's fresh coffee on the stove if you want some.''

"Thanks.'' She could hear his footsteps as he went down the basement stairs. By the time he got back to the kitchen, she was deeply engrossed in the chicken carcass. "That for dinner?'' he surprised her by asking as he poured himself some coffee.

When she looked up, he was sipping the hot liquid while he watched her over the rim of his cup. His gaze was hooded.

"Sure is,'' she said. "Fried chicken is David's favorite.'' The bird slipped from her grasp and fell back into the sink as she made a futile grab for it. Luther was about to leave with his coffee when the phone on the wall by the door rang. She held up one greasy hand and tilted her head. "Would you get that for me?''

He complied, listening for a moment while she rinsed her hands and dried them quickly on a towel. When he held the receiver out to her, his expression was unchanged but his eyes were opaque.

"Warden Bingham, returning your call,'' he said in a toneless voice as he passed her the receiver. He was careful not to let their hands touch.

Automatically, Maddy took the receiver as he brushed past her and headed for the door. Had that been disappointment she glimpsed on his hard face?

Had she been right about his needing someone to trust him?

As she raised the receiver to her ear, feeling as low as if she had just been caught going through his pockets, she spotted his full coffee cup left abandoned on the counter. Somehow the sight of it sitting there made her feel guiltier than ever.

Chapter Three

Maddy didn't see Luther again that afternoon. By the time she had fried the chicken for supper, cooked the carrots that Chelsea had peeled for her and put biscuits in the oven, darkness obscured the view beyond the window. The temperature on the outside thermometer was dropping steadily. When Maddy finally heard the back door open, she smothered a sigh of relief.

"It'll be solid ice in the morning," she heard David say.

"I'll wear my skates." There was no mistaking the deep voice.

Maddy, who had stopped moving when the door opened, began mashing the potatoes vigorously while Chelsea set the table. Even though Luther's faded red pickup had been parked outside all afternoon and she had descended the basement stairs earlier to make sure his duffel bag was still in his room, she'd had the irrational concern that he might not come back.

"Supper's about ready," she called as both he and David discarded their heavy jackets, hats and boots.

Chelsea hugged her big brother and greeted Luther shyly. "We're having smashed potatoes for supper."

He spoke to her in a low voice and then he looked at Maddy. She smiled tentatively, but his expression remained unreadable.

"I smell fried chicken," David said as Luther brushed by her.

"That's right." Maddy beat butter and milk into the potatoes. "Better go wash up before the biscuits burn." From the corner of her eye, she saw that Luther was standing in the doorway.

"Biscuits, too?" David grinned. "You'd think it was Sunday around here. You didn't happen to bake a chocolate cake for dessert, did you?" Chocolate cake was his other favorite food.

Aware of Luther watching, Maddy muttered self-consciously, "There's leftover apple pie for dessert." At least David hadn't commented on the red sweater she had worn that morning. She really had to get herself under control.

"Even for leftovers, your pie's pretty passable," her stepson drawled.

"Passable!" Maddy exclaimed. "David Landers, you watch your mouth or the only chicken you'll get tonight is the neck." It was a hollow threat; Maddy saved the necks for soup. Chelsea giggled and clapped her hands while Maddy gave her stepson a playful shove. "Go on, scrape that dirt off before the food gets cold."

"Yes, ma'am," he replied. "Come on, Luther, before she puts us on bread and water."

"Homemade bread?" she heard him ask as the two of them went down the hall. David's laughter floated back to her. Luther didn't seem to have any trouble talking to her children, Maddy thought with a sigh. She refused to feel guilty for protecting them and doing what anyone with a lick of sense would have done. What counted was that the warden had backed up his story.

By the time the two males had returned, the meal was on the table and she was about to sit down. Before she could, a large hand grasped the back of her chair and pulled it out.

Flustered, she looked up, straight into Luther's steady gaze.

"Thank y-you," she stuttered.

Nodding, he seated her and then himself as David began passing bowls of food. Between bites, Maddy asked him and then Chelsea about school. Luther didn't say anything, but she noticed he seemed to be listening carefully as he ate two hearty helpings of supper.

When she rose from the table to get more butter, Luther allowed himself a fleeting glance at her trim figure in fresh jeans and a bright blue sweatshirt. He couldn't explain the biting disappointment he'd felt when he had answered the phone earlier and realized she had called the warden after all. He only knew he couldn't go on blaming her for something most people would have done before a dangerous con like Luther spent even one night under their roof.

"Thanks for supper," he said gruffly a few moments later, when they had all finished eating and were taking their dishes to the counter. "Fried chicken's one of my favorites, too."

The look of relief on Maddy's face made him feel like a miser who had been hoarding his gold. The idea that anyone might actually care how he felt was one he would have to mull over in the privacy of his basement room. Before he could find himself blurting out more than he had intended, he set his supper dishes by the sink and almost bolted from the kitchen.

There was a beat-up copy of a popular thriller in his duffel bag. He'd distract himself by reading that. Besides, the last thing he wanted was to intrude on Maddy's time with her children. As he hesitated at the top of the basement stairs, he heard her ask David to feed the dogs before starting his homework. Then Luther hurried to his room.

Several days went by as Maddy and Luther worked side by side, battling the snow and the cold. He followed her orders without complaint and he offered suggestions when they were solicited. She began wondering how she had ever managed without him.

Unless she asked him a direct question, he had little to say. He rarely volunteered a comment about anything. Whether they were feeding stock or stringing fence, he kept his head down, his short black lashes screening his eyes, and he was careful not to touch her in any way. Except for an occasional unguarded glance, his defenses seemed impenetrable.

Maddy called for a stock truck and they sorted some of the best-looking calves to be sold, along with the dry cows and those that were over ten years old. Feed had become too expensive to hold them through the rest of the winter.

Luther helped her wean the remaining calves, watching her face as the animals bawled out their anguish. It was easy to see that their suffering got to her. She was as dangerous as dynamite, a woman who cared.

Each morning, Luther drove David and Chelsea to the bus while Maddy cleaned up the kitchen. Then, with the dogs in the truck bed, the two of them headed out together to feed the stock. They took turns chopping through the ice in the water tanks and they checked miles of fencing. The weight of a snowdrift could take out a whole section at a time and the loss of a few animals could mean the difference between survival or defeat.

Maddy couldn't help but notice that when she and Luther worked together, he wore his reserve like a shield against her naturally friendly nature. After a while, her fountain of chatter dried up as she grew tired of hitting the icy wall of his silence. At least he worked hard and knew his way around the ranch.

If being there bothered him, he didn't say and she didn't ask.

On one cold day when she and Luther were out, the wind, reported to be blowing at freeway speeds, drove the snow into her clothing so that it melted each time she returned to the warm truck. At least the hip she had fallen on had stopped aching, the bruise she bore there fading from purple to blue to a sickly yellow-green.

As Luther turned the wheel and eased the ranch truck around a curve in the deeply rutted road, he glanced her way but didn't speak. She wondered what he was thinking. The new arctic blast had turned the snow to ice and driving was treacherous. Maddy didn't enjoy it when the ground was slick, but Luther seemed willing enough.

"Did you run cattle when you had the ranch?" she asked, to get him talking as they went to check on a group of two-year-old heifers that would calve for the first time in the spring. Anything to break the endless silence that chilled her as much as the wind.

"Some," he replied.

Frustrated, Maddy persisted. "What breed?"

"Same as you."

It was clear he didn't feel like making conversation, but she did. During these past desolate months, she had felt isolated from the rest of the world, even though she kept in touch with a few friends by phone. She missed George's steady presence beside her.

Stubbornly she pressed on. "How many head?"

Luther sent her a sideways glance and she could have sworn she saw the ghost of a smile on his hard mouth. The faint softening made her blink.

"More'n you've got, from what I've seen."

She waited, but he didn't add anything more. She was beginning to suspect he was enjoying their odd game. Knowing a question with a one-word reply was a waste of breath, she asked, "How bad was the worst winter you spent here?"

With a sigh, no doubt of relief, he pulled up to a gate and stopped so she could get out and open it. "Bad enough," he drawled as she waited expectantly.

This time she was sure she had seen a gleam in his narrowed eyes. Her hand tightened on the door handle. "Bad as this?" she persisted.

His expression remained grave. "Nope."

Swallowing the chuckle that rose in her throat, Maddy braced herself against the cold and left the cab that suddenly seemed cozy. The icy wind chilled her damp clothes and made her teeth chatter. Sending a glance of pure disgust over her shoulder, she stepped gingerly on the hard-packed snow and opened the gate. After he had driven through, she closed it again. That was the number-one rule of ranching: Always close the gate.

After they had repeated the procedure several more times, Maddy was shivering and her hip had resumed aching. She was too short of breath to bother with questions. Luther must have noticed her discomfort.

"Sit tight," he commanded when they approached the next gate, and then he opened the driver's side door and climbed down.

"Don't be silly," Maddy replied when he came back and put the truck in gear. "There's no point in your getting out twice."

"Then you drive." He set the brake and swung himself down again to close the gate behind them.

"Nothing like a man of few words—and a bossy

one besides,'' Maddy grumbled to herself as she slid over.

Glancing at her through the windshield, Luther circled to the passenger side and took the seat she had just vacated. She thought about thanking him, then decided against it. Thanks would only make him uncomfortable.

Maddy was driving carefully down the icy, rutted road when she glanced to the left and noticed a dozen dark shapes silhouetted against the snow.

''Damn,'' she exclaimed. ''Looks like Oscar's buffaloes found a break in the fence.''

Sure enough, Luther thought as he followed the direction of her gaze. A ragged herd of bison stood huddled in a corner of the pasture where he had once kept bull calves.

''I would have thought the old geezer would be dead by now,'' he commented, remembering the crotchety neighbor whose animals were always getting out.

''No such luck.'' Maddy turned the truck off the road and cut across the pasture. They got stuck twice before she stopped a dozen yards from the woolly brown animals standing with their big heads facing the wind.

Luther followed her through snow that came past her knees. They would have to drive the herd·back through the break in the fence and then mend it. A crust had frozen on top of the snow, and with each step they broke through and sank abruptly. It made walking difficult.

By the time they'd found the spot where the fence

needed fixing, driven the animals back and repaired the hole, most of the morning had been eaten away. Luther had sharp pains in his legs from fighting the snow at each step and he suspected that Maddy did, too.

"It looks like another storm is brewing," she said as she scanned the sky.

Listening to the silence that hung as heavy in the air as the low, spongy clouds, Luther figured she was probably right. A storm bringing more snow was definitely on its way and they still had stock to feed.

After they had finished distributing hay, cake and alfalfa cubes, they hurried back to the house and the promise of a hot meal. After they ate, Luther would tend to the horses while Maddy did inside chores and saw to supper.

He wanted to tell her how much he appreciated her cooking after existing on prison meals for so long. Before he could put the intention into words, though, guilt at his deception rose in his throat and choked off his voice. How could he pay her compliments while he plotted to get back his ranch?

Perhaps he had only to wait out this difficult winter and she would be more than ready to give up the life that was like no other. Either you loved or hated it; there was no middle road. Obviously, Luther belonged in the first group, but he wondered about the woman beside him. Almost any other life would be easier than this one. For her children as well as herself, and for David especially.

Luther had seen how much time the boy put in doing chores before and after school and then studying until late into the night. Just the night before, Luther had wandered upstairs in search of a drink of water, only to find David asleep at the table over his schoolbooks. This morning he'd been feeding chickens before Luther was dressed.

Now he ran a hand over his face, chilled from the bite of the wind. How could a warm, friendly woman like Maddy stand the isolation, the never-ending work and the miserable weather? He would have liked to ask, but again the words stuck in his throat. Better not to know her feelings. Easier, then, to displace her.

Maddy pulled up to the house and killed the engine. "Give me a few minutes to heat up some soup and make sandwiches," she said as she opened the door and let in a blast of cold air. "If you can dig the tractor out of the shed, you could move a load of that feed up from the main road." Chary of getting stuck, the feed-truck driver had refused to come all the way down the long driveway. Instead they'd had to spread a tarp where he could dump his load of alfalfa cubes. Now it had to be brought up to the barn.

Luther nodded his agreement, got out and began walking toward the garage, where a large drift had formed in front of the door. The tractor inside was the same one he had bought new. He had muscled it over and through bigger piles of snow than the one blocking it now. There were some things a man didn't forget how to do.

"I tell you, he's doing fine. He works hard and he keeps his mouth shut." It was a few days later, and Maddy shifted the receiver to her other ear while she sliced carrots to go into the stew she was making for supper that evening. "That's more than I can say for the gossips around here."

She listened impatiently as Beth Weiderman, a friend from church, defended her concern. Beth had all but come out and told Maddy that Luther was probably so woman starved he might jump her if she dared to use scented shampoo.

"Believe me, if he feels any uncontrolled lust around me, he hides it well," Maddy said dryly when Beth stopped for breath. The man barely talked to her, let alone gave any sign of finding her attractive. Maddy glanced at the clock over the stove. "I have to go. We're making a run into town later and I need to get this stew in the oven."

Beth reminded Maddy once again that she had only to call if she needed any help. The woman was tall but bean-pole thin, and she lived fifteen miles away. Nevertheless Maddy thanked her for her concern before they both hung up.

As she peeled and cubed potatoes, she wondered if all her neighbors were waiting to hear that she'd been set upon by her sexually deprived employee.

While she was staring out the window, paring knife in hand, Luther came in the back door with Daisy at his heels. Apparently the collie had overcome her initial shyness; Maddy noticed that she followed Luther almost as diligently as Chelsea would have liked to.

Mindful of the direction her conversation with Beth had taken, Maddy greeted Luther and then looked hastily away as color heated her cheeks. If she lamented his lack of interest in her as a woman, it was obvious that her social life needed work, she thought grimly.

"Lunch is almost ready," she told him as he crossed the kitchen and headed down the hall. He made some grunting reply as she put the pot of stew into the oven and took the kettle of turkey soup, frozen since Thanksgiving, from the stove. Putting out a plate of sandwiches filled with the venison Beth had canned last fall and traded Maddy for stewed tomatoes, she listened for Luther's return.

Sometimes it seemed as if all she did was feed people.

Waiting for him reminded her of all the times she had listened for George's quieter tread. "Let's eat," she said shortly when Luther's wide shoulders filled the doorway. "I want to be back from town in time to finish the chores." George would never come through that door again and give her a kiss on the cheek while she pretended to grumble about his cold nose. She thought she had worked through her grief and dealt with her feelings of loss and abandonment. But apparently she hadn't.

Moments later, Maddy bit into a thick sandwich, made with her own home-baked bread. Pretending that Luther was in any small way a substitute for the husband she had loved was the utmost kind of folly. That she knew without question. So why did the realization make her so melancholy that her eyes filled with sudden, sorrowful tears?

"What is it?" Luther questioned, his coffee cup halfway to his lips. "Is something wrong? Is it the children? Did the school call?"

Maddy blinked and collected her wandering thoughts. "No," she blurted without thinking. "I'm afraid I was just remembering how my husband used to come in from the cold and tease me by pressing his icy cheek against my neck."

For a moment, Luther's expression remained unchanged. Then his mouth pulled down at the corners and he returned his gaze to his coffee cup. "You miss him," he said, and it wasn't a question.

"Of course." Although George had been years older than she was, he had always been good company as well as a solid, supportive presence. Naturally she missed him, although perhaps not in the ways Luther might assume.

The silence grew as he sipped his coffee. There was a lot more that Maddy could have said about her late husband. Instead she rose and shoved back her chair, picking up the plate that held her half-finished sandwich.

"We'll leave whenever you're done," she said, wrapping it for David and putting her dishes in the sink. "The mess here will keep until we get back."

She had put on fresh perfume, Luther realized as she climbed into the truck next to him. The scent of wildflowers was more noticeable than usual. Perhaps there was someone she hoped to see in Caulder Springs.

Silently Luther studied the passing scenery beyond the passenger window. Going to town was not something he was looking forward to. Facing people who had condemned him, answering awkward questions, keeping his temper in check. And doing it all in front of Maddy—that would be the hardest part.

"You okay?" she asked, surprising him with her perception.

He didn't look at her. "I'm fine." The silence stretched between them and he wondered if she had any idea how hard it was for him to maintain the wall he had built around himself. The wall that was there to protect her as well as him.

He shifted his booted feet on the floor of the cab. He doubted that she could even begin to understand just how selfish, how cruel, how downright animalistic a man could be. Luther knew. He had seen it all and more while he had been in the joint. He'd gotten a real education.

Now he lifted his hat and raked his hand through his hair. Not once had he seen Maddy looking at him as if she thought he was the lower life-form most people did once they found out he was a con. Oh, she had checked him out, all right. Only she didn't manage to look down her nose while she was doing it.

Part of him wanted to demand she find something else to study. Part of him—and it sure as hell wasn't the part with the brains—would have liked nothing more than to confront her. To ask if she was so damned frustrated that even an ex-jailbird like him looked good. And part of him, the part he'd tried to forget about while he'd been in the joint, wanted to satisfy his own curiosity about her. It was the last part that scared him the most. Once he let loose that demon inside him, he might not stop until they both found out just what kind of a monster he had become.

Maddy would have liked to ask Luther how he felt about going into town. Did he wonder how people would treat him? If he did, he hadn't confided in her. Instead he muttered something about picking up another set of work clothes at the co-op. Other than the duffel bag he'd brought in that first night, she had seen no other possessions except his battered Stetson and his equally battered pickup truck. Either by choice or necessity, the man traveled light.

"Do you need an advance on your pay?" she asked him now. "I could give you something if you're short." She had little enough money herself until she got the check from the cattle auction, but she felt guilty about the low wages Luther had agreed to. Other ranches paid more.

He gave her a long look before shaking his head. "No, thanks. I'm fine."

Despite his refusal, Maddy suspected that fuel economy was his only motive in consenting to share a ride to town. He had made it crystal clear in half a hundred ways that while he might not openly dislike her, neither had he been incarcerated for so long that he found her remotely attractive. She hadn't once caught him looking at her with anything close to what she might catalog as interest.

Not that she was interested in him, by any long stretch of the imagination. She was just naturally friendly, that was all. In wintertime especially, she liked having another adult to talk to—not that Luther had actually unbent so far as to have a real conversation with her. He had exchanged more words with her six-year-old than with Maddy.

It was obvious that Chelsea found him fascinating. The man even smiled at her. Maddy wasn't jealous; she just wondered what made him tick.

When the silence between them began to draw her nerves tight, she reached over and turned on the radio. Immediately the cab was filled with an old Patsy Cline classic.

During the daytime, when Maddy and Luther did chores together, conversation between them was held to the absolute minimum dictated by necessity. In the evenings, he disappeared after supper, either to his room in the basement or to the barn or one of the other outbuildings. He hadn't left the ranch or gotten any phone calls that Maddy knew of. She wondered if he still had friends in Caulder Springs. If he did, they appeared to be taking their time in welcoming him back.

She slowed for a turn, reminding herself that she had long since lost interest in how Luther Ward filled his spare time. Besides, if she ever wanted to know, she was sure that David could tell her. He often tagged along when Luther disappeared into the darkness beyond the kitchen door.

Apparently the man didn't mind David's company any more than he did Chelsea's. Not that Maddy would stoop to interrogating her own children. If she ever wanted to know anything else about the new hired hand, which was doubtful, she would ask him herself.

"Been a long time since I heard that song," he commented, startling her from her thoughts. When she glanced his way, he was staring out the side window, but the fingers of one hand drummed against his thigh in double time to the song's slow beat. Perhaps he was a little nervous about going to town after all.

"I've always enjoyed her singing," Maddy replied. "Too bad she died so young."

From the corner of her eye, Maddy saw Luther turn his head and look at her. "My cellmate had a radio," he volunteered, "but he liked hard rock."

A dozen questions danced on Maddy's tongue, but she resisted asking. Instead she gave him a small smile before she stopped for the first of the only two traffic lights in Caulder Springs. The weather was still too cold for many people to be out, although there were quite a few pickup trucks and a sprinkling of cars parked along the main street.

Beside her, Luther leaned forward, his shoulders slightly hunched. He was staring out the window and his hat was pulled low on his head.

"We might as well go to the co-op first," Maddy told him as she signaled and turned into the parking lot adjacent to the old, false-fronted wood building. "I have a few things to get here, too, so I'll meet you at the cash register."

Luther didn't reply as they both exited the truck. After he had held open the front door of the store for her, she headed toward the section where the veterinary supplies were kept. She had stopped before a display of bag balm when she heard a male voice address him.

"Heard you got out, Ward. Didn't think you'd come back here, though."

Curious, Maddy moved closer to the end of the aisle

to see who was speaking. It was Ernie Woods, a little weasel of a man who worked here. She knew him only slightly, but she had formed an instant dislike for him the summer before when she heard him giving a family of migrant workers a hard time.

Ignoring the smaller man trailing him, Luther circled the round rack of flannel work shirts. Was Ernie afraid he might try to steal something? He was tempted to ask the clerk to find someone else to bother, but he didn't want a scene. He just wanted to be left in peace while he picked out a shirt.

"Heard you hired on at your old place," Ernie said conversationally as Luther sorted through the hangers, looking for his size.

Luther glanced up impatiently. "That's right." He abandoned that rack of shirts and turned toward another.

Ernie stepped in front of him, blocking his search. Refusing to let his irritation show, Luther moved around him. He found a red plaid shirt and a solid black one he liked.

Ernie shifted so he was again in Luther's way. "Maybe you heard that a widow was runnin' the place and you thought she'd be lonesome. And not too particular about the kind of man she let crawl into—"

A surge of adrenaline hit Luther like a slap across the face. Almost without thinking, he grabbed the front of Ernie's shirt, twisted the fabric and hiked the clerk's spindly body a couple of inches off the floor. Ernie's faded, bloodshot eyes bugged out in shock.

Luther was tempted to beat the little jerk to a pulp. Before he could decide where to plant the first punch, he heard footsteps, and then a hand gripped his upper arm where the thick muscles bulged with tension. "Luther, please. It's not worth it," Maddy's familiar voice said into his ear. She tugged on his arm.

"You heard her," Ernie wheezed. "I didn't mean nothin'."

Shaking with rage and disgust, Luther looked from Ernie's wrinkled face into Maddy's steady blue eyes. He hadn't given a thought to the garbage she might have to endure for hiring him, but Ernie's lewd remark had shocked him like a blow to the side of his head, unseen and unexpected.

Beneath her hand, Maddy could feel Luther's flexed muscles begin to relax. She took a deep breath. "Come on," she urged him in a low voice. "I still have to get groceries and we need to beat the school bus home." So far, no one else had come into the store to witness what might have looked like an unprovoked attack.

"Yeah, lemme go," Ernie whined. "You know I was only teasin' ya." He wiggled and Luther's white-knuckled grip abruptly released him.

Ernie's feet hit the floor and he staggered. His hands shook as he straightened the front of his shirt.

"I could press charges," he sputtered as soon as he had backed out of Luther's reach. "I could have you arrested for assault." His eyes gleamed. "Attempted murder."

"Can it," Maddy warned him before Luther could say anything. "I heard the whole thing. You provoked Mr. Ward and I'd be glad to tell that to the sheriff."

Ernie began to protest, but Maddy ignored him,

turning instead to Luther. She had no idea how much more he could take without exploding, and she wanted to get him out of there before that happened. He was no good to her in jail.

If he appreciated her sticking up for him, he didn't show it. Instead his mouth had flattened into a hard line and his eyes glittered darkly.

The bell over the door tinkled and all three of them looked around. Two men Maddy didn't know came into the co-op and headed for the back corner where the tack was kept.

"Do you have everything you need?" Maddy asked Luther quickly. If only Ernie had the sense to keep his mouth shut.

"I need some jeans."

"What size?" she asked.

When he told her, she looked at Ernie expectantly. He turned to a shelf that held rows of folded jeans and pulled down a pair. When the little clerk thrust them at Luther, he checked the label and tucked them under his arm. Ignoring Maddy, he walked toward the checkout counter.

"Did you have more shopping?" Ernie asked her.

Maddy's chin went up. She could feel her cheeks heating with color at Luther's sudden departure. "I've changed my mind."

For once, Ernie was silent as he followed them over to the register, where he ducked behind the counter and began punching the prices of the clothing into the outdated machine. While Luther dug out his wallet, still ignoring Maddy, Ernie tossed the purchases haphazardly into a paper bag.

Maddy opened her mouth to object and thought better of it. The two men who had come in earlier were walking toward them and she didn't want to cause Luther any more embarrassment.

He gave Ernie some bills and when the older man handed back his change, several pennies bounced to the floor. Ernie took one look at Luther's expression and bent to retrieve them.

The other men had stopped at a display of work gloves and were examining several pair. Without another word, Ernie turned and was about to walk away when Maddy stopped him.

His expression was defiant. "What more do you want?"

"Just one thing." Maddy sensed that Luther had stiffened beside her. She leaned closer to Ernie. "I want you to remember something," she said in a low voice. "When one of my employees comes in here, they represent the Double C. You treat them with respect and courtesy, understand?"

Ernie swallowed and his Adam's apple bobbed.

Maddy felt fresh anger pour through her. "If you don't," she continued, "I'll take my business elsewhere and your boss will know the reason why. Got it?"

Ernie looked as if he were swallowing a live caterpillar. His bloodshot eyes darted to Luther and then back to Maddy. "I got it." His tone was sullen but she didn't care. She had made her point. At least one person in town wasn't going to treat Luther badly. Not if she had anything to say about it.

"Come on, let's go." Luther grabbed his bag and

headed for the door, not stopping until he was seated on the passenger side of Maddy's truck. When she climbed in beside him, he gave her a level stare. She could see that his eyes fairly smoldered with temper.

It was a good thing she had gotten him out of the co-op before he did something to Ernie he would have regretted. Even though she, too, was still upset by the unpleasant scene, she dredged up a smile and touched his arm, about to reassure him.

Before she could utter a word, he shook off her hand and turned so that she was staring at his hard profile.

"Do me a favor," he grated through tightly clenched teeth. "Don't ever do anything like that again."

Chapter Four

Across the wide bench seat of the pickup, Maddy stared at Luther, mouth agape. Then, as he watched intrigued despite himself, anger began to sizzle in the depths of her bright blue eyes. Her chin went up and her lips compressed.

"What do you mean, don't do that again?" Her tone was colder than a side of beef in a walk-in freezer. Her gaze had iced over. And yet, he was still acutely aware of the subtle presence of the wildflower scent she always wore.

He rubbed one hand along his jaw, conscious of the tension between them and his own pent-up frustration. He itched to shake her.

"Don't you realize what the good folks around here will think if you jump in to fight my battles for me?" he demanded. "There's probably talk enough that you

even hired me. Do you want your good name dragged
through the same mud as mine?'' He sucked in a
breath, fighting to control his anger, but it was a losing
battle. He grabbed her arm and felt her stiffen. Her
gaze never wavered as he struggled with his frustration.

''I didn't think about that,'' she murmured.

''When Ernie tells everyone about what went on in
there, they'll draw their own conclusions.'' Reluctantly he released her instead of dragging her closer
the way he wanted. Wouldn't that give her friends and
neighbors something to jaw about?

At his words, Maddy's face flamed. She went to put
the key in the ignition, but her hand was shaking and
it took several tries. While Luther watched, feeling
lower than a wad of gum on the bottom of someone's
boot, she finally got the truck started, glanced into the
mirror and backed carefully out of the parking spot.

''I need a few groceries,'' she said in a rigidly controlled voice.

Swearing under his breath, Luther looked out the
side window to see if anyone had noticed their brief
altercation. A man he didn't recognize pulled in beside
them and got out of his car without glancing in their
direction. Perhaps Luther was only being paranoid
about the whole situation, but he doubted it. The last
thing he wanted was for Maddy to pay with her good
name for giving him a job. Especially when he was
being less than honest with her. They drove past the
bank and he made a mental note to come back when
he was alone.

By the time Maddy found a parking place in front

of the grocery store, Luther had calmed down enough
to realize he owed her a big apology for climbing all
over her when she had only been trying to help. Apol-
ogies always stuck in his throat, but he needed to get
this one out, if only to convince himself he still had a
couple of human tendencies left.

"Maddy, wait," he said as she switched off the engine and shoved open her door. It didn't take a college
degree to see that she was still mad. As she paused,
glaring, Luther saw hurt shimmering beneath her anger. Knowing he had caused it was almost his undoing. How could he make her understand?

As Maddy waited warily to hear what else he had
to say, she realized that this was the first time he had
voluntarily used her first name. She was still smarting
at his unwarranted attack, but part of her knew that
what he'd said made sense. Gossip in Caulder Springs
was as plentiful as dust-covered pickup trucks on Main
Street and could spread as fast as a prairie fire in a
brisk wind.

A lonely widow with an available, attractive man
staying under the same roof... How could she fault
him for being concerned about her reputation? Still,
he had no business being so pompous. Even now, he
looked less than remorseful, his jaw clenched and his
thick brows pulled into a frown as he stared at her.

When he didn't say anything else, she got out of
the truck, slamming the door with more force than was
necessary. How she hated the idea of people gossiping
about the two of them—just as she hated not being
able to control her own speculative thoughts about
him. About how his strong arms would feel around

her and whether his lips were as firm as they looked or if they would be warm and soft. Clearly, she had lost her mind.

While she stood by the truck, doing her best to banish the unwelcome thoughts, he got out and came around to the driver's side. "Are you okay?" His gray eyes were shadowed by the brim of his black Stetson, but his mouth was grim.

"I guess you have a point," she conceded reluctantly.

"I'm sorry." His voice was low. "You didn't deserve what I said."

Maddy studied the toe of her boot. At least he wasn't above apologizing, even if he did look as if he would rather eat dirt. Even though he was probably right.

"I understand why you were upset," she said, in an equally low tone. "I guess I just didn't think."

For a moment, the hard line of his mouth softened. Silence crackled like heat lightning between them, and Maddy wondered if he sensed it, too. Nervously she glanced at her watch.

What was it about this man in particular that made her feel things she had never even suspected she was capable of feeling? Things she hadn't felt with George, her own husband. Maybe it was guilt that kept her tossing and turning at night, listening for the sound of restless footsteps below. And maybe it wasn't.

"Let's get going." Luther's voice was gruff as he glanced toward the store. "I know you want to be home for Chelsea so that David can do his chores."

He looked down at the ground. "Thanks again for getting in Ernie's face, okay?"

Maddy could see that the whole subject made him uncomfortable. "Okay." She led the way up the steps to the door. "This shouldn't take long," she said over her shoulder.

By the time the groceries were paid for and loaded into the back of the truck, Maddy was glad to be headed for home. In the store she had noticed that several other customers gave Luther startled glances, but no one spoke to him. She wondered if he knew any of them and how the stares of disapproval made him feel. Even the cashier ignored him as she rang up Maddy's sale.

The way people treated him, like a leper instead of a man who had been terribly wronged, made Maddy want to scream, and she wasn't even involved. She wondered how they would feel had it been one of their own sons or husbands in Luther's place.

She wanted to confront them. Instead, knowing anything she did would only make a bad situation infinitely more painful, she followed Luther's example and pretended to ignore the whole thing.

"Doesn't it bother you?" she demanded as she braked at a stop sign on the way out of town.

"Doesn't what bother me?" He must find the scenery fascinating, she thought waspishly as she passed a slow-moving sedan with peeling paint and a tattered "Save a rancher, eat a cow" bumper sticker on the trunk.

Glancing at the speedometer, Maddy forced herself

to slow down. "The way people treat you. As if you were a criminal!"

"To a lot of them, I still am a criminal." His voice was an indifferent drawl that didn't fool her for a minute.

"It's so unfair," she burst out, thumping the steering wheel for emphasis.

"Who ever said that life was fair?" Now he was looking at her. She could feel the force of his gaze. "Don't get caught up in my problems," he said coolly. "Remember what I told you about splashing mud. It gets on anyone who stands too close."

It sounded as if he was warning her off, and she wasn't sure how to react. Perhaps he had noticed her attraction to him, and it made him uncomfortable. Oh, God, how humiliating if he had! She risked a glance but he swiftly looked away.

For a moment, Maddy thought she was about to find out if a person really could die of embarrassment. Then she remembered that he was the one going through the rough time, not her. Her feelings weren't important right now.

He had gotten a raw deal and he deserved better. Despite all his dire warnings, if she got the chance to stick up for him, she was going to do it. If it caused talk, she could handle it.

The next day was Saturday. The temperature was unseasonably warm, enough so that the snow was left in patches, the eaves were dripping and the yard was a sea of mud. In the surrounding pastures, enough grass was exposed so that the cattle and horses were grazing when Luther and David checked them that morning.

Now Luther was in the big garage, tuning up the tractor. He straightened, easing the stiffness from his shoulders as he wiped the grease from his hands onto a rag torn from someone's old flannel shirt. Being alone, having some choice in where he went and what he did, was something he still hadn't gotten used to. When he heard David calling him, tension twisted his gut into a hard knot before he remembered that he wasn't in trouble for anything. Not unless Maddy had noticed the pocketful of chocolate chip cookies he'd filched from the batch cooling on the kitchen counter.

"In the garage!" he hollered, wondering what David wanted. He was a nice kid, but he made Luther wonder what his own boy would be like now if he had been allowed to live. The thought made him feel sad and bitterly angry all at once.

"What are you doing?" David asked when he walked in.

Luther took a couple of cookies from his pocket and held one out. "Hiding."

David grinned. "She won't notice." He ate the cookie in two bites. "Is something wrong with the tractor?" He peered at the exposed engine.

"Not yet." Luther popped another cookie into his mouth. Eddie, his cellmate, used to get a package of homemade cookies from his sister once a month, and he always shared them. Luther never got packages, and damned few letters. Except for those from his lawyer, he hadn't answered any of them.

David stood almost eye level to him, but he had an

adolescent's thin build, like a plant that had shot up too quickly. He was wiry, though, and determination made up for his lack of bulky muscle. Luther remembered the protective way David had stood between him and Maddy when he'd first come to the Double C. She was lucky to have a boy like him.

"A rancher has to know how to take care of his machinery," Luther said in response to David's question. Then he hesitated. "When I was about your age I had an old beater I bought with the money I'd saved. If I wanted wheels, I had to keep it running." Luther had managed a job in town and chores on the ranch, but his grades hadn't been much and he'd had no time left for sports or other school activities.

"How about you?" he asked David as he gestured toward the tractor. "Do you know anything besides how to drive it?"

Luther thought back to the day he'd bought the John Deere, and the pride he had felt. Diane hadn't understood, had been angry he'd spent the money on a brand-new tractor instead of a nicer car. He could still remember how she had refused to come outside and see it when it was delivered. By then she had lost much of her power to disappoint him; they had grown too far apart.

David shrugged. "I used to watch my dad work on it and the trucks," he said, "but he didn't have time to show me much before—" His voice broke off abruptly and he looked away.

Luther felt bad for him. "I'm sorry," he said gruffly. He considered giving David's shoulder a squeeze, but wasn't sure if the gesture would be appreciated. "You must miss him."

David raised his head and blinked several times. Luther pretended not to notice.

"Chelsea doesn't remember him before he was sick, but I do." David's voice came out in a rush. "He was always working on something, but he took the time to listen. You know?"

"You're lucky. Not all fathers are so understanding." Luther recalled his own old man—the sarcasm that always edged his voice, the icy disdain. The contempt in his eyes that always made Luther feel like a disappointment. He envied David his memories, even as he cautioned himself to keep his distance from the boy. Better not to get attached. Safer and less painful to feel nothing than to let himself become involved in any way.

He watched as David reached out one hand and ran it down the old tractor's fender as if he were caressing instead a late-model sports car.

"Hell," Luther grumbled, knowing he was going to regret this. "I suppose I could show you a few things if you want."

David's face lit up, surprising Luther. "Cool. Maddy said I might be able to have a car after I get my license." It was clear the idea of a car held more interest for him than an old John Deere.

"Why do you call her that?" Luther demanded. Was this some new form of teenage rebellion? A fad? If David had referred to her by name before, Luther hadn't noticed. All he knew was that if *he'd* had a mother half as warm and caring as she was, he would never have called her by her first name, that was for damned sure.

David looked surprised. "When she and my dad got married, she asked me to call her Maddy," he said with a shrug. "What's the big deal?"

"She's your stepmother?"

"Yeah. Otherwise she would have had me when she was fifteen," David said with a grin. "I know it happens, but I can't picture her and my dad in the back of some car." He made a sound of disbelief as a flush ran up his thin cheeks. "I mean, I know he probably did things like that when he was young, but I don't think about it, you know?"

Luther knew exactly what David meant. He didn't want to think about Maddy in her husband's arms, either. Just why, he refused to analyze. He only knew he would rather picture his mother in the sack with his old man, difficult as that was. Had his father ever been tender or gentle? Luther doubted it.

Nonchalantly he clapped a hand on David's shoulder to distract them both—and was faintly surprised when David didn't pull away.

"So, what happened to your real mom?" Luther asked. "Were your folks divorced or what?" What he really wondered was how much younger than her husband Maddy had been and how she really felt about him. Questions like that didn't belong anywhere in his mind, but he was damned if he could keep them out.

"My mom died in a car accident," David said, setting his jaw. "I was five, but I remember when it happened."

"I'm sure you do." Luther felt a wave of sympathy.

First the boy had lost his mother, and then his father. Undoubtedly he had earned every drop of warmth Maddy lavished on him. Growing uneasy with the emotional content of the conversation, Luther picked up the rag he'd dropped earlier and beckoned to David. "Let me show you how this baby runs," he said on a sigh of relief. Engines were something he knew, something solid and predictable. Unlike emotions and hazy feelings he never could bring himself to talk about, engines had substance.

Eagerly, David crowded closer as Luther began to share with him some of the knowledge passed on from one generation of males to the next.

"Why don't you come to church with us?" Chelsea asked Luther the next morning as Maddy was setting the platter of pancakes on the table. "The sermons are kinda boring, but the singing is nice."

"Chelsea!" Maddy exclaimed, feeling some protest was warranted toward her comment about Reverend Cavanaugh's sermons. "Just because church services aren't as exciting as some video game doesn't mean they're boring."

"Yes, Mom."

Maddy saw the face her daughter made as she helped herself to the bacon.

"Besides," Maddy added rather defensively, "I already invited Luther to join us. He declined." Let him deal with Chelsea's disappointment, she thought as she poured circles of pancake batter onto the griddle. Even though she thought she understood why he had refused her offer, she still found herself wishing he was going with them.

"Why'd you say no?" Chelsea asked him. "Aren't you a Christian?"

"Chelsea," Maddy said warned as she wiped her hands on the apron she had donned to protect her purple wool dress, "that's too personal."

"I don't mind answering." Luther's voice was mild.

When Maddy met his gaze, she could have sworn she saw a twinkle in the stormy depths of his eyes. Must have been a trick of the light.

"Well?" Chelsea prompted him as she forked up a bite of pancake. It was Maddy's turn to smother a grin as she turned back to the stove. A bulldog had nothing on her daughter when it came to determination.

"My family wasn't big on church," Luther explained. "But I wouldn't say that I'm not a Christian."

"Does that mean you are?" Chelsea persisted.

"Why don't you lay off and let the man eat before his breakfast gets cold," David scolded her mildly. "Maybe he has better things to do than spend the morning singing dumb old hymns and listening to the minister tell us what's going to happen if we don't toe the line."

"David!" Maddy had glanced over her shoulder and was about to admonish his rather cavalier paraphrasing when he caught her eye and winked. She sent him a mock glare and then began to flip the pancakes she was cooking. He was such an interesting mixture of mischievous little boy and budding adult. And he loved goading her for a reaction. "Little pitchers..."

she murmured warningly, glancing next at her daughter.

Chelsea was too busy watching Luther to notice. "Do you pray?" she asked. This time Maddy didn't interfere. When he looked at her, she shrugged and waited for his answer.

"Sure, honey," he said. "In the last few years, I said a lot of prayers."

Maddy had been reaching for the empty pancake platter. His words stopped her in her tracks, hand outstretched. Had he ever felt as if God had quit listening to him? A wave of sympathy washed over her. Before she could move, Luther rose and handed her the empty platter. Then he refilled his coffee cup, his face a mask.

"You eating this morning?" he asked her after she had stacked the platter with pancakes.

Maddy could see by his set expression that he thought it was pity she felt. Nothing could be further from the truth. Wordlessly she nodded, swallowing the lump that had risen in her throat. When he held out her chair, she thanked him quietly and sat down, regaining control of her feelings. He watched her, narrow-eyed, until she managed a bland smile.

"More pancakes?" she asked, passing them.

The hard line of his mouth relaxed as he shook his head. "No, thank you."

Maybe his good manners would make an impression on David, who seemed to think Luther walked on water. All she had heard over supper the evening before—to Luther's discomfiture and her secret amusement—had been how cool it was to tune up a tractor.

Afterward when she had found a private moment to thank him for taking the time with her stepson, he had looked even more uncomfortable as he brushed aside her thanks.

"He's a good boy," he'd said. "I thought he was your son." He had sounded almost accusing, but when Maddy attempted to explain, he'd cut her off. "David already told me."

She had wondered at the time if Luther had been angry about something.

"I still don't understand why you aren't going to church with us this morning," Chelsea piped up suddenly.

Maddy hid her smile behind her juice glass. Luther chewed and swallowed a mouthful of pancakes while he eyed her suspiciously. Then he transferred his attention to Chelsea. If he was losing patience with her persistence, Maddy could see no sign of it.

"I work for your family," he answered finally. "That doesn't mean I go everywhere you go."

Chelsea's face reflected her disappointment as clearly as the mirror had reflected the trio of gray hairs Maddy had found just that morning.

"Luther's right," she said as she stirred sweetener into her coffee. "Although he does know that he has a standing invitation to go to church with us anytime he likes," she couldn't resist adding as she flashed him an innocent smile.

He glowered at her in return before he went back to his breakfast.

"Finish up," Maddy told her daughter, glancing at the clock. "It's almost time to leave."

"Wouldn't that just give the gossips something to talk about, if I showed up at church with the three of you!" Luther fumed under his breath the minute David and Chelsea left the kitchen.

Ignoring him, Maddy removed her apron and hung it on the hook inside the pantry.

"If you had a lick of sense, you'd see that I'm right," he continued. She turned to find him towering over her. The force of his somber gaze did funny things to her equilibrium. Now, however, was certainly not the time to speculate on what he would be like if his formidable control ever broke. Thoughts about Luther Ward out of control were the last thing that had any place in her mind on a Sunday morning before church service.

When she remained silent, he leaned closer so that his voice wouldn't carry. "You should have a care toward your reputation, Mrs. Landers."

She looked into his strong face, her senses rioting as she caught the spicy scent of his cologne. He was wearing one of the new shirts he had bought in town, the black one. She wondered what his plans for the day were, but couldn't bring herself to ask.

"My reputation is doing just fine, *Mr. Ward.*" Reaction to his nearness sharpened her tone as she echoed his formality. "And the offer stands. You're welcome to come along with us anytime you like."

His eyes widened. "Maddy, are you in a snit about something?" Humor turned his deep voice to a river of dark velvet. It soothed her jumping nerves.

"I don't do snits," she exclaimed. Her fascinated gaze lurched to his mouth. She watched his smile fade.

The sudden silence stretched between them like a taut rubber band. When she forced her gaze upward, he deliberately dropped his. She felt it against her lips, as searing as a kiss. Helplessly she swayed toward him. The instant she realized what she was doing, she caught herself and backed up against the fridge, hitting it hard enough to rattle the contents.

''Maddy—'' he rasped, pressing one hand against the door of the fridge beside her head.

Before she could humiliate herself any further, she did the only thing possible. She ducked beneath his upraised arm and fled.

''Aren't you afraid, living out there alone with an ex-convict?'' Agatha Finney's expression was avid with curiosity.

Maddy looked her straight in the eye, controlling her temper with an effort. The old bat had made a beeline for Maddy the moment she and the children had entered the basement of the church after the service.

''I'm not alone,'' she said as she glanced down at Chelsea. ''And I'm less afraid now that we have someone as big and strong as Mr. Ward with us.''

''Can I go say hi to Marybeth Perkins?'' Chelsea asked, pointing.

Maddy gave her permission and then turned her attention back to Agatha. She noticed with dismay that several other people were standing around listening unashamedly. Perhaps Luther had been right. Did they all assume the worst, even though they had known her for years?

"If you need any help, be sure to call us," Sam Brown told her. His offer might appear to be a neighborly one, but he had never offered to help before, even right after George died. Maddy knew from his expression that he probably spoke up now only in the hope of collecting some private bit of fuel to feed their speculation. It made her slightly ill.

"Luther's conviction was a mistake," she said firmly. "Everyone knows that. Someone else confessed."

"Yeah, but we don't know why the other man took the blame," Sam's wife declared as she glanced around.

Several other people nodded in support of her comment.

"What do you mean?" Maddy demanded, incensed. "Why would anyone take the blame for a crime he didn't commit? Especially murder?"

"People confess to things they didn't do all the time," another member of the congregation, one she barely knew, interjected. "It's a sickness."

Maddy had little patience left. Apparently people wanted to believe Luther was guilty, even though the facts had proven otherwise. No wonder they watched him as if they expected him to go berserk at any moment.

"What happened to Luther was a crime in itself," she protested. "The man spent eight years in prison for something he didn't do!"

"Maddy's right."

She swung around to see Joe and Emma Sutter from the Blue Moon Ranch standing behind her. The two of them had helped her when George was sick. Emma had brought casseroles and sat with him; Joe had come over with his own men to do the chores. He and Emma still called to see how Maddy and the kids were doing.

"Luther Ward was completely exonerated," Joe drawled, looking at the circle of people who surrounded Maddy. "If anything, this community owes him an apology."

While he waited, the group began breaking up, one after another of Maddy's neighbors drifted away without meeting her gaze.

"Thank you for backing me up," she said as she gave him and then Emma each a grateful hug. "It's sure nice to see you two."

Joe put a supportive arm around her shoulders. "How is everything?" he asked quietly as Emma stood at his side, concern etched on her pretty face. "Do you need any help? You know that all you have to do is call."

Maddy shook her head, thanking him for his offer. He had his own place to run, and he and Emma always had a passel of foster children staying with them. Maddy had often wondered why they didn't have children of their own, but Emma had never mentioned a problem. Anyway, there was only so much help Maddy could accept, even from loyal friends like the Sutters.

"Luther's been wonderful," she said. "He does the work of two men. And, of course, David does more than his share, too."

"I'm glad you gave Luther a chance," Joe replied. "He's a good man."

"How have you been?" Emma asked. "I've missed our visits." When the weather was better, the two women tried to get together fairly often. Joe and George had been good friends for years.

"I miss you, too," Maddy told Emma. "At this time of year I really start feeling like a hermit."

"You let me know if we can do anything," Joe told her as someone hailed him from across the room.

"I will." Maddy would have liked to ask how well he had known Luther, but Chelsea was coming back and she didn't want to discuss him in front of her daughter.

"Call me when you have time," Emma murmured as she gave Maddy another hug. "And I'm glad you have Luther there to help you out."

Maddy found herself wondering if Emma had meant more than her words implied, then decided she must really be getting paranoid where Luther was concerned. Gripping Chelsea's hand, she threaded her way through the crowd, briefly speaking to several people she knew without lingering to visit longer. A headache was starting behind her eyes; it was time to find David and head for home.

As the milder weather continued, Luther was able to handle most of the outdoor chores alone, which freed Maddy to catch up on the housecleaning and a few other inside projects.

When she had more time, she intended to paint the walls of the bedroom she and George had shared and buy a new comforter for the bed. Something in a vivid floral print instead of the blue-and-white-striped spread they'd had for years. It wasn't that she wanted to erase his presence; most of his clothes were still in the back of the huge closet. The room just needed brightening. For today, she could wash the curtains that hung at the windows of the large corner room and do some dusting.

Perhaps Luther would be able to use some of George's clothes. Although not a tall man, her husband had been broad through the shoulders and chest until his illness stripped the weight from him. His shirts should fit Luther. She wasn't sure how she was going to approach him with the offer, but she would find a way.

The house was silent except for the loud music pouring from the clock radio and Maddy's own tuneless accompaniment. George had teased her gently about her voice, but she could never resist singing along, especially when a lively song like the current country hit made her want to dance, as well.

Instead she dragged the only chair in the room over to one window so she could take down the curtains. As she climbed up, the chair teetered on the lumpy rag rug, and she remembered that she had meant to have David even up the legs. She hesitated, thinking about bringing a kitchen chair all the way up from downstairs, then decided against it. She would be safe as long as she was careful.

Taking down one of the striped panels, she realized she hadn't positioned herself close enough to the window to reach all the way across the rod. Instead of climbing down again, she leaned over as far as she could and managed to free all but the last curtain hook.

As her fingers inched toward it, she stepped closer to the edge of the chair.

Something moved on the fringe of her peripheral vision as the chair rocked forward and toppled. Shrieking, she flung out her arms to break her fall.

"Maddy!" Luther lunged toward her, grabbing her before she could hit the hardwood floor. With her in his arms, he managed to twist his body so that they fell across the bed with him lying partly beneath her.

On the radio, a crooner's slow, dreamy voice replaced the driving beat of the previous song. Maddy was sprawled on top of Luther, her breasts flattened against his hard male chest. Immediately he started to ease her away so he could get up. Then he raised his head. His gaze locked with Maddy's and he froze.

As he continued to stare, eyes darkening with awareness, she knew that she should scramble up from the bed. Instead, breath trapped in her throat, she let herself be seduced by his warmth. His body pressed intimately against hers, their legs entwined. He was fully aroused. Deep inside her, heat and yearning began throbbing together.

Luther shifted, bracing himself on one arm. His eyes glittered with raw, stark need as the slow, sweet music swirled around them. Maddy's lips parted on a sigh, but still he didn't move.

"Luther," she said raggedly, unable to hide the longing in her voice.

His jaw clenched and hunger drew his features taut, but still he hesitated, so close she could feel his breath against her mouth. She had only to tip her head for their lips to touch. Sweet heaven, but she wanted his kiss.

Ever so slowly, Maddy slid her hands up his wide chest, her arms circling his neck. Her fingers tangled with the shaggy strands of his black hair. Body on fire, she urged him closer. As his attention shifted to her mouth, a fresh wave of heat roared through her.

Hesitantly he bent his head. She shut her eyes, forgetting to breathe. Her body melted against his.

"No!" he exclaimed in a raw voice. As Maddy's eyes flew open in shock, he shoved her aside and jack-knifed from the bed.

Chapter Five

By the time Maddy had risen to a sitting position, Luther was across the room, standing by the door. His face was stained with color and he was staring hard at the floor.

"I'm sorry," he said, voice flat. Only his hands, balled into fists at his sides, betrayed his tension.

Maddy sucked in a calming breath and rose from the bed. Her legs wobbled dangerously and she bit down hard on her lip to keep it from trembling. Her body still burned with desire, so abruptly denied.

"It was my fault as much as yours," she replied. More so, perhaps. She had wanted him to kiss her, but she couldn't admit that now. Not in the face of his discomfiture. It was plain to see that what had been so welcome to her was only a momentary lapse, now bitterly regretted, to Luther.

His gaze lifted, smoldering, before his eyes narrowed and his dark lashes screened his expression. Perhaps she was mistaken in assuming that all he felt was regret, but she hadn't the nerve to question him.

"Do you want me to leave?" he asked.

"Leave?" she echoed.

His flush deepened and his scar stood out whitely. "Are you going to fire me?"

Stunned, Maddy shook her head. "That wouldn't be fair," she exclaimed. "I was—"

"I'd never hurt you," he cut in. "I don't want you to be afraid, with me sleeping downstairs and all. If you'd rather, I can stay in the barn instead." His jaw clenched resolutely. "I'll move my stuff out there right away," he concluded.

"It's cold in the barn." Maddy's voice was sharp. She wasn't sure which one of them needed protecting more. The realization irritated the heck out of her. "Let's just forget the whole thing happened."

If she expected him to be relieved, she was doomed to disappointment. Instead, he frowned and the corners of his mouth pulled down. "Good idea."

She wanted desperately to know what he was thinking, what he was feeling. If he felt anything. His face could have been carved from stone. Maddy was vaguely aware that a song about a sultry summer affair was playing on the radio.

Before she could say another word, Luther tore his gaze from hers and stalked out the door. Long after the pounding of his feet on the stairs had faded, she remained standing by the bed, wondering how she was going to forget the look she had seen in his eyes, right before his retreat.

Just for an instant, he had wanted that kiss as badly as she had. On that she would bet the ranch.

Luther muttered a steady stream of curses as he crossed the kitchen and grabbed up his jacket, hat and gloves from the mudroom. Barely taking the time to put them on, he hurried out the back door, resisting the urge to slam it shut behind him. His body was still twisted into painful knots of raw need.

As soon as Daisy spotted him, the collie rose from where she had been waiting since he had gone inside. Her tail wagged a feathery welcome.

"You'd better be careful," Luther grumbled at her. "You never know what a man like me might do next."

Daisy cocked her head and whined.

He could still picture the heat in Maddy's eyes and the way her lips had parted, right before he tore himself away from the biggest mistake he could possibly make.

What kind of bastard would even consider taking what she offered, when all he wanted was her ranch?

The ache in Luther's groin told him he was dead wrong, but he ignored it. Maddy was a complication he didn't need. Of course, once she reclaimed her senses, he would be lucky if she didn't come after him with a shotgun—despite what she had told him up there about forgetting the whole thing.

As he tipped back his head and watched a hawk soar overhead, he conceded that, for a fleeting instant,

Maddy might have mistaken loneliness for something else. Maybe she thought she wanted someone to hold her, to kiss her—to share a little human warmth. Luther knew the feeling. Man, how he knew! Almost more than the sex, he missed having someone to hold.

Perhaps she did want a man, but it sure as hell wasn't him. Despite the way her sweet little body had molded itself to his. No doubt she had figured that out by now. No doubt her stomach was churning with revulsion at what could have happened. Involuntarily he glanced around to see if she and her shotgun were coming after him.

Except for Daisy, the yard was empty. As empty as Luther felt.

All he knew was that the glimpse of hot, naked longing he'd seen flash in Maddy's eyes was going to make him lose a lot of sleep before he succeeded in banishing it from his mind. If he ever did. His body was still telling him with painful intensity that he had made a big mistake in turning down what she had offered. It was little consolation that his reason insisted it was his only sensible choice. Being sensible was the last damn thing his hard, aching flesh cared about right now.

As he headed for the barn, his jeans chafing him at every step, Daisy fell in beside him. ''Where's Gator?'' Luther asked her.

The collie cocked her head and let out a joyous yip in reply.

Before the two of them had gone more than a dozen yards, Luther heard a shout from the road. When he looked up, David was coming toward him, waving. Chelsea followed.

The realization of what the kids could have interrupted upstairs in the house, had Luther not come to his senses when he had, was enough to send his heart right into his throat. The sooner he figured out some way to persuade Maddy to sell up and get the hell out of here, the better off they'd all be.

"Wait up!" David called. "Where are you headed?"

Luther stopped, shrugging at the boy's question. "Out to the barn, I guess."

"Hi, Luther," Chelsea cried as she broke into a run and passed her brother. Her red-and-blue knit hat flew from her head and he bent to pick it up by the pom-pom on top. "I brought you a picture I colored at school," she shouted.

There was no way Luther could do anything but wait for them. With mixed feelings, he stood and patted the collie's head, wondering how Maddy would feel about his being around her children now.

Chelsea came to a stop in front of him and began digging in her schoolbag. "Here it is," she said triumphantly, pulling out a sheet of newsprint, which had been carefully folded.

Curious, Luther opened it up. He could recognize the figure of a man with something black on his head. It looked like a crow that had been hit by a car, but he suspected it was meant to be his Stetson. The big figure was holding hands with a smaller one with long hair. Beside the two of them was an orange blob with pointed ears.

"This is very nice," Luther said, squatting down beside Chelsea. "Let's see, this is Tiger and this is me."

"That's right," she exclaimed with a grin.

David had stopped beside them.

"I told you he'd know," she said, elated by Luther's response.

"So this must be you," Luther continued, pointing to the smaller figure with the long hair.

Chelsea giggled. "Yes, it is. Do you like the picture? You can hang it in your room, if you want."

Luther couldn't remember the last time anyone had given him anything without expecting something in return. "Thank you, sweetheart," he said gruffly.

As he squatted there beside her, Chelsea threw her arms around him and gave him a hug. "I'm sorry they put you in prison," she said, surprising him.

Swallowing hard at the sudden emotion that threatened to choke him, Luther returned her hug. As he did, his gaze met David's over her shoulder. Luther would have expected to see a look of teenage derision or, at the least, indifference. Instead, David gave him a wink. It was almost as nice as Chelsea's hug.

Several evenings later, the temperature plummeted. It snowed all night and gusts of wind buffeted the house. Maddy lay in her bed, wondering if the power would be off by morning. Finally, wide-awake despite the lateness of the hour, she got up and shrugged into the thick royal blue robe that George had given her the last Christmas they'd spent together and put on the matching slippers.

When Maddy got halfway down the stairs, she could see that the kitchen light was on. At least the electricity still worked. She had a good idea who was in the kitchen. If David had gotten up, she would have heard him. Besides, both David and Chelsea slept like the dead.

Gripping the banister, Maddy hesitated, her sensible side urging her to go back up the stairs before she was detected. The house was cold at night, and a shiver ran through her. Her fingers tightened on the banister.

From the kitchen, she heard the sound of a spoon hitting the floor, followed by a growl of annoyance. Instantly her stomach twisted into a hard ball of tension and need. Ever since the humiliating scene in her bedroom, she and Luther had managed to avoid being alone together. She kept busy in the house while he tended the animals. On the first day, he threw together a sack lunch and stayed out until suppertime. After that, Maddy had made sandwiches and left them for him in the fridge. If he preferred solitude to a warm midday meal, who was she to dissuade him?

Now she retreated to the top of the stairs and listened to the noises coming from the kitchen, prepared to wait him out. When he returned to his room, she would go down and make herself some herb tea.

The wind died abruptly. She heard Luther open the cupboard, then pour himself a cup of coffee. A kitchen chair scraped back, creaking when it took his weight. Maddy nibbled at her lip and shivered.

She had just turned to go back to her room when a sudden resolution set her jaw. This was her house; no way was she going to allow Luther Ward to keep her from fixing a cup of tea in her own kitchen.

Head high and shoulders back, she swept noiselessly down the stairs. Her momentum lasted until she got to the kitchen doorway. Luther was sitting at the table reading, one big hand wrapped around his coffee mug. Despite the chill in the room, he was wearing only a T-shirt and sweatpants. His shaggy black hair looked as if he had repeatedly run his fingers through it. His eyes, when he lifted his head, were shadowed and wary.

"What are you doing up?" The downright unfriendliness of his tone goaded Maddy. With one hand clutching the lapels of her robe together, she plastered a smile to her face and came into the room.

"I smelled that aroma of your wonderful coffee," she said, knowing as well as Luther that the coffee he made was strong enough to strip varnish and usually as bitter as tree bark. He freely admitted he preferred hers to his own.

If her remark amused him, he didn't show it. Instead he gestured toward the counter. "Help yourself."

"Why, thank you," Maddy cooed, not at all sure why she was acting this way, only knowing that some little devil inside her wanted to kindle some reaction, even a negative one, from him. Aware that he was still watching her, she released the lapels of the robe she knew covered her with complete modesty and sashayed across the room. "Would you like a refill?" She sent him a dulcet smile over her shoulder and barely refrained from batting her eyelashes.

He glowered and returned his attention to the book

in front of him. "No, thanks." His tone was as plain as a Do Not Disturb sign. He wanted to be left alone.

Maddy filled her coffee mug and plunked herself down across the table from him. The furrows on his forehead deepened as he turned a page of his book.

"What are you reading?" she asked, blowing gently on her coffee to cool it.

"Hemingway," Luther answered without looking up.

For several moments, the only sounds Maddy heard were the wind outside and her own breathing. She worked to keep it slow and even.

"Did you read a lot in prison?" Silently she congratulated herself on her casually friendly tone.

Luther didn't reply. Instead he conveyed his impatience by shifting in his chair.

Maddy sipped her coffee and forced herself to swallow, shuddering involuntarily. It was even stronger and more bitter than usual. She didn't know how he managed to turn the identical blend she used into something so vile. "I wonder how deep the snow will be in the morning," she mused aloud.

Luther sighed and turned the page.

"Good coffee," she added sweetly.

That got his attention. His head came up, eyebrows raised. His mouth was twisted into a grimace of disbelief.

"Something wrong with your taste buds?" he demanded.

Maddy shrugged and took another sip of the noxious brew, trying hard not to make a face.

Luther glared at her across the table, wishing she

would take her coffee, her smiles and her wildflower scent back upstairs—before he found himself dragging her onto the table and taking the kiss he had craved since the two of them had landed on her bed. This wasn't the first night since then that he had given up on sleep and come upstairs, but that didn't mean he wanted company—especially Maddy's company.

No, a persistent voice inside him whispered. What he wanted was her mouth. And her scent swirling around him until he was high on it, and then the rest of her, stretched out beneath him.

His body tautened violently, protesting his vivid imagination with an intensity that bordered on pain. Luther bit back a groan and wondered if her husband had ever taken her on the kitchen table. Despite the chill in the room, Luther began to sweat.

"What are you thinking?" Her voice shattered his erotic thoughts.

"Huh?" he asked dumbly.

Maddy's smile widened into a grin. Damn, but she was so pretty she had his tongue tied into a knot that threatened to gag him. His attention slid from her eyes to her soft, full lips, moistened as they were with his own barely drinkable coffee. Heaven only knew how she could stomach the stuff. It nearly made him sick.

"I asked what you're thinking," Maddy repeated, eyes brimming with laughter. "Your expression made me curious."

Luther just bet it did. If she even suspected just how he'd been imagining her lying across the table, she would probably hog-tie him and pour the rest of the coffee down his throat as a punishment.

"I wasn't thinking anything," he lied defensively. "I couldn't sleep so I wanted to read for a while."

"Lucky you," she replied. "You've got me to talk to instead."

Her cheerfulness after the careful way they had been avoiding each other confused him. What was she playing at? Did she enjoy baiting him? Luther stared at his book without reading a word. "I doubt I'm very good company."

"I'm sure you could be if you tried." Her smile was impish, and a dimple he'd never noticed before appeared in her cheek. He thought about pressing his lips against it. Damn. She was enjoying this.

Unbidden, a sudden image of what he would enjoy flashed before him. His body's urgent response was a blatant reminder of the very reason he was sitting here instead of sleeping in his narrow bed. Maybe the best way to get rid of her was to tell her what he *was* thinking. If that didn't send her scurrying back upstairs, she deserved everything she got.

Shoving the book aside, he leaned forward. Clearly startled, Maddy straightened so fast that her elbow hit her coffee mug and its contents spilled onto the tabletop.

"Better wipe it up," Luther drawled. "It'll probably dissolve the finish."

If Maddy was disappointed by his words, she didn't show it. Instead she got a rag from the sink and cleaned up the spill. Before she could sit down again, Luther rose and shoved his hands into his pockets. If he didn't get her to back off, his already shaky control was going to shatter into a million tiny pieces. When that happened, there would be no stopping him, and then they would both end up sorry.

"Do me a favor," he said tersely as she turned and looked up into his face. Her lips parted and he wanted to kiss her so badly it was all he could do to resist.

"What's that?" Her eyes had darkened and a flush stained her cheeks. At that moment, she was the most beautiful thing he'd ever seen.

"Give me what I want," he said, his body rigid with tension. "Sell me back the ranch."

His words were not what Maddy had expected. For a few seconds, shock kept her motionless. Then the meaning behind what he had said sank in, as corrosive as his coffee.

"The ranch!" she cried, and then remembered that it was the middle of the night. "Is that what you want?" she demanded in a stage whisper. "Is that why you're here? Because you honestly think I'd be willing to sell you my ranch?" Her voice rose again. How could she have been such a fool to think it was she who interested him? How could she have convinced herself that beneath the hard, unfeeling shell he wore lurked a man in need of warmth and kindness, even love?

She turned away, anger and humiliation burning through her with equal strength, equal pain, equal devastation.

"That's right." His tone was ruthless. "That's why I came back." She could hear the hunger, the longing. "I lost everything! My freedom, my son, my land."

His son? Maddy whirled around again.

He raised his fist and she thought he was going to

slam it down on the table. Instead he pulled back at the last instant. When he did hit the polished wood, the blow seemed more like a reluctant caress. Controlled. Only a muscle jumping in his cheek revealed his agitation.

"You had a son?" She was still reeling with the pain of rejection. *She* had nothing to do with why he was hanging around here. How could she have believed any differently, even for a moment? One look at his shattered expression and Maddy cast her own pain aside. "What happened to him? Is he with his mother?" She must have heard, years ago, but she couldn't remember.

He looked so broken she thought he wasn't going to answer. It was his turn to look away. He braced his arms against the counter and hung his head.

"Yeah, I had a son." His voice was a harsh whisper in the silent room. Even the wind had stopped again.

With a great deal of effort, Maddy refrained from touching him. "What happened?"

Luther stepped around her and slumped back into the chair, put his locked fists on the table in front of him and stared at them as if they were alien to him. She knew with an awful certainty that something terrible had happened to his boy. Now she did move; she went up behind Luther and put a hand on his shoulder. His muscles were knotted with tension. Absently she massaged him as she would have massaged David.

"Tell me."

Luther glanced up, and for once, he didn't mask what was in his eyes. Maddy braced herself against the raw suffering she saw there and her hand stilled.

She had almost given up when he began to speak. His voice was rusty, as if he hadn't used it for a long time.

"After I got sent away, my wife put the ranch up for sale."

Even though Maddy knew he had been married, the words disappointed her in a way she didn't bother to examine. He'd had a wife, and a child.

"She took my boy, Mark, and she left. He was four." Luther bowed his head. Maddy moved her hand, stroking his hair in an attempt at comfort. Vaguely she was aware that the dark strands were soft and warm beneath her fingers.

He tilted his head, eyes closed, as if he was enjoying her touch. She heard him sigh. Then he shoved back his chair and rose so quickly that she had to scramble out of his way.

"The roads were bad," he continued. "They said she was driving too fast. Halfway between here and Denver, she lost control." Luther's eyes were wild with pain. "The car flipped several times and then it exploded. They were both killed."

Horror poured over Maddy, followed by a mother's awareness. How did one ever survive the loss of a child?

Luther raised his head and looked at her. The torment of the damned burned in his eyes. Overwhelmed with sympathy for his loss, Maddy opened her arms and he stepped into them.

"I'm sorry," she murmured, caressing his bowed head.

For a while, he just stood there like an oversize child, seemingly content to absorb the maternal comfort she offered. She stroked his head, his back, murmuring soft sounds that had no meaning as his breath puffed raggedly against her neck. She could feel his pain and had to blink away tears.

Too soon she felt a hard shudder go through him. She dropped her arms and he stepped away. Fearing what she might see on his face—embarrassment or rejection or merely anger—she looked up.

"I'm sorry," she said again. "I only—"

His mouth had lost its usual tautness. His eyes, though sad, were dry. "You're the sweetest woman I know," he said, voice hoarse.

Then, as she watched, immeasurably pleased by his words, his expression changed. Hardened. As if something inside him, momentarily warmed, had gone cold again. She wondered what was wrong. Had he revealed more than he meant to?

"But all that sweetness doesn't change a thing." His voice had iced over. "My ranch is the only thing left for me and I want it back."

He had shoved her away again as clearly as if he had physically pushed her. An answering challenge rose within Maddy.

"Then you'd better be prepared to kill me," she said without thinking. "Because this ranch ain't for sale." As soon as the words were out, she realized what she had said. Distress threatened to replace the determination humming through her, but she couldn't recall her words without making things worse.

Luther's face darkened. His eyes glittered. "Some people think I've killed before," he growled.

Suddenly Maddy's self-control exploded. "Oh,

that's ridiculous!'' She turned her back on him, shoulders drooping as the emotion of the last few minutes was replaced by sudden, total exhaustion. What was there left for them to say to each other?

''I'm sorry about your son,'' she murmured over her shoulder, unwilling to look at him again. How could she still want him after what he'd said about the ranch?

''Thank you.'' Luther's voice, too, betrayed a weariness that cut clear to the bone.

''I'm going to bed,'' she said, tired. She needed to be alone. To absorb all that he had told her. To sort out her feelings. ''Please turn off the coffee and the light.''

Long after she had settled back under the covers, she replayed what he had told her. Just how much could one man take before the sheer weight of his loss crushed the very life right out of him?

''Did you hear what happened to that guy who confessed to killing Adam Sloan?'' Ernie Woods asked.

Luther glanced up. He'd already been to the bank and now he needed to get work gloves and warm socks. When Maddy offered to come into town for him, he had almost bitten off her head. He had to face his own demons. If anyone could call little Ernie Woods a demon. He was more like a pain in the butt.

Ernie waited for Luther to ask what he meant. Luther didn't intend to, but then curiosity got the better of him.

''What happened?'' he asked with casual indifference as he examined a pair of calfskin gloves. Adam

Sloan was the man Luther had been convicted of killing. His wife Diane's lover.

Ernie sidled closer, like a crab. He lowered his voice. "Somebody bumped him off."

The news was startling. "I thought he was in jail."

Ernie nodded and his beady eyes glittered with excitement. "Somebody stabbed him, right in his cell. It was on the news."

Luther lost interest. People in prison got killed all the time. For cigarettes. For fun. For no reason at all.

"Did you hire it done?" Ernie asked breathlessly.

Luther's head snapped up in astonishment. "What?"

Ernie's face was avid with curiosity. "Did you pay somebody to ice him?"

Under any other circumstances, Luther might have been tempted to laugh at Ernie's self-conscious slang. "Why would I do that?" For the first time, he noticed that two men who looked vaguely familiar were listening to their conversation. Luther glared, and they both began studying the instrument used to inseminate cattle artificially as if it were the latest sex toy.

Disgusted, Luther returned his attention to Ernie. "Why would I spend my money on a hit man?" he asked.

Ernie's voice rose. "Dead men don't talk," he replied in a knowing tone.

Frustration curled Luther's fingers into fists at his sides and tightened his jaw. Prudently he turned away. It was either that or smash the little weasel's face in.

"You probably had him whacked so he couldn't take back his confession," Ernie said, excitement making his voice even louder. "I bet you have lots of friends in the big house who owe you a favor."

"Sure, Ernie," Luther drawled. Why had he listened in the first place? "Maybe I just called up an old buddy back in the slammer and had the guy rubbed out."

"You could have!" Ernie insisted. "How do we know you didn't? How do we know you didn't do it to shut him up?"

Luther turned slowly back around and noticed, with grim satisfaction, that Ernie's mottled skin went pale. "You mean the same way I might shut up a store clerk who's pissin' me off?"

Ernie's bloodshot eyes widened and he scuttled away like a bug. "Now, Lu-Luther," he stuttered. "Do-don't get any wild ideas. I got stuff to do in the back room. Maude will help you if you need anything at the register."

Luther glanced at the other two men who'd heard the whole thing. He half expected them to be grinning at his attempt at humor. Instead, they were both staring as if he had just whipped out a knife and slit old Ernie's throat.

By the time Luther got back to the ranch with his new socks and work gloves, he was still disgusted enough to bite nails in half. Was no one ever going to forget?

The loan officer at the bank had been pleasant enough when he explained why they couldn't give Luther a mortgage. He had glanced at the loan application Luther had filled out and told him the numbers didn't add up. Even with his sizable down payment, his income was too low. No comment was made about the prison term he had listed on the application or his subsequent release. No suggestions were made for alternate financing. Just an oily smile tainted with phony regret, a clammy handshake and a turndown.

Luther should have known it wouldn't be easy. When had anything in his life been easy? That didn't mean he was giving up, though. There had to be something he could do.

When he pulled up in the yard, David came around the house and hurried over to his truck, a serious expression on his young face. Luther's gut tightened in instant response. What if something had happened to Maddy or Chelsea?

"What's wrong?" he demanded.

"Can I talk to you?" David asked.

The tenseness gripping Luther lessened a little. Apparently there was no crisis. Still, from the anxious expression on the boy's face, Luther sensed this wasn't about anything simple.

"Yeah, you can talk to me," he replied, suppressing a sigh as he opened the door of the pickup and got out. "What's up?"

While he stood with his hands jammed into his back pockets, waiting for David to explain, Maddy watched the two of them from the kitchen window. She knew something had been troubling her stepson. He'd been unusually quiet when he got home from school and even refused the snack she offered.

"Are you sure nothing happened on the bus?" she

asked Chelsea, who was seated at the kitchen table behind her, eating cookies.

Chelsea shook her head. "No, only that David was standing in the aisle talking to Brenda Ainsbury and the bus driver made him go back to his seat," she said before she took a swallow of milk. "I heard him telling John Teal that Brenda's hot." Chelsea wiped her mouth with her napkin. "When I'm older, I'm going to be hot, too."

With mixed feelings, Maddy realized how fast her baby was growing up. When she glanced out the window again, both David and Luther had disappeared. The Ainsbury spread was a big one that bred cattle for lineage rather than beef. Maddy hoped the daughter was a nice girl beneath all that adolescent heat.

"What can I do for you?" Luther asked as he followed David into the barn.

Instead of answering immediately, the boy went over to the wall and examined one of the rolls of wire hanging there as if he found it fascinating.

Luther once again jammed his hands into his pockets and rocked back onto his heels, striving for patience. All he really wanted was a cup of Maddy's coffee and a handful of her chocolate chip cookies. Not his first choice, but the only one he would permit himself to consider.

"Did you go to high school around here?" David asked, surprising him.

"Yeah. I grew up on this ranch."

The boy turned to look at him. "I didn't know that." He fell silent again and began to pace across the open area. Luther understood how difficult some things were to talk about, but he still wished David would get to the point. It was cold in the barn.

"Did you, uh, date much in high school?" David asked without looking up. His voice cracked and they both ignored it.

The light began to dawn slowly. Girl trouble. An icy chill shivered down Luther's spine. Surely someone had talked to the boy about all of this. His father, perhaps. Or Maddy. David couldn't expect Luther to explain—

"There's a big dance in a couple of months," the teenager burst out. "And there's this girl I know." His voice ground to a halt as if he had run out of air, and his face flushed deep red.

Oh, shoot. No one had ever bothered talking to Luther about birds, bees or members of the opposite sex. His experience had been an uneasy mix of hearsay and hands on, so to speak. He learned as he went, and his values had been formed as he saw just what carelessness could do.

Surely a boy David's age must know the basics. Didn't they teach the technical stuff in school? Luther hoped so. Perhaps it was only details David needed. Responsibility and restraint. Birth control and disease. Luther's palms were damp and he swallowed past a sudden lump of nerves. Being in a position to influence a boy's attitude toward sex and women was a hell of a lot to take on.

"Just what do you need to know?" he asked.

David looked uncomfortable but determined. Had to give the boy some credit for that.

"Luther?"

He braced himself. "Yeah, son. What is it?"

"Do you think you could teach me how to dance?"

Chapter Six

"I really need to talk to you about something," David told Maddy as she cleaned up the kitchen after supper. Chelsea had already gone into the living room to watch a television program about elephants and Luther was refilling his coffee cup. At David's words, he glanced up.

"I'll be downstairs if you need anything," he said, crossing the kitchen.

Wistfully, Maddy eyed his broad back in the red plaid flannel shirt. Just having him around made her feel safer, and she told herself that was enough. Although she had done her best to make him welcome in the living room during the long winter evenings, she had to assume he preferred his own company to theirs.

"Would you stick around for a minute?" David piped up, before Luther could leave.

Maddy was still curious about what the two of them had been discussing so seriously that afternoon. At supper, David had been unusually quiet and Luther hadn't spoken at all except to ask for the salt and to thank her when she passed it to him.

Now he waited, expression watchful. David swallowed nervously. She would have liked to give him a reassuring hug, but knew it would only embarrass him further. His uncertainty reminded her of the day she had first met him. At seven, he had been shy, but never hostile or resentful of her relationship with his father. He was still a good, responsible boy; she could not have managed without him. Had he gotten himself into some kind of trouble at school?

"What's up?" she prompted him gently.

He lifted his head and his gaze sought Luther's before he turned to her. She tensed at his anxious expression and wondered if Luther was somehow involved. Whatever the problem was, she vowed silently to help David any way she could.

"There's this dance at school in a couple of months," he said, voice high. "I'd like to go, if it's okay with you."

Maddy almost slumped with relief. She noticed one corner of Luther's mouth lift in apparent amusement— almost as if he were aware of the dire thoughts that had been racing through her head. "Oh?" she prompted David as she picked up a wet cloth and began wiping the counter. He had never been interested in school dances before. "I don't suppose that would be a problem unless the roads are bad."

"Great." He let out a gusty sigh. It was all Maddy could do to suppress a grin and she dared not look in Luther's direction.

"What kind of dance is it?" she thought to ask, scrubbing at a spot of dried spaghetti sauce on the stove.

David's tone was studiously casual. "Just a regular dance."

She waited expectantly for details, but none seemed forthcoming. "Will you be going with Kenny and some of your other buddies?" Kenny Sutter was Joe and Emma's boy; he and David were best friends.

Luther leaned against the doorframe and took a swallow of coffee. His gaze was hooded, and Maddy wondered what he was thinking. Was he remembering dances he had attended long ago? From the silence, she deduced that there was more to this business with David than was immediately apparent. Before she could speculate any further, he squared his shoulders and wedged his hands into the back pockets of his jeans.

"Um, there's this girl at school," he muttered as color stained his thin cheeks. "Her name's Brenda. I might go with her."

"Brenda Ainsbury?" Maddy asked, taking pleasure in his look of astonishment.

"How did you know?" he demanded.

She thought she heard Luther turn a chuckle into a cough. With a conscious effort, she kept her gaze riveted on David.

"It's a parent's job to know these things." She hung the wet cloth over the faucet. Staying one step ahead of a teenager, especially one who was just discovering girls, was undoubtedly going to require all the parental mystique she could concoct.

Luther remained silent as he set his cup in the sink and resumed his spot in the doorway. Maddy wondered why David had asked him to stay. Moral support, perhaps?

"Luther's going to teach me to dance, but he said it would be easier if you helped." Her stepson spoke so quickly that the words almost ran together.

Surprised, Maddy glanced at Luther, whose arms were folded across his wide chest. She was hurt that David had consulted him before coming to her.

"I told him I'd show him the steps, but I wasn't about to dance with him," Luther drawled. His face had lost its hard, distant look.

David's answering grin made Maddy's hurt feelings ease. No doubt he missed having a man around. That was probably why he had gone to Luther first. She had done her best to be open with David, but some things needed a man's guidance.

The direction in which Luther might guide David didn't concern her. Maddy was sure that, underneath his crusty shell, Luther was a good man. Still, she made a mental note to discuss the whole situation with him, so he would know that she appreciated any attention he gave either of her children.

"When would you like to start these dancing lessons?" she asked.

David looked relieved, as if he had expected her to

object for some reason. Perhaps it had been too long since the two of them had really talked. She wanted him to know his interest in girls was nothing to be self-conscious about, and to remind him that she was always ready to listen. She couldn't love him any more than if he were her own son. In every way that mattered, he was.

"I'd like to get started tonight, as soon as Chelsea goes to bed." His cheeks grew pink again and he studied his shoes.

Maddy wondered how Luther felt about giving up his precious evening solitude. She looked at him expectantly.

"Okay by me," he replied to her silent question.

Apparently slow dancing was one of those things a person didn't forget, like riding a bicycle or making love. Luther bit back a groan at the unwelcome comparison. He had succeeded in explaining the basic moves to David and in showing him how to hold his partner. Luther had managed all that without touching Maddy himself, and he was feeling rather smug that he had managed to ignore the temptation. If she was disappointed, she hid it well as she stood in her stepson's loose embrace.

"Don't look at your feet," Luther cautioned him as he steered her around the living room with as much care as if she were made of spun sugar. "And try to relax."

"Right." David's tone was dry.

Maddy sent Luther a saucy wink over his shoulder. She hadn't said much, just followed his instructions and David's hesitant lead. As they continued moving to the music, Luther tormented himself by wondering what she would have done had he swept her into his arms and given David an actual demonstration.

A demonstration of what, he wasn't so sure.

While Luther dealt with his body's sudden surging reaction to the idea of holding Maddy close and burying his face in her caramel curls, David eventually stopped moving and lowered his arms.

"I think I get the idea. Thanks for helping, Maddy."

"Sure you've had enough practice?" Luther asked, relieved that the session was almost over. "I guess you've learned all you need for now. If I remember right, slow dancing is mostly standing in one spot and shuffling your feet a little anyway." Hearing the falsely hearty sound of his own voice, he fell abruptly silent. Had Maddy noticed his forced boisterousness?

Her gaze flickered away, and he wondered if she was thinking about other dances, other partners. No doubt she had danced with her husband. Luther's own wife, Diane, had loved to dance. With anyone who asked her. And Luther had been fool enough to let her see how it got to him at the time. He knew now that she had enjoyed his reaction most of all.

He realized both Maddy and David were watching him. Had they been able to read his thoughts? He glowered. Maddy's brows rose haughtily, but David was clearly preoccupied.

"Anything else I can help with?" Luther asked him. If the boy wanted to learn line dancing, he'd best buy a video. Keeping up with the latest steps hadn't been a priority where Luther had spent his last eight years.

"I was just wondering…" David began, frowning thoughtfully at Maddy.

"What is it, dear? You know, we can always go over all this again before the actual dance," she told him.

"Good idea." He studied her for a moment and then turned his attention to Luther.

By now, Luther wanted nothing more than to go downstairs and try to lose himself in an old John Saul thriller he'd picked up at the thrift store. Maddy's familiar scent, the subtle blend of wildflowers and woman he ought to be immune to by now, was wearing away his shaky control.

"I think it would be a big help if I could see the concept in action, so to speak," David said turning to look at his stepmother again.

"I'm not sure what you mean." Her voice had developed an edge.

As Luther watched her, fresh awareness fizzed up inside him like the bubbles from champagne. At the same time, a warning bell began to toll somewhere inside his head.

"Would the two of you mind showing me how this slow dancing is supposed to look?" David's expression was patently innocent, but it wavered when it collided with Luther's hard glare. What the devil was the boy up to now?

Luther opened his mouth to object, then clamped it shut. What could he say without embarrassing Maddy with another rejection? He had already run from her bedroom with so much speed she was probably convinced that he found her repulsive.

He wished to hell he did!

Maddy was having trouble comprehending how the boy she had been thinking of with such parental love and pride could set her up this way. Luther had made it crystal clear he wanted nothing to do with her that required physical contact, and now her smart-aleck stepson was doing his clumsy best to play Cupid. Briefly she considered telling him he could just forget the school dance and anything else that came up for at least the next ten years. The only thing that stopped her was the realization she'd have a tough time explaining her annoyance to either of the two males who stood looking at her.

"I don't think that's really necessary," she protested instead. "Besides, I'm sure Luther's much too tired after the long day he's spent outdoors."

Luther's stormy gray eyes narrowed below eyebrows that reminded her of gathering thunderclouds. From his forbidding expression, it was easy to see that he took her hasty words as some kind of misguided challenge.

While she tried frantically to think of something to defuse him without arousing David's curiosity anymore than she already had, a new song filled the room. Luther's face showed no reaction and Maddy wondered if he even realized it was the same sweet ballad playing that fateful afternoon they had ended up on her bed.

While she struggled to maintain her own composure, Luther took a step toward her and held out his arms.

"Shall we?"

Her heart leapt in response. As the dreamy melody filled the room, she thought she saw a flash of awareness cross his hard face. Before she could be sure, it disappeared, to be replaced by an expression of rigid indifference. Even now he was prepared for rejection. Had he never known the warmth of unconditional acceptance?

Under the circumstances, she had no choice but to step into his arms. When she did, awareness threatened to strip away her veneer of control and leave her quivering helplessly at his nearness, her attraction glaringly obvious both to him and to her adolescent stepson.

Maddy swallowed and bit down hard on her lip. The same determination that had enabled her to get through her husband's long decline, his death and the funeral that followed without shattering into a million pieces kicked in to save her yet again. She even managed a cheeky grin.

Luther held her the same way her stepson had, but there the similarities ended. She had never been more conscious of a man's closeness. His hand warmed her icy one as his other arm circled the body she fought to keep from trembling. She forced her fingers to rest lightly against his shoulder and dragged in a shallow breath. His scent, pine soap and leather, made her head swim.

Together, they began moving to the music, and it was worse than Maddy could have imagined. The harder she tried to unbend and follow Luther's lead, the more her body, taut with nerves, refused to co-operate. She stepped hard on his foot. Mortified, she risked a glance at him, only to blush furiously when she realized he was watching her through narrowed eyes.

"Relax."

His arrogant command was irritating, and for some reason, that irritation succeeded in doing what little else would have. It wiped away her tension as if it had never existed. She went pliant in his arms and found herself suddenly able to follow his lead as easily as if they had partnered each other for years. Her confidence grew as she matched his surefooted steps.

Maddy realized something else, too. She was as drawn to Luther as if he were a magnet and she a piece of iron.

For a breathtaking half minute or so, they moved together as smoothly as synchronized swimmers. Then, just as Maddy was beginning to forget where they were, Luther let her go. Reality crashed down around her, accompanied by the last fading notes of the song.

"I think you get the general idea," he told David in a voice so devoid of feeling that it could have been generated by a computer.

David's gaze darted to Maddy, and she forced herself to give him a reassuring smile. "Thanks for the help," he told them both. It was plain to see that the shimmering tension in the room puzzled him.

Luther surprised her by extending his hand to David, who clasped it briefly. "Anytime," Luther said. "I mean that." He barely glanced at Maddy. "Good night.'' His voice was gruff. Before she could reply, he was gone. The tape player clicked off and the room became silent.

Humiliated by his hasty departure, Maddy blinked away angry tears. Had he been worried she might attack him in front of her stepson?

''I have some things to do in the kitchen.'' She spoke to David through stiff lips as she hurried from the room.

Luther would have liked to take a cold shower, but nothing short of a fire was going to drag him back upstairs tonight. All he could do was stare at the same page he'd been trying to read for a half hour and wonder if Maddy had felt any hint of his body's swift response to having her in his arms. He told himself that it was only because he hadn't been with a woman for so long, but he knew that wasn't entirely true.

His long abstinence was certainly a factor in his reaction to Maddy, but not the only one. His response was more complex, as well as being more focused. His body craved the physical release, but he wanted it with her. And he wanted more than just sex.

He wanted the tenderness she gave the children. Hugs and soft words and warm smiles. Acceptance. Appreciation. Things he had no right to. Luther knew he was in trouble. And that knowledge scared the hell right out of him.

At breakfast the next morning, it was plain to see that Maddy was still upset. While Luther made short work of the eggs and fried potatoes she slapped down in front of him, he watched her. She ignored him.

Chelsea didn't appear to notice, but David did. He kept glancing from Luther to his stepmom and back again. Maddy avoided his eyes and Luther pretended that nothing was wrong.

He hadn't thought how she might interpret his quick retreat, only what she might do if she felt his arousal pressing against her like an unwelcome obscenity. Now it was clear he had some fences to mend as soon as the youngsters left for school. He had no idea what to say.

"The weather report's predicting another storm tonight," Maddy announced as soon as the door slammed behind David's departing back. "I want to bring the heifers from the north pasture closer in this morning."

"That's a good idea." Luther bent to put his dirty dishes in the dishwasher.

"I'm glad you approve." Her voice had an edge as she wiped off the table, and their gazes collided. The hurt and puzzlement he saw in her eyes was nearly his undoing. The last thing he had meant to do was cause her any distress.

"I'd like you to load up the horses while I finish here," she said as if that look had never passed between them.

"Maddy, about last night—"

"I want to go right away," she cut in. "The storm could come early, and I don't intend on losing any more animals." She started to step around him, and

Luther moved, blocking her way. Obviously startled, she glared up at him. "I *said*—" she began, frowning.

"Maddy." He caught her elbow. While his tongue got tangled around his apology, he felt the warmth of her arm through her sleeve and dropped his hand. "We need to talk," he finally managed to say.

"I don't think so." Again, she tried to move around him.

Again, he shifted, feeling like a cutting horse after a stubborn calf. Finally he reached out and clamped his hands around her waist to still her movements. Then he leaned down until they were almost nose to nose.

"I'm sorry," he muttered.

Her eyes grew dark. For a timeless moment, he felt as if he were falling into their bottomless navy depths.

As he held her effortlessly, so close that Maddy could see the fine cross-hatching of lines around his eyes, she fought to keep from betraying her reaction to his nearness. How dare he manhandle her like this after giving her the brush-off last night. Just what was he playing at anyway?

"You have nothing to be sorry for." She kept her voice impersonal, although she would have loved to demand an explanation. She knew that David was almost as confused as she was by Luther's behavior. He couldn't figure out what was going on between the two of them, if anything, and neither could she.

"I didn't mean to embarrass you last night," Luther continued as his hands at her waist tightened briefly and then let go. Inexplicably his cheeks darkened. "I needed to put some space between us and I didn't think about how you'd take it, or how it might look to David. I'm sorry if I upset you.''

Maddy tried to brazen it out, although she had never been a good liar. ''I don't know what you're talking about.'' What did he mean about needing to put space between them? Wasn't that big brick wall he'd erected protection enough?

Luther straightened away from her. ''Have it your own way then.''

Maddy took a deep breath, unable to figure him out. ''I want to get those cows moved so I can get to town later, if the storm's still holding off.''

''I don't like your going alone.'' It was obvious that his bossy words surprised him as much as they did her. ''I'll go with you.''

She arched her brows. ''That's not necessary.'' She wanted to see her lawyer, but she didn't feel inclined to tell Luther that she intended to make sure he didn't have any legal grounds to take back the ranch considering that he hadn't wanted to sell it in the first place. She was sorry as she could be that he had lost it, but the Double C was her home now, hers and her children's.

His frown deepened. ''I don't want you getting stuck alone in the storm halfway between the ranch and town. It was hard enough for me to make my way here after my truck went off the road.''

''I'm tougher than I look.'' He stared silently, making her feel ashamed of her flippant response to his concern for her safety. ''Oh, all right,'' she conceded finally. ''I'll keep one eye on the sky.''

"Don't act foolishly because you're ticked off at me," he replied. "I told you I was sorry."

Suddenly Maddy was furious. "I don't act foolishly. And I don't get ticked off at one of my hired hands over some imagined slight." Before the words were out, she knew she had gone too far.

Luther's hands wrapped around her shoulders, biting into her flesh, and he hauled her against him. "Then let's see if this ticks you off," he growled, bending his head.

The touch of his lips on hers was explosive. There was no tenderness in the kiss; it was too carnal, too blatantly erotic. Too hot. Pride urged her to resist, but pride was no match for the passion Luther aroused in her between one heartbeat and the next. Her resistance went up in flames. All she could do was hang on tight and kiss him back as his powerful arms closed around her.

Her trembling fingers touched his cheek, and his mouth gentled on hers. His passion set her afire, but his tenderness broke her heart. She slipped her arms around his neck and hugged him hard against her.

A shudder racked him. Groaning deep in his throat, he released her mouth to nuzzle the sensitive place below her ear. She gasped and pressed closer. Sensations raced along her nerve endings and pooled deep inside her. Blindly she sought his mouth again. His lips branded hers with a series of hot, quick kisses that left her breathless and made her feel like a fairy princess, coming alive after a long sleep. The strength of his passion fanned her response. Her fingers sank into his hair as she anchored his mouth against her own.

Standing on tiptoe, Maddy tried to absorb him into her flesh. It had been such a long time, and her sensors were on overload. Luther shuddered again and slid his hands down to her hips. She was vaguely aware of being lifted as he set her on the edge of the kitchen table and made a place for himself between her parted thighs. When she looked at him, his eyes were dark and intent, his face taut. Sliding one arm around her shoulders to support her back, he leaned closer and kissed her again. As she held onto him, her fingers dug into the hard muscles of his upper arms.

His free hand slipped beneath the hem of her top and his touch on her bare skin sent a rush of sizzling tremors racing through her. His callused fingers skated up to close over her breast, covered by her plain cotton bra. Her nipple puckered and he rubbed it with his thumb. She arched into his hand, her voice breaking on a sob of hunger.

"You feel so damn good," he muttered, bending his head to press his face against the rounded swell above her bra. "You're so warm and you smell like flowers." He rubbed his cheek against her as if he couldn't get enough of her feminine softness. "Put your arms around me, sweetheart," he begged. "No one's held me in so long."

His voice throbbed with raw need, and her heart went out to him. Just as she had suspected, there hadn't been enough tenderness in his life, enough caring, enough love.

Her own responses were out of her control. She squirmed against him, seeking more of the hard, heated power of his big body. A thousand sensations assailed her, both sweet and hot, and she wanted more. Reason had gone the way of her pride, abandoned in the flare of desire that raged between them.

With a hand that trembled, she tugged at the snaps of his shirt, freeing several so she could touch him. His hard muscles jumped beneath her exploring fingers. The soft mat of hair was curly. She felt his chest expand on a sigh as he groaned out her name.

Maddy was pulling his head down to hers when she felt him tense. "Noo," she whimpered. He couldn't reject her, not again. How could he, when he made her feel so good? Her hands tightened possessively and she kept her legs wrapped around him. "Luther, please." Despite her efforts, she could feel him withdrawing emotionally as well as physically.

Like a dash of cold water, his rejection doused her desires. Pride came roaring back as she forced herself to release him and tried to scramble off the kitchen table.

"Maddy, wait." His voice was thick with strain.

She didn't care. How could she have let him kiss her like that, hold her so tight, stroke her so tenderly, when he had already admitted that all he wanted was her ranch? It was painfully clear to her now that he was willing to use any means—even seducing the present owner—to attain his own ends.

So why had he stopped?

Her feet hit the floor and she glared at him with loathing made all the stronger by the lust it replaced. "Let me past." Her voice was icy.

He tried to haul her back against him. When she resisted, he immediately released her. "You don't understand,'' he said, spreading his hands wide in silent supplication.

"Oh, I think I understand just fine.''

"Sweetheart, listen to me,'' he pleaded.

"I'm not your sweetheart.'' She was in no mood for excuses. She tried shoving him aside, but his big body didn't budge.

"I don't have anything to protect you.'' The bald admission stopped her in her tracks. "Maddy, I didn't plan this and I didn't come prepared.''

When she remained silent, he grabbed her hand and pressed it to the fly of his jeans. At her touch, he trembled.

"Does this feel like I don't want you?''

Overwhelmed by his blatant masculinity, she jerked her hand away, her mouth too dry to speak.

"I'm sorry,'' he repeated.

She had to stop herself from flying back into his arms. Her first impression had been right; he did want her. As badly as she wanted him. And still he had denied himself, denied them both, all because he had wanted to protect her, too.

"Oh, Luther,'' she murmured softly, overwhelmed by his selflessness. She was tempted to take a chance, to urge him to gamble, but the impulse quickly died. It wasn't in her nature to take that kind of risk.

Before she could think of anything to say, the phone on the wall rang shrilly. They sprang apart, the guilt in his eyes matching her own. The phone rang again and she wanted to smash it into silence.

Instead she smiled ruefully. Luther's expression was

so wary that it tore at her heart. "I'd better get that," she murmured. "It might be the school."

He nodded and stepped aside.

When she answered, an unfamiliar male voice asked for him by name. Curious, Maddy handed over the receiver and listened brazenly to the one-sided conversation.

Luther identified himself and then listened for a moment. Shock flared in his eyes and then they narrowed. "I have no idea who could have killed him," he said in a flat voice. "It has nothing to do with me."

Another murder? Ice slithered down Maddy's spine. She folded her arms and wished she could hear what the caller was saying.

Luther's expression reflected his growing anger. "No comment," he finally snapped and slammed down the receiver.

He glared at Maddy and she thought he was going to stalk out of the kitchen without another word. Then he hesitated, distractedly raking a hand through his hair. "That was a reporter. The other day I heard that someone killed the man who confessed to Adam Sloan's murder. This guy was calling to see if I knew anything about it."

Maddy was astonished. "Why would anyone kill him?"

Luther shrugged. "Who knows. People in prison get taken out all the time."

For a moment, Maddy felt sick. Despite his innocence, Luther could have been killed there, too. Sudden tears came to her eyes. Blinking them away, she realized he was watching her intently.

"Why did he call here?" she asked.

"He implied that I might have had something to do with it."

It was the last thing she expected to hear. "That's ridiculous," she cried. "How could you get to him in prison?"

Luther's mouth curved in a humorless smile. "According to Ernie at the co-op, I still have buddies in the joint who'd do just about anything for a price."

"Ernie?"

Luther brushed her question aside. "No big deal."

"Why would you want to kill the man responsible for your release?" she asked, confused.

"A dead man couldn't recant his confession."

Maddy was shocked by the lack of emotion in Luther's voice. "Why can't they all just leave you alone?" she demanded. "You didn't do anything. You could *never* do anything like that."

To her surprise, Luther's frozen features began to thaw. His rigid stance relaxed. She would have loved to go after the reporter who had called just now and rip his tongue out. The violent impulse astounded her; normally she was a peaceful woman.

"Thanks, honey." Luther's voice was little more than a whisper. While she watched anxiously, his chest expanded on a deep breath. His shirt still gaped open where she had unsnapped it, revealing an inviting glimpse of black curls and smooth skin. Her fingers itched to stroke him again. While she struggled against her renewed attraction toward him, he surprised her again by gathering her into a loose embrace and resting his forehead against hers.

"What am I going to do with you?" he sighed.

His heat and closeness fueled the desire still riding her. For a moment, she was unbearably tempted, despite all that had happened since he had let her go before.

Then reality returned. "Nothing, I guess, at least not until one of us gets to town," she drawled.

Grinning, he let her go. "You would have to remind me."

Maddy felt that, somehow, they had just taken a giant step forward.

As it turned out, neither of them made it to town that day. The storm rolled in as they were moving the cows, and the snow was already coming down hard when they loaded the horses into the trailer.

At supper, Maddy's hand accidentally brushed Luther's when she passed him a bowl of beets. Her gaze flew to his. His narrowed eyes reflected her own simmering hunger. The knowledge that he shared her feelings was both a comfort and an added torment.

"Don't let the storm get to you," he said softly before he left the kitchen after supper. "It will be over before you know it."

She didn't reply, just stared as he gave her a slight grin and left her to wonder how to read his comment. Normally Luther wasn't a man for idle conversation.

It snowed all that night, and school was canceled the next day. In the morning, all four of them, bundled to the eyebrows, crowded into the truck to check out the stock. The dogs rode in the back. By the time they got back to the house for lunch, they were all cold and wet.

"I'll be in shortly," Luther said, as they piled out of the cab. "I want to look for something in the barn."

When Maddy had the pea soup heated up and sandwiches on the table, he still hadn't come in. She was about to ask David to find him when the phone rang. Kenny Sutter, David's best friend, was on the line.

As soon as he'd picked up the receiver in the living room, Maddy looked out the window again. Still no sign of Luther, and she was starting to feel genuine concern. Turning down the burner under the soup, she put on her heavy coat and her gloves.

"I'll be back in a few minutes," she told Chelsea. "Stay here with David."

When Maddy reached the barn, there was no sign of Luther. She called his name, but he didn't respond. Growing more worried by the second, she circled the big pieces of machinery that were stored there and called again.

Thinking she heard a noise, she stopped and listened intently. For a moment, there was silence. Then Luther called out, "I'm over here, in the storage room." His voice sounded terrible, drained of all feeling.

Maddy hurried past the tack room and around the corner to the room George had always meant to clean out. It was full of junk. Inside, a bare bulb on the ceiling glowed dimly, revealing Luther's slumped form seated in a rickety chair, surrounded by dusty old furniture and boxes. His bowed head was in profile as he gazed down at the rusty sled he held on his lap.

Though she was relieved to find him in one piece,

it slowly dawned on Maddy that the possessions stored in this room were things that must have belonged to him and to his family.

She stood in the doorway, reluctant to intrude. "Are you all right?" she asked softly.

At the sound of her voice, Luther raised his head. His face was ravaged by pain and his cheeks were streaked with tears.

Chapter Seven

Luther had never looked less like a hardened criminal.

With a soft cry, Maddy ran over to where he sat slumped in the rickety chair.

"This sled was my son's," he choked, setting it down beside him. "He loved for me to pull him on it."

For once Luther wasn't masking the feelings tearing at him. There in his eyes she could see the pain and the terrible loss. Acting on instinct, Maddy gathered him into her arms. At first he resisted, but then he sighed and leaned against her. How she wished she could take his pain away! He pulled her onto his lap and she cradled his head against her breast. For a long time, they stayed that way, hugging each other tightly as she rocked him and murmured wordless sounds of comfort.

Finally he loosened his desperate hold on her. "I thought if the sled was still here, the kids might enjoy riding it," he said after he had cleared his throat. "I didn't think seeing it would bother me so much."

Maddy could hear the retreat in his voice. He was slapping up those walls she hated as fast as he could. She stayed on his lap and kept her arms around him, doing her best to prevent him from distancing himself from her again.

"What was your son like?" she asked, stroking Luther's black hair. He needed love so desperately. If only he could learn to trust in it—in her—just a little. He stayed quiet for so long she thought he was going to ignore her question. She felt the muscles of his thighs flex beneath her as if he meant to get up and dump her from his lap. Her arms tightened.

"Mark was a terrific kid." Luther's deep voice rumbled against her chest. He kept his head down as he talked. "He was bright and funny, and as curious as a puppy." He fell silent, undoubtedly lost in memories.

Maddy bit back the questions she was dying to ask and let him go at his own speed.

"I didn't spend a lot of time with him, and now I wish I had. Mostly Diane raised him while I took care of the ranch. The important stuff that took up all my time." Luther's voice was heavy with regret. "About the most I'd see him was for a few minutes in the evening before he went to bed."

Maddy wished she could see Luther's face. "You

did what you had to," she said when he didn't continue. "You took care of your family the best way you could." She knew how much time and energy were eaten up trying to run a ranch. A person made choices all the time and prayed they were the right ones. "And you found the time to go sledding with him. I bet you did other things together, too."

"He was only four when he was killed, so we didn't have a lot of time together. And I'd been gone for several months by then." Luther sounded weary, like a man nearly worn out by the burden he carried.

Maddy wished there was some way to comfort him.

"I hope he never knew where I was, or why," Luther muttered.

"Oh, I'm sure he didn't," she exclaimed. "His mother wouldn't have told him something like that when he was too little to really understand."

Luther tipped back his head and looked up at Maddy. Although the moisture on his cheeks had dried, his face was still ravaged by regret.

"Don't bet on it," he said. "You didn't know Diane."

Maddy was having trouble thinking of this woman as Luther's wife, but thinking of her as the mother of his child was at least as difficult for her. Resolutely she thrust aside her own feelings of misguided possessiveness. They were the last thing Luther needed now. "Surely she wouldn't have told him you were in prison for murder."

Luther's jaw was set as if he had braced himself against the pain. "She could have. In the end, she hated me."

His bald words were a shock. "Why would she hate you so much?"

She could feel his hesitation. Silently she willed him to trust her. "I thought you knew...had been told what happened," he began slowly. "I was convicted of killing her lover. From the very beginning, she believed I was guilty."

Stunned, Maddy bowed her head and rubbed her cheek against the top of his head in a gesture of comfort she would have used on Chelsea or even David. "I'm so sorry."

His breath caught. His hand flattened against her back and she became achingly aware of his hard thighs beneath her. What had begun as a desire to comfort him was rapidly changing into something else.

He lifted his head, dark gray eyes wary. Slowly Maddy traced a finger down the faint scar on his cheek. From somewhere outside, a cow bawled, breaking the spell.

As if he had revealed too much of himself, Luther untangled her arms and pushed Maddy gently aside. His expression lacked its usual remoteness, so perhaps she had chipped away a little of the ice. She hoped so.

"We'd better get back to the house," he suggested, reminding her for the first time of her children and the lunch awaiting them. "Afterward, I thought we could take the sled out, have a little fun."

She searched his eyes, but found no ghosts lurking in the shadows she saw there. "Are you sure you want to do that?"

His mouth softened slightly. "I think we could all

use a break,'' he replied in a steady voice as he helped her up and got to his feet. "I think we've earned it."

By the time the four of them got to the rise behind the hay shed, Chelsea, who had been sledding before over at the Sutters' ranch, could barely contain her excitement. Her eyes sparkled as she danced circles around Maddy and she hadn't stopped talking since they had left the house.

"Can I go first?" Chelsea asked Luther, grabbing his gloved hand as they trudged through the snow up the long, gentle rise on the front side of the hill. He was pulling the sled along behind him. "Would you go with me?"

Beneath the wide brim of his black Stetson, his face was ruddy. Maddy wasn't sure if it was the cold or being singled out for Chelsea's attention that had given his cheeks their hearty color. She did know he was pleased by the enthusiasm displayed by both David and her daughter. The suggestion that they go sledding rather than spend the afternoon on chores and schoolwork had been met with whoops and cheers.

Now Maddy hung back and watched the other three. Chelsea was still tugging on Luther's free hand while he pretended to slow down, and David was talking about the school basketball team and their successful season. As they crested the rise, Luther managed to give the impression of listening to both of them at the same time. It was a feat that had taken Maddy years to master.

The thought occurred to her that he was a natural-born parent. It must have broken his heart to lose Mark.

Realizing that Maddy wasn't with them, Luther turned around to see what had happened to her. Her smile, when she caught his eye, almost took his breath away. Instead of returning it, he looked down at Chelsea, who was trying to get his attention.

"Can we, Luther? Can you and me go down first?"

He glanced at David, who shrugged indulgently. "I guess we'd better let her, before she wets her pants or something."

Chelsea let go of Luther and shoved her brother. "I don't wet my pants!" she cried.

"Stop teasing your sister," Maddy scolded as Luther swept the little girl into his arms.

"Don't pay any attention to David," he told her, appalled by the angry tears he saw in the eyes that reminded him so much of Maddy's. "Come on, let's you and me make that first run."

With a shout of agreement and a smug glance at David, Chelsea allowed Luther to seat her on the front of the sled. Then he lowered himself behind her, shoved his hat more firmly on his head and pushed off the back of the hill.

For the next two hours, they took turns hauling the sled up the hill and riding it back down. Since there was room on the sled for only one adult and one child at a time, Chelsea made each trip while the other three took turns accompanying her. Finally, David's stomach rumbled loudly.

"I'm cold," Chelsea announced. "My fingers hurt."

Maddy glanced at Luther. "Time to stop, I think. There are chores to do before supper."

With a nod, he agreed. "Here," he said to David. "You take this." He handed him the sled and turned to Chelsea. "How about a piggyback ride up to the house?"

At her little girl's beaming expression, Maddy had to blink back sudden tears. For a couple of hours, they had been just like any regular family, happy and boisterous.

She sent Luther a grateful smile. He looked a little uncomfortable, as if he wasn't quite sure how to handle her glowing approval. Swallowing the lump in her throat, Maddy grabbed David's hand.

"Cocoa with marshmallows for everyone when we get to the house," she announced. "Last team to get there unloads the dishwasher." She tugged on David's hand and the two of them broke into a clumsy run through the snow.

"No fair!" Luther hollered. "You got a head start."

Glancing over her shoulder, Maddy let out a peal of laughter at his disgruntled expression. With Chelsea bouncing around on his wide shoulders like a miniature jockey, he didn't stand a chance of overtaking them.

Although another snowstorm blew in that evening, it was warm and cozy in the ranch house. Luther didn't have much to say at supper; he was content to listen while Chelsea and David talked almost nonstop. Too often for his own peace of mind, he found himself watching Maddy.

She, too, was quiet, but he caught her eye more than once. Each time he did, she looked quickly away, but he saw her smiling as she did so. Apparently she didn't consider what had almost happened between them too great a calamity. What was driving him crazy was wondering how she felt about what they *hadn't* done.

Was she glad they had stopped or did she feel as tormented as he did? He could tell nothing from her expression and it was driving him nuts.

That night, he stood at the window and looked out. The snow had stopped and the temperature had plummeted. Being outdoors the next day was a brutal reminder of just how difficult ranching could be. Luther tried to spare Maddy from the worst of it, but she insisted on doing what she considered her share.

"If David is going to be in the house with Chelsea all morning, at least send him out with me this afternoon and stay inside yourself," Luther told her as they loaded feed into the back of the truck. "He can help me and you can get your cooking done."

Her eyes sparkled up at him in the clear, cold light and her breath hung in the air like mist. "Afraid we'll end up having peanut butter and jelly sandwiches for supper if I stay outside?" she teased.

He resisted the urge to plant a kiss on her lips before the rugged weather could chap them, but it wasn't easy. He had tossed and turned most of the night and today he was tired. His resistance was dangerously low and he was on his guard.

"I've had worse food," he said gruffly, thinking of the prison meals he had endured for all those years. It had been the lack of choice rather than the lack of quality that wore him down the most. After a while he got used to just eating what they gave him without thinking about it too much.

Somehow it seemed that Maddy understood what having choices meant to him; at least a couple of times a week she asked what he wanted for breakfast or supper the next day. The idea of being able to have a say in what he ate still gave him a huge amount of pleasure.

Now she shot him a sympathetic glance before she bent to heft a heavy bag of feed.

''I'll do that,'' he said automatically. She had told him more than once that working side by side left no room for niceties, but he acted on instinct, and on the manners his mother had tried to instill in him when his father wasn't enforcing them with a hard swat or a chilling comment.

''Tell me about the man you were convicted of killing,'' Maddy said as they left the yard.

Luther was driving and she was sipping coffee from the thermos they had brought. Her question stunned him. Up to now, she had respected his reluctance to talk about himself. She must think he was more willing to share the details with someone he wanted to sleep with.

He meant to tell her he didn't want to discuss it. ''Like I told you, he was having an affair with Diane,'' he heard himself saying instead.

Maddy's expression was sympathetic but she only held on to her coffee with care as they bounced over the frozen ruts in the road.

Luther cleared his throat and glared past the windshield. "She finally admitted it to me. I'd been over to confront him earlier that same day he was killed. We argued and I punched him." Luther could still recall the way he'd felt when he found out about the two of them. He had been mildly suspicious before, but he had expected Diane to deny it, to convince him it wasn't so. Instead she had told him defiantly that Adam understood her. He respected her.

Luther remembered his initial disbelief and then the anger that roared through him. And, underneath both, the pain and the disappointment that he hadn't been enough for her. Had never been enough.

Now he tightened his hands on the wheel. "When the feed-truck driver found Sloan the next morning, it looked as if the place had been robbed. Someone reported seeing my truck around there and they figured I'd set up the robbery to divert suspicion from myself."

"How was he killed?" Maddy asked quietly.

Luther glanced at her. Her face bore none of the avid curiosity for grisly details or the condemnation he had seen so often on the faces of people he'd thought were his friends.

"His skull was crushed. The crowbar they found outside had been wiped clean of prints. After they determined that I had been there that day and they found out about Diane, they didn't bother to look any further for suspects. My bruised knuckles and the marks on his face didn't hurt their case, either."

Luther heard the bitterness in his own voice, remembered his shock when he'd been charged, the gut-wrenching fear and the sense of aloneness when he was convicted—and then remembered the things in prison he hated remembering, but would never forget. Thank God he had been big enough and tough enough to avoid the worst.

"I'm sorry." Maddy's voice brought him back to the present. He almost groaned with relief when he looked around and saw that he was still on the ranch, that getting out hadn't all been a dream.

"Thanks." He didn't look at her again and she didn't ask anymore questions as they stopped in front of the first gate. She hopped out to open it and he watched her, his body tightening when he thought of the way she had looked with her lips swollen from his kisses and her eyes heavy with desire.

Was she merely lonely or did she feel some of the fierce attraction that he felt for her? he wondered. He had failed miserably with Diane, had never been able to open up and share what he was feeling, too afraid that she would laugh or use it against him in some way later.

How was he supposed to warn Maddy away now when he wanted her so badly? Surely keeping his hands off her was more of a sacrifice than one man should be expected to make.

For the next two days, it snowed off and on and once again school was canceled. Maddy's body became bruised from falling on the slippery snow and her joints were stiff from the cold. Despite her gloves, her hands had gotten chapped and cracked. She suspected that David and Luther were just as sore as she was. Chelsea had asked several times if they could go sledding again and David had spent an hour with her one afternoon, but that was all. The adults were too battered and bruised for sledding.

Surprisingly neither the electricity nor the telephone went out. In the evenings, they read, watched old movies on the VCR and played board games, bundled in extra clothing to keep warm, despite the heat from the propane stove. Luther stayed in the living room with them instead of retreating to the basement, but when Maddy asked if it was cold down there, he said no. She didn't press him further, just enjoyed his presence instead.

"It's supposed to warm up tomorrow," she mentioned to him after both David and Chelsea had gone upstairs, the former to listen to tapes on his headphones and the latter to sleep. "There'll be an announcement about school first thing, and we need groceries if the roads aren't too bad."

His gaze was steady on hers. "I have errands in town if you want to give me a list."

Maddy recalled just what one of those errands might be and felt her cheeks begin to heat. "So do I."

He lifted his brows in question. "Sounds like we'd better both go as soon as the stock's fed."

"Mmm." It was an effort to keep her voice calm. What was she going to do if he confronted her with the supplies he'd been lacking the other day? She hadn't decided yet, but she knew she wanted him. And she suspected that he needed from someone the caring and tenderness that went with a closer relationship. Why not from her?

Why not, indeed? He might desire only a warm

body in his bed, but what did she want? And had she a prayer of getting it from him? He had come right out and admitted that the ranch was what he was really after. How far would he go to get it?

"Do you intend to try to buy me out?" she asked him now, shattering the peaceful silence in the living room.

Her question caught him off guard. He studied her for a long moment before he spoke. "If I can."

"The ranch isn't for sale." She couldn't have sold it even if she wanted to. She and the children had nowhere else to go. If she bought a house in town, she would have to find a decent job or the capital would eventually be gone and she would have nothing. Perhaps she could invest in some kind of business. But this ranch had been George's dream. Hers, too. Surely Luther couldn't force her to sell.

"Ranching's a hell of a hard way to make a living," he said. His expression was bleak as he glanced around. "Especially around these parts in the winter."

"But it's a good life, and winter will be over eventually."

"It'll come again."

She shrugged. "I still won't sell."

He glanced away, obviously mulling over her words in his mind. "I won't give up," he said at last.

Unexpected tears threatened Maddy. Blinking them away, she got to her feet. "It sounds as if we're at a standstill then." She glanced at the clock on the wall over the bookcase. "I'm tired. I'll see you in the morning."

As she crossed the room to the foot of the stairs,

she felt his gaze on her back. She wanted to turn around and insist again that she would never sell, but she didn't. Luther was obviously as determined as she, and there seemed to be no answer to their mutual dilemma that would satisfy them both.

That Saturday after chores were done, they all headed to the Blue Moon Ranch. Emma Sutter had invited them to dinner, and then Chelsea and David were going to stay overnight. It had been a while since David had been able to see his best friend, Kenny, except at school, and there were always other children around the Blue Moon for Chelsea to play with.

"I've sure missed you," Emma told Maddy as she climbed down from the truck and gave her friend a hug.

"I've missed you, too." How Maddy wished she could confide in the other woman about the feelings that had been plaguing her almost since Luther had first showed up. At the very least, she was dying to ask Emma what he had been like before prison.

Emma turned to give Chelsea and then David a hug. "Kenny's down at the horse barn with Joe," she said, including Luther in her greeting. "Tell him I want everyone back here for dinner in an hour."

Luther grinned at her. They both had black hair, but there any similarities stopped. Emma was beautiful, and Luther—

As always, Maddy was stunned at the way his face was transformed when he shed his habitual closed expression. Even his scar, almost hidden in one of the grooves formed by his smile, added to his rakish ap-

peal. Laugh lines fanned out from his smoky gray
eyes, and the sensual curve of his mouth made her
stomach lurch in response.

"I'll tell Joe what you said," he replied to Emma.

It was easy to see that being with friends had caused
him to lower his guard, at least slightly. He had been
downright talkative during the ride over, answering
Chelsea's endless questions as he and David debated
whether professional wrestling should be considered a
sport. When Maddy had ventured an opinion, he had
actually winked at her as he sided with David. The
two males agreed that women didn't appreciate the
concept behind competitive matches with predeter-
mined outcomes.

Now Emma directed her attention to Chelsea.
"There's a litter of puppies down at the barn, too, if
you'd like to go along with the guys. And make sure
that Kenny introduces you to Iris. She's almost eight,
but I think you'll like her."

"Okay with you if we go?" David asked Maddy.

"Keep an eye on your sister," she cautioned him,
buoyed by the chance to speak to her friend alone.

"I'll watch out for both of them," Luther volunteered.

Maddy thanked him self-consciously, aware that
Emma was watching her closely.

"What gives between you and Luther?" she asked
when the others were out of earshot and the two
women were inside the Sutters' beautifully decorated
old-style ranch house.

Maddy took the mug of coffee Emma handed her,
feeling color spread over her cheeks as fast as spilled

paint. She knew she couldn't hide her feelings. Not around Emma, whose curiosity stemmed only from kindness and concern.

"Something smells wonderful," Maddy commented, stalling for time as she sniffed appreciatively at the good kitchen aromas.

"It's pot roast," Emma replied impatiently. "I usually don't get much chance to cook except during roundup, but Joe's mother has been visiting friends in Arizona for the past couple of weeks. I get to play in the kitchen while she's gone and then she'll be back to take over before I get really tired of it." A slight frown marred Emma's smooth brow. "Now quit trying to distract me," she scolded. "What gives?"

"Am I that easy to read?" Maddy asked before biting into one of Emma's home-baked macadamia nut brownies. What if Luther had also seen the feelings she tried so hard to hide? It was enough that she had thrown herself at him on more than one occasion. Must he know that her emotions were involved as well as her hormones?

Emma reached across the scarred kitchen table and patted Maddy's hand as she played with the handle of her mug. "Not everyone knows you as well as I do," Emma said lightly. "Besides, I could feel the tension between the two of you out there." She gestured toward the window.

"You could?"

Emma's blue eyes danced with gentle laughter as she pushed a hand through her black curls. Then her expression sobered. "Luther's had a terrible time of it, but beneath all that male pride, he's a good man."

"Did you know his wife?" Maddy asked, curiosity eating her alive.

Emma made a face. "Not well. Joe knew Luther from cattlemen's association meetings, and he always felt that Luther had gotten treated very unfairly when Adam Sloan was killed." She hesitated, looking down at her hands. "Did Luther tell you that his wife and Adam were involved?"

Guilt assailed Maddy at discussing his private affairs. He would hate it if he knew. Then her concern for him superceded her guilt. Her curiosity wasn't idle; she wanted to understand him better. "He mentioned it," she said in reply to Emma's question. "His wife's affair must have been a terrible blow."

Emma took a sip of her coffee. "I'm sure it was. From what I could tell, he and Diane weren't very well matched anyway. Luther's so quiet, so self-contained, and she was just the opposite."

"How do you mean?" Maddy asked. Apparently prison hadn't changed him that much after all.

"Joe knew Diane from school, and he told me that she always wanted to be on the go. You know how hard it is to run a ranch, even with help. If Luther's anything like Joe, he probably wanted to stay home in the evenings. Diane seemed to need other people. We ran into them several times at dances and parties, and we don't go out that much. Diane would be out on the floor with anyone who asked, while Luther sat on the sidelines and watched."

Maddy remembered the brief moments she had been in Luther's arms. She wondered why he hadn't danced more with Diane himself. And why hadn't his wife preferred him as a partner over anyone else? Maddy would.

She was getting in too deep. As she stared into her coffee mug, she shook her head slowly. "Having different personalities is no reason to get involved with someone else. Or to abandon your husband when he needs you the most." She swallowed, recalling how Luther had told her Diane believed he was guilty, right from the beginning. "Or to sell his ranch out from under him when he can't stop you."

"Or to take his son away," Emma added softly. "It was such a tragedy, after everything else he went through, when we heard that both Diane and his little boy had been killed on the way to Denver."

Maddy was silent, wondering how much a man could take, and whether Luther would ever be able to move beyond the pain and be whole again. And be able to trust. *Not without a lot of love,* she thought. Whether he realized it or not.

"You just be careful, okay?" Emma said quietly. "Luther must have scars that neither you nor I can even begin to guess at. And he's got a lot to overcome around here, even though he was cleared. Some folks aren't that eager to admit they were wrong about him, and they'll turn against him before they'll own up to their mistakes."

"I know," Maddy replied, remembering the way the clerk at the co-op had acted. "But Luther shouldn't have to keep dealing with what's in the past."

Emma shrugged. "That's human nature for you. I just don't want you taking him on as some kind of project and ending up getting hurt yourself. You have your own losses to deal with.''

"I know. I'll be careful." Even as she said the words, Maddy wondered if she had any intention of following them. There was such a need in Luther that it was hard for her to even think about turning away.

Emma glanced at the wall clock and scraped back her chair. "I guess I'd better see to dinner, since I made such a big deal about everyone getting back in on time."

Maddy looked up. "What can I do to help?"

A warm smile flashed across Emma's face. "Glad you asked me that."

The noisy bunch of children, including the girl, Iris, and her older brother, Jay, who were staying at Joe's ranch while their father, a single parent, was in the hospital recuperating from a car accident, surged on ahead. Joe and Luther followed at a slower pace.

"I'm sorry I never answered your letters," Luther said gruffly. "I mean, while I was away."

Joe made a dismissive gesture with his gloved hand. "That's okay. I can't pretend to know what you were going through."

"I was going through hell," Luther replied baldly. "But that's all behind me now."

"I was real sorry to hear about your boy," Joe said as they trudged along, their booted feet crunching in the snow. "And your wife."

Luther shot him a sidewise glance. "Thanks." His breath made puffs in the cold air. Except for the excited shouts of the kids pulling farther and farther ahead of them and the occasional lowing of the cattle in the distance, they were surrounded by a wall of quiet. Luther took a deep breath, unable to picture any other way of life besides ranching.

"Kenny's getting to be quite a boy," he commented, both to divert his own thoughts and to redirect Joe's attention away from himself.

"We're real proud of him."

Luther remembered vaguely that Kenny had been adopted by the Sutters shortly after they were married. "I see you're still taking in strays," he said, gesturing toward the group that was cutting across the yard.

Joe tugged at the brim of his light blue Stetson. "We both like having kids around," he said.

They walked on in companionable silence.

"How are you and Maddy getting along?" Joe asked as they reached the edge of the lawn surrounding the old house.

Luther kept his gaze straight ahead and began walking a little faster. He still felt like a fool for breaking down in front of her when he had first found Mark's sled. She had caught him crying like a baby and all she had done was hold him as if he were one of her own kids. Since then, she'd been acting as if it had never happened, so maybe she didn't think less of him for blubbering the way he had. The memory still made him uncomfortable.

"Maddy and I get along okay, I guess," he told Joe as they paused by the back porch.

"Maddy's a fine woman," the tall rancher said as he looked up at the roof. Smoke poured from the chimney, almost the same color as the pale sky.

"She's had a hard time, but she's strong and warm-hearted, despite everything that's happened."

Luther clamped his hands on his hips and gave Joe an exasperated glance. "Something you're trying to say?"

Joe was grinning from ear to ear, clearly unaffected by Luther's annoyance. "Just making an observation," he said. "She's pretty, too."

Luther made a sweeping gesture with one hand. "Yeah, and she's sexy and she smells good," he blurted without thinking, fed up with Joe's meddling. "So, what's your point?"

Joe's grin widened even more and he took the porch steps two at a time. "Just wanted to make sure you noticed," he said over his shoulder.

With a shout of laughter, he ducked inside as the snowball Luther hurled at him smashed harmlessly against the screen door.

Chapter Eight

By the time Maddy and Luther had driven home from the Sutters' ranch, changed clothes and finished up the chores, it was full dark. She still had the dogs to feed and beans to soak for dinner the next day. She wasn't really tired, but strain over the night ahead had shaped a headache behind her eyes.

Ever since they had bidden Emma and Joe goodbye, Luther had been his usual taciturn self. Could he be thinking about their spending the night alone together in the house, too?

Maddy hung up her coat and went into the kitchen. Did he wonder how she felt about the situation? She wished she knew.

She found Luther devastatingly attractive. She could have admired his hard weathered face for hours, and she enjoyed watching the way he moved. Even his loose-hipped walk was fascinating. Sometimes she caught herself trying to imagine his big male body without its bulky layers of clothing. Her own response to his powerful masculinity was like nothing she had ever felt, not even for her own husband.

Of course, Luther had already admitted that he wanted the ranch. Would he be willing to seduce her in order to up his chances of getting it?

The possibility was so distasteful that it made her shudder. And what of her own feelings? Even if the ranch wasn't part of the equation, would one stolen night of passion be worth the pain she might suffer later? Could she continue to work side by side with him and face him across the kitchen table if they slept together and it didn't work out? Or even if it did? How would an affair between them affect David and Chelsea? They already liked Luther; what if they came to love him—or Maddy did—and then he moved on?

It was all so complicated. Her head throbbed dully and she rubbed at her aching temple as she closed her eyes against the bright light of the kitchen.

Luther had followed her through the back door and was in the mudroom hanging up his jacket and hat. As the silence in the house closed in around her, Maddy caught herself staring hungrily at his broad back. He was so overwhelmingly masculine. Shaken, she turned away.

"Do you want a couple of sandwiches?" she asked. Her voice sounded loud in her own ears, but he didn't seem to notice.

"Thanks, but I can make my own sandwiches." His reply surprised her. "Want me to throw a couple together for you while you take something for that headache?''

"How do you know about my headache?" she asked.

The hard line of his mouth softened for a moment. "I'm not blind."

Headache or not, Maddy wasn't used to having a man volunteer to do anything in the kitchen unless it was unstopping a sink or eating the food she'd prepared. George had never done any cooking, not even when she had Chelsea. Many times, the two of them had worked side by side all day, and then she had fixed a meal while he'd read the newspaper. She had never thought to resent it until now.

Luther cleared his throat impatiently. "Well? Do you want a sandwich or not?"

Maddy was no fool and a little food might make her feel better. "That would be nice," she replied. "I'll fix the coffee as soon as I've had some aspirin."

"Anyone would think you had something against my coffee," he drawled. There was a light in his eyes and one corner of his mouth was hitched up.

"You can make it if you want." She barely succeeded in keeping her own face noncommittal, since she knew that he didn't like his own coffee, either.

Luther wasn't sure if she was teasing him or not, but he wasn't about to take any chances when it came to the choice between a dark, aromatic brew and burned, bitter sludge. "No, no, you go ahead." He gave her what he hoped was a look of encouragement before he started making the sandwiches.

He was gratified to see her smile as she got the

aspirin out of the cupboard. He knew he had been less than friendly since they had left Joe's earlier, but the only thing he had been able to think about was the long night that stretched ahead of them. Ever since Emma had invited both Chelsea and David to stay over, his mind had bounced back and forth between wondering what Maddy was thinking and reviewing all the reasons why he should leave her strictly alone and forget about the condoms he'd bought in a weak moment.

He smeared mustard on the bread and dealt out slices of lunch meat like playing cards. Wanting her was tearing him apart. Ever since he had kissed her, he had known that kissing her again was guaranteed, like death and taxes. Like more snow before spring. Like anything between them ending in crash-and-burn disaster.

He stacked lettuce leaves on the open sandwiches while Maddy got out coffee mugs and plates. It was easy to convince himself that he had a right to the ranch; it had been taken and sold without his consent. But he had no rights at all when it came to Maddy, and at this moment, he wanted her more than anything else, even the damned land.

The realization shocked him. With the big knife, he chopped through each sandwich, so aware of her that he barely missed severing a finger.

When they worked outside, she was always so bundled up against the cold that she appeared shapeless. He knew better. Now he swallowed, and a silent curse danced through his mind. Who was he trying to kid? He hadn't a prayer of staying away from her.

Dumping the sandwiches onto two plates, he put them on the table and sat down. Maddy poured their coffee.

"Want some chips?" she asked, pulling a bag from the pantry.

He shook his head and took a bite from his sandwich without waiting for her to join him. By the time she did, he was half-done.

"Okay if I take a shower?" he asked as she sipped her coffee.

"Of course. You don't have to ask."

"I'm going to town." He told himself it wasn't disappointment he saw flash across her face; it was relief. "I haven't been anywhere since I got back. 'Bout time I checked out a couple of the local watering holes."

Her recovery was almost immediate. She smiled brightly, but the way her hand trembled when she set down her mug convinced him he was doing the right thing. He planned to get very drunk and then spend the rest of the night in his truck. With a couple of extra blankets, he might not even freeze to death. When he didn't show up until morning, Maddy would draw her own conclusions. She wasn't the kind of woman who would crawl in bed with him after she thought he'd been with someone else.

The announcement that he was going to town made Maddy feel like a fool. All her mental hand-wringing over whether she would sleep with him if he asked, and he wasn't even going to be here.

"Sounds like a good idea," she said before she bit into her sandwich. It stuck to the roof of her mouth like damp cotton.

They finished their meal in silence. She was still forcing down the rest of hers when he pushed back his chair, grabbed his dishes and got to his feet. "Want some more coffee?"

She shook her head. "Thanks, no."

"What are you going to do tonight?" he asked, catching her off guard.

Wonder who you're with, she thought grimly. "Maybe I'll take advantage of the solitude and have a long bath and an early night." She was proud of her quick answer. Actually, a bath did sound good. It was something she rarely indulged in, and Chelsea had given her some scented oil for Christmas that she hadn't even opened. Perhaps she'd paint her toenails while she was at it.

"How's your headache?" His intense gaze made her want to squirm in her chair as he towered over her.

Fighting down the impulse to ask him to stay with her, she realized that her headache had disappeared. "It's gone. I guess the sandwich helped."

"Good."

After he left the room, she breathed a sigh of relief. Another minute and she wouldn't have given a fig for his possible motives; she would have been begging him not to leave. When he came back up the basement stairs a little while later, Maddy was in the living room with her feet up. She was looking at a magazine, waiting for the house to be empty so she could go upstairs and take her bath in peace.

"I'll see you later," he said as he walked into the room.

The sight of him made her eyes widen. Even his shaggy hair, in need of a trim, didn't detract from his rugged male appeal. He had on snug, dark jeans and a leather vest over the black flannel shirt he'd bought at the co-op. All he needed to complete the picture was his Stetson and a pistol strapped to his hip.

Maddy itched to run her hands over the width of his shoulders and down the smooth leather covering his chest, to touch her mouth to his and feel the firm heat of his lips. Instead, she stayed where she was and managed a casual smile. "Have a good time."

Still, he hesitated. "You be okay alone?"

It was a struggle to answer. "I'll be fine." She stared down at the magazine again and held her breath until she heard him walk away. The back door shut, his truck fired up and then the sound of the engine faded to nothingness before she trusted herself to move. It was humiliating to realize how hard she had been hoping for him to turn around and come back.

Come back and do what? She had no answer.

Hours later, she still had no answer as she lay in bed, wide-awake, with her ears straining for the sound of a returning truck. The night crawled by as she tossed and turned, fighting to keep her mind blank. What time did the taverns close? She didn't know.

She peered at the clock on the nightstand. Perhaps he had found a willing companion and gone home with her. The sharp pain in Maddy's chest made her gasp and sit up in bed as the sheet slipped down the silky fabric of her nightgown. The black lace made her feel a little foolish, but it had seemed like the right thing to put on after the bubble bath. Besides, there was always her electric blanket if she got cold.

The soft growl of an engine captured her attention. She listened hard until she was certain it was Luther's truck. Another minute passed before she heard the engine quit and the back door open and close, a few more until the bathroom pipes rattled. She heard his footsteps on the basement stairs and the house fell silent once again.

Too tired to dissect the feeling of relief that he was home, Maddy lay back down and pulled up the covers. What had she expected? That he would come in and wish her good-night? That he would sit casually on the edge of the bed and tell her about his evening?

She was so busy reminding herself it was better this way that she almost missed the sound of his footsteps until they came down the hallway to her room. Light showed beneath her door. She sat up again and the covers slid to her waist. Before she could grab them or reach for the lamp, her door swung open. Luther stood silhouetted in the light from the hallway, still wearing his hat.

"What do you want?" Maddy squeaked as she grabbed for the covers. She wished she could make out his expression, but his face was in shadow.

"I tried, Maddy, I really did." His voice was soft but it wasn't slurred as she might have expected. If anything, he sounded tired, even resigned.

Before she could ask what he meant about trying, he came into the room, tossed aside his hat and sank to his knees by the side of her bed. He smelled of smoke and whiskey and spicy after-shave. The glow from the hall light hit one side of his face, revealing his tense features and the rigid set to his jaw.

"Are you all right?" she asked.

His laugh was humorless. "I tried to get drunk. I tried to find a woman. I tried to stay away from you." As he recited the litany, his voice roughened and he anchored one arm across her. His hand clasped her hip, swaddled by the bedclothes. "And I didn't succeed at one damn thing."

Maddy swallowed, not sure what to say. "Sounds like you had a pretty full evening." It was hard to believe that he was really here. She hadn't expected him back until morning, unless the women of Caulder Springs had all gone blind. Even now, in the half-light from the hall, he was breathtaking.

"Actually, it was a pretty empty evening," he contradicted, arm tightening.

Maddy knew he could see her even though his own eyes remained in shadow. She let go of her death grip on the sheet and touched his arm.

"Is that why you came back? Because you couldn't find what you wanted in town?" she asked quietly, needing to know.

He shook his head and she saw a muscle jump in his cheek. "I went to town knowing that what I wanted was right here."

"The ranch?" she asked.

He lowered his head for a moment. She heard him sigh. "I won't lie to you," he said when he looked up. "But I swear the ranch is the last thing on my mind tonight."

Maddy stroked his arm, longing to believe him.

Wondering if he thought the black nightie with the tiny straps and the lace trim was for him. Realizing it was.

"Do you want me to go?" he demanded. "Or do you want me to stay? I'll do whatever you say, but you have to tell me now or it will be too late."

She wanted him so badly that her voice failed her.

He must have misinterpreted her silence because she felt him start to pull away, felt the muscles of his forearm flex beneath her hand.

"No," she cried softly, but he released her and got to his feet.

"I'll just go back downstairs," he said, taking a step away from the bed. "Maybe you can forget I ever came up here."

Terrified now that he really would leave, Maddy threw aside the covers and scrambled to her knees. "No!" she cried again. "Don't go." She grabbed the lapels of his vest and tried to pull him back down with her.

Luther went rigid, so she slid her arms around his neck and pressed herself wantonly against him. Heat radiated from his body and she started to melt. He took her arms and held her away from him while he searched her face. Trembling with desire, she fought to keep her gaze steady even though her head threatened to loll back on her neck, like a flower on a broken stem.

"Are you sure?" he rasped. "If I stay, I want more than kisses." She saw a swallow contract the muscles of his throat. "And I can't promise to be gentle."

His confession made ribbons of longing twist hotly

inside her. "I want more than kisses, too," she whispered, leaning back so her lower body pressed more boldly against his. "And I don't want you to be gentle."

He was fully aroused. At the intimate contact with her, he released a hiss of reaction. "You better be sure. Another five seconds and you couldn't run me out of here with a posse of armed men." Humor softened his tone. "Not that I want an audience. I've been thinking about being alone with you since Emma Sutter first called."

"Then why did you leave?" Maddy wailed, still hurt by his earlier abandonment.

"Trying to do the right thing. I should have saved us both the trouble."

She didn't ask what he meant, just reached up and planted a kiss on the side of his jaw. Immediately he bent his head, his breath hot as his mouth found hers. One rough hand slid up her body and cupped her breast.

"This is pretty," he said, tracing the lace trim at the top of the nightie. Before Maddy could thank him, he was smoothing the flimsy straps off her shoulders and replacing them with wet, openmouthed kisses.

Shivering with pleasure, she tunneled her fingers into his hair and held him close. At her touch, he went still.

"Damn," he growled as she wondered if she had done something wrong. "I knew you'd shoot my control all to hell."

He lifted his head again and kissed her passionately, insistently, irresistibly. She touched her tongue against his and a hard shudder went through him. A feeling of feminine exultation made her heart soar as he coaxed her mouth open wider. Then she was lost in the wet heat of his kiss.

Before she could recover, he released her and got to his feet.

"Where are you going?" she cried.

"Nowhere." He shut the door, stripped away his shirt and yanked off his boots.

When he came back and pulled her down with him, her hands reached for him eagerly. His skin was hot to her touch. As she traced the muscles of his chest and rubbed the soft hair with her fingers, he sighed with pleasure. She hadn't gotten nearly enough of touching him when he slid one big hand up her bare leg beneath her nightie and spread it across her stomach.

"You've got skin like satin," he breathed as he bent his head to kiss her again. Then he reached for the hem of her nightgown and pulled it over her head. He leaned over her until her bare breasts were cradled against his chest, and then he moved slowly across her so his skin abraded her nipples. They hardened immediately as he pulled her closer. Maddy took the opportunity to get her hands on his broad back. To her dismay, he stiffened and drew slightly away.

"What's wrong?" she demanded.

He looked down at her in the near darkness of the room. "You touch me as if you enjoy it," he said wonderingly.

"I do," she replied, surprised. "I love touching you."

"Ah, Maddy," he sighed. "You don't know how good you make me feel." Before she could say anything else, he bent his head to her breast. At the touch of his lips on her distended nipple, she moaned and arched her back. Flames shot through her body and moist heat pooled between her legs. As if he knew exactly what she was feeling, Luther skimmed one hand up the inside of her thigh and touched her intimately. At the same time, he plunged his tongue deep into her mouth.

As new sensations poured through her, Maddy's hands found the fastening of his jeans, but she was too overwhelmed by everything she was feeling to manage the snaps. Instead she caressed his hard length through the heavy denim.

Luther pushed himself against her hand and groaned. Then, breathing hard, he rolled away from her and shucked off the rest of his clothing.

"Good thing I got to town the other day," he growled as he fumbled with a small packet. Even as Maddy reached eagerly for him, he stroked her again with his fingers and delved into her liquid heat. When she moaned and shifted restlessly, he settled himself between her thighs.

"I'm sorry I couldn't wait any longer," he whispered as his arousal nudged her. "I'll make it up to you next time."

"No, please, don't wait." As he filled her, Maddy's last rational thought was to wonder how it could possibly get any better than this. She wrapped her legs around his hips and held him tight with her arms. As he began to move inside her, faster and faster, she crested with a speed that was breathtaking. As soon as he felt her contractions, his hands tightened on her hips and he slammed into her, deeper and harder than ever. Almost immediately, she felt his climax shudder through him, and reveled in his ragged groan of pleasure. When he finally collapsed against her, she hugged him close. Her heart raced. After a moment, he shifted onto his side, still anchoring her next to him.

"Lady, you're unbelievable," he murmured.

Maddy snuggled closer yet as a kind of dreamy peace drifted over her. When their breathing finally slowed to a more normal pace, he began tracing an intricate pattern down her back with his fingers. When he touched the sensitive skin of her hip, she shivered.

"Mmm, don't start something you can't finish," she teased softly.

His answering laugh filled her with quiet happiness. "I promised you better," he breathed in her ear. "But I can't imagine it getting much better than it just was."

His words warmed her, soothing the lingering doubt that he might still use her as a means to an end. Surely she hadn't been the only one to feel that special bonding, that moment of unison. "Me, too," she whispered as she raised her head to kiss him.

In moments, she was again transported by the intimate spell he wove around the two of them so capably, so lovingly. For a silent, withdrawn man who seemed to know little about trust, the gentleness and generosity he showed her warmed Maddy's heart.

The first time they had joined, he'd overwhelmed

her with hunger and need. This time, in the midst of their shared passion, he wooed her with a glimpse of his own lonely soul.

When Maddy drove home from church the next morning with Chelsea and David, it was a good thing the two kids were talking nonstop about what a fantastic visit they'd had at the Sutters'. Maddy would have had a hard time holding up her end of a rational conversation. For once her attention wasn't on her children.

Luther had wakened her that morning before the alarm went off. They'd started out slowly, but almost immediately the passion between them had flared out of control and swept them along with an almost savage intensity. Afterward, she had been shocked to notice a dark bruise on his jaw, but all he would tell her was that he had gotten into a disagreement with someone in the bar the night before.

Reluctant to ask more questions, she had settled on pressing a light kiss to the discoloration. After she did, Luther had studied her for a long moment, fingers sifting gently through her hair, before he climbed out of bed gloriously nude. Without another word, he had scooped up his clothing and left her gaping at the sheer male beauty of his powerful body.

She had hoped he might accompany her to church this morning after the chores were done, but she accepted his refusal without an argument. If he had been with her, she wouldn't have heard a word of the service anyway.

After she had changed into her purple dress and come downstairs, the shower was running. She resisted the temptation to poke her head in the bathroom and tell him she was leaving, but she hated missing the chance for one last private moment. Before she could leave the house, however, he had come out of the bathroom with only a towel knotted at one lean hip.

After she stared at his shoulders and chest in mute appreciation, he kissed her soundly and actually winked before he padded back to the bathroom.

The man was full of surprises. Now, as she struggled to follow her children's comments, she couldn't help but wonder where this new development between her and Luther would lead.

"Iris is so cool," Chelsea said for the half-dozenth time. "She's already had two boyfriends, and she was the goalie on her soccer team." She barely paused for breath. "Did Tiger miss me?"

"Yes, he sure did," Maddy replied absently.

"Kenny and Jay and I played games on Kenny's dad's computer," David said. "Kenny's had lots more practice, but I beat him three times straight. Then his mom made popcorn and we watched a movie on TV."

"Good for you, honey." What was Luther doing now? Was he thinking about her? About last night? Would he be there when they got back? How would he act toward her?

"We watched *Aladdin*." Chelsea snuggled closer to Maddy, who smiled into her daughter's eyes. "While they were playing their dumb old computer games." She motioned toward David. "Emma let us stay up really late."

"Yeah, late for little kids," he teased.

"Almost as late as you," she retorted.

"Did either of you get any sleep?" Maddy asked, turning into the driveway of the Double C.

"Some," David replied.

Chelsea only giggled. "Not much."

Glancing in her mirror, Maddy saw a sheriff's car slow and follow her onto her road. Puzzled, she braked and rolled down her window. Charlie Horton, one of the deputies, got out of his car and walked up to hers. He was wearing his hat and a heavy tan jacket with the official county insignia on the pocket flap.

"How are you?" Maddy asked, smiling up at him. Charlie and his wife belonged to her church, although she hadn't seen either of them there this morning.

Charlie touched his hand to his hat brim. "Morning, Maddy. Hi, kids." He didn't return her smile, and a little shiver of apprehension worked its way down her spine. She hoped that nothing was wrong.

"What can I do for you?" she asked.

Charlie frowned. "Actually it's Luther Ward I need to talk to." He squinted as he looked down her road. "Do you know if he's home?"

Heat washed over Maddy as she remembered how Luther had looked first thing that morning, rumpled and unshaven. Despite the shadow of dark whiskers, the bruise on his chin stood out clearly. Could Charlie be here about that?

Had someone pressed charges?

"He was here when I left for church," she admitted cautiously. "Why do you want to see him?"

"I'd rather discuss that with Luther." Before Maddy could think of anything else to say, Charlie went back to his patrol car. She had no choice but to put the truck in gear and lead the way to the house.

"What's Luther done?" David asked.

"I don't know any more about it than you do," Maddy replied, anxiety swirling in her stomach like a flock of magpies. She resisted the urge to push the accelerator to the floor and race ahead to warn him. "I'm sure it's just a misunderstanding."

"Will he have to go back to jail?" Chelsea asked tearfully. "I don't want him to leave."

"Neither do I," Maddy admitted. "He's a big help around the ranch and I don't know how we could manage without him."

A single tear slid down Chelsea's cheek.

"I'm sure it won't come to that," Maddy said firmly. More images from the night before danced across her consciousness and she fought to maintain her composure.

Luther must have noticed Charlie's car following hers. When she pulled into the yard and stopped, he was waiting with his hands on his hips and a dog on either side of him. His hat was pulled low over his eyes and his body was braced for trouble. Who had he gotten into the fight with and why? Surely Luther wouldn't have been foolish enough to really hurt someone? Not after all he had already been through?

"David, take Chelsea inside," Maddy instructed as soon as they had all piled out of the truck. They both started to argue, but she gave them a quelling look. "Do it." Something in her tone must have gotten through to David, who took Chelsea's hand and shot

Luther a worried frown. The boy's shoulders drooped as he led his sister to the house.

"It'll be okay," she reassured them, praying she was right.

"Aren't you coming?" David asked.

She shook her head, determined to give Luther whatever support she could.

Silently the three adults waited until the back door had shut before Luther and Charlie squared off. Their stances reminded Maddy of an Old West shoot-out. Swallowing nervously, she moved closer to Luther. Charlie's eyebrows rose and Luther turned to glare at her.

"Don't you have something else to do?" he demanded.

"No." Returning his stare with a defiant one of her own, she thought she saw a glimmer of appreciation in his gaze. Then he turned his attention to Charlie.

"So, what can I do for you?"

Charlie must have realized Maddy had no intention of leaving. "There was a break-in at the Dykstra place last night," he began.

"What does that have to do with Luther?" Maddy demanded, bristling. "He was cleared of everything from before."

"It's okay," Luther told her. "Don't be upset."

"Of course I'm upset," Maddy replied impatiently. "Are you questioning all the ranch hands?" she asked Charlie, "or just mine?"

Charlie looked uncomfortable. "It's the sheriff's idea," he said. "I know Luther's been cleared, but this burglary had the same MO as the one where Adam

Sloan was killed. I'm just going around asking a few questions.''

He made his visit sound so casual, almost random, but Maddy realized the sheriff must not believe the confession that had cleared Luther or Charlie wouldn't be here. Was Luther going to be questioned about every petty crime committed in Washington County?

"Would you mind telling me where you were between seven yesterday evening and 2:00 a.m.?" Charlie asked him.

"You don't have to answer," Maddy cut in. "You were cleared. If the sheriff can't accept that, it's his problem.''

"If you won't talk to me here, I'll have to take you in for questioning," Charlie warned him. "It's up to you." His hand shifted to the butt of his gun and Maddy glared.

"I don't mind talking to you." Luther's color was high; he must find this whole thing humiliating after everything he had already been through.

Maddy couldn't resist a snort of disgust. Both men frowned at her.

"I went into town last night," Luther said. "I had a few beers at Smitty's and then I went to The Watering Hole.''

"What time did you leave here?" Charlie asked.

Luther thought for a moment and then looked at Maddy. "Around eight?" he ventured. "I didn't pay much attention.''

She nibbled at her lip, trying to remember. "I guess. I really didn't notice, either." She gave him an apologetic glance. Some alibi.

"Could it have been earlier?" Charlie asked as he wrote in his notebook.

Luther shrugged. "I suppose."

Maddy remained silent. She hadn't glanced at the clock until after nine, and she had no idea how much time had crawled past by then. All she knew was it barely seemed to move at all until Luther finally got back.

"How'd you get that bruise?" Charlie asked, pointing to Luther's jaw.

"Had a disagreement with a guy at Smitty's—Duane Snyder."

Maddy knew Duane. His ranch bordered hers on the short side and he had come around to see her a few times after George died. She hadn't trusted his motives and took no pains to hide her feelings.

Charlie nodded and kept writing. "What about?"

Luther hesitated. "Nothing much."

When he didn't add anything, Charlie asked him for a list of people who might remember seeing him at both taverns. Then he asked when Luther had gotten back to the ranch. He and Maddy both knew the answer to that, but she stayed quiet, only nodding curtly when Charlie glanced at her for confirmation. Finally he shut his notebook with a faint slap and put it back into his pocket.

Ordinarily she would have invited him in for a cup of coffee. Today she didn't.

Luther's face was carefully blank. "That all?" he asked Charlie. "I have chores to do."

The deputy had the grace to look uncomfortable.

"Sorry about all this," he said as he zipped up his heavy jacket. "It's just routine."

"Was anyone hurt at the Dykstras'?" Maddy thought to ask.

"No one was home. A few things were taken. Some jars of peaches and a bag of sugar were broken and scattered around the kitchen. It made quite a mess." He raised his hand to his hat brim. "Well, I'll be going," he said. "Again, I'm sorry to trouble you." He gave Luther a sharp glance, but Luther only stared impassively.

"I didn't see your wife at church this morning," Maddy told Charlie in an attempt to lessen the awkwardness. "I hope she's feeling okay."

He gave her a grateful smile. "She's fine. Actually, she and the kids are visiting her folks in Golden for the weekend, but I expect them back this evening."

"Tell her hello for me," Maddy said as she walked him to his car.

Before he got in, Charlie waved to Luther, who merely nodded, and apologized again to Maddy for bothering them.

After he drove off, she turned back to see how Luther was doing, but he was nowhere in sight. Before she could go and look for him, David and Chelsea spilled out the back door.

"What happened?" David asked.

"Is Luther going to be arrested?" Chelsea cried.

Luther was in the bunkhouse ripping up the floorboards that had been damaged by the water from the broken pipe when his prison-honed instincts warned him he was no longer alone. He straightened and looked over his shoulder, expecting to see David. Instead it was Maddy who stood watching him with a worried expression on her face.

"Are you okay?" she asked.

Luther emitted a bark of laughter. "I bet you never had the police coming around in their official capacity to question one of your employees before," he said bitterly. "All part of being involved with an ex-con, though, so you might as well get used to it as long as I'm around." He pried another board loose with the crowbar and tossed it onto a growing pile of rubble.

Maddy circled around so that she was in his line of vision. "I don't have the money for new lumber right now," she said, indicating the bunkhouse floor. "This will have to wait, you know."

"I know." Furious with her and with himself, Luther was about to toss down the crowbar when he remembered that one similar to it had been the weapon of choice in Adam Sloan's murder. With an oath, he hurled the crowbar across the room, where it hit the wall with a gratifying crash.

Maddy flinched. Then, to his surprise, she came right up to him and stroked his chest. Wasn't the fool woman afraid of anything?

"What do you want?" he growled, twisting away.

"I want you to kiss me."

He almost said something nasty and hurtful, but then he caught the expression on her face. She looked upset. Her concern was for him, he realized slowly, all for him with no thought for her own safety. With a groan, he pulled her into his arms and buried his face in her hair.

"God, I'm sorry," he whispered raggedly.

She shook her head, bumping his nose. "Don't be sorry. None of it was your fault. Can't that stupid sheriff accept reality?"

Luther rubbed his face against her sweet-smelling curls and then he made himself let her go. "He just hates admitting that he was wrong. He'd rather believe that the poor bastard who confessed was coerced or something, I guess. No matter, though. You shouldn't have to—"

"Don't worry about me," she said sharply. "I'm okay. It's you I'm worried about."

He set her away from him and grinned at her. "Then I guess I'm okay, too," he told her, startled to realize that it was true. At least for now. The way that Maddy was looking at him, it would be easy to believe that no one could hurt him as long as she was around.

"Honey, you're amazing." A shiver of longing went through him, a longing to belong somewhere and to have someone who would always have the faith in him that Maddy seemed to have now.

With a sigh, he took her in his arms and bent his head to hers. A little voice at the back of his mind asked just how long he expected a good woman like Maddy to believe in a man like him, but he did his best to shut it out as he buried himself in the sweetness of her kiss.

Chapter Nine

"I'll be happy when it warms up a little," Maddy said as she stared out the kitchen window at the icicles hanging from the eaves. Another storm had blown in last night, dumping several inches of snow on the frozen ground. It made walking even more treacherous, and she was glad Luther had driven Chelsea and David out to the bus stop.

"Getting sick of winter yet?" Luther asked now as he tossed his denim jacket over a kitchen chair and helped himself to more coffee.

"I was sick of winter before Christmas," she replied, wiping her hands on a kitchen towel and applying a squirt of lotion to her hands. Keeping them soft in this weather was futile, but she kept trying.

As she worked the lotion between her fingers, she glanced at Luther. He was watching her, narrow-eyed.

It was the first time they had been alone together since he had kissed her in the bunkhouse. If her appearance in heavy wool pants roomy enough to fit over her thermal underwear and thick, shapeless yellow-and-black-striped sweater was giving him lustful thoughts, he hid them well behind the impenetrable wall of his gaze.

A sudden burst of self-consciousness made her glance away. "I'm ready to go if you are."

"Not just yet." He set down his cup and came closer, trapping her against the counter. Bracing his hands on either side of her, he bent his head and touched his mouth to hers. The kiss was light, almost fleeting. Maddy barely swallowed a protest when he buried his face in the side of her neck. He wrapped his arms around her in a gentle hug.

For several moments, she stood motionless in his embrace. She was beginning to think physical closeness was almost as important to him as making love. Then he lifted his head and his burning gaze strayed to her mouth.

"Any reason I shouldn't tote you upstairs?" he asked thickly. "School bus won't be back for hours."

Maddy struggled against the nearly unbearable temptation to be with him again. Already her blood was pulsing thickly through her like hot, sweet syrup.

"I can think of more than a hundred reasons why we can't," she said reluctantly. "It might be hard to concentrate with all that bawling going on so close to the house."

"Nothing's going to interrupt my concentration." His deep voice sent tendrils of desire curling through her. Then his chest expanded on a sigh. "I guess you're right, though.'' He leaned over and kissed her again, exploring her mouth with leisurely expertise. By the time he let her go, breathing took an effort.

"Come on," he drawled as she was about to reconsider the whole thing. His eyes were as soft as smoke. "Duty calls."

Luther didn't have much to say as they hauled feed and checked water tanks for ice, but he felt a pleasant glow each time Maddy's gaze met his. Her cheeks were ruddy from the wind, which blew the snow into huge drifts, and yet her eyes reminded him of summer. Even the bleak sky and the biting cold weren't enough to wear away at his deep sense of contentment. He found himself constantly making excuses to touch her or to brush up against her.

Maddy had been passionately responsive in bed. The intensity of their joining had sent him into sensory overload. Afterward, when he thought he was recovered, she proceeded to show him how good it could feel to be held, to be touched, to be treated like someone special. Like someone who mattered.

In her arms he had been reminded of all he had missed for so long. If he wasn't careful, he was going to suddenly find that he was in a hell of a lot deeper than was good for either of them, he realized as he chucked another bale of hay off the tailgate.

He was losing his enthusiasm for finding the financing to buy back the ranch. Or for his campaign to persuade Maddy to sell. Not that he had been making a lick of progress at either front.

"Hey!" Maddy exclaimed, reclaiming his attention.

"Watch where you throw those bales, big fella. That last one almost clobbered me."

"Sorry." He felt his cheeks heat with embarrassment, and then she grinned up at him and banished his discomfort.

"You flatten me and you'll have to finish the job by yourself," she teased as she spread the hay for the hungry cattle.

"In that case, I'll have to be extra careful." Luther couldn't get over how easily the banter came to his lips. Some women would have had second thoughts after scratching an itch with the hired hand. He'd been prepared for just about anything. Up to and including being fired. He should have known that wasn't Maddy Landers's style.

He heaved the last bale off the tailgate and jumped down to the ground.

"Hustle your buns, Ward," she said without looking up. "We haven't got all day."

He was tempted to kiss her again, just to remind her that some things were worth the delay, but he resisted. If he gave in to temptation, he'd have her in the cab of the truck or down on the snow before either of them could draw two breaths. For someone who had been celibate for longer than he cared to remember, his current state of constant semiarousal was both a blessing and a curse.

"I'm hustlin', boss," he replied meekly, chuckling when her head popped up. "Anything you say."

When they stopped to share coffee and sandwiches, Maddy watched Luther out of the corner of her eye and wondered what he was thinking. There were still so many unanswered questions between them, questions she was reluctant to ask about his background and his intentions—not to mention the years he had spent in prison and how they had changed him. Maybe she couldn't ask about any of those things without making him scramble to put distance between them, but she could ask about the bruise on his jaw, which was turning a lurid blue-green.

"What caused the fight between you and Duane Snyder?"

Without looking at her, Luther drained his coffee cup and started the engine. She could feel his withdrawal as surely as if he had moved closer to the door. Then they began bouncing over the rutted road, and she decided he had no intention of answering.

"I told you," he said finally when the silence became oppressive, "we exchanged punches. No big deal."

"I'm curious about what started it." Again there was a long pause before he pulled up to the next gate. Instead of hopping out to open it, Maddy merely looked at him until he set the brake and reached for the door handle. She stopped him with a hand on his arm. The hard muscle shifted beneath her fingers, making her shiver with awareness.

"Wait," she pleaded. "Tell me what you're hiding."

"Nothing!" His voice rose sharply. "Damnation, woman, what gives you the right to pick through my brain like some guard searching my cell? Just because we're sleeping together doesn't mean I can't have my privacy, does it?"

His words were like blows. Vaguely she was aware that he had said "sleeping together" as if it were an ongoing situation, rather than a onetime roll in the hay, but she didn't let herself be distracted.

"I'm not trying to be nosy." Keeping her voice down was a struggle, but she managed. "Why do you have to treat the simplest question like some major invasion of privacy?"

He stared out the window, his thick brows drawn into a frown and his gloved fingers tapping out a tattoo on the wheel. "Ever had a body cavity search?" he asked quietly.

Shocked, she shook her head. Whatever that was, it sounded horrible.

"I have." He turned to look at her, eyes opaque and impossible to read. "More times than I could count. For eight years, the only place I had left to keep anything private was up here." He jabbed a finger at his head.

As she was reminded of what he had been through, her eyes filled with sudden tears. Impatiently she blinked them away. "I'm sorry. I didn't mean to pry." Her voice came out high and thin.

For a moment he stared, but then he turned his attention back to the road ahead. "It's okay. Open the gate, would you?" he asked gruffly.

Maddy nodded and got out. Suddenly she heard his voice raised over the sound of the engine.

"If you really want to know, Snyder and I were fighting about you."

Shocked, Maddy went ahead and dragged open the gate with shaking hands. After he drove on through, she shut it carefully and climbed back into the truck, bursting with curiosity.

Luther made a sound of annoyance. He twisted the key in the ignition and sat looking at her in the sudden silence. "What happened between you and Snyder?" he asked, catching her off guard.

"Me?" she squeaked. "What about you and Duane? You're the one who got into a fight with him."

Luther's expression was grim. "You first."

"Nothing happened between us. Maybe you know his land runs along the Double C's east border. Duane and his wife moved up from Texas, I think, three or four years ago. He stayed—she didn't."

Luther was frowning impatiently. "I don't care about that. Get to the part about you and him."

The possessiveness in Luther's tone ignited a little flame of pleasure deep inside her. Was he jealous? He would never admit it if he was, probably didn't even realize it himself, but she found the idea fascinating.

He leaned closer. His jaw was set and a muscle jumped in his cheek. It wasn't possessiveness that glittered in his eyes, but annoyance.

"What was Snyder to you after George died?" he growled.

She resisted the urge to point out that it was way before he had come down the pike and that she didn't owe him any explanations anyway. "Nothing happened!" she exclaimed instead. "What happened at the bar?"

"Nothing happened," he mimicked.

She looked pointedly at the bruise on his jaw. "Did you land any punches?" she asked sweetly.

Luther's glower deepened. "Yeah, I did. Right after he asked me how I liked screwing my boss."

Maddy mouth fell open. "Why, that pig," she cried out. "I always knew he had a slimy underside. After George died, he pretended he was interested in me, but all he really wanted was the ranch." She fell abruptly silent when she recognized the awkwardness of what she had just said. "I didn't mean—" she began.

Luther looked away. "Yeah, you did, and I don't blame you." He fired up the engine and shoved the truck into gear. "We've got work to do," he said without looking at her. "We'd better get to it."

Maddy wished he would say something, anything, to banish the sudden tension between them. Even if it was a lie.

It was late and the house was quiet, but Luther couldn't sleep. Instead he was sitting up in bed, staring at a book that couldn't hold his interest. Despite the chill in the basement room, his chest was bare and he had kicked one hairy leg free of the blankets.

For eight years, each night after lights out, he had gone over in his mind everything he would have done at the ranch that day. He had followed the seasons and the breeding schedule of his livestock. Mentally he had ridden miles of fence, irrigated acres of fields and baled tons of hay. He had imagined the land baked by the sun, scoured by the wind, flooded by the rain. He had conjured up images of the ranch as it was now, covered with snow. The only thing he had never imagined, not even once, was coming back for real.

And when he finally did, feeling the crunch of frozen ground beneath his feet and the bite of pure, cold air in his lungs, a fierce longing had filled him. He felt alive again.

Then he met Maddy. Against his wishes, his world and his list of priorities had once again been turned upside down—leaving him lost and confused and not liking the feeling one damned bit. He had thought he'd found a purpose, one he could sink his teeth into. Now he was more confused than ever.

He wanted Maddy, but he didn't deserve her. This place, though, was another matter entirely. If he didn't keep in mind what he had a right to and what he didn't, he was going to end up with nothing.

Frustrated, he raised his arm to hurl the paperback against the wall. Muffled footsteps thumped softly on the stairs. He froze as the door to his room opened slowly. In a turnabout replay of a few nights before, Maddy stood poised in the doorway.

She was wearing a quilted pink bathrobe buttoned up to her chin. Her eyes were huge in her delicate face. Luther's heart slammed up into his throat and wedged itself there as he dropped his arm and let the paperback fall to the floor.

"I saw your light," she whispered as he stared, wondering if he had fallen asleep and dreamed her up. "Couldn't you sleep either?"

He sat up straighter in the twin bed, the blood draining from his head to his lower regions so fast it made him dizzy. "Couldn't you?" he countered like a dull-witted idiot.

Mutely she shook her head. "May I come in?"

"It's your house."

"It's your room." Her hands were shoved into the pockets of her robe. Fuzzy slippers poked out below the hem. She looked as seductive as a stuffed bunny and still he was so aroused he could barely breathe. Surely his alarm would go off any minute now and wake him up.

"Aren't you cold?" she asked, and he saw that her gaze was riveted on his bare chest.

"Have you come down here to warm me up?" With an effort, he kept his tone light though his tongue felt thick. He had been unable to get her out of his thoughts and now she was here. He could even smell the scent of her bubble bath. His first impulse was to fall on her like a rabid dog. Luckily, sanity prevailed, but just barely.

She moved closer to the bed, her gaze lowered as if she had never seen the old quilted spread. Her long curly lashes screened her eyes and her cheeks were as pink as her robe. "I wasn't sure if I should come," she murmured, smoothing a wrinkle out of the bedspread. "Do you have everything you need? Are you comfortable here?"

He was rock hard and throbbing, about as uncomfortable as a man could get. Beads of sweat popped out on his forehead.

"Yeah, thanks," he said in a strangled voice.

She looked as if she was going to bolt, so he reached over and snared her hand. His heart was thudding so loudly that the sound filled his ears. He wondered if she could hear it.

"Have you really come to make sure I've got enough blankets?" he asked. What if he was totally misinterpreting her reason for being here? What if he just couldn't sleep and had decided to check up on him?

Sure, Ward, he thought wryly. *She came down here at one in the morning to see if you needed to have your pillow fluffed.* It seemed pretty unlikely, but he had learned the hard way to be cautious, and it wasn't in him to jump to conclusions, no matter how obvious they seemed. Or how tempting.

When she didn't say anything more, he cleared his throat. "Anything else you wanted?"

She raised her head and he saw the answer in her eyes. The pure honesty of it stunned him. Before he could react, her gaze skittered away. "I guess not."

"Whoa there," he said softly before she could retreat. Slowly, barely breathing so as not to spook her, he drew her closer, until her legs bumped the edge of the bed. Then he slid over and lifted up the corner of the covers in silent invitation.

He was sure the hunger twisting his insides glowed on his face like a neon sign. Watching him, she raised one trembling hand to the buttons of her robe. While he waited, almost afraid to breathe, she freed them. Underneath she had on a practical flannel nightgown. For some reason it made him remember the handful of black lace she had been wearing the other night. In its own way, the flannel, hiding and hinting at what lay beneath it, was every bit as seductive.

"You look pretty," he whispered, gratified when a pleased smile lit up her face.

"You don't have to say that."

"It's true." The soft material clung to her high breasts, making him ache with impatience to bare them, to touch and taste them. As she dropped the robe on a chair and hesitated, heat rose in Luther like a fire in dry hay.

"Come here, honey," he urged, struggling for some shred of control as he patted the mattress. When she perched on the edge, he wrapped his eager arms around her and claimed her mouth. Her fingers tangled in his hair, the sweet scent of her satiny skin filled his nostrils and the soft flannel of her gown rubbed against him like a gentle caress.

His hunger growing, he forced himself to release her mouth. "I've missed you," he groaned.

"Me, too." She stroked his cheek, gentle fingers tracing the long scar. "How did you get this?"

"One of the guards at the joint wore a snake's-head ring," he told her quietly, remembering the beating he had gotten his first week there. His indoctrination, Conroy had called it.

She must have felt him shudder. Her lips moved over the scar. "I couldn't stay away from you tonight," she murmured, distracting him from the memory of Conroy's fists.

The confession brought color to her cheeks and a deep, throbbing response low in Luther's body. "When do you have to go back?" he asked, thinking of the children asleep upstairs.

"Well before dawn."

He glanced at the clock and then he went to work on the small mother-of-pearl buttons at her throat. When they were free, he reached for the hem of her gown.

"What about the light?" she whispered.

"All in good time," he replied. "Okay?"

When she nodded, he stripped off the gown and tossed it aside. She was even lovelier than he remembered, and he wished he had the words to tell her so. Instead, he studied her intently until she began to squirm under his gaze, and then he lowered his mouth to the creamy skin of her breasts. Her nipples puckered like sweet, wild berries. Slowly he drew first one and then the other into his mouth as she arched her back and pulled him closer. Her fingers tightened in his hair and her breath caught.

Again his control wavered and threatened to crumble. Trying to slow things down, he lifted his head. Allowing himself one quick look at her breasts, flushed and moistened by his mouth, he switched off the bedside lamp. The darkness proved to be even more seductive as she smoothed her hands over his bare chest, making his nerves dance in wild response to her touch. Gliding downward, her fingers barely reached the waistband of his shorts before his control began to completely unravel.

He let her pull them down and trail her fingers back up his legs. When he could stand it no longer, he urged her above him. Arms at his sides, hands tangled in the sheets, he gritted his teeth as she settled down onto his straining flesh. The rhythm she set soon had him arching off the bed as, totally at her mercy, he exploded inside her.

Afterward, as they lay together and rational thought came slipping back, he realized that she'd touched a part of him he had forgotten even existed. The part that made him more than an animal. She made him feel good, but she also made him feel wanted and accepted. And safe. Being with her reminded him of all the things he had missed besides sex.

"I should go." Her voice was a husky whisper, her breath an angel's kiss on his damp chest.

His arm tightened around her while he fought the need to keep her close. Reluctantly he forced himself to loosen his hold. "I wish you didn't have to leave."

"I know," she murmured longingly. "So do I, but David—"

"I understand." Luther dropped a kiss on her forehead and lifted his arm. He could barely make her out in the gloom as she sat up and slipped her nightgown over her head.

"Shall I turn on the light?" he asked.

"No. Go to sleep."

Instead he caught her hand before she could reach for her robe. "What about you?" he asked. "Will you be able to sleep now? I don't want you to be tired."

She leaned close and caressed his cheek. "I'll sleep like a baby," she murmured.

It was all Luther could do to keep his hands still instead of pulling her back into bed with him. After she left, padding up the stairs in her fuzzy slippers, he spent the few hours left before dawn trying to figure out how his life had suddenly gotten so damned complicated.

There was a break in the weather the next day, so Maddy took the opportunity to drive into town to see her lawyer and pick up some much-needed groceries. It would probably be her last free moment before the first of the new calves made an appearance.

After a kiss that made her toes curl in her thick woolen socks, Luther let her go and went back to repairing the corral fence. The next day, they would begin bringing in cows that looked ready to calve.

It took only a few minutes for her attorney to confirm there was no way Luther could force her to sell him the ranch. She was relieved to hear it, but she felt as if she had been sneaking around behind Luther's back.

The first person she ran into after she'd left the attorney's office was Agatha Finney from church. "Did you hear there's been another burglary?" Agatha demanded, stopping Maddy on the sidewalk.

"No, I hadn't." She would have liked to ask when and where the break-in had taken place, but she hated giving Agatha any more fuel for gossip by appearing too curious.

"Funny, they started up again right after Luther Ward came back," Agatha speculated, watching Maddy avidly. "And I hear they're similar to the burglary he committed when he killed Adam Sloan."

Maddy stiffened with anger. "He was cleared of all that," she replied, struggling to keep her voice level. "Why won't people just leave him alone?"

"A jury found him guilty," Agatha countered sharply. "There had to be something to that."

"Someone else confessed." Maddy was weary of the whole argument, but she knew Agatha wouldn't listen to anything she said in Luther's defense. Did the whole town feel the same way?

"And now we'll never know why that other man said that he did it." Agatha stepped closer and lowered her voice. "I think your hired hand had him killed before the truth could come out."

The unfairness of Agatha's accusation made Maddy want to scream. "You're being ridiculous," she snapped instead.

"I don't see why it matters to you what people think," Agatha said slyly. "Unless he's become more than your hired hand."

"I'll see you at church next Sunday," Maddy said before she turned away, through listening to the other woman's poison.

"Letting him stay with you isn't doing your reputation any good, either," Agatha called after her.

Maddy didn't bother to reply. She didn't really care what people said about her, but she worried if David, or even Chelsea, had been hearing things at school. It didn't make her feel any better that, as of a few nights ago, at least some of the gossip was true. He had become much more to her than just her hired hand.

She passed the school bus on the way home, and concern for her children again filled her thoughts. Luther must have heard her coming, because he walked into the yard as she hopped down from the cab.

"Help you with the groceries?" he offered.

Maddy smiled at the utter timelessness of his appeal. He looked so ruggedly attractive in his worn jeans and denim jacket, the familiar Stetson on his dark head and scarred Western boots on his feet. "Thanks, I'd appreciate it."

She had no intention of passing on to him what Agatha Finney had said, but she couldn't help but wonder how the news of the second burglary was going to affect him when he did hear. Would he feel the talk about him would never stop? The notoriety might even drive him away. What would she do if he left? She was in too deep to come out of this with her heart unscathed.

"Charlie was here again," Luther said as he took two bags of groceries from the truck.

"What did he want?" As Maddy grabbed a case of canned soup and followed him into the house, Luther repeated what Agatha had told her about the second break-in. "When did it happen?" Maddy asked. Luther had been here every day doing chores.

"One night when the people weren't home. Maybe the sheriff figures I sneaked out after you and the kids went to bed."

"That's ridiculous," Maddy said as she dumped the soup on the floor of the pantry. "Surely they have other suspects?" She remembered Luther telling her how the last time they stopped looking when they found him. How hard would they look this time?

Luther set the bags on the table. "Charlie still insists he's just asking questions."

Maddy let a snort of disbelief convey her scorn for that explanation. Then she studied Luther's expression, trying to decide how much he was letting this bother him. As usual, his stoic features revealed nothing.

"Sooner or later, they'll find the real culprit," she said quietly.

The leap of emotion in his eyes sent a tremor through her. Before she could study that look more closely, he hauled her up against him. Her pulse rate went into instant overdrive. Just the feel of his big body pressed against hers was enough to make her knees go weak. She clutched at him to keep from falling.

"Honey, you're going to spoil me for sure," he muttered, and then he let her go.

She was about to pull his head back down to hers when the back door flew open. The children! And she hadn't even given them a thought.

It was amazing how much privacy two people who wanted to be alone together could find. One afternoon, Luther surprised Maddy in the barn. Despite the chill in the air, he kept her toasty warm as he spread an old sleeping bag down on the tack-room floor and persuaded her to take a half hour away from her chores.

There was something distinctly erotic in having his hands slip beneath her thermal shirt and unfastened bra to caress her breasts while she rose above him, her lower half completely bare except for two pairs of warm woolen boot socks. Luther's shirt hung open; his undershirt was pulled up under his arms and his jeans were around his knees. Hands grasping her hips, he encouraged her to establish a rhythm that sent them both quickly over the edge. Afterward, as she collapsed along his length, struggling for breath, he caressed her bare bottom with his callused hands. When the dreamy lassitude that followed began to ebb at last, they rearranged their garments, shared a last quick kiss and went back to their separate tasks.

His appetite for her seemed insatiable, and hers was rapidly growing to match it. Thoughts of him crowded her mind and filled her body with heat and longing. In her desire to bring warmth to his bleak eyes and smiles to his hard mouth, she had also managed to fulfill some of her own forgotten dreams, as well.

Almost every night, she slipped downstairs for a few stolen hours. Sometimes they barely exchanged any words at all as she climbed into his bed and shared with him all the tenderness and loving that had been missing from both their lives for so long. At other times, she talked quietly as he listened and made an occasional murmured reply. Her attempts to draw him out were mostly unsuccessful, but she didn't give up. Luther couldn't seem to get enough of her, apparently content to cuddle her close when they weren't exploring every sexual position Maddy had ever heard of and a couple she hadn't.

One night he caressed her intimately with his fingers while he slid into her heated core from behind. No matter how urgent their lovemaking became, he always took care not to let his superior size and strength hurt her in any way.

After an explosive climax that shuddered through them both, he shifted to his side, still holding her close. He didn't speak, but held her tightly until she fell asleep. When she woke up, his hand still cupped her breast and his steady breathing fanned her cheek. She managed to extricate herself without waking him and made it back to her room only moments before David came out of his.

Later that same morning, as she sliced up potatoes to fry, she wondered how he and Chelsea would react if she quit trying to hide the change in her relationship with Luther. No, she decided reluctantly, it was not something she could expose them to. Not yet. They were already fond of him. If they thought there was something going on between him and Maddy, they would only be more vulnerable when he finally left. As Maddy was sure he would do when he realized she had no intention of selling.

If everyone in Caulder Springs, including the sheriff's office, kept treating Luther like a criminal and Maddy didn't sell him back the ranch, what possible reason would he have to stay?

For a moment, she let loose her imagination. The two of them could become partners and run the ranch together. They could get married. Maddy's imagination drifted for a few more seconds before reality took over. There was no emotional commitment between them. The truth was that she could end up with a heart in pieces, as could her children. No matter what kind of pain she was willing to risk for herself, she had no right to take that risk for them.

Chapter Ten

"Didn't he look all grown up?" Maddy asked for the third time. "I can't believe he's only fifteen."

Luther grinned at her as he urged his horse across a patch of bare ground. With the first of the pregnant heifers almost ready to give birth and another storm blowing in, they were moving the herd nearer to the barn. Despite the cold, it still felt damn good to Luther to be on a horse. Riding was just one of the many small freedoms he would never take for granted again.

"You've done a good job with David," he told Maddy, who rode beside him. She looked completely at home on horseback, even though she had confessed that she'd never been on one until she and George bought the ranch.

Now she flashed Luther a look of gratitude. "I can't take all the credit for David. He's a lot like his father."

Luther wanted to ask her more about her marriage, but the words wouldn't come. There were so many things he wanted to know. Did she still miss her husband? Had they been happy together? Had he pleased her in bed? But they were none of Luther's business.

He noticed one of the heavily pregnant cows lagging behind. Before he could urge his black gelding into a trot, Daisy bounded after the cow and soon had her back with the rest.

"It sounds as if I would have liked David's father," Luther suddenly found himself saying.

Maddy looked thoughtful. "I think you would have. He was a good man and he loved this ranch. He grew up on a spread in South Dakota, and having a place of his own was his dream."

She looked so sad that Luther groped for a change of subject. "Do you remember a chestnut gelding called Reno?" he asked. He had wondered if his favorite mount had been sold. "Big for a quarter horse, with a white streak in his mane."

Maddy frowned thoughtfully. "I do remember. He had a long scar on his right flank."

Luther nodded. "That's the horse. He got that scar from barbed wire that snapped back on him."

"George rode him a lot the first couple of years. Then one day when he was walking Reno across the yard, a bone snapped in his fetlock. The pop was so loud that I heard it from where I was standing by the back door. The vet came out and took X rays, but there was nothing he could do." Her gaze was sympathetic. "Reno was a good horse. Sweet tempered. Was he yours?"

Luther nodded grimly. "I bought him as a two-year-old."

"I'm sorry." Another cow began to drift off and Maddy whistled to Daisy.

"Don't worry about David," Luther told her when they stopped and he leaned over to wrestle with the gate. His saddle creaked beneath his shifting weight. "With Joe driving the boys and their dates to the dance, they'll be fine."

"You're reading my mind." She did look worried. Her capacity for warmth and love was a constant wonder to Luther, whose own parents had been undemonstrative at best. No surprise he'd been an only child.

Maddy showered acceptance and approval on her children and now she had expanded the loving circle to include him. He would find things like his torn shirt, neatly mended, hanging on his doorknob, or lemon meringue pie, his favorite, for dessert on a weeknight. Maddy had insisted he take some of George's work clothes, too, but he felt funny about wearing them.

When he and Maddy were together, she was so open in her need that she stole his breath away. Her response to him restored his faith in himself as a man; her hunger made him burn. At times, she would lie beneath him, melting at his touch. At others, she would climb him like a tree, all raw desperation and clinging hands, and ride him until they were both damp, winded and totally satiated. Or she would cuddle him like a child, stroking his skin as if just touching him pleased her. She made him feel warm and safe. Special.

Since he'd long since given up any hope of keeping

his hands off her, all he could do in return was to try to show her how beautiful and special she was to him. He wished he could find the words, but he had never been good about laying out his feelings. That was asking for rejection.

"It was nice of Joe to offer to drive the boys and their dates," she said after they had herded the reluctant cows through the gate and closed it again. "I don't worry so much with him taking them."

"David will be old enough to get his license in a few months," Luther reminded her. David had already been after Luther to help him find a car to drive.

Maddy made a face. "Joe said that Kenny's getting his license next weekend. He and David can hardly wait."

"Joe won't let him run wild." Luther cleared his throat. "You know, he wrote to me a few times when I was away."

"Joe did? That was good of him."

"I never read his letters. The only ones I opened were from my lawyer."

"Why?" Maddy asked. "Weren't you homesick?"

"At the time, cutting ties seemed to be the only way of surviving," he admitted, remembering his overwhelming feeling of hopelessness. After Mark had been killed, he had wallowed in despair for months.

Maddy's eyes darkened with sympathy. He hadn't told her to make her feel sorry for him.

"David and Kenny seem to be real good friends," he commented, hoping to distract her.

"They sure are. Kenny's a nice boy." She chuckled deep in her throat and his senses sprang to attention.

When she smiled, he could barely breathe. "And they're both so nervous about this evening." The two of them rode in silence for a while, and then she shook her head. "In some ways they seem so young, but they're really growing up fast. I wish I could have seen the girls in their dresses, though."

"There'll probably be a photographer at the dance." David was staying at Kenny's tonight to save Joe having to bring him home so late. Since Chelsea was too young to leave in the house alone while Maddy did chores, Emma had once again suggested that she spend the night, too.

Luther didn't let himself dwell on the evening ahead, but he was well aware that he and Maddy would be alone. No need to sneak around. Anticipation raced through him, settling low in his body. Would he ever get enough of her sweet fire?

By the time the cattle were secured in their new pasture and the horses were fed and cared for, Luther was bone tired and as hungry as a grizzly in springtime. The last thing he wanted to see when he and Maddy walked out of the stable arm in arm was a patrol car sitting in the yard.

As Luther dropped his arm from Maddy's waist, swearing under his breath, Sheriff Thomas got out of his car.

"Afternoon, Maddy," he said, hitching up his belt.

Luther was secretly pleased when she merely nodded coolly. "What can we do for you, Sheriff?"

"There's been another burglary," he replied, glanc-

ing at Luther and then back to her. "I have a few
questions for your hired hand."

Luther saw Maddy start to bristle, and he put a hand
on her shoulder. No way was he going to let her hide
him behind her skirts.

"I can handle this," he said, ignoring the tension
in his gut. "Why don't you go on into the house and
get warmed up? I won't be long." He shot a grim look
at the sheriff. "Unless you're here to arrest me?"

Sheriff Thomas shook his head, looking displeased.
"Not today."

Maddy wore a worried frown as she searched Luther's face. "Okay." It was clear she had doubts about
leaving. "Holler if you need me."

He wondered how far she would be willing to go if
he really did need her help.

Before she could walk away, the sheriff spoke up.
"Actually, if you wouldn't mind sticking around for
a minute, I might have a couple of questions for you,
too."

"Is she a suspect?" Luther asked.

Without bothering to reply, Thomas unzipped his
jacket and got out a notebook and a pencil stub. The
eraser end was badly chewed. "Where were you last
Wednesday afternoon between twelve and four?" His
beady eyes were fixed on Luther.

"Why do you need to know?" Maddy asked.

"There was a burglary near Sterling, same MO as
the others. We think it might have been the same fella
who's been busy around here."

Luther felt a spasm in his gut. The whole business
made him nervous and he knew how Sheriff Thomas

felt about him. The man hated seeing Luther out of prison. He was a walking advertisement that Sheriff Thomas had made a big mistake, and it was obvious that he didn't like it one bit.

"I was right here all day Wednesday," Luther said, tempted to ask where the sheriff had been but knowing from long experience that the man had no sense of humor. "A cow slipped on some ice and went down in a gully full of water. I spent most of the afternoon trying to get her out." Attempting to give the impression that the whole subject of burglaries bored him instead of filling him with impotent frustration, he shoved his hands into his jacket pockets and studied a flock of geese overhead.

"Is that right?" the sheriff asked Maddy.

Clearly, Luther's word wasn't good enough for him.

When she didn't immediately reply, Luther forgot about the geese and willed her to say something. An icy fist wrapped itself around his heart and he held his breath, dependent on her goodwill and hating it. His stomach was churning.

What if they did manage to pin these burglaries on him? They'd been wrong before, and look where it had gotten him. He'd rather die than go back to that place. Bile rose in his throat. For a moment, he thought he was going to disgrace himself, and then he fought the urge down.

"Maddy?" the sheriff questioned, pencil poised.

To Luther, her hesitation seemed to go on forever while she nibbled on her lower lip. Did she doubt him, too?

"Yes, he was here." It had taken Maddy a moment

to mentally sort out the past week in her mind. She'd gone to the dentist on Tuesday, and it was Wednesday that Luther had rescued the cow. He had been late coming in and she'd almost sent David to look for him.

She glanced at Luther and tried to smile her encouragement, but he looked away. A muscle worked in his scarred cheek. He must find these visits by the sheriff's department alarming, since he had been mistakenly convicted for a crime once before. How could he help but worry about the same nightmare happening all over again?

"You sure about that?" The pencil quivered in the sheriff's beefy hand.

"Yes," she said firmly. "Absolutely."

He slapped the notebook shut. "Thanks for your time." He seemed to hesitate. "People might get the wrong idea if you was to leave town," he told Luther. Touching the brim of his hat, he fixed Maddy with a hard stare. "You take care now."

Before she could think of a suitable reply to his heavy-handed warning, he ambled back to his car. The man was a toad, she thought as she watched him drive away. She should have told him so.

If she was tired of his questions, how must Luther feel? "I'll be glad when they find the man who's doing this."

Luther's expression was so bitter that it made her heart ache. "I'll just bet you will," he muttered. Before she could ask what he meant by that, he headed for the house. His movements were uncharacteristically stiff, making her realize again how degrading this must all be to him.

She called out to him as he opened the back door. When he didn't stop, she hurried after him. Something was wrong; she could feel it.

She caught up with him in the mudroom. Ignoring her, he hung his hat on a hook and shed his coat.

"I'm sorry about what happened out there," she offered, trying to gauge his temperament.

He glanced at her, his expression blank, but he didn't say anything. Quickly she peeled off her own outer garments while he used the bootjack. She had planned a special dinner for the two of them. He must be starved. With one last worried peek at his grim face, she went around him into the kitchen.

"I'll start supper," she said as she washed her hands at the sink. "It won't take too long. I hope you're hungry." Realizing that she was chattering, she sent him an anxious glance, which he ignored. What was he thinking? If only he would tell her.

Instead, he walked through the kitchen without a word. Moments later, she heard the pipes in the bathroom and then his footsteps on the stairs. Her stomach fluttering nervously over the evening ahead, she turned on the oven and took the pan of lasagna she had made earlier out of the refrigerator. He had told her once that he liked Italian food. While it baked, she would have time to make a salad, then to shower and change.

Nothing had been said about the evening ahead; she hoped he was looking forward to it as much as she was. Earlier, she had caught him watching her several times with a gleam in his eyes that made her heart race. Now she wondered if she had just been seeing what she wanted to.

After she shut the oven door, she took the salad fixings out of the refrigerator and nearly collided with Luther. He had changed his shirt and combed his hair.

"Supper will be ready in a little while," she said breathlessly. As always, his nearness affected her on a primal level. "I made lasagna."

"I'll eat in town."

The words were so unexpected that she could only stare. Had she misinterpreted him so totally? His eyes were narrowed, unreadable, but his mouth was pressed into a thin line.

"What's wrong?" she demanded.

He shook his head and tried to step around her. She shifted quickly, dumping the vegetables she was holding onto the counter, and put a detaining hand on his arm. A bad feeling clawed at her insides.

"Never mind." His voice was cold, the way it had been when he had first arrived. He shrugged off her touch.

"I want to know." She hated the pleading she heard in her own voice, but this was no time for pride.

"Doesn't being alone with me make you a little nervous?" he asked, baffling her.

"What on earth do you mean?" Tiger rubbed against her leg and meowed, but Maddy merely shoved him away with her foot. "You know I'm not afraid of you."

"But you don't trust me," he accused. "You think I might be guilty of those burglaries."

"That's the craziest thing I ever heard."

His gaze locked on hers, and the expression in his eyes chilled her to the bone. It was empty, unfeeling, as if all the emotion had been sucked out of him. "Forget it," he said. "It's not important."

"Not important! How can you say that?" Dear Lord, what had happened?

For a moment, he looked utterly weary. Then he stiffened. "Leave it alone," he warned.

"No. Please, we need to talk."

His lip curled in a sneer. "I'm all talked out."

As Maddy fought tears of frustration, she began to feel angry, too. Didn't he know how she felt? How much she cared about him? Didn't any of that matter?

As she stared into his face, holding her breath, something in his eyes began to change. Their attraction to each other, always there, began to grow and expand until she would have sworn she could feel it in the room with them.

Clearly unwilling, he leaned closer. If she hadn't known him as well as she did, she might have found the gesture threatening. Instead, all she felt was a ribbon of desire curling low inside her.

"I told you," he grated through clenched teeth, "I'm not in the mood for talking right now. You'd best just let me go or we might both end up real sorry."

Eyes widening at the threat behind his words, Maddy reached out a shaking hand and touched his cheek. She sensed he was fighting some kind of inner battle and she ached to help. "Don't leave," she pleaded.

"Then don't say I didn't warn you," he growled as

he wrapped his hands around her wrists. With one sharp tug, he yanked her closer. Her body collided with his and she could feel his arousal. Despite her confusion, her own body reacted. Knowing this was no answer, she tried to ignore the sudden rush of desire that flooded her. "Let's be honest," he whispered harshly as he rubbed his hips against her. "This is why you keep me around."

Incensed by his words, she tried arching away from him, but she only bumped the wall behind her. He curled his fingers around her jaw.

"I don't want—" she began.

"The hell you don't." Eyes locked with hers, he bent his head and crushed her mouth in a voracious kiss. Her blood pounded in her ears as equal measures of fury and passion poured through her. Did he think he could sidetrack her so easily? Her body thought he could.

Luther released her jaw, only to clamp his arms around her like barrel staves. Her hands were trapped between them. She tried pushing at his chest, but he was solid strength. Unyielding. She was about to twist her head away when he pressed his open mouth to hers. His tongue traced her lips, seeking entrance. Dizzy, lost in sensation, she moaned low in her throat. Her resistance melted like snow in the sun.

He leaned back to study her. "Want me to stop?"

Her answer was to touch her mouth to his. Parting her lips, she invited him inside. He kissed her wildly until they were both gasping for breath. Releasing her mouth, he slid his hands down to her bottom and lifted her to the counter. She spread her knees and he stepped between them. His hands gripped her hips. When he pressed intimately against her, she dug her fingers into his waist and wrapped her legs around him.

Throwing back his head, he dragged in a shuddering breath and swore. Then he swooped again, claiming her mouth the way a pirate claimed plunder. Passion rose between them, hot as a branding iron. Compelling as the need to breathe. Impossible to resist. Trembling, Maddy began to melt against his hard body.

"You like this," he growled, chest heaving.

Her only reply was a groan of pleasure. Again and again he kissed her, with hot, openmouthed, erotic kisses. His tongue plunged repeatedly as she stroked his hair, his jaw, his neck. All Maddy could think about was how much she wanted him, needed him. How he made her body burn for him alone. She arched her back and pressed closer, aching to take him deep inside her.

"Luther," she whimpered. "Please."

He let her go so abruptly that she almost hit her head on the cupboard behind her. Her eyes flew open as he backed away. Although color stained his cheeks, his expression was impossible to read, his eyes opaque.

"What is it?" she cried as she straightened. Why had he stopped when she was on fire with longing? She knew how much he wanted her—she had felt it. He was staring accusingly, mouth compressed. An icy chill cut through her and she shivered.

"I can't do this." His voice was low, bitter. He raked a hand through his hair.

Maddy slid down from the counter, trying to collect her scattered wits. Her legs wobbled and her face grew hot as she folded her arms protectively across her chest. Her body felt like one raw nerve.

"What's wrong?" she asked again.

He raised his hand as if to warn her off. His chin thrust out. "We're wrong."

Her heart seemed to explode in her chest. "I don't understand," she cried. "Tell me—tell me what's happened."

"No," he growled, sounding like an animal in pain. "I need to get the hell out of here."

Maddy swallowed her pride. "But I want you," she confessed, her voice shaky.

Luther turned slowly, his face an unreadable mask. "But all I want from you," he said in a deadly quiet voice, "is this ranch. Have you decided to sell yet?"

His words sliced through her like the blade of a broadsword. "No," she whispered. "I can't." He didn't mean it. He cared about her!

His gaze raked her from head to foot, contemptuous. "Then we have nothing to talk about."

As she braced herself against the counter, fighting to keep from collapsing under the sheer pain of his words, he strode to the mudroom and shrugged into his jacket. He jammed his hat onto his head, grabbed his gloves and stalked out.

Dazed, Maddy watched him cross the yard to his truck. He didn't look back. All around her, the aroma of spicy lasagna filled the kitchen. How had everything gone so wrong so quickly?

As soon as Luther got outside, he wanted to go back in. He had seen the flash of pain in her eyes. Knowing he was the one who had put it there damn near killed him.

Hell, her doubts had hurt him, too. If he went back now, fury and pain warring inside him, he'd either say something to hurt her even more or put his fist through a wall in sheer frustration.

He had known better than to touch her, to kiss her, but her face showed every emotion like a billboard and he just plain hadn't been able to stop himself. His own emotions were running too high. Another moment and he would have taken her right there on the counter. As if her doubts didn't matter to him. As if nothing mattered but her tight, heated flesh surrounding him like a velvet fist. His body clenched as he got into the truck and he almost turned around, despite everything.

He had been starting to think she believed in him, even when no one else did. That she cared about him, when nothing about him deserved her caring. What a fool he had become! A soft, sentimental fool. He had come back for the ranch and let himself believe he had found something more.

He knew he'd been born lacking something. He'd seen the truth in his father's disapproving frown, had felt it in the indifference of his mother's touch. No one was going to love a man who was frozen and empty inside. He couldn't hide it forever and he would do well to remember that when his hormones went on a rampage. Maddy might want him, but she would

never love him—not the way his whole being longed
to be loved. Not the way he was terrified he might
already love her.

Maddy was feeding the dogs the next morning when
she heard a truck coming down the road. For a moment, her heart lurched. Luther hadn't come back last
night and she had barely slept, too upset by his parting
words. She had spent a good part of the night trying
to concentrate on the ranch accounts, a job she hated
under the best of circumstances.

Looking up, she saw that it was Joe's blue truck
and not Luther's faded red one pulling up in the yard.
She found a smile and wiped off her hands as David
and Chelsea got out. Joe rolled down his window.

"Thanks for everything," she called from the
porch.

He grinned and waved. "No problem. See you at
church."

As he drove away, Chelsea ran over and gave
Maddy an exuberant hug. David followed at a more
sedate pace, carrying his duffel bag and Chelsea's Bar-
bie suitcase.

"You forgot this," he told her as he thumped it
gently against the little girl's backside.

"How was the dance?" Maddy asked quickly, to
head off a squabble.

"It was okay."

"Did you have a good time?"

David bent over to rub Gator's back as the dog
wolfed down his breakfast. "Yeah, I guess."

Maddy would have liked to hear all about the evening, but she knew that was unlikely. Especially in

front of Chelsea. "I'm glad it went okay," she said, quelling her curiosity. "Go ahead and do your chores, then change clothes for church. Did you have any breakfast?"

He was bounding up the back steps, no doubt relieved to escape from her prying. "Joe's mom fed us."

"Blueberry pancakes," Chelsea added. "They were yummy. Did you miss me?"

"I always miss you, honey," Maddy told her daughter. "Did you and Iris have fun?" One day soon, they would have to have the other little girl over for a visit. Emma Sutter had done more than her share in taking Maddy's kids.

Before Chelsea could answer, they both heard the low rumble of another truck. Maddy's stomach tightened with mingled longing and dread. She couldn't forget the last thing Luther had said to her before he left. Had he meant it? Was the ranch the only reason he was still here? How far would he go to get what he wanted? The silent questions brought with them a surge of pain she had no time to deal with now.

Brushing her thoughts aside, she watched Chelsea run over to greet him. He looked tired. He glanced at Maddy before bending down to give Chelsea a hug. Seeing the easy way her daughter flung her arms around his neck filled Maddy with sadness. Had he meant those painful words? If he had, she wasn't the only one who stood to be hurt.

All day, Luther braced himself for Maddy's questions, but they never came. Perhaps she really didn't care where he'd spent the night and whether or not she was important to him.

No, he knew that wasn't true; he'd seen the pain in her eyes before he left. She cared. Only problem now was how could he ever convince her that he did, too? She would always wonder if he wanted her for herself or because of the land she stood on. Just as he would wonder if she trusted him, down deep inside.

He went downstairs right after the evening meal, knowing he was still too confused himself to stick around and field any questions she might come up with.

Ever since she had hesitated over vouching for him with Sheriff Thomas, his feelings had been in such a snarl he didn't know which way was up. He'd gotten so drunk last night that he hadn't dared drive back to the ranch. All he needed was a DWI ticket to add to his popularity with the local police. Luckily for him, he had run into an old cowboy who had worked for him at the Double C. Scooter had insisted that Luther crash on his lumpy couch.

Apparently there was at least one person in Caulder Springs who didn't still hold his past against him after all.

As far as his relationship with Maddy went, though, Luther could see only one solution that would keep him from hurting her any more than he already had. He opened the closet door and stared at the meager contents. Despite the recent additions to his wardrobe, there wasn't much to pack. Trying not to think about how badly he wanted to stay, he began folding shirts and stacking them on the bed.

She would never know it, but in leaving he would be showing her in the only way he could what was really important to him. He'd go the next day, he decided, after he had helped her with the chores. He knew he would be leaving her shorthanded, but she had managed before he got there and she would manage after he had left. Just like everyone else in his life had been, she and the children would be better off without him.

For a moment, he recalled the pleasure he'd felt when David had awkwardly asked him for the dancing lessons. But hell, helping the boy hadn't been a big deal; it didn't make Luther a hero. And it didn't make him indispensable.

For a moment, the cover of the paperback he was holding blurred. He blinked and shook his head. This was the best way. He would always be an ex-con. She and the kids didn't need that, and other people would forget once he'd left. Even if he never did forget what he'd almost had. And then lost.

The strength of his regret was nearly enough to send him to his knees. But he clenched his fists and forced himself to get on with his packing.

Realizing that the clothes and books he had accumulated since he first got back wouldn't all fit into his battered duffel bag, he went upstairs in his stocking feet to find some kind of box or bag he could use. As he did, he wondered where Maddy was now. His emotions were too raw for a confrontation. Tomorrow was soon enough to tell her he was leaving.

"Just a damn minute," he heard her exclaim as he padded silently down the hall. He froze and looked around. Her voice was coming from the living room, but her back was turned and the telephone receiver was pressed to her ear. Her next words floored him.

"I have better things to do than listen to that kind of talk, Sam," she said. "He's innocent. Anyone who doesn't believe what I'm saying is no friend of mine. Goodbye."

While Luther stood in the hall, eavesdropping unashamedly, she slammed down the receiver. Why was she still sticking up for him if she doubted his innocence? Was she embarrassed to admit she could have been wrong?

His thoughts were in turmoil as he continued on to the kitchen to get a garbage bag to hold his clothes. Maybe she hadn't made up her mind completely, but she was only hurting herself more by defending him. Leaving was still the best thing to do. The best thing for Maddy and her little family, even if it was the worst possible thing for Luther.

The next day, Luther tried without success to find the right moment to tell her he was going. The weather had warmed up and the sun was shining. Luther's horse was following Maddy's as she headed for a creek filled with snowmelt. Its steep banks were still coated with a thick layer of ice, packed down by the cattle. The water itself was freezing cold.

They hadn't talked much, only when it was necessary. Maddy looked tired and she seemed preoccupied. Guilt kept Luther from asking how she felt.

"Careful," he called out as Maddy's horse left the

water and scrambled up the opposite bank, slipping and sliding as she lurched in the saddle.

His warning came too late. Her mount lost its footing and went to its knees, sending Maddy over its head. As she hit the ground, the frightened horse ran over the top of her.

Luther cried out her name, urging his own mount forward as Maddy tumbled back down the bank into the icy stream. Before she went under, he was out of the saddle. Barely conscious of the swiftly running water, he scooped her into his arms and staggered to the bank, sliding with every step.

"Maddy," he cried again as he looked down at her deathly white face. When her eyes opened and she groaned, relief exploded inside him. "Where do you hurt?" he demanded, laying her down on the ground with care and gently feeling for broken bones.

"All over." Her voice was thin, her eyes full of pain, but she managed to move her arms and legs.

"You're soaked," he told her. "I have to get you home."

"I feel like I've been trampled by a horse," she joked feebly. "Is Rowdy okay?"

Luther glanced around. The horse was standing a few feet away. "Yeah, he's okay. Do you think you can ride with me back to the truck?"

Her lips curved into a faint smile although she was shivering. "What kind of a sadist are you?" Before he could reply, she struggled to sit up. "Of course I can ride."

Working quickly, he helped her onto his gelding and then mounted behind her. Leading her horse, who was limping slightly, he took them back to the truck. He knew that every moment she spent in her wet clothes increased the chance of hypothermia. As he urged his horse to go faster, cradling her shaking body against his, a sickening realization gripped him.

What if he had left the night before and she had been alone when her horse threw her into that freezing stream? What would have happened to the woman he loved then? And how could he possibly leave her now, before the dangers of the brutal winter were behind them?

Chapter Eleven

"I'm s-so c-cold." Maddy's teeth were chattering so hard it was difficult to talk. Her whole body shook. Her back and hip throbbed. She knew that Rowdy had stepped on her several times in his attempts to get up the steep, icy bank.

Luther held her in front of him on his horse. When they got to the pickup, he dismounted and lifted her carefully from the saddle. "Take it easy, darlin'. We'll have you warm again in no time." His deep voice was gravelly as he set her in the cab of the truck, started the engine and cranked the heater up to high. "Can you get those clothes off?" he asked as he reached behind the seat for a faded blanket and an old sweatshirt of David's.

The harsh lines in Luther's face were deeper than usual, but he avoided meeting Maddy's gaze as she struggled with her sodden jacket. She tried to unbutton it, but her hands in their wet gloves refused to work. Finally Luther stripped the jacket and her sweater and thermal underwear away, yanked the old sweatshirt down over her head and wrapped her in the blanket. As warm air began to pour from the heater vents, he rubbed her arms vigorously.

"You're hurting me," she moaned as he wrestled with her boots and jeans in the confines of the cab. Feeling was coming back to her hands and feet. With it came renewed pain.

"Sorry, honey. I know it's uncomfortable, but we have to get you warm."

She glanced at his jeans. He was wet from the knees down from jumping into the creek and grabbing her.

"What about you?" she asked. His feet must be frozen.

"I'm okay." His expression was grim, but fury smoldered in his eyes. As she huddled in the blanket, he poured a cup of coffee from the thermos. "Drink this while I get the horses loaded. We'll have you back to the house before you know it."

He sounded like a man who was used to giving orders. Maddy was grateful for his presence and his level head. Her shivering had almost stopped and the hot coffee warmed her insides enough for her to smile when she heard him swear at Rowdy. Her horse always balked when he was being loaded into a trailer.

Luther's obvious concern was gratifying to Maddy after the puzzling way he had been acting. Finishing the coffee, she sighed and let her head fall back against the seat. Lord, but she ached everywhere. Her knee stung; she must have torn her jeans and scraped it when she fell. The heels of her hands throbbed. They were red and smeared with dirt.

Luther scrambled back into the cab, still swearing about her horse. "Damned jughead belongs in a slaughterhouse."

"Is he okay?" Maddy asked.

Luther's glare softened when he looked at her. "Except for being stupid," he said shortly. "Are you getting warm yet?"

"Yes, thanks." If he kept looking at her the way he was, hypothermia didn't stand a chance, she mused.

He drove back to the house faster than usual, but his hands on the wheel were utterly competent. He left the horses in the trailer for David to unload and scooped Maddy into his arms. "Keep that blanket wrapped around you."

She clutched at the edges, painfully aware of being almost naked beneath it. Her bare feet poked out and she rubbed them together. "I can walk, you know." Despite her protest and the pain, she wasn't too far gone to appreciate the feel of his strong arms cradling her against the hard wall of his chest. If only he were carrying her for a totally different reason.

"You better see the doctor," he urged as he took the stairs two at a time.

"No. That's not necessary." When they reached the second floor, she noticed he wasn't even breathing hard. His heart was beating, slow and even, beneath her hand. "I'll just have a hot bath and I'll be fine," she added.

His eyes locked with hers. "I want to see where

you're hurt." His tone brooked no argument as he set her on her feet in the bathroom and turned on the faucets in the tub.

Maddy wrapped the blanket tighter. He had seen her naked body before, but that didn't mean she wanted him looking at a bunch of ugly bruises. "I can handle the rest of this alone."

His thick brows rose skeptically. "You sure?"

"I'm sure. Thanks for getting me back here so quickly." She hesitated. There was so much more she wanted to say, but she could feel his withdrawal. Nothing had really changed between them.

"How do you feel?" he asked. "Any nausea? Headache?"

She shook her head. "Just my back and hip. That's probably where Rowdy's hooves got me." For a moment, she remembered her sudden terror when she realized she was going to be trampled. Now she blinked back tears of relief. "I thought he was going to crush me." Her voice was hoarse and she cleared her throat. "Then I hit the water. It was so cold but I felt like I was on fire. Thank you for hauling me out so fast."

As she had known he would, Luther shrugged off her gratitude. A look of pure torment flashed across his face. "I should have gotten to you sooner." Before she could contradict him, he glanced at the partially filled tub and reached for a jar of bath salts. "Go ahead and take your bath," he said after he had dumped a handful under the flow from the faucet. The scent of cinnamon and peaches filled the air. "The hot water will help keep you from getting a chill." He put his hand on the door. "Do you need my help?" Something blazed in his eyes and was quickly hidden.

"No, thanks." She shifted her grip on the blanket.

"Do you want me to wait in the hallway?" Despite the wall he'd retreated behind once again, he was clearly reluctant to leave her.

Regardless of her condition, erotic images of the two of them in the tub together danced before her eyes. "No. That's okay."

"Do you want some aspirin? Some tea?"

She shook her head. "You need to change, too. Your feet must be soaked."

He glanced down at his jeans and boots as if noticing them for the first time. "Well," he said finally, "I guess you're all set."

Awareness floated between them like the steam coming from the tub. Another minute and she would be inviting him—no, begging him—to stay. Then she heard David shout from downstairs.

"You'd better get out of here," she told Luther.

"Yeah. I'll head him off." Still, he hesitated. Then they heard David's footsteps at the bottom of the stairs.

"Mommy, where are you?" Chelsea hollered.

"Okay, I'm going." Luther gave her one last look, his gaze raking down her body swathed in the old blanket. Then he slipped through the door, shutting it softly behind him.

"What happened?" she heard David demand. "Are you okay? Why are the horses still in the trailer? Where's Maddy?"

"I want to see Mommy." Chelsea sounded alarmed.

"Maddy's fine." Luther's deep voice was a reassuring rumble.

"I'm okay, sweetie," Maddy called through the door as the water soothed her. Mmm, it felt good. "I'll be out in a few minutes."

"Is she really okay?" she heard Chelsea ask Luther.

He must have squatted down as he often did when he talked to her, because his voice was fainter and Maddy couldn't make out his words. Chelsea would accept what he told her. She trusted him. After a moment, Maddy heard receding footsteps as the three of them went back downstairs.

Maddy had two purple hoofprints on her back and one on her hip, where Rowdy had struck her. She was lucky it hadn't been worse. Lucky that Luther had been there with her or her accident might have ended much differently. She knew better than to thank him again, though. Since she had come downstairs after her bath, swaddled in her quilted robe, he had retreated back into his shell. Only his eyes were black with suppressed emotion.

"Don't worry about supper," David told her when she ventured stiffly into the kitchen. Her hip was going to be even worse tomorrow, and they were just at the beginning of calving season. Supper was the least of her worries. "Luther's making pancakes."

At his insistence, Maddy ate a couple with strawberry syrup and then rose to go up to bed.

"An early night is probably a good idea," Luther told her. "Do you want me to carry you?"

She was tempted to say yes, but pride stopped her.

She refused his offer, thanked him again and made her own way slowly up the stairs. With each painful step, she could feel his gaze, but she refused to look back. Suddenly she was exhausted, but she knew she was too sore to actually sleep.

Sometime later, something woke her up. She opened her eyes to see the outline of a man sitting on the edge of her bed.

"Luther?"

He smoothed a hand over her forehead. "I didn't mean to wake you," he whispered. "I just wanted to make sure you were okay."

Deeply touched by his concern, Maddy glanced at her bedside clock. It was very late. All of a sudden she was overwhelmed by what had happened. She could feel Rowdy's hooves hitting her, could taste her own fear. A sob rose in her throat. Without giving herself time to reconsider, she launched herself at Luther's dark shape.

"Oh, honey," he groaned as his arms closed around her protectively. "I'm so sorry that I couldn't get to you sooner. I should have been able to catch you, to keep you from falling."

She stiffened in his embrace. "Don't you dare think that way," she scolded softly. "You did everything you could. I might be dead if you hadn't acted so quickly. What if you hadn't been there at all?"

At her words, his arms tightened and a hard shudder went through him. He pressed his rough, warm cheek against hers.

"Don't think about that," he murmured in her ear. As usual, his nearness distracted her from everything else. When he found her mouth, she was more than ready to return his kiss.

Shivers of longing rippled through her as his lips caressed hers. She melted into his embrace, wanting never to let him go again. He stroked her shoulders carefully. His breath was hot against her skin as his lips prowled the sensitive spot at the base of her throat. When he pushed aside the collar of her flannel gown, she felt his fingers tremble.

"Maddy," he whispered softly as he gathered her closer. "I should leave. You're sore and I don't want to hurt you."

"You'll only hurt me if you leave," she chided him gently. Ignoring the twinge in her back when she lifted her arm, she tangled her hand in the coarse silk of his hair. She wanted to feel his naked body against hers, despite her discomfort. Wanted to know he was as caught up in the passion that flowered between them as she was. Wanted to celebrate being alive and in love.

"Stay with me," she breathed, raising her head to trail kisses along his hard jaw, swallowing the words she really wanted to say.

He skimmed his hand over her ribs and settled it on the underside of her breast. "What about the kids?" His voice had grown hoarse. "What about your bruises?"

"The kids could sleep through anything and my bruises aren't what's aching right now," she admitted, pressing closer.

She heard his breath catch. He kissed her again, easing his tongue between her lips to duel with her

own. He was half lying across her but he supported
most of his weight on his forearms and she was fast
forgetting about her injuries.

Urging his mouth back to hers, Maddy did her best
to convince him to stay. When his hand touched the
bruise on her hip, though, she couldn't stop herself
from flinching.

He froze. "You're in a lot more pain than you're
letting on."

"It's okay. I still don't want you to leave."

Wordlessly he sat up, stripping off his T-shirt and
sweatpants. Then he eased himself down beside her
and gathered her into his arms, turning her onto the
side that hadn't been trampled.

"Okay?" he asked, stretching out behind her and
curling one arm around her protectively.

Heart overflowing at his generosity and understanding, Maddy sighed and closed her eyes. "Mmm, you
bet."

Luther held her until he felt her breathing slow and
deepen. His own body clamored fiercely but he ignored it. He knew what she needed right now and it
wasn't sex. He knew because he needed it, too. He
had never realized how very empty his life was until
he met her, but now as he lay in the darkness, he was
perfectly content to hold her close and feel her heart
beat against his hand.

For a while, he dozed as he continued to cradle her
against him. Once or twice she stirred in the darkness
and shifted as her body undoubtedly started to ache.
He wished he could shoulder part of her pain, wished

again that there had been something he could have done to keep her from getting hurt at all.

It had happened so fast, one of those flukes that made ranching so dangerous. In his heart, he knew there was nothing he could have done differently, but still he felt regret. Thank God he had been there.

Maddy groaned in her sleep and turned so that one of her breasts filled his hand. Fire raced up his arm and down his body, spreading to his groin and pooling there. He allowed his fingers to touch her nipple and he smiled in the darkness when it tightened. Then she arched her back, tucking her bottom against him, and his smile disappeared.

After what seemed to him like hours, he glanced at the clock and saw that it was time for him to leave. Carefully he slid his arm out from under her. She rolled onto her back, her eyes still closed. When he dropped a kiss on her mouth, she responded in her sleep. He thought about parting her thighs and slipping into her warmth, waking her when he was already buried deep inside her, and beads of sweat broke out on his forehead. Then he realized how stiff and sore her body undoubtedly was and he found the willpower to ignore his own throbbing stiffness and tear himself away.

Leaving her there in the early-morning darkness was one of the most difficult things he'd ever had to do.

Before she opened her eyes, Maddy knew he was gone. She tried to stretch and pain slammed through her like a runaway train. Before she could catch her breath, there was a soft knock on her door and then it opened. Luther stood there with a glass of water and a bottle of pain pills.

Without saying a word, he helped her into a sitting position and gave them to her. He was dressed in his work clothes and his hair was still damp from the shower. His expression was unreadable, but his gaze never left her face.

"How are you feeling?" he finally asked.

"I need to get up," Maddy said, struggling against the pain that seemed to grow only more intense with each tiny movement. She shifted her leg. Her injured hip protested violently, bringing tears to her eyes.

"I can fix breakfast and get the kids off to school," Luther said. "You stay in bed. I already called Emma Sutter and she'll be over in an hour. David's doing his chores and Chelsea's getting your coffee."

Maddy choked on the lump that rose in her throat. It was wonderful being looked after like this. "Thank you."

Luther patted her shoulder awkwardly and stood up. "No one's indispensable," he said lightly. "You take it easy today."

She wanted to thank him for all he was doing, for staying with her the night before, for just being there with his strength and reassurance. She was battling tears and the words stuck in her throat. Finally she managed to look up and she could see from the expression on his face that he didn't need the words.

Maddy spent two days working on the ranch accounts before she felt well enough to venture outside. Despite her impatience, Luther had refused to let her do anything more physical than pushing a pen across the page. When the numbers began dancing with each other, she finally pulled rank and threatened to fire him if he didn't at least let her get some air.

"Be careful," he cautioned, hovering like a new mother as she made her way down the back steps. Her hip was agonizingly stiff and her back felt as if someone had run her through with a pikestaff. If it hadn't been for Luther at her side, clumsily trying to coddle her, she might have given up and gone back in the house.

"I'm fine," she muttered through clenched teeth. "I just need to loosen up a little after sitting around on my butt for so long."

His expression was disbelieving. They were on their way to the corral to check on the cows with the most imminent chance of delivering. Three others had already done so while Maddy was trapped in the house, the calves healthy and nursing well.

Not ready to go back inside, she insisted on riding in the truck with Luther when he went to check on the rest of the cattle. By the time they got back to the house, she was exhausted. Every bone in her body ached, her muscles were screaming with pain and her body was bathed in perspiration. He must have become all too aware of her discomfort.

"Stay put," he said, parking the truck in the yard and shutting off the engine. He got out and reached for her as she did her best to slide across the seat without groaning.

"I can manage." Her voice came out more sharply than she intended.

Ignoring her protest, he lifted her down. Before he set her back on her feet, he lowered his head and kissed her.

"You're such a tyrant," he whispered, making her chuckle. With an arm around her waist, he walked her slowly to the house and helped her up the steps.

Maddy was bitterly disappointed at the way her body was letting her down. She had expected to be fully recovered by now. Instead, it was all she could do to heat up the pot of stew Emma had left along with a loaf of homemade bread and then collapse onto the couch.

"Will you be okay until the kids get home?" Luther asked after he had brought her more pain pills and spread an afghan over her. "I was going to go to Joe's to pick up that extra calf puller he said we could use. Emma forgot to bring it with her, and I haven't been able to fix the one that broke."

Maddy knew they had to have it. Sometimes a calf was turned the wrong way, or a young heifer was small and had problems delivering by herself. If she couldn't expel the calf, chains were attached to its front feet and the calf puller was used. Otherwise both mother and baby could be lost. It was lucky for Maddy that Joe had a spare.

"Go ahead," she told Luther. "I'm not an invalid. I'll be fine."

He looked at her anxiously and then he leaned down to kiss her cheek. She turned her head so their lips would meet, but he raised his head instead. "They kids'll be home in a few minutes," he said, straightening.

He hated leaving her, but he could see she was too exhausted and sore to accompany him. He wished that David had his driver's license; then he could have gone when he got home.

When Luther arrived at the Blue Moon, another rancher he knew slightly was looking over a young black-and-white filly. Luther found a spot at the railing and watched as Joe put the filly through her paces. He was unsaddling her when one of the hands hurried in, carrying a cordless phone.

"Call for you, Mr. Wilson," he told the other man. "It's your wife and she sounds upset."

Wilson took the phone while Luther and Joe exchanged curious glances. From his side of the conversation, it became clear immediately that something was seriously wrong.

"Are you hurt?" Wilson demanded. His leathery face had gone pale.

Luther assumed his wife had had some kind of accident. Too bad. Wilson seemed like a nice enough guy and he had mentioned that he had children, too.

"Did you call the police?"

Joe put a bracing hand on Wilson's shoulder as he assured his wife that he was on his way. His hand trembled as he switched off the phone and handed it back to Joe.

"I've gotta get home," he said. "Someone attacked Marie."

"My God!" Joe exclaimed. "Is she okay?"

"Hell, no, she's scared and upset." Wilson began walking swiftly to his truck, as Joe and Luther hurried after him. "She came home from work early. When she walked into the kitchen, someone hit her from behind and knocked her down. By the time she got back up, the bastard was gone. She called the sheriff and then she called me."

His words sent a deep chill of fear through Luther. It could have been Maddy. "Was your wife badly hurt?" he asked.

Wilson's jaw worked. "She sounded okay, just real scared. I'd like to get my hands on the bastard who hit her, though." He glanced at Joe. "I'll call you about the horse."

"No hurry," Joe said as Wilson climbed into his pickup. "Let me know if there's anything I can do."

With a curt wave, the other rancher went barreling down the road as if the devil himself were after him.

"I'd better go, too," Luther said. He didn't like the idea of Maddy and the kids being alone at the ranch. "It sounds like this guy is getting bolder. Or more careless. I want to check on Maddy."

Joe eyed him for a moment, expression thoughtful. "How are you two getting along?"

Luther might have resented the question, but Joe had been a good friend to both of them, and Luther sure as hell didn't have many friends. That didn't mean he felt like discussing his feelings toward her, though. "We get along okay," he said, shrugging.

Joe slapped his back and grinned. "Don't worry," he said finally. "Those dogs of hers won't let anyone sneak up on her. But I know how you feel. I'd kill anyone who touched Emma." He paused as if waiting for Luther to make a comment. When he didn't, too busy thinking about all the things that could happen when he wasn't around to stop them, Joe said, "Let me get that calf puller and you can be on your way."

As they walked to the other barn, all Luther could think about was Maddy. Her fall had been scary enough; if anything really bad happened to her, he doubted he could survive it.

"Well, I guess this settles one thing," Joe drawled.

Luther threw the calf puller into the back of his truck, thanked him and got behind the wheel. "What's that?"

"If this was our serial burglar who attacked Wilson's wife, I'd say you've got yourself an airtight alibi."

Maddy hoped that Luther would take down the wall he'd put up, now that suspicion for the burglaries had shifted away from him. Instead, he seemed only more quiet and withdrawn. He hardly ever left the ranch, unless she wanted to go somewhere, and then he insisted on accompanying her.

Her bruises were gradually fading, turning from purple to green to a sickly yellow, but her hip still ached like a bad tooth if she was on her feet for too long. And too long was the rule during calving season. Everyone, including David, put in endless hours. He and Luther tried to spare her as much as possible, but there was just too much work to do.

Luther stuck as close to Maddy as a tick on a dog, but he didn't have much to say. Apparently he had forgiven or forgotten whatever had sent him to town that one night when he hadn't returned until morning. Despite the increased work the new calves brought with them, he still managed to find time to be alone with her. At night, if she didn't limp down the stairs to his room, he would come to her as soon as he was sure that David and Chelsea were asleep.

Now that her bruises were healing, he took her fiercely and often, as if he was driven by an insatiable hunger, and sometimes without uttering a word. He plunged harder and deeper, shoving her over the edge into mindless ecstasy and then joining her there as his body quaked with his own release.

Any guilt that Maddy felt at their secret affair was burned away in the heat of the passion they shared and the growing love she felt for him. Nothing more had been said by either of them about the ranch. Although she sometimes wondered how much it influenced his obvious desire for her, she always managed to shove her concerns aside as soon as he took her in his arms.

The only thing she missed was some sign from him that his emotions were even half as involved as her own. She knew he cared; it was in the dark glow of his eyes and the raw possession of his touch. Still, she would have given a lot to hear the words.

"This calf needs help," Luther said as he examined a young heifer that had been struggling to give birth for hours. "Do you want to see if you can turn it?"

Maddy nodded. It didn't take long to ascertain that the calf wasn't going to be born on its own—not the way it was positioned inside its increasingly frantic and exhausted mother.

Unable to turn the calf, Maddy found its tiny feet

and attached the chains of the calf puller while Luther did his best to keep the heifer still. From then on, everything went smoothly as they helped her to dilate and then pulled out her baby. Soon the new mother had the little bull calf washed off and was encouraging him to nurse.

As they watched the pair, Luther put his arm around Maddy's shoulders. "There's nothing like it," he murmured. "No matter how many animals I help give birth, it always affects me the same."

Maddy sensed that his admission was an attempt to share some of his feelings with her. "Me, too," she said as she slipped an arm around his waist and rested her head against his chest, which was covered by several thick layers of work clothes. They were both coated with slime and filth, but once again they had outsmarted death. It was worth getting dirty to bring a being into the world, alive and healthy.

Somehow the peaceful tableau renewed Maddy's faith that her own life would eventually sort itself out, too. She was tempted to try to explain to Luther how much the ranch and the life here fulfilled her, but she was reluctant to spoil the moment of peaceful camaraderie.

"I guess we'd better turn them out and get cleaned up," she said instead. "Before the next crisis hits."

While the successful birth of the little bull calf renewed Maddy's belief in the general rightness of the world, what Luther found in the pasture a few days later reminded her how precarious life could be.

"You don't want to go over there," he said as he

walked back to the truck to get a shovel and a burlap sack.

"What is it?" she demanded as she got out of the cab. They had been driving along the fence line, getting stuck in the ooze twice, when they failed to see another recent arrival that should have been with its mother. The sun had come out and the temperature had shot up well above freezing. All around them was a sea of mud and wet brown grass.

Maddy had managed to convince herself that the missing calf was probably resting in a nearby hollow. Now a helpless feeling of resignation stole through her before Luther could even say the words.

"I found the calf." He shook his head. "There were coyote tracks all around his body."

"But they don't usually bother healthy calves," Maddy protested, as if a good argument would change the poor thing's fate.

"I've heard stories of them killing calves before," Luther replied. "But I've never had it happen to me." He glanced at the shotgun on the rack behind her head. "I'll come back later and look around some more."

"I don't know that I want you to shoot the coyotes." Maddy thought of the hours of entertainment the local pair had provided, playing in the snow like children, calling to each other in the night, keeping the rodent population under control. They were only doing what came naturally, she knew, but if the two she had seen hanging around had turned into calf killers, something would have to be done.

Luther studied her for a long moment. "I'd prefer not to kill them, either. They're only trying to survive.

A couple of shots over their heads should convince them it's not healthy for them around here, though.''

Maddy was glad he felt the same way she did. With a sad smile, she nodded. ''Good idea.''

''I don't like leaving you alone.'' Maddy was admiring the stubborn thrust of Luther's jaw. He had just finished kissing her thoroughly and was shrugging into a quilted vest that once belonged to George. ''I'll take the dogs to the vet some other day.''

''No, they really should go today.'' She loved seeing his concern. How much longer could he keep up that final wall of reserve he had erected against her, when they were getting closer in so many ways? ''Their vaccinations are way overdue, and I want the vet to look at Daisy's tooth. I'm sure it pains her.''

She knew that Luther worried about the burglar, still on the loose, and she knew he had been going out at night to patrol the grounds when he thought she was asleep. Ever since Marie Wilson had been assaulted and Luther cleared as a suspect, he had become increasingly vigilant in guarding the Double C and its inhabitants. Maddy took his protectiveness as another sign that he cared much more than he was yet willing to admit, even to himself.

''Don't worry. I'll be careful,'' Maddy promised him now, smiling.

His expression remained somber. ''I don't want anything to happen to you,'' he said gruffly as he touched her cheek.

She rubbed it against his callused fingers. ''I know.'' He still held a big part of himself closed off from her, but she didn't let that get her down. Somehow they would manage to resolve the problems that still lay between them, including the ranch. She had to believe that. Even when they made love, she could feel Luther holding back as long as possible, fighting his feelings. When he finally did let go, exploding inside her, it seemed to be as much a defeat for him as a triumph.

Now, as he lingered, she searched his face for clues. She was learning to read the small signs there—the softening of his mouth, the glint of humor in his eyes. Today, though, his expression revealed nothing of what he might be feeling.

Luther returned her perusal with a worried one of his own. Her nose was red and she kept sneezing. She might be nearly recovered from her plunge in the icy creek, but it was obvious to his untutored eyes that she was coming down with David's cold.

They were due at the Blue Moon in less than an hour, and her compliance when he suggested she stay home had him convinced she felt worse than she was willing to admit.

One of Joe's dry heifers had gone lame, so he was butchering it that afternoon. Maddy and Luther had planned to help cut and wrap the carcass in exchange for a share of the beef. On the way, they intended to take the dogs to the vet.

It never ceased to amaze Luther how hard Maddy drove herself. Even after she had been hurt in the fall from her horse, her idea of taking it easy had been to spend long hours with the account books. For a little thing, she had reserves of strength he had barely begun to discover. He had tried to get her to take it easy, with minimal results. She hated it when he bossed her around, but sometimes he thought she needed a keeper.

Beside him, Maddy sneezed explosively and her head began to pound. She felt like hell. Maybe Luther was right, and what she needed was a nap. It certainly sounded appealing.

"You go upstairs," he said in that confident male tone that took instant compliance for granted. "I'll lock up on my way out."

She wanted to put up a token resistance, just for the sake of principle, but her head was throbbing too fiercely. By the time he left and she was settled beneath the covers, she was halfway to oblivion. Before she drifted off, the last thing she heard was his sharp whistle summoning Daisy and Gator.

The next thing she heard was the sound of glass breaking. It woke her from a sound sleep. Confused, she lay on the bed and listened, ears straining in the silence, while she wondered if she had only been dreaming.

Footsteps and the scraping sound the top drawer of her desk always made convinced her she hadn't been. Cautiously she rolled over on the bed and picked up the telephone, but there was no dial tone. The downstairs phone must be off the hook.

Hands shaking, Maddy slipped noiselessly off the bed and got out George's gun. Avoiding the squeaky board in front of the dresser, she found the ammunition. There was a knot of fear in her stomach and she could taste it in her throat. As she tried to think what to do, wishing Luther were here with her, she heard more loud noises from below. The intruder was making no attempt to be quiet; he must have some reason to think he had the house to himself.

Tucking that thought away, she gripped the gun tightly. Her knees and hands shaking, she began to creep slowly down the stairs.

Chapter Twelve

Luther stared down at his bandaged hand in disgust as he pulled into the yard and turned off the ignition. Talk about clumsy. Since he had been thinking about Maddy instead of paying attention to the sharp knife he'd been using on the side of beef, he supposed he was lucky he hadn't lopped off a couple of fingers.

The cut across his palm, though not deep enough to need stitches, made it too painful to finish cutting up the meat. He had offered to stay and do something else instead, but Joe would have none of it. He had insisted that Luther go on home.

At least the cut was on his left hand, he thought as he went up the back steps. It could have been worse. He was reaching for the doorknob when he noticed the broken window. Then he heard Maddy scream.

Luther's blood turned to ice and he bolted through the mudroom, boots crunching on broken glass.

"Don't move or I'll shoot," he heard Maddy say.

"Honey, where are you?" he shouted. "Are you okay?"

"I—I'm in the living room." Her voice was unnaturally high.

What Luther saw when he got to the archway stopped him in his tracks. A thin man with long, dirty blond hair and a scraggly beard was holding a knife. Maddy was pointing a gun at him. When she glanced at Luther, the intruder leapt at her and knocked the gun from her hand. Maddy screamed again and managed to roll away from the blade.

Terrified for her, Luther lunged forward, grabbed a handful of the intruder's long hair and pulled him around. The man bellowed and slashed the knife in a deadly arc. Dodging it, Luther planted a fist in his face. Bone and cartilage gave way, splattering blood. He cried out and dropped the knife.

Rage pumped through Luther like adrenaline and he swung again, hitting the man in the gut and doubling him over. When Luther let go of his hair, he slid to the floor, groaning. Blood seeped between the fingers protecting his injured nose.

"Are you okay?" Maddy cried as Luther straightened.

"Yeah, are you?" He kicked the knife out of the assailant's reach. Then he glanced at Maddy.

"I'm just a little scared." Luther was pleased to see that she had gotten her hands on the gun again and that it was aimed at the bastard cowering on the floor.

Maddy's bottom lip quivered, but her eyes were snapping with fury.

Fresh anger roared through Luther as he realized how frightened she must have been under all that bravado. He wanted to hit the son of a bitch again, just for his own satisfaction. Instead, he looped one shaking arm around Maddy's shoulders.

"Are you sure you're okay?"

She nodded, but he could feel her trembling.

He was still shaking, too, and his hand ached. "What happened?" he asked raggedly.

"I woke up when I heard glass breaking. I got George's gun and sneaked down here. I'd just gotten the drop on him when you walked in."

Luther managed to swallow down the wave of sick fear that rose in his throat. Dear God, she could have been killed.

"Stand up," he snarled, releasing Maddy to grab the cowering man by the front of his shirt and haul him to his feet.

"Don't hurt me," he whined, flinching away. He dropped his hand from his bloody nose and Luther blinked in surprise.

"You work for Joe Sutter," he blurted. "Isn't your name Kendall?"

"Crandall." Completely subdued, the man was still partly bent over, one arm curled protectively around his stomach and the other cradled beneath his dripping nose.

"Honey, why don't you give me the gun and call the sheriff," Luther asked Maddy without taking his eyes off Crandall. All he wanted to do was to take her into his arms, make sure she really was unharmed and then never let her go again. Instead, he gave her what he hoped was a reassuring smile, although it felt pretty wobbly around the edges. She handed him the gun and went to the phone.

What if he had gotten home a few minutes later? Would she have been able to defend herself against this scum or might he have overpowered her? Luther could feel cold sweat popping out on his forehead.

He barely resisted the sudden impulse to shoot Joe's part-time cowhand where he stood, his eyes darting nervously like those of a rat in a trap. "You move," Luther told him in a hoarse voice, "and you're a dead man."

As soon as Maddy was done calling the sheriff, she hurried back to the living room carrying a pair of long leather bootlaces. "Sheriff Thomas is on his way. Meanwhile, could you tie him up with these?"

Luther glanced at the laces.

"I ain't goin' nowhere," Crandall protested. "There's no reason to hog-tie me."

Luther raised the gun. "Shut up," he said.

Crandall shut up.

"Can you cover him while I tie him?" Luther asked Maddy.

Her face was still pale and her freckles stood out. "Of course I can," she said, obviously regaining a little of the spunk Luther had come to expect from her. "I had him covered when you got here, didn't I?"

Luther remembered with heart-stopping clarity the scene he'd walked in on. He didn't want to think how it might have turned out if Crandall had been any good with the knife he'd been wielding. And he didn't bother to tell her it had looked more like a standoff than a victory on her part.

"Come here," he told her instead. When she did, he wrapped his free arm around her and hugged her close again without taking his gaze off the other man. She was still shaking, despite her courageous facade, and he wished he'd landed a few more punches before he let Crandall go.

The sound of an approaching car, followed by the scrape of tires against gravel, made Maddy straighten and pull away.

"I guess we won't have to tie him up after all," she told Luther.

Sheriff Thomas pounded on the back door and Luther hollered for him to come in. Charlie, the deputy, was right on his heels, followed by David and Chelsea. It was obvious from their flushed faces and heaving chests that they had run all the way from the bus stop.

Thank God they hadn't been the ones to walk in on Crandall and his knife, Luther thought distractedly. When he looked at Maddy, he could tell she was thinking the same thing.

Her stomach churned at the knowledge of what could have happened; her knees began to shake from delayed reaction. Abruptly she sank to the couch. Both David and Chelsea ran over and hugged her as Charlie slapped handcuffs on Crandall and escorted him outside to the patrol car.

It took a few minutes for Maddy to explain what had happened to the sheriff's satisfaction, but finally he had all the information he needed for the moment. Getting to his feet, Thomas glanced at Luther, who was leaning against the doorjamb with some ice on his knuckles.

Maddy caught his glance and wondered how the sheriff felt about Luther's innocence now. She hoped he might have learned something about jumping to conclusions, but somehow she doubted it. Old dogs didn't usually learn new tricks.

"I wouldn't be surprised to find out this guy's responsible for all the burglaries we've had around here lately," he told her. "Meanwhile, you all take care. I'm sure glad none of you was hurt." Again he glanced at Luther, but he didn't add anything more.

"Thanks for getting here so quickly," Luther told him as he turned to leave.

The sheriff looked flustered, and then he grinned. "Thanks for handling things until I could." He held out his hand. Barely hesitating, Luther shook it.

Maddy didn't even care that he was getting the credit when she was the one who had gotten the drop on Crandall in the first place.

"Are you really okay?" Luther asked again that night as they lay in each other's arms in his basement room.

"I'd be better if you'd quit fretting and pay me a little more attention," she whispered in a deliberately throaty voice.

He had already made love to her with barely controlled violence that stole her breath and sent her over the edge into a shattering climax. When he followed, he had muffled his harsh cry of fulfillment in the pillow next to her head and he hadn't let her go since.

Now that she had finally caught her breath, she wanted to make love again, but this time she wanted to savor every slow step of the way until they were both wild from wanting. Until she finally felt in control of her life again.

His chuckle rumbled deep in his chest. "You trying to kill me?" he asked conversationally.

Maddy stroked one hand down his chest, following the line of hair to his navel. It pleased her to hear his breath catch and to feel his muscles quiver beneath her light touch. She let her fingers trail a leisurely path around the indentation of his navel and then she wandered lower.

"It's going to be a slow, painful death," she murmured.

His ragged groan brought a smile to her lips as she rose over him and bent her head.

As soon as Luther guessed her intention he sat up straight in bed and tangled the fingers of one hand in her hair. She could tie him in knots faster than anyone he had ever known, but the scare he'd had that afternoon was still with him. Even his frantic possession of her hadn't been enough to erase the sharp taste of fear and helplessness that still plagued him.

And now she was trying to drive him totally insane. How much did she think one man could take? And why was she so eager to minister to him when she was the one who deserved the love and attention? All he had done was to show up when the crisis was all but over.

She raised her head and he realized he was still holding on to her hair. Carefully he forced his fingers to relax their grip as she put a hand against his chest and pushed.

"Lie down," she crooned. "It's my turn."

The temptation was too great, his need of her too raw for him to protest any further. In the darkness of that basement room, she proceeded to show him how unselfish the love between a man and a woman could be. Completely overwhelmed, unable to hold back the smallest part of himself, Luther finally gave himself up to the total trust he had always feared so much— and to the love he had always believed he would never find.

Afterward, astounded by the full surrender of his response, Maddy lay back down beside him. When he whispered her name, she placed her fingers against his mouth.

"Don't talk." She felt the warmth of his breath.

His arm came around her and he pulled her closer. She shifted her hand to stroke his cheek and felt something wet beneath her fingertips.

It was a tear.

Her lonely warrior, so strong, so unbreachable in his fortress, had stepped out from behind the wall. Silently, her own heart threatening to burst with love, she gathered him close and held him.

This was her favorite time of year, Maddy realized as she sat on Rowdy's back and looked at the newly sprouted carpet of green on the pasture where they kept the bulls. When she first got back in the saddle, she had expected to be nervous, but there had been no time for that kind of nonsense. The bulls they had come up to move had broken through the fence and were scattered across the road that bordered the ranch.

While two neighbors who had been driving by watched for other traffic, she and Luther had mounted quickly. Her nervousness had been forgotten until the animals were safe, and then it was too late to be afraid.

As soon as Maddy had thanked the other couple and they drove off, Luther rode up close and gave her a hug. "You were great. How's the hip?"

She grinned at him, handsome as the devil in his Stetson and Western gear. "Not bad." Neither of them had ever mentioned the tear she'd felt on his face that night. To her dismay, he had retreated once again behind his wall. At least this time, she didn't think he had gone quite as far back as before, and there was reason to believe his feelings for her were growing stronger.

Now admiration glinted in his eyes before he leaned toward her. His saddle creaked and his horse shook his head impatiently, rattling its bridle. "You're a hell of a woman," Luther murmured before he kissed her hard. Way too soon, he straightened again and glanced around self-consciously. Before she could stop him, he backed his horse away from hers. "We're too close to the road here," he said. "Someone might drive by and see us."

"So what?" she challenged. "We're both unattached adults. Or is there something you haven't told me?"

His expression darkened. "Come on, Maddy, you

don't want people talking any more than they already are about you and your ex-con hired hand, do you? Where's your pride?''

His question startled her. She thought he had gotten over the idea that being linked with him was going to ruin her socially. Apparently not.

She crowded closer to his black gelding. ''If I had any pride, would I be involved with a man who's more interested in the ground under our feet than he is in me?''

''That's not true,'' Luther said hotly, stunned by her question. It was his fault that she thought he felt that way. He knew now that his feelings had changed, but how was he ever going to convince her?

Maddy shrugged. She was smiling, but her eyes were serious. ''It doesn't matter anyway.''

What could he say? His mind came up empty. The more he argued, the more convinced she'd become that she knew the truth. And he had no one to blame but himself. While he debated the issue, she began herding the bulls toward the gate.

He loved her. And he couldn't tell her. Not now, and probably not ever. No matter what he said, she would never be sure which it was he really wanted— her or the ranch. Working the dilemma like a piece of jerky, he urged his horse forward.

For a moment, he thought about giving Maddy the money that sat in the bank, his share from the original sale. Then he realized that she would never accept it without making him a partner. He would get what he wanted and his grand gesture would prove nothing.

He heard her shout and looked around. A bull had

bolted for freedom. Automatically Luther headed him off.

There was only one thing to do, and he knew it. Heart-wrenching as the idea was, he had no choice.

"You can't leave now." Joe had come by to bring the frozen beef, and he stood in the middle of the barn with a look of incredulity stamped on his face. "How can you do this when she needs you? She gave you a job when most people around here wouldn't have given you a cup of coffee. You can't let her down."

Luther shook his head, too ashamed to tell Joe the real reason he was leaving. "I can't stay," he said stubbornly. "I was hoping you could spare a man to help her out. Just until things slow down a little or she hires someone else."

"You think you're that easy to replace?"

Luther felt the heat climb up his cheeks. What did Joe Sutter think he knew? Luther wasn't about to ask. He shrugged. "Anybody'd be better than me" was all he said.

Joe paced the length of the barn and back. "What about the kids?" Joe demanded. "Kenny says that David talks about you nonstop. Even little Chelsea thinks you're better than a talking Barney doll."

For a moment, Luther felt a shaft of pure agony rip through him. He had lost one child. How could he give up two more? But how could he stay, knowing what Maddy thought? And what if the kids found out? How would they feel then? Worse than if he left now, that was for damn sure.

"They'll get over it," he said gruffly.

Joe frowned and rubbed at his sideburn with one finger. "I don't know, man. I guess if your mind's made up I could send Dallas over for a couple of weeks." His expression was resigned, but it was obvious he disapproved of what Luther was doing. "Dal thinks he's a real ladies' man, but I expect Maddy can handle him."

Luther refused to rise to Joe's bait, but something twisted hard in his gut. "I expect she can."

"How soon are you leaving?" Joe asked.

"Day after tomorrow." If he waited any longer, he would never be able to tear himself away.

David seemed to have gotten over the effects of the break-in, Maddy thought as she bade him good-night a week after the incident and watched him take the stairs two at a time. Crandall had finally admitted to using information he picked up at Joe's ranch to plan the burglaries. Knowing he was safely behind bars, Maddy, too, was able to begin putting the terror of that afternoon behind her.

Chelsea had recovered from the trauma more slowly. She'd had nightmares and had slept with Maddy until she was ready to go back to her own room a couple of nights ago.

This evening, she had asked Luther to read her a story and tuck her in. Clearly flattered, he had glanced at Maddy for permission. When she watched the tall man and the little girl ascend the stairs, hand in hand, she thought of the son he had lost. He had never said whether he wanted more children, but she knew he would make a good father, despite his doubts. On one of the few occasions he had mentioned Mark, he'd commented that he didn't have what it took to be a parent. Maddy had seen for herself how wrong he was.

She heard his tread on the stairs.

"Chelsea's asleep," he said.

Maddy saw the tenderness in his eyes as well as the fatigue she knew was mirrored in her own. They were all exhausted, and spring calving was only half-over. At least they hadn't lost any more animals and they hadn't seen the coyotes hanging around since Luther had run them off with the shotgun.

She thanked him for tucking Chelsea in and then he wished her and David good-night. When David left a few minutes later, Maddy was tired but not sleepy. She turned the television on low and tried to concentrate on the news, but soon she was thinking about Luther instead.

She had come to depend on him. He knew ranching and he knew the Double C, but that was only part of it. She depended on him in so many other ways—they all did. She wondered if he had any idea how much of himself he shared with the three of them. One day soon, she would have to try to tell him, and hope he didn't bolt. She suspected that he thought of himself as a private man who needed space, not people, but she knew how mistaken that assessment really was.

Luther was a man in desperate need of love and warmth. A man she firmly believed could learn to trust and to share the emotions inside him struggling to get out. He was the man she loved with all her heart—the one she refused to give up on.

Joe had brought her some beef yesterday and had

sought Luther out before he left. The two men had stood by Joe's truck talking earnestly for several minutes, but Luther hadn't mentioned what Joe wanted.

After Maddy turned off the television and went to her room, she heard the faint sound of her door opening. Luther stood in the doorway. When the thought that he was just using her to get the ranch raised its ugly head, she quickly squashed it and held out her arms. He was here. That was enough for now. If it took the ranch to hold him, so be it. She wanted him to stay. Was it so unreasonable to think he deserved to get something he wanted, too?

Luther feasted his eyes. The curtains were open to the moonlight and Maddy appeared to be bathed in silver. A lump of regret rose in his throat and he swallowed it back down. God, how he hated leaving her— and the home and family she had let him be a part of. He would use the money from the sale of the ranch to start over somewhere else and pray she understood what he was trying to tell her. If she didn't, it was no more than a man like him deserved, but it was the only way he could think to show her what really mattered.

He had said his silent goodbyes to the children. He and David had discussed what to look for in a car when he got his license, and Luther had told Chelsea stories until she fell asleep. Losing the two of them was almost as bad as losing his son, but at least he would know they were alive and well. Maddy would take good care of them.

Now he stood in her bedroom doorway, trying to

memorize the way she looked with her arms out-stretched and a smile of welcome on her beautiful face. When she whispered his name, he could resist her no longer. Heart aching, he crossed the room and sank to his knees by the bed. This time, he was going to make it last all night. He was going to make it last until he could return to her with something to offer besides his own emptiness.

Luther's touch had never been so gentle and yet so compelling. It seemed to Maddy as if he was trying to show her something he couldn't put into words. With his mouth and hands and body, he wooed and wor-shiped her until she burned for his touch. Until she begged for his possession. Until she yearned for his love.

In turn, she stroked and coaxed and seduced, but still he held back. As if he meant to spend the entire night loving her. "Luther, please," she finally moaned, driven almost beyond rational thought. "I love you so much."

She hadn't meant to tell him. Not yet. While she held her breath, he stiffened and levered himself away from her. For a moment, she thought he was going to leave, but he only sighed and stroked her hair.

"I don't deserve you," he whispered.

Her heart cried out for other words, three in partic-ular, but he didn't say them. Perhaps he never would. It was up to her to show him that he deserved to be loved. That he had it in him to love in return. All she needed was time.

When he pulled her back into his arms and kissed her, she was caught up once again in the passion he ignited so effortlessly. This time when she begged him to take her, he complied. Together, they soared in perfect, breathtaking unison. Afterward, it was Maddy's turn for silent tears.

When Maddy awoke the next morning, she didn't expect to find Luther beside her. He always went back to his own basement room well before David got up to start his chores. Neither did she expect to find a note with her name on it propped up in front of her clock radio.

A terrible premonition slithered through her as she picked up the folded sheet of lined paper. Holding it with shaking hands, she sat up in the bed that suddenly seemed too big and lonely. For a moment, she clutched the note tightly, without opening it, and willed it to be some sentiment he couldn't yet express aloud.

In her heart, she knew that wouldn't be the case. Tears were already filling her eyes when she read it.

By the time you get this, I'll be gone.

She gasped as pain threatened to take her under.

I came back for my ranch, and then I met you. I'm sorry I tried to get you to sell it. Thank you for sticking up for me when no one else would. I can't let you give up anything else for me when I have nothing to give you in return. I never meant to hurt you.

Luther

Maddy stared at the note for a long time as tears rolled down her face. Finally a knock at the door made her heart lurch in her chest.

Had he changed his mind?

"Luther!" she cried, scrambling from the bed and wiping away the tears. Before she could get to the door, it opened cautiously.

"It's me, Mommy," Chelsea said. "Aren't you going to fix breakfast this morning?"

Maddy glanced back at the clock. She hadn't realized how late it was getting. "Yes, honey, I overslept, but I'll be right down."

Chelsea pushed the door open wider. "What's wrong?"

Maddy reached down deep for some of the grit she'd had to find when George first got sick. She smiled at her daughter. "Nothing's wrong, baby. You go ahead and get dressed and I'll be ready in just a minute, okay?"

When Chelsea acquiesced and turned away, she sank back onto the bed with a sigh of relief. It had taken every bit of determination she contained to keep that smile in place. Now, in the next few minutes, she had to dredge up some more of that same grit and convince her children that all three of them would survive Luther's leaving. Maybe, while she was at it, she could also convince herself.

Chapter Thirteen

"**Y**ou can sleep here and take your meals up at the house," Daniel Sixkiller told Luther as the two men stood in the doorway of a small room in the barn. A little girl, younger than Chelsea, perched on Daniel's shoulders and watched Luther with big brown eyes. She had straight black hair like her father's and honey-toned skin. "Bathroom's through there," Daniel added, pointing.

"Thanks," Luther replied as he tossed his duffel bag onto the bunk. "I really appreciate this."

Daniel grinned, revealing even white teeth. His black eyes crinkled at the corners. "Any friend of Joe's," he said with a shrug. "Besides, I can use the help. You haven't really worked until you've done time at a sheep ranch during lambing season."

The words he used made Luther briefly uncomfortable and he wondered how much Joe had told his old foreman. Would Luther's past never let him go?

Daniel's easy smile didn't waver as he curled his dark hands around his daughter's chubby legs, dangling over his shoulders. "Go ahead and get settled. Supper's in an hour. Just come on up to the house." He brushed off Luther's thanks and turned away. His black hair hung in a single braid down his back. "We'll see you in a little while."

Luther stepped into the small, plain room and looked out the high window. The rolling pasture was dotted with sheep. Luther shook his head. Sheep!

When Joe had finally accepted Luther's determination to leave, he had offered to make some phone calls. Now Luther found himself a couple of hundred miles away from the Double C, working for a man he barely knew. Until he figured out what to do, one place was as good as another.

Damn, but he missed Maddy. Missed the kids. For a moment, a terrible sense of loss threatened to engulf him. It was all he could do to keep from giving in to despair. Several times during the drive to Craig he had almost succumbed to temptation and turned his truck around. Only the knowledge that he was doing the right thing for Maddy, if not for himself, kept him headed west.

He wondered if she missed him. Was she angry at the way he had left, sneaking off in the night? If he'd had to say goodbye to her face, he never would have been able to go.

Absently he chewed on his lower lip, watching a pair of lambs as they circled their mother. It was hard to believe that a dedicated cattleman like Joe's fore-man could stand to raise sheep, but Luther understood that Daniel's coming here had been a real fluke.

Life certainly dealt its share of surprises, Luther thought with a rueful shake of his head. Just look at him. All he had been able to think about was getting that damned ranch back, and now he would have given it away just to show Maddy how much he loved her. Only problem was, that wasn't an option.

He wondered what she was doing right at this moment. Probably fixing supper for the extra man Joe had promised to send over. Dallas, the ladies' man. Luther frowned darkly. If Dallas took advantage of her while she was feeling sad and vulnerable, he'd—

Luther spun away from the window, fists clenched. He'd do nothing, that was what. He'd forfeited that right when he had turned his back on her. Damn, he screwed up everything he touched.

He relaxed his hands and shoved them into the back pockets of his jeans. A ragged sigh tore through him. Knowing Maddy, she was coping with his desertion just fine. Part of him wanted her to be okay, but a selfish little voice he tried to ignore wanted her to miss him the way he missed her.

Hell, he should be used to losing by now, should be used to ending up alone. When it came to the things other people took for granted, he had never measured up. Had never figured out how to find the courage to try. To trust. He had tried with Diane, but he had failed. Only with Mark, his son, had he felt a small measure of acceptance, and then Mark had been taken from him forever.

Maddy would probably never forgive him for leaving her and the children. He wondered if any of it was worth the pain of losing. With Maddy, it had been, he realized. What they had found together was special, and then he'd spoiled it by telling her the ranch was the only thing he wanted. He'd had his second chance and he had blown it sky-high. This time he deserved whatever he got.

Tossing his battered duffel bag to the floor, Luther unfolded the sheets Daniel had left for him. If the other man was telling the truth about lambing, Luther would be too tired later to do more than fall into bed, so he might as well make it up now.

"Do you know where he went?" Maddy demanded, hands on her hips.

Joe shifted from one foot to the other, looking uncomfortable. He and Emma exchanged glances. "He didn't want you to know," Joe said gently. "All I can tell you is that he's got a place to stay and he's okay." Maddy saw Emma touch his arm, but Joe just shook his head. "He's convinced it's for the best." Joe's head was bowed, his expression hidden.

"You know better than that," Maddy exclaimed. "The kids and I are what he needs. Not being alone again."

"I'm sorry." Emma's blue eyes were brimming with sympathy.

"Me, too." Joe looked as if he would have liked to add something. In the end, he shrugged. "For a while, I thought things were going to work out between you."

"So did I." Maddy didn't try to keep the bitterness from her voice. She stood in the middle of their kitchen indecisively. She had already refused Emma's offer of coffee and she felt like a fool for coming here in the first place. This wasn't their fault, and she wasn't the first woman who had been dumped by a man.

"I know it's no consolation," Joe said with a wry grin, "but Luther's a hardheaded fool and I told him so. He should have stayed here and worked things out instead of taking off."

Maddy swallowed past the lump of pain in her throat. "Thanks," she said, fighting to keep her voice steady. "And thanks for sending Dallas and Henry to help me."

Joe made a dismissive gesture. "No thanks necessary. I just wish things had turned out differently."

"Me, too." Maddy gave Emma a hug, fighting back tears, and headed for the back door. No point in humiliating herself any more than she already had. She'd promised David and Chelsea that she would try to find out where Luther had gone. Knowing how stubborn he could be and how little value he put on his own worth, she didn't expect him to come back.

Emma followed her onto the porch. "Let me know if I can do anything," she said. "If I hear any news, I'll call you."

"Thanks." Maddy hesitated, reluctant to go home and face an empty house. "Do you know where he is?"

Emma shook her head. "Stupid male loyalty," she muttered. "Men, you gotta love 'em."

"Luther thought he was doing the best thing for me by leaving," Maddy admitted. "I wish there had been some way to convince him he was wrong." She gave Emma a rueful grin. "Like beating some sense into him."

Emma glanced behind her, but Joe had disappeared. "Why do men always manage to break our hearts when they insist on giving us what they think we want?" she asked. "I went through the same thing with Joe."

"You did? Did he leave you?" Maddy asked, curious. She would have bet that Joe and Emma had the perfect marriage. The love that shimmered between them was there for anyone to see and it surprised Maddy to hear they'd ever had any problems.

Emma leaned against the porch railing and her smile softened tenderly. "Joe did worse than leave me. He almost let me go back to Seattle. He was convinced he'd make me unhappy. Being a typical noble but misguided male, he decided to make the ultimate sacrifice and give me up." She rolled her eyes expressively. "Believe me, it was the last thing I wanted."

"What did you do?"

Emma was silent for a moment. "It wasn't easy, considering how stubborn Joe can be, but I finally made him see that what he thought I wanted wasn't worth anything without him to share it."

A crow flew by, calling noisily. Maddy considered what Emma had said. "Well, I'd say you did the right thing in not letting him send you away."

Emma's eyes were moist. "I almost gave up," she confessed, dabbing at them. "Then I realized that if I lost Joe, nothing else mattered. It was getting him to see that his sacrifice was pointless that was difficult.''

''I'm glad things worked out,'' Maddy told her sincerely. Emma was lucky, but there was no way Maddy could change Luther's mind. He was already gone.

Maddy was standing at the kitchen sink when she heard a car come down the road and stop in the yard. Her heart faltered in her chest when she saw Charlie get out. Had something happened to one of the children? She dropped the towel she'd been holding and ran to the door. What about Luther? Perhaps he had been hurt and Charlie was coming to tell her.

Gator was barking when she grabbed a jacket and rushed out the back door. ''Quiet!'' she ordered the shepherd mix.

Daisy watched her silently. Since Luther had been gone, the collie stayed around the yard, watching the road with her head resting on her forepaws. Maddy knew just how she felt.

''What can I do for you?'' she asked Charlie, hiding her fear. She still hadn't forgiven him for following Sheriff Thomas's lead in suspecting Luther of the burglaries.

Charlie stopped a couple of feet away and removed his hat. ''I just thought you might like to know that Crandall, the fellow who broke in here, has pleaded guilty to everything,'' he said, turning the brim of his hat around and around in his hands. ''You won't have to testify or anything.''

Maddy was relieved to hear it. ''Thank you for coming all the way out to tell me.''

Charlie glanced around. "Is Luther here?"

A fierce pain stole her voice and she had to swallow twice before she could get the words out. "No. He left. Why?"

Charlie looked distinctly uncomfortable. "I was going to tell him how sorry I was about all this," he admitted quietly. "Luther deserved a better break than he got when he came back here."

Maddy had to blink back sudden tears. If only Charlie had reached this conclusion a little sooner! "That's true. He deserved better."

Charlie must have realized that she wasn't going to invite him in for coffee the way she used to do. It would take her some time to forgive him and everyone else who had been so quick to turn against the man she had loved and lost. The wound was still too new.

When Charlie left, she went back inside. As she began to mix the ingredients for meat loaf together in a big bowl, she wondered where Luther was and whether he was thinking about her. Suddenly the tears she had been trying so hard to contain burst from her like a flood. Leaning over, she laid her cheek against the counter and sobbed.

"I'm a desperate woman, so you might as well give me what I want." Maddy searched Joe's wary face as she brandished the pitchfork. It had been three weeks since Luther left. Sick of moping around, she had finally decided to take matters into her own hands. She'd thought long and hard about what Emma had told her and finally come up with a plan. It all hinged on finding out where Luther had gone. Joe knew, and she wasn't letting him leave her barn without telling her.

Joe gave her a grin she found infuriating. "Now, Maddy," he began in a soothing tone he no doubt used on skittish horses. "I think you're overreacting here." He'd backed up a couple of steps and one hand was extended placatingly.

She made a jabbing motion with the pitchfork and he backed up a little more. Then he must have seen some of the fierce determination in her eyes because his smile vanished.

"He insisted that I not tell you where he went." Joe's voice had become edged with nervousness.

"Did you promise him?" Maddy demanded. If he had given his word, she didn't have a prayer of getting him to talk, no matter if she threatened him with a pitchfork, a branding iron or a castrating knife. Men like Joe could be disgustingly stubborn when it came to things like honor and giving their word.

Without taking his eyes off the gleaming tines of the pitchfork she waved at him, Joe pulled at his lower lip. "Well, no, I guess I didn't exactly promise him," he admitted.

Maddy released the breath she had been holding and gripped the handle tighter. "Then I guess you have a decision to make," she drawled.

With a shrug, Joe told her what she wanted to know.

When she let him in on what she was going to do, he offered to take David and Chelsea home with him after he helped Dallas with the chores.

"It's the least I can do," he said with a smile of understanding. "Good luck with your man."

Maddy tried to thank him for his help, tears swimming in her eyes. Apparently, crying females made Joe more nervous than pitchforks did. He brushed aside her thanks and urged her to hit the road.

She called her attorney and told him what she wanted. He argued, but she didn't listen. After a quick stop at his office to collect the legal document he drew up under protest, she gassed up the truck and headed west.

Following Joe's map, she finally turned down a private road, driving past an attractive house and pulling up in front of the barn. When she got out of the truck, her knees were shaking from sheer nerves and her hands were trembling so badly she could barely grip the document she had brought with her.

While she stood in the deserted yard and looked around, wondering what to do next, an old man came around the corner. When he saw her, he stopped in his tracks and a wide grin split his wizened face.

"You must be my Christmas present," he exclaimed. "Late as usual."

Before she could think of a reply, another man appeared. He was a Native American, and one of the most attractive men Maddy had ever seen. Next to Luther, of course.

"I'm Maddy Landers," she said. "I'm looking for Luther Ward."

"Damn," the old man muttered. "I knew you was too good to be true."

The other man smiled and approached her with his hand outstretched. "Joe called," he said. "I'm Daniel

Sixkiller and this is Cully. We've been expecting you.''

Maddy gave his hand an impatient shake. Her determination had been unwavering all the way here, but now she was assailed with a thousand doubts. This had to be the dumbest idea she had ever thought up. Another minute or two and she was going to lose her nerve and bolt like a runaway horse.

Daniel must have seen something of her rising panic in her face. ''Luther didn't know you were coming,'' he said. ''I'll send Cully to get him.'' The old man ambled off, grumbling under his breath, while Daniel did his obvious best to put Maddy at ease. ''Luther's been like a bear with a sore paw ever since he got here,'' he told her conversationally. ''Even though he's been a big help, I don't think he likes sheep and I can't say that I'm all that sorry to see you.''

''How do you know I'm going to make the situation any better?'' Maddy asked.

Daniel threw back his head and laughed. ''You and my wife are really going to hit it off,'' he predicted, white teeth flashing in a wide grin. ''You'll have to come up to the house and meet her before you leave.''

Maddy didn't answer. If this whole thing turned out as disastrously as she feared it might, she wasn't going to be sticking around to meet anyone.

''Karen's seven months pregnant,'' Daniel elaborated. ''She's had to stay off her feet a lot. Having Luther around has freed up some of my time so I could spend it with her and our kids, Twyla and Jamie.''

''That's nice,'' Maddy murmured with a sinking

heart. It sounded like Daniel really needed Luther's help. "How old are they?"

"Jamie's eight, Twyla's almost four and we're expecting twins. Don't worry, though," he added. "One of my summer herders is coming up from Mexico early. He'll be here day after tomorrow." Daniel pushed back the brim of his hat, revealing twinkling black eyes. "In case Luther has to leave suddenly."

Despite his best efforts to put her at her ease, Maddy was growing more nervous by the minute. Her hands were damp and she realized she had been wrinkling the legal document she had brought with her. Bowing her head, she tried to smooth it out.

"You love him, don't you?" Daniel asked quietly.

She jerked up her head. "Does it show?" This was going to be even more humiliating than she had first thought.

Her defensive reply seemed to amuse him. "It shows to me," he said, removing his hat and smoothing back his hair. The hatband was silver, studded with turquoise stones. "Just like Luther's feelings show. Now that I've met you, I can see why he's been so miserable."

"Did he say anything to you about me?" Maddy asked disbelievingly.

"Luther? Are you kidding?"

She couldn't help but smile at Daniel's expression. "No, I guess he wouldn't have."

"He didn't have to tell me anything. I could spot his problem a mile off." Daniel's lips quirked as if he was thinking about something that amused him. "I'm glad you came," he declared warmly.

Before Maddy could reply, she heard hoofbeats approaching. Saddle leather creaked as the rider pulled up on the other side of her pickup and dismounted. "Daniel, you wanted to talk to me?"

Luther's voice shot a bolt of feeling through Maddy that threatened to knock her down. As he came around the truck, leading his horse, Daniel gave her an encouraging smile.

"Someone here to see you," he told Luther.

When he saw Maddy, Luther could only stare in disbelief. Wearing her jeans and denim jacket, she was even more beautiful than he remembered.

"Hello, Luther," she said quietly.

His horse snorted noisily and pulled at the reins, but he was barely aware of it. "Hello," he managed despite throat muscles that were locked with tension. "What are you doing here?" Vaguely he heard Daniel make a sound of disgust. Luther flushed.

"I came to see you." Her eyes flashed and she thrust out her chin.

"How did you know where to find me? Joe promised—".

She shook her head. "He never actually promised. When I threatened him with the pitchfork—"

. It was Luther's turn to interrupt. "Pitchfork!" he exclaimed.

"Karen's going to love you," Daniel muttered.

Maddy looked slightly abashed. "Well, I had to get him to tell me where you went," she said defensively.

Luther ground his teeth. Was there going to be no end to his torment? Despite Daniel's presence, it was all he could do to fight the nearly overwhelming urge to yank her into his arms and kiss the breath from her. Damn, but he had missed her!

Instead of touching her, he held his body rigid, hands clenched at his sides, and gave her his most intimidating glare. The one that had kept the other cons at bay.

"What the hell are you doing here?"

She marched up to him and slapped a paper against his chest. It looked like his divorce papers. "I came to give you this."

Automatically he took it. "What's this?"

"A bill of sale," she said. "Sign it and give me a dollar."

"Huh?" Her words caught him totally off guard.

"I'm selling you back the Double C for a dollar," she said briskly as she stuck out a pen. "It's a legal document. Sign and we'll get Mr. Sixkiller to witness it."

Luther frowned and took a step back from her. "Wait just a damned minute. What are you trying to do?" Had she flipped out? Where was she going to go if she sold him the ranch? What was she going to use for money if she sold it for a buck? What about David and Chelsea? Luther's head was spinning. None of this made any sense.

She put her hands on her trim hips and stared up at him. "You thought the ranch came between us," she stated. "Am I right?"

Confused, he nodded. "That's right. I—"

She ignored his interruption. "You were afraid I'd think you were only after it, didn't you?"

Again he nodded. "Yeah, but—"

"If you already own the ranch, you don't have to pretend to care about me to get it, do you?" she persisted.

"Yeah, but—" he tried again.

"It's no good to me without you," she said. "I realized after you left that the ranch isn't a home anymore. It's just a place. A place I can't bear to be if you aren't there, too." He opened his mouth to speak, but she rushed on. There were angry tears in her eyes. "So what's keeping you from accepting my offer?" she demanded. "Too complicated for you?"

Luther might have grinned at the bite in her tone if his heart hadn't been beating so fast he was afraid it might burst right out of his chest. Hardly able to trust what he was hearing, he began to see where she was going with this, and he couldn't let her do it. Not for a man like him.

Before he could find the words to explain why he had to turn down her crazy offer, Daniel stepped forward. Luther had forgotten all about him.

"If you aren't going to take her up on this, I will," he said, taking his wallet from his back pocket.

Maddy realized what Daniel was trying to do, and she could have kissed him for it. Before she could say anything, Luther made a noise deep in his throat, which sounded suspiciously like a growl, and grabbed her arm possessively. "The hell you are." Glaring at Daniel, he marched her toward the barn. "Let me see if I have this right," Luther said to her as soon as they were inside. "You're willing to sell my ranch back to me for a dollar."

"That's right."

"This bill of sale is legal?" He waved the folded paper at her.

"That's right," she repeated.

"If I sign it and give you the dollar, you and the children are prepared to move out. I'll own everything, no strings attached?"

She swallowed nervously. From his forbidding expression, she had no idea what he was thinking. "Yes." Oh, God. What if she had been wrong about his feelings? She was risking her children's futures as well as her own.

He seemed to mull over what she had told him. His eyes never left her face. "You dreamed up this grandstand gesture, gambling everything you've got, on how much I love you," he said softly, and it wasn't a question.

She answered anyway. "Yes."

Something glittered in his eyes, but she couldn't decipher it. This wasn't going at all the way she had hoped. His face seemed to be carved from stone.

"You threatened Joe with a pitchfork." Luther seemed to choke. He bowed his head and cleared his throat. "You left your children God-knows-where and you drove over two hundred miles to spring this on me."

"That's about it," she agreed, fighting tears.

"I see." He stared past her, gaze unfocused.

Furious with herself, Maddy felt a tear spill over and slide down her cheek. While she wiped it away, Luther grabbed the pen. Holding the paper up against a wooden beam, he scrawled his signature at the bottom. Then he fished a crumpled bill from his pocket and leaned forward to tuck it into the neckline of her shirt. Her skin tingled where his fingers brushed the top of her breast.

She almost cried out.

Luther ducked his head so that the brim of his Stetson hid his face. The bill of sale slipped from his fingers and fluttered to the floor of the barn as Maddy watched him, waiting for him to speak the words that would evict her and her children from the only home they had.

Man, oh man, had she been wrong.

While she waited, trembling with hurt and disappointment, Luther stunned her by sinking to his knees in front of her. He took her hand in his and tipped back his head to look into her eyes.

His hard face seemed frozen, but then his mouth curved into the most beautiful smile she had ever seen. His eyes blazed.

"Maddy," he said, his voice gruff, "you believed in me when I didn't believe in myself. You taught me how to feel when I didn't know I could. You showed me that it was safe to trust. And now you've convinced me that you think I'm worth loving. I reckon you've already figured out how I feel about you." He took a deep breath. "Will you do me the honor of becoming my wife?"

She stared as his words sank in. Then, with a whoop of pure joy, she threw her arms around him, almost knocking him over.

"What's wrong?" Daniel shouted as he appeared in the doorway. "Are you okay?" When he saw Luther and Maddy, arms around each other, he skidded to a stop. "Oops, sorry. I heard Maddy cry out."

Luther continued to stare up at her. "Well?" he asked softly. All his feelings for her were there to see in his eyes.

"Yes," she whispered as her tears spilled over. "I'll marry you." She glanced from Luther to Daniel and began to laugh with pure joy.

Luther got to his feet and held up the bill of sale. While Maddy watched, puzzled, he tore it in two.

"What did you do that for?"

He shrugged, grinning like a boy. "It wasn't legal anyway since Daniel didn't actually see me sign it. What do you say we modify the agreement a little?"

"Modify it how?" she asked warily.

"I've still got the money from my share of the sale," he said. "I'd like to buy into the ranch as a partner."

Relief drained through Maddy, leaving her light-headed. For a moment, she had been worried that something was going to go wrong. Now she stuck out her hand. "Cowboy, you've got yourself a deal," she said.

Luther looked down at her outstretched hand. Then he looked at Daniel, who was grinning from ear to ear. He gave Luther a thumbs-up.

"I'd go for it if I were you."

While Maddy looked up at Luther, love shining in her eyes, he slipped his arms around her and lowered his head. The kiss he gave her laid his feelings bare.

"Honey," he said tenderly, "let's go home."

* * * * *

LEGACIES . LIES . LOVE .

**Experience the mystery, passion and glamour
of Harlequin's *brand-new* 12-book continuity,
FORRESTER SQUARE.**

Coming in September 2003...

TWICE AND FOR ALWAYS

by *USA TODAY* bestselling author
Cathy Gillen Thacker

Kevin Taylor and Kelly Bassett are Forrester Square Day Care's
five-year-old pranksters. Their latest scheme: switching their
single parents' beepers! Little do the kids know that their parents,
Brody Taylor and Meg Bassett, are former spouses—and that
Kevin and Kelly are actually fraternal twins!

Forrester Square... Legacies. Lies. Love.

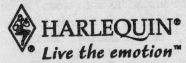

Visit us at www.forrestersquare.com

PHFSU

If you enjoyed what you just read,
then we've got an offer you can't resist!

Take 2
bestselling novels FREE!
Plus get a FREE surprise gift!

Clip this page and mail it to The Best of the Best™

IN U.S.A.	IN CANADA
3010 Walden Ave.	P.O. Box 609
P.O. Box 1867	Fort Erie, Ontario
Buffalo, N.Y. 14240-1867	L2A 5X3

YES! Please send me 2 free Best of the Best™ novels and my free surprise gift. After receiving them, if I don't wish to receive anymore, I can return the shipping statement marked cancel. If I don't cancel, I will receive 4 brand-new novels every month, before they're available in stores! In the U.S.A., bill me at the bargain price of $4.74 plus 25¢ shipping and handling per book and applicable sales tax, if any*. In Canada, bill me at the bargain price of $5.24 plus 25¢ shipping and handling per book and applicable taxes**. That's the complete price and a savings of over 20% off the cover prices—what a great deal! I understand that accepting the 2 free books and gift places me under no obligation ever to buy any books. I can always return a shipment and cancel at any time. Even if I never buy another The Best of the Best™ book, the 2 free books and gift are mine to keep forever.

185 MDN DNWF
385 MDN DNWG

Name	(PLEASE PRINT)	
Address	Apt.#	
City	State/Prov.	Zip/Postal Code

* Terms and prices subject to change without notice. Sales tax applicable in N.Y.
** Canadian residents will be charged applicable provincial taxes and GST.
All orders subject to approval. Offer limited to one per household and not valid to current The Best of the Best™ subscribers.
® are registered trademarks of Harlequin Enterprises Limited.

BOB02-R
©1998 Harlequin Enterprises Limited

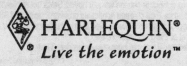

**Treat yourself to some festive
reading this holiday season
with a fun and jolly volume...**

TEMPORARY
Santa

**Two full-length novels
at one remarkable low price!**

Favorite authors

Cathy Gillen
THACKER

Leigh
MICHAELS

**Two sexy heroes find true love at Christmas
in this romantic collection.**

Coming in November 2003—just in time for the holidays!

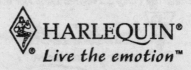

HARLEQUIN®
Live the emotion™

Visit us at www.eHarlequin.com

BR2TS